The Nearly-Weds

Also by Jane Costello

Bridesmaids

The Nearly-Weds

Jane Costello

POCKET
BOOKS

LONDON • NEW YORK • TORONTO • SYDNEY

First published in Great Britain by Pocket Books, 2009
An imprint of Simon & Schuster UK Ltd
A CBS COMPANY

1 3 5 7 9 8 6 4 2

Simon & Schuster UK Ltd
1st Floor, 222 Gray's Inn Road
London WC1X 8HB

www.simonandschuster.co.uk

Simon & Schuster Australia
Sydney

A CIP catalogue record for this book is available from the British Library

ISBN 978-1-47115-738-7

Typeset by Rowland Phototypesetting Ltd, Bury St Edmunds, Suffolk
Printed and bound by
CPI Group (UK) Ltd, Croydon, CR0 4YY

For Lucas, with all my love

Acknowledgements

Thank you to all those people behind the scenes who have played such a crucial part in the creation of this book.

They are my agent Darley Anderson (I haven't stopped feeling lucky since he agreed to represent me) and the immensely talented team at Simon and Schuster UK, particularly Suzanne Baboneau, Julie Wright and Libby Vernon.

Thanks also to Doris Alexander and Sarah and Jack Shulman for their help with the Americanisms.

As ever, I am indebted to my parents, Jean and Phil Wolstenholme, for their love and support.

Finally, thank you to Jon, whose input I value enormously, despite my suspicion that he'd prefer to be reading *Middlemarch*.

Chapter 1

I'm trying my best to create the air of a sophisticated world traveller but am not entirely sure I'm pulling it off.

With hindsight, I probably gave the game away immediately by enthusiastically testing one too many fragrances at Duty Free, leaving me now exuding an aroma so pungent it could wake someone from a coma.

I've also been let down by my ethnic-style cotton top, the one I was convinced looked like an item I'd picked up somewhere fabulously exotic in the South Pacific – until I discovered the price tag poking out, revealing that I in fact paid £44.99 for it in Monsoon.

And maybe I didn't look quite as streetwise as I'd hoped by being the very first to camp out at Gate 65, beating a large group of Saga holidaymakers by at least half an hour.

Now I'm actually in the air, it's still happening: my status as a long-haul travel amateur is being ruthlessly exposed at every turn.

I'm currently attempting to balance all the empty packaging from my in-flight meal on top of a ludicrously proportioned tray and an undrinkable cup of coffee without it tumbling on to my neighbour's lap and leaving his tackle with third-degree burns. It's like a real-life version of Kerplunk, with every item threatening to wobble off at the slightest hint of turbulence.

Unlike the American gentleman sitting next to me – he has cleverly tucked his lemon-scented freshening wipe into his empty teacup and neatly stacked the salt and pepper packets, plus the mini butter tub, in his tasty beef casserole container – I have ended up with an unruly compost heap of plastic and foil debris.

'Shall I take that for you, madam?' asks a stewardess, swiping it away before I can prevent a knife clattering on to my table.

'Whoopsadaisy!' I hoot, sounding not very like the cosmopolitan member of the jet-set I'm hoping to appear. I pick it up and attempt to hand it to her, but she's off already, steamrolling her trolley down the aisle and nearly taking the skin off several passengers' knuckles.

I glance to my side and realize my neighbour is eyeing my knife dubiously.

'Oh, well.' I shrug. 'Who knows when I might need a plastic knife complete with generous smothering of butter?'

He smiles.

It isn't a particularly conspiratorial smile, though, one that belies a flicker of amusement. It's sympathetic, revealing pity for the poor creature next to him who must surely be on day-release from a psychiatric ward.

I lean back in my seat, mentally humming a song that

was always on the radio when I was little and Mum was cremating the Sunday dinner: 'I'm leaving on a jet plane . . . la la la . . . la la la la la la la . . .'

Oh, never mind. I'm sure the words will come back to me. And, anyway, it's the sentiment behind them that matters. The song, I assume, is about embracing new beginnings. About moving on. About discovering a whole new world.

Which is exactly what I'm doing right now.

As you may have guessed, however, flying halfway across the world by myself isn't something I've ever done before: easyJet to Barcelona for a two-night hen weekend, yes; two weeks in Turkey with boyfriend in tow, not a problem; a week with the girls in the South of France, bring it on.

But three and a half thousand miles across the Atlantic? *And possibly for good?*

No.

Except here I am. Actually doing it. Even if I wish it was with rather more panache.

Chapter 2

When I was at primary school, my best friend was called Elizabeth. She was of Jamaican origin but she was Scouse through and through – and had an accent so thick it could have unblocked a toilet.

Even at ten, Elizabeth knew what she wanted to do with her life: to see the world. She wanted to climb mountains, trek through rainforests and see as many different places and meet as many different people as she could. I found out last year that she'd graduated from Oxford, travelled for two years and now works for the Red Cross in Stockholm.

I mention this merely to illustrate a point: that if a scale existed to measure how adventurous your twenties were – according to conventional wisdom, at least – Elizabeth's life would be at one end and mine would probably be at the other.

For the past seven years, until last Friday, in fact, I've worked as a nursery nurse in Woolton, a suburb of Liverpool that fancies itself posh. Actually, I'm doing myself down a bit: by the time I left, I'd risen to deputy manager (the youngest they'd ever had, as my mother informs anyone she meets within the first thirty-two seconds of conversation).

This achievement doesn't so much reflect ruthless ambition, as the simple fact that I love my work. *Really* love it. Which is a constant relief, given that I embarked on this career after dropping out of my first year of a law degree (something my mother informs anyone she meets within the next thirty-two seconds of conversation).

The real point is that Bumblebees Nursery is precisely six minutes' walk from the house in which I grew up, twenty-one minutes' drive from the hospital in which I was born, and so close to my former secondary school that if you look out of the nursery's attic on tiptoe you can still see some graffiti referring to a snog I allegedly had with Christopher Timms in the lower sixth. (This, by the way, was someone's attempt at irony. At seventeen, Christopher Timms was renowned for lighting his own farts with such regularity he needed his own Fire Incident Support Unit.)

The pond-like existence I have somehow maintained for my entire twenty-eight years on this earth is – I am fully aware – slightly tragic, but, in my defence, I've got a good excuse. No, two good excuses: I found a job I adored and a man I adored.

So, why would I want to give them up?

I shift in my seat in another vain attempt to make myself comfortable. It's a space that would fail EU regulations for transporting poultry, never mind people. But it's no good. I lost all sensation in my bum cheeks a good two hours ago and I'm not likely to get it back any time soon.

I pick up my rucksack for want of something – anything – to do and take out my compact mirror to examine my reflection. It isn't a pleasant experience.

I'm not saying that under normal circumstances I'd threaten any of Eva Longoria's L'Oréal contracts but until recently I've been relatively okay with my looks. I inherited good bone structure from Dad's side of the family, good legs from Mum's and I've even – after many years of angst – learned to live with the washboard stomach I sadly didn't inherit from either.

At the moment, though, my most striking feature is not the dark eyes or full mouth I used to be complimented on, but my skin – which is so pale I look as if I need basting. I went for one of those spray tans a couple of weeks ago to see if its advertised 'natural, golden glow' would sort me out. Unfortunately, my knees and elbows ended up with such an alarmingly orange tinge that I'm convinced the beautician who applied it must have been sniffing glue.

To add insult to injury, in less than a month, my size ten–twelve frame – the one I took so utterly for granted that I even managed to complain about it at least twice a day – has somehow been replaced with one that is precisely sixteen and a half pounds heavier (and counting).

Yes, you read that right: sixteen and a half pounds. If you hadn't realized until now that it was physiologically possible to put on that much weight in such a short time, then I assure you, neither had I. But it is – and I have. Probably because I've spent the last couple of months comfort-eating for Britain.

What has caused all this?

Oh, what do you think? A man. Obviously. My man. At least, he *used* to be my man.

I can now say categorically that Jason Redmond – high-flying accountant, pool champion, charmer of friends and parents alike, oh, and love of my life – no longer answers to that description.

No matter how many nights I spend weeping bitter tears into my pillow. No matter how many hours I spend with Leona Lewis crooning out of my iPod. No matter how many times I've accompanied well-meaning friends to karaoke bars and tried my best to look convincing while belting out 'I Will Survive'. (Okay, so, 'I Will Plummet Into The Depths Of Despair Until He Phones Me Again' hasn't quite got the same ring.)

I snap my compact closed and throw it back into my rucksack.

'Do you need an I-94W form, madam?' asks the stewardess, appearing at my shoulder.

'Um, why not?' I reply, taking it from her as casually as someone who fills in one of these every other weekend when they pop over to Buenos Aires for a spot of polo.

When she's gone, I peer at the lines on the form, wondering whether I'm meant to have one.

'You got a UK passport?' asks my American neighbour, repositioning his U-shaped cushion, an item I've been coveting for the last six hours.

'Um . . . yes,' I reply, suspiciously.

'Then if you're just going to the States on holiday you need to fill it in.' He smiles.

'Oh, um . . . yes, I know,' I lie. 'I mean, it's a bit more than a holiday I'm going for but . . .'

'You emigrating?'

'I've got a year-long working visa,' I explain, stuffing the form into the pocket of the chair in front, next to the butter knife and two plastic cups with Diet Pepsi dregs in the bottom. 'So, I'll be there for at least twelve months. Assuming they don't throw me out first, that is!'

He smiles again, but this time it isn't even the sympathetic one. It's the sort of smile you'd give a shoe bomber to instil an air of calm while trying to work out where the emergency exits are.

'Ladies and gentlemen, this is your captain speaking,' announces a reassuringly plummy voice over a crackly speaker. 'We will shortly be making our descent into JFK . . .'

I sit up in my seat and take a deep breath.

New life, here I come.

Chapter 3

We are so bombarded by American culture in the UK that it's sometimes impossible to think of the United States as a foreign country. Yet the second I step off the plane, JFK couldn't feel more foreign if it were situated on the far side of Jupiter. I wander round the airport lounge, trying not to spend too long scrutinizing the flight information boards with a hopeless look on my face in case I give anybody the impression I don't know what I'm doing, and am enveloped in unfamiliar sights and sounds: accents that make my own vowels sound so British I feel like someone auditioning to read the BBC news in 1953; language I recognize – *diapers, cell phones, mommies, zip codes* – but have never used. And there's a bustling, gaudy, fast-food whirlwind of an atmosphere that makes half of me giddy with excitement and the other half long for somewhere that sells a nice sausage roll, and tea that's been brewed to the correct strength for several days.

I had an inkling of this sensation when I spoke to my new employers on the phone last week. I'm on my way to be a nanny for Summer (three and a half) and Katie (two), daughters of Josh and Karen Ockerbloom. The Ockerblooms run their own real-estate company just outside Kalamazoo, Michigan – my ultimate destination – and they sound lovely. Really lovely. And unbelievably, well, *American*.

Karen was at pains to stress how excited she and Josh were about welcoming me – 'a bona-fide British nanny' – into their home.

On top of that, I get my own car (an SUV – which, thanks to Google, I now know does not refer to the filters in a sun-tan lotion), I won't be expected to do any chores (they have staff) and they'd like me to go on holiday with them to Bermuda next month, *all expenses paid*.

I feel my mobile vibrate. There's a new message from the agency I've registered with, British Supernannies. They're apparently very good – the fastest-growing UK agency in America – although, judging by their choice of name, understatement isn't a speciality.

'This is a message for Zoe Moore,' begins the voice of Margaret, the slightly doddery secretary I've been dealing with for the past few weeks. 'I'm terribly sorry about this, Zoe, but there's been a change of plan. Please do give me a ring when you have a chance – and, most importantly, before you get on your connecting flight.'

A long conversation ensues, during which it emerges – as I try not to get too exasperated – that I'm no longer going to Kalamazoo. I'm now going to Hope Falls, which is near Boston. Which means I'm no longer going to live with Karen and Josh. Or to drive their SUV. Or to go to Bermuda. Hope Falls? You can say that again.

I'm now going to Mrs R. Miller, a single mother, to

look after her two children, Ruby, who is nearly six, and Samuel, who's just turned three. There was a last-minute change of plan, apparently. Karen and Josh have a nanny, a girl from Surrey who was with them last year and suddenly became available again after they came to an agreement about a pay rise.

I grip my rucksack and force myself to come over all Thelma and Louise-like. To remind myself that I'm a strong, confident, independent woman who is more than happy to live life on the edge and change her plans when required – even when it means Bermuda's out.

I head towards a shop to buy a bottle of water, and when I get to the till to pay for it, the generously proportioned African-American assistant flashes me a smile.

No, no. That's not right. To call it a smile doesn't cover it. This is the sort of grin you'd expect from a woman who'd just lost a stone in weight, won the lottery and found the most glorious pair of shoes she's ever set eyes on . . . in a sale.

'Going anywhere nice, ma'am?' She beams.

'Oh, Boston. For work,' I reply, keeping it vague enough for the others in the queue to imagine me an off-duty human-rights lawyer on her way to reverse a miscarriage of justice or two.

'Boston, huh? Well, you be sure to have a good time.'

'I will. Thank you.'

I take the bottle from her and attempt to put it into my rucksack before I move away. But the cord at the top isn't budging. I free my hands by shoving my purse into my mouth, then try stuffing the bottle into the front pocket. But it just isn't happening. Not easily, anyway.

Pushing, pulling and scrambling, I'm no nearer to getting the bottle into my bag, and painfully conscious now of the growing queue.

With the woman behind me tutting and rolling her eyes, I rip open the back pocket, stuff in the bottle and straighten my back indignantly.

It is at this point that the clasp on my purse, still squashed between my teeth, takes on a life of its own. It bursts open, coins projecting out as if I'm vomiting two-pence pieces. The woman behind looks as if she has lost the will to live. Others rush forward offering help as I scrabble around, clumsily trying to pick up my money. My cheeks redden violently.

'Um, thanks, ooh, sorry, I, em, thanks a lot, sorry, um . . .' I babble. Wanting to escape, I shove my empty purse between my knees and hobble out, my arms full of coins, plastic bank cards and my rucksack, forcing myself to ignore the suppressed giggles.

'Have a nice day, ma'am!' the assistant calls after me, as I disappear round a corner, hoping she'll understand why I don't reply.

Chapter 4

Having taken the monorail to Grand Central Station I settle down to wait for my train to Boston and dig out my magazine. As I flick through it, I sense somebody sitting next to me and catch a waft of aftershave that immediately pricks my senses.

Calvin Klein Truth. I'd know it anywhere. It's the aftershave Jason would splash on religiously every morning, just after he'd checked his hair and straightened his tie in the uniquely meticulous way I came to know so well. Forgetting where I am, I glance upwards, pulse racing.

But it's not Jason. Of course it isn't. I haven't seen him for nearly two months, so why would I think he'd be here in the States?

My neighbour – a heavy-set guy in his late thirties with a wonky fringe – flashes me a shy smile. I smile back and return to my magazine, even though I've been through all its pages at least three times now.

Jason and I met when I was twenty and he was twenty-three – a small age difference, really, but at the time it felt like one of Michael Douglas and Catherine Zeta-Jones proportions.

By then, I'd dropped the law degree I hated and was a trainee at Bumblebees; he'd already left college, had spent a gap year bumming around Europe and had just been accepted on to a graduate-trainee scheme for one of the UK's biggest firms of accountants.

The first thing I should point out about Jason is that he's the least likely accountant you could ever meet. Not that I've got anything against accountants, but public perception of the profession doesn't put them up there in the excitement stakes with your average NASA scientist.

Jason dispels that myth comprehensively. The life and soul of any party, he's one of those people who gels so instantly with everyone he meets he's like a human tube of Vidal Sassoon Shockwaves. I found him charming, engaging and utterly gorgeous. He turned heads everywhere we went. Admittedly, that had something to do with the fact that, in the year we met, Gareth Gates had recently been named runner-up in *Pop Idol* and it's fair to say that there's more than a passing resemblance between him and my ex.

Jason had classic boy-band good looks and, at thirty now, he retains them. He's slightly skinny and only a few inches taller than me, but his face and smile are to die for. He was my own personal heart-throb and I was smitten.

My feelings blossomed into what I became sure – no, I *knew* – was deep, everlasting love. By that I don't mean that, seven years on, we were still gazing into each other's eyes like lovelorn puppies. But we knew each other's flaws and continued to love each other despite them. After that length of time together, our love wasn't as all-consuming as it had been in the early days. But it was solid. A real love. The basis for a lifetime together. At least, that was what I'd thought.

How wrong could I have been?

Chapter 5

I have been on the train for more than three hours and have spent approximately 95 per cent of that time talking. This, like anything that stops me thinking about Jason (albeit temporarily), can only be a positive thing. Even if my jaw feels as if it might seize up.

The first person to sit next to me was George Garfield II, a big old bear of a man who retired eighteen years ago after a career as a fire-fighter. He'd been in the Big Apple to see his grandchildren and was so impressed that I was from Liverpool (because that was where the Beatles were from) you'd think I'd just won an Olympic medal.

Then there was Janice Weisberger, a former model in her fifties with a chignon so perfect I'm convinced it must have been sprayed with Superglue. She was on her way back from a two-day beauty convention and was kind enough to present me with a facial wash for problem skin. She lived next door but one to someone who had a cousin who'd been to Liverpool in the mid-eighties. As she put it, she and I had so much in common.

Next came Earl, the struggling artist, who talked so fast I only managed to catch every fifth word, and Kate, the library assistant, who'd just dumped her boyfriend after walking in on him trying on her mom's flannel nightgown.

When Kate has gone, it strikes me how much I'm getting into the spirit of this lone-traveller lark. In fact, what on earth was I worried about?

At the next stop, an elderly lady with candyfloss hair, a smart buttoned-up coat and a gingham shopping trolley scuttles over and sits next to me.

'Hello!' I offer, smiling in the warm, American manner to which I am now becoming accustomed.

She doesn't respond.

Not too concerned – and ready for a break from talking – I dig out the copy of *OK!* I bought at Manchester airport, enticed by the prospect of studying such matters as the type of wallpaper Jordan and Peter André have on their loo walls. I'm engrossed for about five minutes when I can't help noticing what my neighbour is up to.

With my head fixed forward – so that to anyone else it would appear that I'm focusing intently on Jordan's nose – my eyes swivel sideways.

The little old lady is reaching into her shopping trolley and producing a bottle, covered with a paper bag. Which would be fine except that I suspect it does *not* contain a litre of Appletize. It smells like a 70 per cent proof home-brew that has been fermenting in someone's basement for the last two millennia.

As she proceeds to down mouthfuls of this noxious substance, I wonder whether I should sneak away to another seat or simply continue to watch in fascination. But the train is packed and I'm stuck.

I spend the next twenty minutes of the journey studying my magazine and pretending to be enthralled. Eventually I stuff it back into my bag, only then noticing an envelope that has been hidden at the bottom. I pick it up and examine the front, where 'Zoe' is written in my mum's handwriting.

At forty-four, my mum is relatively young – at least, compared with the parents of most of my peer group. And despite the wild-child tag she must have acquired after falling pregnant with me at just sixteen, the reality – as far as I've ever seen – is that she's anything but.

She and Dad dashed up the aisle before they were old enough to buy shandy legally, and have spent the last twenty-eight years in domestic circumstances that are happy, unremarkable and as traditional as they come.

And Mum, although she's young enough to shop at River Island still and attend a step class four times a week with Desy (her gay best friend), is in lots of ways no different from anyone else's mother. She's certainly no less over-protective, as I discovered when I announced I was going on this trip. She made it no secret that she'd prefer me not to go. And when my mother has an opinion about something, she doesn't hesitate to let it be known . . .

15th June

Dear Zoe,
Well, if you're reading this letter, it means you've gone through with it and are now on your way to America.

18

You already know what I think about this, so we won't rehearse the arguments again.

If this is what you feel you've got to do then, obviously, you've got to do it. Personally, I think you'd be sticking two fingers up to That Bloody Swine far more effectively if you stayed here. What better way to show him that life goes on without him?

Desy agrees with me, by the way. And his love life makes Gone with the Wind look short on drama, so he should know. This morning we went for a latte after step and he admitted Jason always reminded him of that bloke he brought home from his holiday in Sunny Beach in Bolivia a couple of years back (or was it Bulgaria?). You remember him, don't you? Good-looking fellow with only one leg. He was talking about opening a bar with Desy, then buggered off with a newsagent from South Shields. Desy was devastated. And while it might not compare with what you've just been through, the point is, you're not alone. There are plenty of us around you who know what it's like.

Oh, there's no point in me going over old ground.

The only thing I would ask is that you heed a few pieces of advice from someone who's been around a lot longer than you have.

First, watch out for terrorists. If you see anyone acting suspiciously, then phone me immediately (or the police). Second, if you're thinking of taking the opportunity of this travelling business to get a tattoo, then at least make sure it's one of those tasteful Arabic type ones, like Angelina Jolie has. I mention this only after what happened to Mandy at work (the one in Accounts who went on Who Wants to Be A Millionaire?, *not the one in Marketing who's got alopecia). She's still distraught after her Brian came back from his trip to Australia with a tattoo of a koala bear on his bottom. If you're even slightly tempted by this, then please, Zoe, just close your eyes and imagine it on your backside when you're ninety.*

Also – and don't take this the wrong way – you need to watch your weight. You used to have lovely legs. And I know dieting might be the last thing on your mind at the moment, but that was probably what Britney Spears once thought.

Anyway, I've said my piece now. Which means the only thing left to say – for one final time – is goodbye. Goodbye, my sweetheart, my little girl. I'll miss you.

Love and kisses,
Mum
XXX

As I finish reading it, I look up and realize we're minutes away from Boston. I start to pack away my belongings, when something unexpected happens.

The train jolts. The lady next to me – the one with the bottle of moonshine – clearly isn't the steadiest on her feet at the best of times and now shunts forward, nearly falling off her seat. I lean down to help her up, but the train jolts again and this time she flies backwards into the seat.

Unfortunately, it isn't just she who flies backwards. The second jolt is enough to propel the bottle out of her hand and straight towards me, in a movement remarkably similar to something Tom Cruise did in *Cocktail*.

As its contents spill over my hair, my face, my clothes, they seem to seep into my every pore. I'm stunned and unable to comprehend anything more than that I now smell as if I've been washing my armpits with Glenfiddich for most of my adult life.

'I – uh, wha—' I'm dumbfounded.

'BASTARD DRIVER!' she howls, ignoring me and shaking her fist in the air. She looks like a cross between Miss Marple and Linda Blair in *The Exorcist*.

I fight my way past her with my luggage in tow and squeeze myself – and it – into the toilet at the end of the carriage. I have just minutes before the train draws into the station. The cubicle is desperately small, but I know that my only hope is to push my hand through the suitcase zip to get out a change of clothes.

As I force my hand in, though, almost drawing blood, to root around inside, I know that the only thing I'll be able to get my hands on is whatever's closest to the top. Panicking, I brush my alcohol-soaked hair out of my face and eventually pull out some things.

'Oh, God,' I mutter, as I examine them. 'Oh, God, oh, God, oh, God.'

But the train is pulling into the station and I have two options. The first is to stay as I am: soaked, so that my top is now see-through and emitting the sort of stench that can only be described as *eau-de-bail-hostel*. The second is to change into the only outfit I've been able to reach, no matter how unsuited to the occasion.

It's close. It's bloody close. Even as I wrestle my way into my clean clothes, aware of the train emptying, I wonder whether the second option really was preferable.

The only positive thought that runs through my mind is that at least Jason can't see me. It would only confirm to him that leaving me had been the right thing to do.

Oh, God, Mrs R. Miller, I hope you're an understanding woman, I really do.

Chapter 6

It is immediately obvious that the person holding a sign with my name on it isn't Mrs R. Miller. It's not that the sign doesn't say 'Zoe Moore' in such huge black letters I suspect it's probably visible from space. Or that this person is not waiting directly under the clock, which was where the agency told me to go. Or even that the two children leaping about in the background couldn't feasibly fit the description of Ruby and Samuel. It's something else. The person holding a sign with my name on it is *a man*.

Clearly, I can't let on that this has fazed me – first impressions and all that – so I stride across the concourse attempting to seem enthusiastic, confident and, above all, so utterly professional I'd intimidate Hillary Clinton.

He fixes his eyes on me. His expression is stern, but he's not unattractive. Not by any means. In fact, he's . . . *oh, God* . . . he's stunning. *Scarily* handsome.

He has dark blond hair, penetrating blue eyes and, although he's a few years older than I am, a physique that would make anyone go weak at the knees: tall and toned, broad-shouldered, with just the right amount of muscle. It's a physique that's far more obvious than Jason's, far more in-your-face, but no less attractive.

On the other hand, this beautiful stranger isn't exactly what my mother would refer to as 'well turned-out'. He clearly hasn't shaved in a week, and his T-shirt and Levi's might have been laundered on the banks of the Ganges. But somehow he carries off the look spectacularly well. He's very good-looking, but wild and dishevelled too. His brand of gorgeousness is rough and raw, dirty almost. Very different from . . . Oh, God, why do I compare every man I meet with Jason?

'Hi!' I find myself mouthing involuntarily as I approach.

But he doesn't move and he doesn't smile.

There is no doubt that the children belong to him. Both have the same striking eyes and distinctive hair, the little girl's falling in wavy tresses down her back, her brother's shorter, but overgrown and unruly.

I continue towards them. It's only when I'm within a couple of feet that I realize their father's expression reveals his alarm.

'You must be . . . Zoe?' he says, almost reluctantly.

'*I am!*' I reply, rather more loudly than I'd intended. I drop my suitcase and hold out my hand. '*Really* pleased to meet you,' I continue, shaking his vigorously. 'How did you know I was Zoe? I guess you'd heard about the famous British sense of style, hey?' I glance down at my clothes. It's no wonder he's unimpressed.

My trousers are the bottom half of a pair of pyjamas that Great Auntie Iris bought me as a going-away present. Aside from the obvious problem, they are not even *nice* pyjamas – although I feel terrible for saying it. I'm convinced they're made of 140 per cent polyester and I know they were purchased from one of Iris's favourite stalls at St John's Market, the ones that specialize in bras the size of a decent two-man tent. Then there's the pattern: *fluorescent* pink tartan.

I only wish I could say my top half made up for them. But while my silver boob tube was fabulous at Garlands nightclub when I was a size ten, right now I look as if I've dressed for my first day at work in a roll of Bacofoil.

I pull my denim jacket closed as my mind whirs with possible excuses for this attire: I'm experimenting with the new look *Vogue* have dubbed 'lunatic chic'; in the UK everyone catches a train wearing fancy dress; I've lost my mind.

'Follow me,' he instructs, grabbing my suitcase and marching off, with the children galloping behind.

'Oh, that's – that's really kind of you,' I mutter, and try to keep up.

He beats me to the car, has the suitcase in the boot, both children strapped in and the engine running before I've disentangled myself from my rucksack and hauled myself into the passenger seat.

As we pull out of the car park, my heart is hammering with a combination of excitement and nerves – and, although I can barely believe it, because it's been so long since it's put in an appearance, a flicker of *lust*.

Partly to take my mind off the contours of his arms, I decide now might be a good time to clear something up. '*Sooo* . . . where is Mrs Miller?'

25

His eyes narrow and for a second he looks very much like the Terminator considering whether or not to tear someone's legs off. 'Is that supposed to be funny?' he says.

'No.' I frown. 'I mean, I just had a conversation with the agency who told me I'd be working for Mrs R. Miller.'

'Sorry, honey. I'm R. Miller. *Ryan* Miller. And, as you can see, I ain't no *Mrs.*'

Chapter 7

Ryan Miller, I decide, is a bit of a puzzle. First, he has produced two of the politest, most adorable children I could ever have wished for. Samuel talks non-stop throughout the car journey, pointing out in the uniquely random way of three-year-olds every branch of McDonald's (which he refers to as 'Old McDonald's'), and declaring five minutes into our relationship that I am his 'bess friend'. I am gratified by the apparently instantaneous bonding I've achieved with one of my new charges, until he adds, 'And Daddy is my bess friend and Ruby is my bess friend and Benjamin is my bess friend and Big Bear is my bess friend', and so on, until he has named everyone from their neighbour to the dentist he visited last week.

As well as entertaining Samuel – whom she clearly adores and constantly fusses over – Ruby spends much of the journey telling me, in her soft American lilt, how wonderful her father is ('Our daddy works in a big office'; 'He used to play baseball for his school'; 'Did I tell you our daddy once went to New Zealand? *And* he's been to New Jersey'). In Ruby's eyes, Ryan Miller is

Superman, God and the Tooth Fairy rolled into one.

While the kids and I make friends easily, however, the same cannot be said for their dad and me.

Aside from Ryan's undeniably impressive six-pack (which is so defined you could play 'Chopsticks' on it) I can't say he's charm personified. Throughout the journey, he has been barking orders through his earpiece to various unfortunate individuals who apparently work for him. Only now does he pause to make conversation with me, but he's not in the mood for small-talk.

'Occasionally I leave the car at the office so I'll need you to drive me to catch the T,' he tells me. Despite his brusqueness, the accent is deep and unbelievably exotic.

'Right, no problem,' I reply, hoping to appear familiar with 'the T' until I can get hold of a guidebook to translate.

'The subway,' he says, sensing my bewilderment.

'Hmm?'

'The T. That's what we call it here.'

'Oh, um, right. Of course.'

We're thundering along a dual carriageway full of unfamiliar road signs and huge cars. The colour and sound of my surroundings are totally foreign, completely new. And yet for some reason I find my mind drifting as I breathe in Ryan's smell and try to work out which aftershave he's wearing, which is nothing I recognize from the counter at Boots. Intense, musky, masculine. And disturbingly sexy.

'So you'll need to get the kids dressed and ready to go out at seven fifteen a.m. and no later,' he continues, interrupting my thoughts. 'The train's at seven twenty-eight, and if I miss it I'm screwed. Okay?'

'You betcha,' I reply, but regret it. It was a pathetic attempt to demonstrate how I'm getting into the spirit of my new surroundings, but his expression says he thinks I'm being sarcastic.

'Give them dinner whenever you want, and don't wait for me to get home before you put them to bed. I work late a lot so I can't guarantee I'll be back in time.'

I frown. The contract I signed with the agency said I was supposed to finish at five thirty, apart from on pre-agreed occasions.

'You're flexible on hours, right?' he says, as if sensing my thoughts.

'Um, of course.' I assume he's referring to the odd evening and I don't want to make a fuss at this stage. 'And bedtime is when?'

He pauses for so long I get the impression it's not an issue he's considered before. 'Ten. Ten thirty?' he says finally.

'Really?' I blurt.

'Look, whenever you want,' he shoots back.

'Right, right.'

Okay, I'll admit it. Alarm bells are already going off about the complete lack of warmth emanating from my new boss. Despite this, or perhaps because of it, I find myself trying even harder to come up with ways to impress him, to make him see how brilliant I'm going to be at the job.

'*Sooo* . . . the agency passed you my CV, did they?' I bring this up so that I can slip into the conversation that

I was second in command in my last job, have recently passed my umpteenth early-years qualification at night school and have a reputation for potty-training children faster than you can say 'magnetic sticker chart'.

'Yeah.' He glances over and makes eye contact with me for the first time. It's only for a split second but it makes my heart jump.

'You okay with house cleaning?' he asks, his eyes returning to the road.

'House cleaning?'

'Yeah. Vacuuming, the kitchen, you know the kind of thing.'

'Well, yes, but—'

'And the kids' laundry?'

'Um, yes, I can, although—'

'Good,' he replies.

I deflate and have to force myself not to think about Karen and Josh Ockenbloom's army of domestic staff.

'The odd chore isn't a problem,' I continue, feeling that some clarification of my professional boundaries is essential at this point. 'I mean, the main focus needs to be the children – a key plank of early-years teaching is—'

'Sure,' he interrupts. 'Well, you might need to go out and buy some Clorox and stuff. I've left a coupla bucks on the table for you.'

'Okay. Great.'

'It's cleaning fluid,' he says.

'What is?'

'Clorox.'

'Oh.'

There is a long pause. Awkward silences with Ryan Miller are more awkward than most awkward silences. So I decide to take a different tack. Perhaps if I ask some intelligent, searching questions about the place that will be my new home for the foreseeable future I might be able to engage him in a more meaningful conversation. I mean, now I'm an experienced traveller, I ought to try to get a feel for Hope Falls. I think about Michael Palin interviewing the indigenous people of far-flung places for his travelogues and clear my throat. 'So, Hope Falls . . . um, what's it like?'

Okay, so maybe I'd struggle to get a job on *Newsround* with that one.

He flicks on his indicator, slows down and turns on to a wide driveway. 'Your average American suburb,' he replies.

'Right.' I try to look as if this fascinating insight has surpassed all my expectations. 'Good.'

'You'll see for yourself,' he adds.

'I hope you never apply for a job as a tour guide.' I chuckle, hoping that just the right amount of cheek might endear me to him.

He ignores me. 'We're here.'

As Ryan opens his door, I follow his lead and take in my surroundings as I step out of the car.

We are in a large, crescent-shaped road that would be immediately identifiable as American to even the most culturally naïve ten-year-old. Maybe it's the fact that the houses all have slatted wooden exteriors and front porches on stilts – the kind designed for sitting on, in a rocking-chair, to ponder the meaning of life. Maybe it's the mailboxes at the end of every driveway or the fire hydrants that play a bit-part in every cop show in the history of television.

Whatever it is, it isn't Woolton, Liverpool.

There is one crucial difference, though, between the house we're outside and all the others. The front of this one is so overgrown it must be hosting species of flora and fauna that usually thrive in far-off corners of Brazilian rainforests.

I follow the children up the steps, battling exhaustion. But as I reach the door I notice something: my bags have been abandoned on the porch. And so, apparently, have I. Because my new employer is heading in the opposite direction. 'Gotta go,' he throws over his shoulder.

'What?'

'Ruby'll show you your room. The spare car's in the garage, keys are on the table in the hall and – uh, you'll find your way around.'

I'm panicking. 'Where are you going?' I try to ask casually, but sound as though I've just discovered my trousers are on fire.

'The office,' he replies, pulling his mobile out of his pocket again. 'I gotta catch up with some work.'

'But it's Saturday,' I point out.

'Yeah,' he says, as if I've just told him my favourite brand of exfoliator. 'Like I said, I gotta catch up. Now, come on, you guys—'

He leans through the rails on the steps to kiss the children, then dives into his car and speeds away. I'm left standing there with my mouth open like a stunned turbot's.

Not for the first time since I left the UK less than twenty-four hours ago, I feel way out of my comfort zone. The effect this has on me is the exact opposite of what I'm trying to achieve by leaving home: it makes me *long* for Jason. I want him to put his familiar arms round me and tell me everything will be all right. I want him to kiss my forehead tenderly in the way he always did when I was nervous. I yearn for the reassuring stability I was convinced our relationship represented, ironic as that now seems.

Ruby appears at my side. 'Do you like my daddy?' she asks anxiously.

How to answer this? I can hardly tell her that, while I think he's heart-stoppingly sexy, my first impression of Ryan is that he's also arrogant, evasive and downright rude. I take her hand, squeeze it and smile. 'Your daddy's great,' I tell her.

Her little face beams, leaving me in no doubt that that's not something she hears very often. 'You really think so?'

'Oh, yes,' I say.

She looks overwhelmed with happiness. 'I just knew you'd be different from all those other nannies we had.'

Chapter 8

My mother has a beautifully euphemistic phrase she uses to describe other people's houses when she thinks they could do with a bloody good clean: 'lived in' – as in, 'Well, yes . . . it could be a nice house if it wasn't quite so *lived in*.'

It's a phrase that springs to mind as I walk into the Miller residence, except it may not be strong enough. This house is so *lived in* that squatters might have taken it over.

You can tell that the large hallway has been decorated – at some point in the distant past – by someone with taste. But the cream walls are now camouflaged with grubby handprints, the stylish antique tables so battered they're ready for the dump, and the once bold abstract paintings now hang on the walls so haphazardly they might have been put there by a hyperactive chimpanzee.

I cast my eyes down. It's difficult to identify the floor between the toys, books, shoes, old fast-food cartons and random stacks of office paper.

There's something about the state of the hallway that

makes me hold my breath before I walk into the living room. But I still let out a tiny gasp on entering it.

Yes, at some time in its history, someone has made the most of its high-beamed ceiling and imposing stone fireplace by adorning it with what were once three stylish sofas and various tasteful antiques. The problem is, the sofas are now smothered with kiddy-food debris, including what I suspect are chocolate ice cream, peanut butter and a hideous, sticky pink concoction. Several empty coffee cups are lying around, along with black-soled children's socks, trodden-on crisps and beakers of fermented juice. In short, the room looks as if it has just suffered a heavy night of bombing.

Samuel marches past me, switches on the TV and, with his nose about a foot and a half from the screen, is immediately in a semi-hypnotic daze.

'Samuel, wouldn't you prefer to do a puzzle or something?' I ask, sitting down on a sofa.

'Huh?'

'A puzzle, Samuel,' I suggest, 'or . . . we could do some drawing?'

'*Noooooo!*' He shakes his head.

'Ruby,' I say decisively, 'what are your dad's rules on watching TV? I presume you're not allowed to in the daytime?'

She looks at me as if she fears for my mental health. 'Sure,' she replies, plonking herself next to her brother.

I am a dedicated early-years professional, so it is obviously out of the question for me to allow the children to watch television on my first day. I mean, I'm trained to conjure up all manner of stimulating exercises aimed at broadening young minds and rewarding their progress. I can sing 'Twinkle Twinkle Little Star' in Urdu and construct a detailed model of a farmyard from old egg cartons. I suspect I know the words from *Aliens Love Underpants*, *The Gruffalo* and *Harry and His Bucketful of Dinosaurs* better than their authors do. So letting Ruby and Samuel sit in front of the goggle-box all afternoon just isn't on. Not on my watch.

'Well, I think we should play something,' I persevere. 'Or maybe go outside. It's a gorgeous day.'

As I attempt to usher them outside, I realize I can't. Such is my exhaustion that trying to lift myself off the sofa feels like hoisting a six-ton rag-doll. Overwhelmed by fatigue, I slump back – just for a second, you understand – as my eyes plead to close.

'We usually watch TV,' Ruby tells me, flicking to *Dora the Explorer*, then wiping Samuel's nose with a piece of tissue she keeps tucked in her sleeve.

'Really?' I whimper, trying to summon up the collective power of my principles, training and energy.

'Uh-huh,' she confirms.

'Oh. Well, why not, then?'

I feel myself drift into semi-slumber as I fight to keep awake and alert to what the children are up to. I have no idea how long my eyes are closed. It might have been seconds. I suspect it's at least minutes. It's certainly long enough for the voice that ultimately wakes me to startle me so much I almost leap out of my chair.

'*Hiiiyyaaaa!*'

It's coming from the porch and has the pitch of a tribal

warrior announcing that battle is about to commence. I glance at the children, but they look as bemused as I suspect I do.

Chapter 9

It's fair to say that Trudie Woodcock is not your arche-typal British nanny. I don't know why exactly, but it may have something to do with the generous cleavage, *Charlie's Angels* hair and vertiginous wedge heels.

Within half an hour of meeting her, however, it's clear that Trudie's Wagtastic sense of glamour is of little interest to Andrew and Eamonn, the two-year-old twins she looks after on the other side of the crescent. To them, Trudie is the most entertaining individual they've ever come across. She has boundless energy, with a discernible naughty streak, and they seem to see her as the human equivalent of a Labrador puppy – perma-nently in the mood for fun.

This quality is illustrated to spectacular effect each time she breaks off from a grown-up conversation – without warning – to dive towards her charges and tickle them so vigorously that they look likely to end up in Casualty from laughing so much.

'Now, come on, you two, calm down,' Trudie gasps, attempting to catch her breath between guffaws. 'God, I gave up smoking just before I came out here and thought

I'd be super-fit by now. I don't know what's gone wrong.'

'Not ready to run your first triathlon yet, then?'

'I'd be better prepared to run for president,' she puffs.

I giggle. 'How long have you been here?'

'A month and a half. And I hope you haven't come here to meet a fella because, let me warn you, the talent here isn't exactly world class. In Hope Falls, at least.'

I don't bother telling her that that's the last thing on my mind. I've already found the man of my dreams – even though the end of our relationship was the stuff of nightmares.

'I'd make an exception, though,' continues Trudie, lowering her voice.

'Oh?'

'Your man.'

'What man?'

'Your man here! Ryan!'

'Ssssh!' I check the children didn't hear. 'Do you really think so?' I ask casually. 'I hadn't noticed.'

'Bloody right I think so!'

'Well,' I whisper, 'he couldn't be grumpier if he'd had private tuition from Ebenezer Scrooge.'

'Grumpy? *Brooding*, you mean,' she murmurs. 'Like Mr Darcy. Or the one that was on *The X Factor* last year.'

'Whatever you say.' I grin.

'And he's a bit of a heartbreaker, apparently.'

'Oh? Well, I can't see it.'

'Then there must be something wrong with your eyesight.'

Mercifully, the conversation is cut short when Samuel

ventures on to the sofa next to us. 'Are you from England, Zoe?' he asks.

'I am, sweetheart,' I tell him, straightening his T-shirt.

'I am from Hope Falls,' he declares.

'I know,' I say. 'And I'm going to stay with you here, aren't I?'

'Can I come to England?' he asks.

'Well, one day I'm *sure* you'll be able to,' I say, thinking that perhaps in fifteen years' time he might join the throngs of US students backpacking round Europe.

'Today?' he says hopefully.

Ruby bursts into fits of giggles and leans over to hug him. This starts Samuel giggling. 'You silly thing,' she says, kissing his head. 'England's too far away to go to today. It's even further than Maine.'

Trudie and I are quizzed on everything from what language is spoken in England to whether we have ever eaten a Gummi Bear. When, eventually, they go back to the TV I turn to Trudie again. 'I take it your earlier comment – about the men here – means you're not attached?'

'*Au contraire*,' she replies, raising her eyebrows. It's the first time I've ever heard someone utter a French phrase in quite such a thick Yorkshire accent. 'I've met my ideal man while I've been over here. I said the talent isn't world class *in Hope Falls*. My bloke lives on the other side of town.'

'Ah,' I say.

'He's absolutely bloody spectacular,' she continues dreamily. 'I love him to bits.'

'How did you meet?' I ask.

'Ritchie's a tree surgeon and was doing a job at our

place in the first week I was here. He was sorting out one of the sugar maples at the bottom of the garden. I first saw him when he was halfway up it with a chainsaw. Took one look at those biceps and, let me tell you, *I was his!*'

'Can't resist a bloke with a power tool, hey?'

'Something like that.' She giggles. 'It's not just that, though. He's *lovely*. So kind and thoughtful. Always telling me how gorgeous I am – even if I've got a zit on my nose – and he's for ever buying me flowers. That might sound corny but I'm a sucker for it.'

'It doesn't sound corny at all,' I tell her truthfully. 'It sounds absolutely fantastic.'

'Listen,' she says suddenly, 'why don't you go and get yourself unpacked and have a shower? I'll watch the kids and then we can all go out for something to eat. There's a place down the road that does pizzas so big they must have about four thousand calories per slice.'

'Really? You don't mind?' I whimper. I couldn't have been happier if she'd offered to pay off a lifetime of parking tickets, resit my French GCSE and remember to buy Great Auntie Iris some lavender talcum powder for her birthday each year.

'Go!' she instructs.

Ruby leaps up and grabs my hand. 'I'll show you the way, Zoe.'

We climb the stairs. As we approach the spare bed-room, I can almost picture what I'm about to face: the sort of room about which a Wormwood Scrubs resident would be entitled to send off a stern letter of complaint. But as I open the door I'm well and truly shocked.

It's small, sunny and astonishingly neat. There's a white and pastel patchwork throw draped over the bed. The walls are the colour of ripe lemons and the curtains at the window are covered with bright yellow roses and tied back with matching ribbons. I wouldn't say it's my style – a bit too Laura Ashley-meets-*Seven Brides for Seven Brothers* – but it's such an improvement on everywhere else, you'd hardly think it was in the same house.

'Do you think it's pretty?' asks Ruby.

'It's gorgeous,' I reply, squeezing her hand. 'It really is.'

'I told Daddy he had to make it nice for you,' she adds proudly. 'He didn't do that for any of our other nannies.'

'Oh. What makes me so honoured?'

'I guess he doesn't want to lose another.'

On the bedside table there's a little filigree picture frame with a photo of Ruby and Samuel in it.

'Look!' exclaims Ruby, pointing at it.

'Wow!' I smile. 'It's you and Samuel! Thank you so much.'

'You can put somebody else in it, if you like,' adds Ruby. 'We don't mind.'

'I'd like to keep your picture in it. I can't think of anything nicer.'

Which is almost true. Even if the reason I don't want anyone else's picture in there is a bit more complicated than that.

That's all it takes – a comment about a picture frame – and Jason invades my thoughts. This time, for no particular reason, I have a flashback to when we first met, all those years ago.

In films, romances never begin in a scruffy pub with a soundtrack courtesy of a karaoke machine programmed to play nothing but Chesney Hawkes tracks. Yet in real life such mundane settings are often where the seeds of a big relationship are sown – at least, that was the case with Jason and me.

We met during a night out with the girls for me and a night out with the boys for him. Our paths converged at a Mathew Street hot spot in the days before they spruced up the area for the tourists and when hens and stags threw back tequila slammers in heroic quantities.

While I can't recall the exact path of our conversation, I know that Jason and I hit it off so well that I kept expecting to see a little fellow with wings and a harp hovering in the background.

When I woke up the next morning I remembered he'd asked for my phone number but didn't think he'd follow it up. But he did. He phoned me that very day – and when my mother heard his accent she went into a veritable tizz. Jason is originally from Cheshire, which, as far as my mum is concerned, makes him practically aristocracy.

That was how it started. Seven years down the line we were still together, still – I assumed – very much in love. But, then, it turned out I'd assumed a lot of things.

I'd assumed we were soul-mates. I'd assumed we'd be together for ever. I'd assumed that on our wedding day, as I arrived at the church where he was supposed to meet me at the altar, he'd turn up too.

Silly me. I'd assumed wrong.

Chapter 10

Given that Boston is going to be my new home town, I'm keen to blend in with the indigenous population as quickly as possible. Or, at least, not to look like a hapless tourist who can't find their way to the loo without an in-depth destination guide and a pop-up street map.

I saunter into American Jack's in a bid to appear as at ease with my surroundings as Norm walking into Cheers. Instead I trip over a step, nearly knocking over a waitress. It isn't a subtle restaurant, with its Stars-and-Stripes banners behind the bar, baseball matches on the TVs in each corner and diners' plates piled so high they should have been supplied with JCBs instead of cutlery.

We make our way past the oak-panelled bar and up some stairs on to a warm patio drenched in early evening sun. It's here that we're pounced on by a hyperactive redhead, so cheery you'd think she'd spent the morning snorting fairy dust. 'Hey, guys! How are y'all today? I'm Ci-Ci and I'm your waitress! What can I getcha?'

I fumble through the menu, trying to pick something before I'm caught slacking.

'You can just order drinks right now, if you like,'

Ci-Ci squeaks, 'then look through the menu at your leisure.'

'Oh, um, okay,' I say, sliding my menu down. 'I'll have a coffee, please.'

My energy level might have risen slightly in the last couple of hours, but I still haven't slept for what feels like weeks and know that without a pick-me-up I'll keel over at any moment.

'No problem, ma'am,' chirps Ci-Ci. 'Would that be a regular filter, cappuccino, latte, espresso, iced . . . ?'

'Iced,' I interrupt, quietly impressed that I haven't just gone for a boring old cappuccino as I would at home.

'Sure thing. Would that be small, regular, large, extra large or super-sized?'

'Oh, um, just a kind of . . . medium, please.'

'I'm sorry?'

'A med— Oh, um, regular.'

'No problem. De-caff, half-caff or regular strength?'

'Regular strength.'

'Gotcha. Full-fat, non-fat or fifty-fifty?'

'Fifty-fifty,' I reply, as if I indulge in it twice a day.

'Sure. Any syrup?'

I smile. 'Not today.'

'Great!'

Now she turns to Trudie. 'How 'bout you, ma'am?'

Every member of our party is treated to the same smiley grilling and I'm slightly miffed with myself when Ruby places her order with significantly more aplomb than I managed.

When it comes to food, I glance down the list, past

Chicken, Broccoli and Ziti, Jack's New England Clam Chowder, and Fresh Boston Schrod. I remind myself that I have recently gained sixteen and a half pounds, which has probably risen to seventeen and a half after all the Pringles I devoured on the flight. I owe it to myself to pick out the lowest-fat dish on the menu, then eat only half of it.

'Some of the salads sound nice, don't they?' I muse, trying to convince myself more than anyone else.

Oh, sod it. I order Jack's Rack of Slow-roasted Pork Ribs with coleslaw, hand-cut fries and a side order of onion rings. It arrives on a plate the size of Malta.

'You look starving, love,' Trudie says, halfway through the meal.

'I should be on a diet.' I sigh, chomping a chip.

'Oh, you're joking! You don't need to diet. I've got more spare tyres than Kwik Fit and it's never bothered me.'

That's all the encouragement I require to demolish the rest of my meal, which should have come with its own cardiac-support unit. Maybe that's just one of the reasons why I like Trudie.

It turns out she became a nanny two years ago, having given up her less than lucrative job as a barmaid back home in a nightclub called Crazy Brian's. 'I loved every minute of it,' she says, her voice dripping with sarcasm. 'It was a dream job, apart from the pervy boss, obnoxious customers and crap pay.'

'How did you get into childcare?' I ask.

'I'm the eldest of seven, so I was quite well qualified,' she begins. 'To be honest, though, I just got to a stage in my life where I wanted to change things. I grew up on a council estate that was as rough as hell. You needed a flak-jacket some nights just to go out of your front door. By the time I'd left school, my prospects weren't much better. I took a hard look at my life and thought, I want more than this.'

'So you went back to college?' I ask.

She nods. 'I left school with virtually no qualifications. God knows why – I was always being told I was quite bright. Something just went horribly wrong in my schooling. I fell in with a bad crowd, I suppose – I was more interested in trying to cadge my next Benson & Hedges than I was in getting an education. But when I went to college at twenty-three it was different, maybe cos I love kids. Or maybe it was just the idea of telling Brian he'd have to get someone else to order his Big D nuts from then on.' She giggles. 'Whatever it was, well . . . I passed.'

She's trying to keep a straight face when she tells me this, but it's clear she's bursting with a sense of accomplishment and pride.

'I couldn't believe it,' she continues, flicking back a wave of blonde hair. 'I'd never been good at anything before. Except fruit machines. And smoking.'

By the time the children are eating their ice cream, we have moved on to the subject of my new workplace. 'So, what's Mrs Miller like?' I ask, lowering my voice. 'I mean, I've already worked out she isn't exactly a stickler for standards of household cleanliness. But am I going to get on better with her than I have so far with her other half?'

Trudie nearly chokes. 'Bloody he— I mean, heck,' she says, glancing at the children. 'I thought you knew.'

'Knew what?' I frown.

She wipes her mouth. 'There *is* no Mrs Miller.'

'You mean they're divorced?'

'I *mean*,' Trudie hisses, 'she's dead.'

For a split second I think my heart has stopped beating.

'I don't want to sound sexist,' she continues, and slurps some Diet Coke, 'but how many women have you met who would let their living room get like that? The place is like the set of a disaster movie.'

I shake my head. 'I hadn't realized. I mean, I just assumed . . .'

'Well, you weren't to know. Poor little buggers, eh?'

Ruby and Samuel are still tucking into their ice cream. Samuel has so much of his in his hair that he looks as though he's been shampooing with it.

'How long ago did it happen?' I ask.

'According to Barbara – that's my boss – it was just after Samuel was born. So, two and a half years, maybe.'

I think about Ruby, then just three, having a parent there one day but not the next – and the unthinkable bewilderment and sadness she must have felt. Two children are growing up without a mum to watch nativity plays, kiss their knees when they fall over, or tuck them up in bed in the way that only mothers can.

I think about my own happy upbringing, with two parents who adored me – and still do – and feel incredibly sad.

I also feel a pang of guilt about Ryan. Okay, so strains

of E. Coli have displayed more charm than he'd directed towards me that morning, but this puts him in a new light. Suddenly I'm determined to rise to the challenge of working with the family and proving the strength of my moral fibre.

'How did she die?' I ask Trudie.

'A car crash,' she says. 'Although I think Barbara has convinced herself she's under the patio.'

I must look alarmed.

'Not really,' Trudie adds. 'Barbara's just like that. She and Ryan aren't what you'd call best buddies.'

'Why not?'

'Because his lawn isn't mown to her standards, the kids don't go to church and he hasn't told her recently how fabulous she's looking.'

I smile. 'How well do you get on with her?'

'Oh, fine,' she replies. 'We're not what you'd call peas in a pod, but Barbara's fundamentally okay. Apart from anything else, she puts up with me when I'm sure I'm not what she was hoping for when she ordered a British nanny.'

'What do you think she was hoping for?'

Trudie pulls up the strap on her Wonderbra and tries, but fails, to suppress a burp. 'Mary Poppins.'

Chapter 11

It's ten twenty-five. Bedtime – if your approach to childcare is totally demented, completely half-hearted and utterly nuts. Which is exactly what I am starting to suspect Ryan Miller is.

Sorry. I'll calm down.

And not least because I should have seen this coming. To somebody who has lived and breathed children for the past seven years, the fact that this is too late for them should have been as obvious as the answers on *Family Fortunes*.

The trouble is, Ryan is the parent – even though he hasn't put in an appearance since he dumped me, my bags and his children on the porch this morning.

His status as their dad foolishly made me think he might know some secret I didn't. That there must be some logic in his advice to keep the children up so late. I honestly thought I'd be playing it safe by allowing them to stick to their usual schedule – no matter how odd it seemed. That both children are still awake – exhausted to the point of tantrums and tears – would tend to indicate that there is not.

I take a deep breath and remind myself not to be fazed. The words of my first boss at Bumblebees are for ever ingrained in my memory: a good child-carer is an *unflappable* child-carer.

What a smartarse she could be.

Here's what I'm up against: those two polite, almost subdued children – whom I've been attempting to cajole into activity all day – now resemble a pair of juvenile delinquents after an overdose of Pro Plus.

'Nooooooooo!' Samuel howls, as he flings himself on to the sofa.

All I'd done was suggest it was time we switched off *Curious George* for some wind-down time before we go up to bed, but you'd think I was threatening him with the gallows.

'*It's too early!*' shrieks Ruby, her cheeks ruddy with tiredness as she throws Strawberry Shortcake at the table.

'It's not too early,' I repeat, for the twelfth time. 'It's ten twenty-five. That's your bedtime.'

I'm using my special nursery-nurse voice, which strikes just the right balance between caring and authoritative. The Sugar Plum Fairy, with overtones of Genghis Khan. It *usually* works.

'Daddy said it was ten to ten thirty,' Ruby sobs, screwing up her face.

'Which is what ten twenty-five is,' I reason.

'No, it's not,' she wails. 'That's *before* ten thirty. I'm not *stupid*, you know!'

'Not stupid! Not stupid!' echoes Samuel, stamping his feet.

There's only one thing for it. Forget the stacks of qualifications and years of experience. What the hell did Supernanny do with that family from South Wales – the toddler who was close to being issued with an ASBO and the ten-year-old who'd perfected the art of breaking and entering?

I kneel down to Ruby's level and hold her hands, hoping to put her in a semi-meditative state with my calming get commanding manner. 'Listen to me, Ruby,' I say softly. 'You've been a good girl all day, so I know you're a good girl really. But good girls go to bed when they're told to and—'

'*I don't want to go to bed!*' she squeals, and the windows rattle. 'I don't *like* going to bed!'

I'm attempting to maintain a composed, temperate and compassionate exterior. My head feels like the inner chamber of a volcano, mid-eruption. Think, Zoe. What is at the root of all this? Why the hell aren't they settling down?

I glance over at the TV in the corner, which is blaring *Go, Diego, Go!*. This is not going to make them happier, but it has to be done. I take another deep breath, stride across the room and flick it off, with a formidable, matronly air. 'Now—'

'Arrrgh!' Samuel howls, as he throws himself on to the floor, pounding his fists so furiously that he nearly knocks a hole through to the cellar.

It is eleven twenty-five by the time I get them to bed. And – after repeated escape attempts, followed by reasoning, bribery and outright threats (largely to disconnect the television) – it's twelve fifteen before they are finally asleep.

And it's about twelve sixteen when I wonder if there's any beer in the house. I should stress that, under normal circumstances, I have a healthy relationship with alcohol. In fact, I like to describe myself as one of those people who can take it or leave it.

So, don't be fooled by the fact that when I locate a cold bottle of Coors, I open it with trembling hands and immediately feel like Nicolas Cage when he poured vodka over himself in *Leaving Las Vegas*.

However, when I've slugged half of it – and even though I've been awake now for about two days and am exhausted – I'm not sleepy. No matter how I try, I can't relax. I'm wired. And I know what's causing it: this chaotic house. *Nobody* could mentally unwind while they were surrounded by so much crap. At least, I can't. I lived with Jason too long to be able to put up with a mess.

The house where Jason and I used to live was always immaculate, thanks largely to his influence. It wasn't a huge, flashy place like this one, just a sweet little terrace off Sudley Road. We fell in love with it the minute we first saw it. We spent months doing it up so I could see why Jason was obsessed with keeping it clean and tidy. Even though it didn't come naturally to me, I soon came to appreciate a permanently glistening chrome bathroom, and our living-room carpet was still lusciously cream two years after it had been fitted.

Which is more than I can say for this carpet. I pick up Island Princess Barbie from under the table. She looks as if she's spent the day drinking methylated spirits.

I make a half-hearted attempt at tidying her hair before I throw her into the toy box. Then I pick up a Lego sheep and throw it in after her. The spinning top is next. Then a Bratz hairbrush. Followed by a Mr Potato Head. And by the time I've dealt with the My Little Pony Teapot Palace, the fluffy orang-utan with bits of yoghurt stuck to his fur and the Sing-along Spiderman, I'm going at a hell of a pace.

I just can't help it. When I've cleared all the shoes from the hallway, done the dirty dishes I found in the downstairs loo (I kid you not), mopped the kitchen floor, tidied the bathroom *and* swept up the layer of muck that was making the hall floor look like a third-world street market, it's three twenty-five.

And I'm sleepy. Not just sleepy, in fact, properly tired. Beautifully, gloriously, perfectly, doggedly *tired*. I'm just about to head for bed when I hear a key in the door.

I straighten my back.

I'm ridiculously pleased to be bumping into my new boss because I can't wait to see his reaction to my handiwork. This is a guy who seemed more concerned about my abilities to scrub his toilet than care for his children, and on that basis he'll be knocked sideways when he sees my achievements.

I lean casually on a work surface as Ryan enters the kitchen.

He's even more dishevelled than he was when I first set eyes on him – but even sexier too. My eyes are magnetically drawn to the top of his jeans, where half of his T-shirt is tucked in. His hair is enticingly unkempt, his swagger effortlessly self-assured.

It strikes me that Ryan, without having to say a word, exudes something bewitching and mysterious. His sexual presence is such that he'd turn heads in a room with a thousand people in it.

'Hi!' I say, trying to read his face as he sets eyes on his newly pristine kitchen.

As he walks past I'm enveloped in an aroma that almost makes me faint, subtle but unmistakable, of booze, perfume and cigarette smoke. The whiff of a big night out.

'Did you get much done?' I ask, heart thudding. 'At work, I mean.'

'Hmm?' he says absently, opening the fridge.

'You were going to work,' I remind him, wishing he'd turn round.

'Oh. Yeah. Yeah, I did. Thanks for asking,' he replies. I can't help noticing his speech is slightly slurred.

'Um, the children had a bit of trouble settling before bed,' I inform him. I walk over to the table and lean across it to draw attention to its gleaming surface.

'Oh, yeah?' He shuts the fridge door, leaving the beer, and takes a bottle of whiskey out of a cupboard instead.

'I think they were overtired,' I offer.

'Sure.'

I stand up straight, fold my arms and frown. Ryan is utterly uninterested in this conversation *and* the state of the kitchen.

'They really didn't want to go to bed,' I persevere. 'It was a bit of a struggle.'

'Yeah. They get like that sometimes.'

He fills his glass with whiskey. It's the sort of amount that would put the Jolly Green Giant ten times over the limit.

'Right. Well, if you don't mind, I'd like to try putting them to bed a bit earlier tomorrow.'

He shrugs. 'Whatever you think. I already said that, didn't I?'

'Yes. But . . . Yes, I suppose you did.'

There's another long silence.

'Well, I think I'll go to bed,' I say. But I don't move. I wait. And wait. And wait. I wait for him to say, 'My God, Zoe, the house is amazing, truly unrecognizable. It was barely fit for human habitation before, but now it's like something the Sultan of Brunei wouldn't mind crashing out in. And I've got you to thank, you wonderful, wonderful woman.'

When he finally looks up, his eyes skim across my face, as if he's taking in my features properly for the first time. He doesn't say anything but the attention sends my stomach into freefall. 'Sure,' he replies, and gulps his whiskey.

Chapter 12

The minor fixation I seem to have developed with my new boss's body is juvenile, difficult to ignore and baffling. While I haven't known Ryan long enough to form a detailed judgement on his personality, I have seen enough to want to remind myself that I am not – and have never been – one of those women who are attracted to bastards. The idea appals me.

The only conclusion I can come to, therefore, as I undress and jump under my duvet, is that this is another example of how being jilted on my wedding day has left me mentally unstable. *Jilted*. Now there's a word no prospective bride ever thinks she'll use in relation to herself. Oh, how wrong I was.

With hindsight – a word I've used so often since – I should have heard certain alarm bells ringing in the run-up to the wedding. I'm only talking little bells – travel clocks as opposed to Big Ben. One of the things that has nagged at me is when Jason asked me to marry him. I don't think he ever actually did. Certainly there was no dramatic moment when he got down on one knee with a ring that I spent the next twelve months brandishing at friends, family and anyone else who'd look. Somehow we just slipped into it. We both assumed we'd eventually take the plunge.

At the time I didn't think anything of this. If anything, I saw it as a positive affirmation of the extent to which we were on the same wavelength. I felt I didn't need some showy proposal because it was *obvious* we both wanted the same thing.

The earliest recollection I have of us talking about our wedding was just after Jason's best friend Neil and his fiancée Jessica threw an engagement party. Poor Jessica's mum had slaved for days over the catering, but twelve hundred mushroom vol-au-vents (or canapés, as she insisted Jess's dad refer to them when he offered them round) didn't provide much in the way of variety. Jason and I decided to join a couple of others in a curry house on the way home and I remember him turning to me as he passed me a bowl of lime pickle and asking, 'Where do you think we should get married?'

Yet, now I think about it, that can't have been the first time it was mentioned because I wasn't shocked by the question. In fact, at the time it had barely registered because 'getting married' was something we'd always known we'd end up doing.

So assumed was this state of affairs that, with only six weeks to go before the big day, I had to point out that I didn't possess an engagement ring. Jason agreed we should buy one using some of the loan we'd taken out to pay for the wedding – I'm convinced it was bigger than the mortgage on a small stately home. I'd envisaged paying it off over five years. In fact, I got rid of the outstanding balance all at once by selling our house after everything went pear-shaped.

The house was one thing, but getting rid of everything else proved slightly more of a challenge. When you've purchased 122 silk bags of sugared almonds, twelve table centrepieces and a three-tiered white-chocolate gateau, believe me, you're stuck with them.

And while I was happy that my cousin Tanya and her new boyfriend Darren enjoyed our five-star honeymoon in Mauritius, I would have preferred a cash contribution to the knock-off Ralph Lauren T-shirt she sent me to say thanks.

But none of that compares with the horror of what happened on the day itself.

We'd wanted to follow tradition and spend the night before the wedding apart. When Jason kissed me good-night on my mum's doorstep, I had no doubt that he intended to go through with it.

I'm not saying he wasn't nervous. He clearly was. But aren't pre-wedding nerves as normal a part of it as ructions over the guest list and the bridesmaids being guaranteed a snog?

Perhaps the fact that he hugged me so hard I couldn't breathe should have told me there was more turmoil in his head than in a Middle Eastern war zone. But it didn't.

The wedding was booked for two o'clock at St Michael's, Woolton, the church where, as a child, I'd spent many a Sunday morning, tucked away with the other kids attempting to re-create the nativity scene with bits of newspaper and a Fairy Liquid bottle.

The really strange thing is that the first half of that day was one of the most enjoyable times of my life. If what happened later hadn't happened, I would still be reminiscing about it.

I woke at four thirty, after a fitful night in my mum's spare room – so small and stuffy it was like trying to sleep in the airing cupboard. Dropping off again proved impossible so I resorted to skimming through the only book I could see – a dog-eared children's Bible that had been printed in the early seventies, judging by how strongly Jesus resembled David Cassidy.

Later, my hairdresser told me that all the brides she 'did' had a terrible night before their big day, and advised, if I was ever in that situation again, to try a Temazepam (which apparently works a treat, although it can have unwanted side-effects the next day if you go at the champagne too early).

It was at the hairdresser's that we really got into the swing of things. Jessica, my matron of honour, my bridesmaids, Heather (old friend from school) and Win (my cousin), and I were curled and sprayed so much our hair follicles must have been close to meltdown.

When we got back to Mum's, we were ushered to the kitchen table and Dad brought out massive plates of breakfast – scrambled eggs piled high with smoked salmon. That moment, when we were sitting around the table, merry with Buck's fizz and happiness, was one of the most perfect of my life.

Desy had just done my mum's makeup. After an intensive three-week training programme from his sister Caroline – who works on the Clinique counter at Boots

– he was an expert at applying light-reflecting foundation and high-definition mascara. She joined us still wearing her Juicy Couture dressing-gown and a head full of pink Velcro rollers that looked like the insulated pipes in an alien spacecraft. My dad was already in his tails, which he'd put on at about six fifteen that morning.

Then there was me: excited, elated, nervous – and with not a shred of doubt that I was doing the right thing. Jason was the man I loved, with whom I'd effortlessly spent the last seven years and would happily spend ten times that.

That was the thought going through my mind as the car pulled up outside St Michael's on one of the hottest April days ever recorded. Dad squeezed my hand and tried to hide a tear as I stepped out of the car, careful not to let the hem of my dress touch the dusty ground. The sun warmed my shoulders as I gazed into the cloudless, cornflower-blue sky and smiled.

'Right, Zoe, let's have one of you and your dad,' called the photographer, as he attempted to prop up Dad's already wilting buttonhole.

But as we laughed and posed, I couldn't help noticing that something didn't look right. Andrew, one of Jason's ushers, was pacing up and down next to the church door, his phone glued to his ear, his face white.

When he turned to us, I frowned.

His eyes widened and he glanced around as if he was searching for somewhere to run.

'You okay?' I mouthed.

He hesitated before he headed towards us. 'Can you . . . just give us a minute?' he asked the photographer.

The photographer recognized the look in his eyes and backed away.

'Listen, Zoe,' Andrew began, his neck red with nerves. 'There's been a bit of a – a hiccup.'

'A hiccup?' I asked calmly.

'What do you mean, a hiccup?' added Dad.

Andrew gulped.

'Oh, God, don't tell me the flowers didn't turn up!' I said. The colour-blind church housekeeper had been determined to provide them and I'd had visions of a gaudy array of fit-inducing hydrangeas.

'No, nothing like that,' said Andrew, loosening his collar.

'The organist? Oh, shit – Jess warned me he was a bit of a pisshead but I thought—'

'No, Zoe. Stop!' said Andrew. 'It's nothing like that.'

'Then what is it?'

'It's – it's Jason.'

My mind went blank. I tried to swallow, but couldn't. 'He's . . . been in an accident?'

'No,' said Andrew. 'He's fine. I mean, he's not fine . . .'

'*What*, Andrew?' I said, suddenly impatient. 'What is the matter with Jason?'

'He's not coming,' said Andrew, lowering his eyes. 'Zoe, he's not coming.'

Chapter 13

'Zoe! Wake up, Zoe!'

It's a nightmare. It must be a nightmare.

'We want our breakfast, Zoe!'

I roll over and put a pillow over my head, willing myself to go back to a semi-erotic dream involving Jason, a plush hotel room and a six-pack of Cadbury's Creme Eggs.

'Zoe! *Come on!*'

The voice is soft and not particularly loud. But what it lacks in volume it makes up for in insistence.

'Zo-eeeeee!'

I open one eye and see Ruby and Samuel standing there, perky as two little bunnies on a spring day. 'What time is it?'

'Um, not sure,' says Ruby, unconvincingly.

'You could tell the time last night,' I point out.

'Um, six twenty-five,' she replies sheepishly.

I groan. 'You shouldn't be up yet.'

'But we always get up at this time,' says Ruby.

'Oh, goody.' I rub my eyes. 'Excellent news.'

I turn to look at them. 'You've only had a few hours'

sleep,' I remind them. 'You'll be exhausted today.'

'We're not exh– exh– tired,' says Ruby, as Samuel stands behind her, yawning.

'I want *SpongeBob*,' he says, rubbing his eyes.

'Not sleep?' I ask, hopefully.

'Uh-uh,' they confirm.

As I hobble out of bed, I can't help reflecting that I'm supposed to have Sundays off. And, while I know I've only just got here, part of me had hoped that would apply today so I could at least try to get over my jet-lag. Problem is, Mr Talkative and I never got round to discussing that.

'Come *on*, Zoe!' the children shout.

I head downstairs in my dressing-gown, holding Samuel's hand and looking, I suspect, like a Victorian charlady after a forty-two-hour shift. We go into the kitchen, where Ruby puts on the TV – yes, there's one in there too.

'Okay,' I say, trying to sound upbeat. 'What do you normally have for breakfast?'

'Hmm, we had Hershey's yesterday,' Ruby tells me.

'Isn't that a chocolate bar?' I frown.

'Uh-huh,' says Ruby, as if that was the most reasonable thing in the world.

'Now, come on, I can't believe your daddy would let you ha—' I begin. 'No, hang on, maybe I can believe it. Okay, what did your last nanny give you for breakfast?'

'French toast,' declares Ruby.

My heart sinks. I was hoping for something no more taxing than a bowl of Cheerios. 'How about cereal?' I ask, hopefully.

'Whatever.'

I'm about to look for some cereal, when I stop myself. What am I thinking? This is an opportunity to win the kids over, especially after last night's dramatics. Of course they can have French toast. It's virtually a speciality of mine. And, besides, there's no way I'm refusing them something a previous nanny gave them.

'Okay,' I reply jauntily. 'Seeing as it's you two, French toast it is.'

I have visions of the children greedily tucking into my home-cooked breakfast and viewing me as some sort of Nigella Lawson figure, primed to rustle up a luscious culinary delight from nothing more than half a pound of self-raising flour, a couple of pistachios and the odd free-range vanilla pod.

I head for the fridge to seek out what Nigella would refer to as the 'store-cupboard ingredients' required for this particular dish: a couple of nice fresh eggs, a little butter and some thick-cut bread, preferably the organic wholegrain kind with super-healthy nutty bits and bobs.

Then I open the fridge.

The only consumables inside it are alcoholic. Although there are several items of food, the majority are so old they could be classed as Jurassic. There's a semi-decomposed tomato in the salad tray, several crusty-lidded sauce jars on the top shelf and a piece of cheese so hard Roger Federer could have served an ace with it.

There are certainly no eggs. And a quick glance in the bread bin confirms there is no bread, unless you count one amorphous lump of carbohydrate with enough mould spores on it to provide an entire hospital with antibiotics.

'I'm afraid it'll have to be cereal,' I tell the children.

But, sadly, when I open the cupboard I realize it isn't going to be cereal either.

'Well,' I say, spinning round. This is the sort of challenge that nannies like me can rise to without a second thought. 'Where's the nearest shop?'

Ruby giggles. 'You mean *store*, don't you?'

I can see I'm going to be a source of some amusement round here.

Chapter 14

I'd assumed Ryan was sleeping off his hangover while I dressed the children, stocked the fridge with half the contents of the local 7/11 and made sure the place remained so immaculate that an OCD sufferer would have eaten their dinner off the floor.

Apparently not. I hear the door slam at ten thirty, followed by footsteps bolting up the stairs.

'Is that your daddy coming in?' I ask.

'He's been for a run,' Ruby informs me proudly. 'He runs a lot.'

'Oh, right.' I'm reluctantly impressed. Actually, *amazed* is probably a better word. After the bender he went on yesterday, I can't believe he's managed to roll out of bed at all, let alone go for a jog.

'He does ten miles every morning,' adds Ruby.

Fifteen minutes later – long enough for me to have satisfied a mysterious urge to dash to the bathroom and apply a slick of mascara and nude lip gloss – Ryan enters the kitchen.

He smells deliciously clean and his hair is so wet from the shower that it's still dripping, moistening the skin on one side of his now clean-shaven jaw. Despite that, he still has the rough-round-the-edges quality and has obviously thrown on the first pair of jeans he could find. But he's so glamorous somehow that I feel embarrassed to be in the same room. I get a flash of paranoia that my subtle makeup is fighting a losing battle against the bags under my eyes, which, when I glanced into the mirror earlier, were of a colour best described as 'ecclesiastical purple'.

'*Daddy!*' hollers Ruby, jumping up and skipping across the kitchen to hug him.

'Daddy, daddy, daddy!' echoes Samuel, running over to join in.

'Hey, you two, what's up?' He gives them a cursory hug, prises them off and picks up the newspaper – the one I nearly tripped over when I opened the front door.

'Um ... good morning,' I say brightly, flicking back my hair.

He looks up briefly, and in the split second that he catches my eye, I'm shocked at the extent to which my pulse quickens.

'Howya doing?' He sits down and examines the front page. It wasn't a particularly enthusiastic greeting.

'Can I get you some coffee?' I ask, picking up the pot I've just made and bringing it to the table.

'Hmm, great,' mutters Ryan, starting to dismantle the paper's sections.

'Daddy, we had French toast for breakfast,' Ruby tells him brightly.

'Uh-huh.'

'Zoe made it for us. She's a real good cook.'

I swell with pride – and not just because Ruby apparently hadn't minded that I'd burned hers twice and broken the piece she ended up with when I slid it on to her plate.

'Good, honey,' he mumbles, turning a page. I note that his hands don't look like those of an office worker, although I gleaned from his phone conversations in the car yesterday that that's exactly what he is. They are big, tanned, hard-working hands. There's a vein running along one that I want to trace with my fingertips.

Ryan takes a sip of coffee and pulls the sort of face you see on contestants undertaking a bushtucker trial on *I'm A Celebrity . . . Get Me Out Of Here!* 'Think I'll stick with juice,' he says, handing the cup back to me.

As I take it from him, our fingertips touch and an electric current shivers through me. I take a deep breath and tell myself to get a grip. 'So, you work in the city?' I ask, hoping to spark something approaching a conversation.

'Yup,' he replies, turning a page of his newspaper.

'What is it you do?' I ask.

It takes him a second to register that I'm still speaking. 'Oh, I work for a global sportswear company.'

'Ooooh.' I nod approvingly, wishing I could think of a more intelligent comment. It hardly seems to matter, though, because I don't think he's listening. 'So, are you a salesman or something?'

'Vice-president of communications.'

'That sounds . . . fascinating,' I add, although I can't help thinking that communication hasn't struck me as his forte so far. 'Did you have any plans for today? Only

I need to sit down with you for ten minutes to go over a few matters. About the children's regime, what activities you'd like me to do with them and, um, my days off.'

'Well, I gotta be somewhere today,' he replies unapologetically. 'I'll be gone for most of the day so it'll have to keep for now.'

'Right. If you've got five minutes now—'

'I haven't,' he snaps.

I feel ridiculously wounded by the sharpness of his response, as well as infuriated. Is asking for a couple of minutes so unreasonable?

'Daddy,' says Ruby, tentatively, 'can't we do something together today?'

'Sorry, honey, not today,' he replies, at least looking a little sorrier than he had when he addressed me.

'But, *Daddy*.'

'Come on, no buts,' he says, putting down the paper as he pulls her on to his knee. As she puts her arm round his neck, she looks tiny compared with him.

'But I made a card for you, Daddy.' She hands him the collage to which she's spent the last half-hour gluing bits of dried pasta and rice.

'That's sweet,' he tells her, barely glancing at it. Then, as if hit by a flash of guilt, he pulls her to him and kisses her head. His eyes close as he breathes in the scent of her hair. When he opens them, they're softer than before and his smile intended to be bright and reassuring, is almost melancholy.

'We'll do something next weekend, I promise,' he murmurs.

Now Samuel is at his daddy's side and clambers on to

Ryan's other leg. Ryan laughs and ruffles his hair. 'Okay,' he says finally, disentangling himself from the children and standing up. 'I really have to go.'

'Awwww,' says Samuel, but Ruby grabs his hand and squeezes, perhaps to prevent a tantrum. I glimpse her dejection as she puts an arm round him.

'Come on, Samuel,' she says, with an authoritative air, as she guides him to the TV and turns it on.

I wonder if I should persuade her to turn it off and do some more drawing, but something compels me to run after Ryan.

Now, I know that questioning a parent's decision is not part of my remit. And that Anita – my old boss back at Bumblebees – would have given me such a bollocking if I'd done so that my ears would have been ringing for three weeks.

But something in Ruby's face drives me to action. Besides, I can be diplomatic when I want to be. I could give Kofi Annan lessons. All I need to do is think of a subtle but effective way of suggesting that Ryan spends some time today with his kids.

'Er, um!' I say, as I reach him in the hallway.

He spins round and my heart somersaults.

'Um, this thing you've got to do today,' I begin.

'Yup?'

'Well, is there anything I could do to help? So that perhaps you could spend some time with Ruby and Samuel.' My intention is to sound thoughtful and efficient.

Ryan stares at me as if I'm something unpleasant stuck to the sole of his shoe.

'It's just that Ruby is obviously dying to spend some

time with you this weekend,' I continue, 'and if there was anything I could do for you so you could . . . well . . .'

Okay, it doesn't sound as persuasive as I'd hoped.

Ryan is taking a deep breath. The sort of deep breath parole officers take when they've learned that one of their charges has broken another bail condition.

'No,' he says. 'There isn't.'

'It's just that—'

'Listen to me,' he snaps. 'You and I will get on really well if we understand each other.'

'Okay.' I'm already wishing someone had taped my mouth shut before I'd got out of bed this morning.

'You may have come to the conclusion that I'm a bad father –'

'Oh, God, no,' I bluster, feeling heat rising to my face. 'I didn't mean to imply—'

'– and maybe I am. Although, I gotta say, it usually takes longer than twenty-four hours for someone to work that out.'

'But I—'

'This is the way I do things,' he continues. 'And it isn't going to change. Okay?'

My neck and chest are blazing like a rampant forest fire. 'Fine,' I manage.

'Good. Because I'm not employing you for your opinion. I'm employing you to look after my kids.'

I cross my arms, suddenly defiant. 'Fine,' I repeat, refusing to look away as his eyes bore into mine.

After a couple of seconds it becomes apparent to both of us that we're engaged in a playground staring competition. But I'm not to going to wimp out. My pulse is still racing but now it's for a different reason than how chiselled his features are. Now an overwhelming thought whizzes through my mind: I might have felt sorry for this guy, I might have developed an annoying obsession with his bone structure – but there's no way I'm going to let myself be pushed around. Not by him or anyone else.

'You can do that, right?' he continues, still glaring at me. 'You can look after my kids?'

'Of course,' I reply frostily, my pupils dilating as I refuse to move.

'Good. Now, I suggest you go back in there, pour yourself a glass of water and sit down.' He turns his back on me and opens the front door. ''Cause you look a little stressed.'

Chapter 15

I read somewhere that sleep deprivation can be used as a form of torture. Well, move over the KGB, because my first weekend in the Miller household is proving so bad on this front that I must look like a chronic narcoleptic.

My eyes keep closing spontaneously because I still haven't caught up on my jet-lag, and despite my determination to get the children to bed at a decent hour, it isn't proving as straightforward as I'd hoped.

In Samuel's case, this is because he insisted on having an afternoon nap – something he really shouldn't be having at his age. Not just that, but he proved as easy to wake as an Egyptian mummy – and what was supposed to be a short sleep stretched for almost three hours.

Meanwhile Ruby, who *definitely* shouldn't be having a day-time nap at her age, sneaked off to the sofa for forty winks while I was making lunch and wouldn't move until I threatened to eat her Reece's Peanut Butter Cups.

All of this means that at eight thirty p.m. (new bedtime), I'm treated again to the Jekyll and Hyde routine.

But what about Daddy, you must be thinking. Isn't he around this time?

Although tonight he *has* graced us with his presence in the house, he has spent most of the evening holed up in the living room in front of series six of *The Sopranos*, a mountain of documents and his laptop.

When I *finally* get the children to sleep I decide that now is the time to have that conversation with him: the one about a plethora of matters we haven't yet broached, the rules, Ruby's reading, Samuel's toilet skills (which, it has become apparent, are haphazard) and my day off.

I push open the living-room door. Ryan is still ploughing intently through his paperwork.

'Um, hi,' I pipe up. He doesn't turn so I scrutinize his face, trying to work out whether or not he's heard me. I am hit again by an overwhelming sense of how alluring his features are and blood rushes to my neck.

'I wonder if now is a good time to have a chat about a couple of things,' I say, slightly louder.

Ryan looks up momentarily, but only to witness Tony Soprano putting his hands round someone's throat. 'Not really,' he replies.

My heart sinks. 'Well,' I persevere, 'I know you'll be at work tomorrow so there won't be a chance then and I really need to discuss a couple of things with you.'

'Look,' he sighs, 'I have a stack of work to get through before tomorrow. Is this *really* urgent or can we do it tomorrow night?'

'Well . . . "urgent" probably isn't the word I'd use,' I'm forced to admit. 'It's not life or death but there are some practical things that—'

'Okay, if it's not life or death then let's do it

tomorrow.' He picks up a file from the floor and drags it on to the sofa next to him.

Clearly I don't have much choice.

When I don't move, he flashes a look as if to say: 'Are you still standing there for a reason?'

'I'll go, then,' I say despondently. I'm starting to feel quite depressed about the whole thing.

When the kids and I wake up the next morning, my first thought is whether I really will get to pin Ryan down – or whether I'll just have to wing it. My answer comes in the form of a Post-it note on the kitchen table. The handwriting is surprisingly graceful. 'Late tonight – don't wait up. R.'

Winging it, then.

Later in the morning, the kids and I venture over to Trudie's place and we are soon ensconced in her employers' vast kitchen.

This room, like the rest of the house, is gorgeous: trendily traditional with duck-egg blue Shaker cabinets, an island bursting with sparkling utensils and the odd hand-woven basket as if Little Red Riding Hood had dropped by on the way to Grandma's.

The purpose of the visit is a 'play date' – an exercise designed to broaden the children's life experiences by allowing them to interact with other youngsters in a safe environment. And, of course, for their nannies to have a good gossip.

We have been joined today by Amber, another British nanny who has washed up in Hope Falls and with whom Trudie got together a couple of weeks ago. A pretty blonde with dreadlocks Bob Marley would have coveted, Amber has a cannabis-leaf-shaped stud in her nose, and so many bangles on her arms it's a wonder she hasn't the biceps of a Russian shot-putter. The overall look is of someone brought up by a family of tree-hugging political activists on a diet of reggae and space cakes. The accent, however, couldn't have been more Sloaney if it had come with a certificate from Cheltenham Ladies' College.

'I'm considering getting another tattoo,' she tells us excitedly, as Trudie prepares lunch and I oversee a game of Snap. 'I mean, I like the one I've got, but it's true what they say about them being addictive.'

'What are you thinking of having?' I ask.

'Well,' she begins, flicking back her dreadlocks and leaning over the breakfast bar, 'I've been reading a lot lately about the women warriors of Skrang Iban in Borneo.'

'The who?' asks Trudie.

'Skrang Iban,' she replies. 'In between doing warrior-type things and weaving their sacred *pua kumbu* blankets, they were trailblazers in the art of tattooing. The Iban's ultimate aim was to provide balance and harmony in the cosmos, which is *so* where I'm at in my life right now. I thought I'd get a design that emulated one of theirs.'

'Top banana,' says Trudie. 'What does the one you've already got say?'

Amber pushes up the sleeve on her *baba* blouse and examines the symbol at the top of her arm. 'It's Tibetan *kanji*.'

'Right,' says Trudie. 'But what's it say?'

'Well, um, it's just some words surrounding a philosophy I used to feel strongly about.'

'I know, but what's the translation?'

'Well, um . . . "Mind, soul and spirit are my strength."'

'Oh, right,' says Trudie. 'Nice.'

'At least,' Amber coughs, 'that's what it's supposed to say.'

Trudie frowns questioningly.

'I found out about a year ago that it might not quite say that.'

'Might not?' repeats Trudie.

'Um . . . doesn't.'

'So what does it say?' asks Trudie, scrunching up her nose.

'Well, I had no reason to question the chap who did it when he said he was a Buddhist. I mean, it could have happened to anyone, really, so before I—'

'So what does it say?' Trudie persists.

Amber flicks a dreadlock defensively. 'Batteries not included.'

Chapter 16

I'm already learning that Trudie isn't what you'd call a stickler for the golden nutritional guidelines as laid out by the nanny books. In fact, the spread she's put on for us today is enough to give Jamie Oliver heart failure.

The feast began with a mountain of anaemic bread spread haphazardly with an indefinable gunk that Trudie advises is 'spray cheese', an ingredient she champions as one of America's greatest culinary inventions. It's piled on plates overflowing with crisps, doughnuts, M&Ms and other items so laden with saturated fat that just looking at them would make your cellulite explode.

Unsurprisingly, none of the children is complaining.

Trudie's twins begin excitedly to demolish the sky-scrapers on their plates and while Brett, Amber's four-year-old charge, is somewhat alarmed at first, one bite of a nacho confirms that he's more than prepared to forfeit his usual roughage-packed lunch.

'How did you end up here as a nanny?' I ask Amber.

'Au pair,' she corrects me. 'It's just a stop-gap for the summer. I'd been travelling in India and went back to the UK to apply for a job teaching aromatherapy to reformed drug addicts but I didn't get it. My sister came out here last year as an au pair and enjoyed it, so I thought I might give it a go.'

'And do you like it?'

'Yeah, I do, actually,' she replies. 'I mean, I'm not in it for the long term or anything, and I'm nothing like as qualified as you, but—'

Andrew burps – so loudly that you'd never have guessed he was only three foot tall.

'Bless him, I don't think he's used to food like this,' says Trudie, throwing a handful of M&Ms into her mouth. 'His mum likes me to feed them dead healthily – and I do usually. Despite what it does to the contents of their nappies.'

'So she wouldn't approve of all this?' I ask.

'Well,' shrugs Trudie, dismissively, 'I thought I'd do a special lunch today since you lot were coming over. Just for a treat. I mean, nobody would mind that, would they?'

'Probably not,' I agree. 'But if you were giving them this every day, some parents would wheel you off to social services.'

A door slams. Trudie's face registers such alarm you'd think she'd come face to face with King Kong. 'Bloody hell! It's Barbara!' she hisses. 'Quick! Get rid of some of this food, please! Come on – quick.'

'But I thought you said she'd be okay about it for a treat?' I say.

'It's not a theory I want to test, love.' She sprints to the fridge. 'Now – help!'

There's something about the way she delivers this order that sends me and Amber into a panic.

I drop my doughnut and bundle food into the nearest bin, to the children's stunned bewilderment.

'Green stuff on the kids' plates – pronto!' Trudie chucks a bag of pre-prepared lettuce at Amber, who fumbles to catch it.

The three of us have become a crack SAS squad, just parachuted in.

'Zoe – some apples. Quick!' barks Trudie, convincing as commander-in-chief.

I grab random items of fruit from the large bowl in the centre of the table and rapidly plonk one of each on the children's plates. Trudie is in the process of shovelling a handful of crisps from Eamonn's plate into her own mouth when the kitchen door flies open.

'Mrs K! Hiya! You're home early!' splutters Trudie, as hickory BBQ flavour Lays escape from the side of her mouth.

Barbara King enters the room like a Roman empress surveying her kingdom. She is wearing a designer suit, suede high-heeled shoes, and carrying an expensive handbag. Her dark hair is cut in a short, sleek bob and her makeup is so perfect you'd think she'd been made over by Max Factor himself.

'Why is there a lemon on that child's plate?' she asks.

Damn. My mistake. 'Um, it's a traditional British party game,' I pipe up. 'It's called "Pass the Lemon". We always played it at the nursery where I used to work. Here, Ruby, you next.'

Ruby takes the lemon and regards me as if I'm demented. Then she shrugs and passes it on to Samuel.

'I'm Zoe,' I say, holding out my hand.

Barbara shakes it and frowns, still deciding what she thinks of my party game. At least, she almost frowns. Barbara has apparently had enough Botox sessions to paralyse the forehead of a Tyrannosaurus Rex, so it's more of a twitch.

'Now, where are my boys?' she cries. 'Mommy was on her way to a meeting so she thought she'd stop by to surprise you!'

The twins leap from their seats and hurtle towards her open arms, their hands and faces covered with so much artificial cheese and non-Fair Trade chocolate that they can barely prise their fingers apart.

'Oooh, er, hang on a min!' hollers Trudie. 'Let me wipe that *peach juice* off your hands.'

She grabs a baby wipe and deals with Andrew but Eamonn is too quick for her. As he reaches his mother, she recoils. 'What in God's name have you been eating?' she demands, with such horror you'd think a live mouse was hanging out of his mouth.

'Oooh, Eamonn, you're all sticky,' observes Trudie, innocently, as she jumps in to remove the offending debris from his hands. 'That juice really is a nightmare, isn't it?'

'Tru*die*,' says Barbara, sternly, as she scans the kitchen table. 'Have you forgotten my rules about what the children can and cannot eat? About them having lots of fruit and vegetables?'

'Course I haven't, Mrs K!' says Trudie, brandishing a limp piece of lettuce, apparently as evidence. 'Five a day! I've not forgotten!'

'Seven in this household,' corrects Barbara, wiping

Andrew's mouth with a pristine handkerchief produced from somewhere in her bag. 'And I want no trans-fats whatsoever. Okay? And sugar – absolutely no more than ten per cent of their daily calorific intake. Okay?'

'Don't you worry,' says Trudie, strategically placing herself in front of a plate of brownies. 'I think of nothing *but* the state of their arteries, Mrs K.'

'Hmm,' says Barbara, clearly unconvinced, 'and you're not giving them any tonic, are you?' Tonic is what Bostonians call fizzy drinks.

'Tonic? Ho! As if!' laughs Trudie.

Barbara straightens up and eyes Trudie suspiciously. 'Good. Because heart-disease rates being as they are, these days, I firmly believe that failing to feed children a properly balanced diet is tantamount to cruelty. Half the pre-schoolers in this country have chronic constipation.'

Trudie nods obediently.

'Well,' continues Barbara, 'I'll leave you to it. Now, you two, come and give Mommy a big hug!' She bends down to the twins, closing her eyes tightly and nuzzling her face in their hair.

'*I* have a tonic,' announces Ruby, unhelpfully, as she holds up a can of Coke.

Barbara's eyes ping open.

'Oh,' I say, grabbing the can from her, 'that's just for you, sweetheart.' I turn to Barbara, feeling the need to explain. 'The other children had something different,' I tell her. 'Ruby's daddy doesn't mind her having fizzy drinks.'

She purses her lips. 'So Ryan Miller lets his little girl drink Coke all day. Why doesn't that surprise me?'

'Oh, well, I wouldn't say *all day*,' I mumble, wondering why I'm trying to defend him. 'It's just—'

'Don't worry, honey,' says Barbara. 'If you're living with Ryan Miller, that's the least of your worries, believe me.'

Chapter 17

The keys to the garage are apparently in the hall drawer. The problem is, so is everything else. Determined to dig out the children's bikes so we can do something active and fun this afternoon, I spend ten minutes rifling through the drawer before giving up and tipping it out on the floor.

The kids think sifting through the contents is enormous fun, at least for the first five minutes. I'm less impressed, largely because I've got better things to do than untangling phone chargers from balls of Plasticine, old bandages, a tape-measure, a half-eaten jam tart and various other bits of detritus.

When I locate the keys, I fight my instinct to sort through the rubbish and instead pile it back into the drawer. I'm about to call the kids back to tell them we're one step closer to getting at their bikes, when I spot a mildly intriguing piece of paper. Slightly creased, but relatively unscathed compared with the other items in the drawer, I open it up and am unable to stop myself reading it.

Darling Ryan,

I have so many conflicting thoughts about you at the moment, I barely know where to begin. So, I suppose I'll get straight to the point. I love you. There, I've said it. Whether you like it or not, that's the situation. Which both of us now have to deal with, one way or the other.

Predictable as this sounds, I knew I loved you the minute I met you. It wasn't just your looks that won me over. It was your soul, your mind – a mind most women couldn't begin to understand. I knew instinctively that beyond your impenetrable exterior was a man with so much to give. I believe I have reached out and seen the real Ryan – and now I'm determined to see more of him.

I should tell you that the very fact I'd loved you in secret for so long before something happened between us made that moment all the more perfect. As I'm sure you already know, I'm a woman who strives for perfection. And that is why I don't want to let this go. The first night we spent together wasn't just special, it was beautiful. Life-changing, in fact. And I will not let you throw it away like yesterday's pizza.

Now that I've opened my heart to you, Ryan, it's time to be frank – so forgive me in advance for being so, but this is my request: I want you to reconsider what you said about not seeing me again. A simple one, I know you'll agree, but one that could change both of our lives for the better.

Yours for ever,
Juliet
XXX

'Zoe, have you found them yet?' asks Ruby, impatiently.

'Here we are!' I reply, dangling them in front of her.

'Great! Come on, Samuel – race you to the garage!' she cries, grabbing his hand and deliberately letting him get ahead of her.

I fold the letter, and stuff it into the back of the drawer, which I close decisively. Then I follow the children outside to focus on what I *should* be focusing on.

Chapter 18

To: Zoemmoore@hotnet.co.uk
From: Helen@Hmoore.mailserve.co.uk

Dear Zoe,

How is America? I've been watching a lot of TV lately and thinking about you and what life is like over there. I had to turn *Cagney and Lacey* off the other night – you know what it's like when your mind runs away with itself.

Desy kept going on at me that *Cagney and Lacey* is set in a completely different city, is twenty-odd years old, is based on the lives of two New York police officers and completely fictional. As if I didn't know all that! He can be bloody dismissive sometimes, honestly. Thankfully, your dad suggested I might take in a bit of the *Happy Days* season that's been on satellite for the last week. I feel much better about the whole thing already.

Anyway, let me tell you what happened to me the other day. I'd popped into Sainsbury's to get the ingredients for a new twist on a Delia recipe I thought I'd experiment with – satsuma crumble – and I was standing in the queue when I suddenly went really dizzy. I almost fainted. Well, I didn't exactly lose consciousness or anything but it was enough for me to have to sit down. One of the staff brought me a glass of water. I'd just started to feel a bit better when I looked up and your old boss from nursery – Anita, isn't it? – was standing beside me.

She went on and on about how I should see a doctor because it's happened with her staff in the past and you can never be too careful (what a hypochondriac I'd be if I shuffled off to the doctor's every time I felt a bit queasy!). The point is, when I managed to get a word in edgeways, I finally got her to tell me about the girl who's replaced you at work.

Reading between the lines, she isn't anywhere near as good as you. Anita said so, near as damn it. And that she'd have you back like a shot. I just thought I'd mention that, in case you were thinking of coming home.

I know your dad thinks you need to do your own thing at your own pace, but he doesn't understand you like I do, Zoe. Never has. And, anyway, it doesn't do any harm me just laying out your options for you, does it? So *if* you were thinking of coming home then your old room is still there. Don't forget that, will you?

Just so you know, people have stopped gossiping. Well, to me they have. I mean, I saw Judy Stephenson in Andrew Herbert the other day when I went in to get my top lip bleached and she made a pointed comment – but she doesn't count. I've always said she was an old boot. (And that's before you get me on to her hair. I swear, that woman's roots were so bad I'm surprised she wasn't mistaken for a prostitute.)

Apart from that, there isn't a great deal of news for you. Your cousin Kylie has been picked for the school play. It's

The Wizard of Oz and she plays a chicken. I don't remember any chickens in *The Wizard of Oz* but, as Desy said, we can't all be Judy Garland. Besides, I've heard that poor child's singing voice and I think she's lucky to have won a part as poultry.

The weather's terrible. It's been throwing it down for days now. Where's this global warming they keep promising us? That's what I want to know.

Love and kisses,

Mum

XXX

Chapter 19

Although I'm glad to be away from Liverpool, my first few weeks in America pass slowly. It takes longer than I'd expected to get used to things. To not having my own space. To not having my friends and family around me. To being almost permanently on duty.

Most of all, though, I'm shocked by how little the move affects my feelings for Jason. I'm thousands of miles away from my old life yet he's forever in my thoughts. Okay, so I'm doing nothing like the amount of crying I did in the immediate aftermath of our wedding day. My emotions aren't as raw as they were then, but I'm still harbouring this horrible dull ache that nothing can shift.

I still feel angry about what he did to me, to us. But that isn't my overwhelming feeling. More than anything, I miss him. Desperately. I long to feel his arms round me, to revel in the embrace I once took for granted.

Some mornings I wake up, forgetting where I am, and roll over, expecting to find him there. When I realize I'm in a single bed all by myself the sensation hits me like a ton of bricks.

I also find myself – more often than I can believe – drifting into a dream world in the middle of the day, luxuriating in memories of key events in our relationship. Like the day I took him home to meet my parents all those years ago. I was touched by the effort he'd made to impress my mum, bringing with him the most stunning bouquet of yellow roses I'd ever seen. He pretended to enjoy her cooking, even though she'd misread the recipe for *salsa verde*. The resulting concoction contained approximately seven times the number of anchovies that Rick Stein recommends. Between that and the Jersey Royals – so hard that Dad dislodged a filling – it's a wonder he ever went back.

Except he was wonderful with both of my parents. I watched him turn on the charm to the extent that they enthused for weeks about him, everything from his fascinating views about recent items on *This Morning* (Mum) and his impressive grasp of the state of refereeing in today's Premiership (Dad).

Jason had the same effect on my friends. You could see their minds whirring when they first met him, wondering whether he was too gorgeous for his own good – the sort of bloke who fancies himself more than any woman and whose only meaningful relationship is with his bathroom mirror.

They soon discovered, as I had, that despite the pretty-boy tag Jason was genuinely nice.

At least when I came here I left all my pictures of him at home. The idea was that, with time, I'd be unable to visualize what he looked like.

The theory sometimes works. Occasionally, I find it

impossible to conjure up an exact image of him and am left with a frustratingly hazy outline. At other times, his face is crystal clear.

Either way, it doesn't really matter, because what I loved – still do – wasn't Jason's looks. It was the whole package. A package I've well and truly lost.

Chapter 20

'Oh, for Chrissake, can't someone else deal with it for once?'

It didn't take me long to learn that Ryan doesn't *do* good moods. He only does bad moods. Or terrible moods. Or just moods. Today his temper is so far from good that if he were a dog someone would put him down.

'Tell me, please,' he thunders into his cell phone, 'which *asshole* in Accounts has not managed to process this invoice when they've had fourteen full days to do so? What *exactly* is so difficult about that?'

I can't hear how the person at the other end is trying to justify whatever horrendous cock-up has so infuriated him, but I can see he's no closer to launching into a rousing rendition of 'I'm Walking On Sunshine'.

This morning he's wearing a battered green T-shirt with a faded logo on the front. His combats sit low on the hips, as if his waist was slightly bigger when he bought them. He hasn't shaved, which he only ever does when duty requires it. I came to the conclusion the other day that he's sexier with day-old stubble.

'I don't want excuses,' he interrupts, pacing up and down the kitchen, 'I want a cash transfer. For Wolfe and Co. Now. As in *today*.' He hangs up, takes an exasperated breath and marches over to the coffee-maker, beside me.

He's got that fresh-out-of-the-shower smell again and I find myself inhaling deeply and surreptitiously. A wave of heat surges through my body, then concentrates around the knicker area. I bite my lip. Thank God nobody is aware of this but me.

'Where – is – the – coffee?' asks Ryan.

The answer to this question is that he drank the entire pot I made – to replace his own disastrous attempt – about forty-five minutes ago. Instead of saying this, I turn to him, a vision of calm composure compared with his thermonuclear demeanour. It's a skill I've mastered since I've been living with Ryan. 'Would you like me to make some?' I offer.

'I'd have preferred it to be there already, given that *I've* made some this morning.' His eyebrow twitches. 'But since it isn't, yes, please.'

I take in the accusatory implication of this statement. 'No problem.' I smile. 'Happy to replace the one *I* made this morning.'

He's about to start pacing again when he pauses. 'I think you'll find *I* made the coffee this morning.'

'Well, yes,' I concede, hoping my tone is soft enough for me to get away with this, 'but you might have got the quantities wrong because it wasn't very nice. So I replaced it.'

'You replaced it?'

I nod.

'Because it wasn't very nice?'

I nod again.

'Well,' he says, crossing his arms, 'that won't be necessary in future.'

I look into his eyes. The staring competition is on again. 'Right,' I say.

'Because *my* coffee was fine,' he explains.

I grit my teeth and refuse to break eye contact. 'It wasn't.'

'I make great coffee,' he tells me defiantly.

'I'm sure you do. But that *particular* coffee was not great.'

'I'm sure it was.'

'It really wasn't.'

'Yes,' he insists. 'It was.'

I'm tempted to tell him it was barely fit for human consumption when Ruby appears and cuts the conversation short – which is probably a good thing.

'Daddy, I've drawn a picture of you and Zoe,' she announces, tugging at his shirt. I look down at her and smile.

'Not now, honey. Daddy's trying to get some work done,' Ryan replies. When I turn back to him I notice he hasn't stopped staring at me. I blush violently.

Fortunately, he walks away, hammering another number into his handset as the kids and I watch.

'Jim, it's Ryan,' he begins. 'That invoice still hasn't been dealt with yet ... Hey, don't even *think* about starting on me about it.'

Ryan continues to pound round the room as I pour

some coffee and, as soon as I'm confident my face and neck have returned to their normal colour, put the cup into his hand.

He catches my eye and mouths, 'Thank you,' in a way that can only be interpreted as sarcastic.

'Listen, phone me back – but on my cell, not at work,' he continues. 'What? Oh, yeah, I'm working from home today. Trouble with the air-con in my office ... Don't ask.'

As Ryan marches into the study like an imperial storm trooper heading for the Millennium Falcon, I say to Ruby, 'Can I look at your picture?'

Shyly, she holds it out.

'Oh, wow! It's lovely! I like the dress you've put me in. It's much more stylish than my jeans, hey?'

Ruby giggles. 'Do you think it looks like you and Daddy?'

In the picture, my hair is so curly I'm like a cross between Little Miss Muffet and a poodle. 'You've got us to a T,' I tell her.

There's something odd about the picture, though. Ruby has drawn Ryan and me holding hands. Which is unlikely, given that he and I seem unable to be in the same room together without the conversation disintegrating into a heated exchange.

It isn't as if I'm not trying. The day before yesterday Ryan instructed me to 'Just throw my washing in with the kids', wouldya?' Even though the agency I'm with specifies that the only laundry nannies should do is the children's, I don't want to win myself a reputation for pedantry, so I ended up doing two and a half loads for him. I don't think that man has washed a pair of his own underpants since Christmas.

And what did I get in return? I'm not saying I expected chocolates, but a plain old 'Thank you' might have been nice. Instead, Ryan picked up his freshly laundered clothes without a word and took them to his bedroom.

Then there was last night's phone call. The children were playing up again before they went to bed – I've got them down to nine o'clock now, after a good two-hour wind-down period. And Ruby refused to go near her bedroom unless I let her phone Daddy to say goodnight.

I duly made the call, let her 'kiss' him goodnight and was about to hang up when he asked to speak to me.

'Kids aren't meant to be awake at this time of night,' he informed me. 'I was speaking to one of the guys at work and his kids are in bed by seven thirty.'

'I know!' I was overwhelmed with relief that, finally, he might be prepared to recognize what I've been battling with for weeks. 'It's been so difficult to handle. If there's anything you can do to help I'd—'

'Well, can you deal with it?' he said.

'Deal with it?'

'Yeah. It can't be good for them.'

'If *only* you'd said that before!' I almost cried, but restrained myself. 'Of course,' I told him flatly. 'No problem.'

I put the phone down, heart pounding with frustration. Ryan Miller might have been through the mill emotionally but that didn't mean I'd let him walk all over me.

'What's the matter?' asked Ruby. 'You're not sick, are you?'

'No, sweetheart,' I smiled, squeezing her hand. Not unless a severe pain in the backside counts.

Chapter 21

Ryan's BlackBerry has a ring tone so irritatingly high-pitched that it's a wonder the entire canine population of the neighbourhood doesn't turn up on our doorstep each time it goes off. As its manic beeping grows ever more frantic, I pick it up from the kitchen table and scurry to the study. It stops as I reach the door. Ryan's thunderous brow is buried in his laptop and he's typing so hard and fast he seems liable to break a couple of fingers at any moment.

I hand him the BlackBerry. 'You just missed a call.'

He takes it from me. 'Uh-huh,' he grunts, which, for my own sanity, I choose to interpret as thanks. I'm about to leave when he says, 'About the laundry.'

I'm stunned. I couldn't have misjudged him, could I? Could it really be that even Ryan Miller isn't so bad that he'll let someone do nearly three loads of washing for him without saying, 'Thank you'? 'Don't worry about it,' I say, feeling strangely elated. 'There was quite a lot, but I don't mind doing—'

'You turned one of my shirts pink.'

'What?'

'One of my shirts,' he continues flatly, 'is now pink.'

Take a deep breath. Ryan is half right. He does now have a pink shirt. The fact of the matter, however – the *crucial* fact of the matter – is that it was pink when it went into the machine. How am I so certain? Because so pink was that shirt that I remember thinking it looked like something you'd choose for a Barbara Cartland tribute evening.

'I'm pretty sure it was already pink,' I tell him. 'I do remember the one you're talking about and—'

'Are you trying to tell me I don't know my own shirts?' he says.

That's exactly what I'm trying to tell you.

'Well, I'm just pointing out—'

'Look, I'm not going to sack you for it, I'm just telling you,' he continues, 'so it doesn't happen next time.'

There wasn't supposed to be a sodding first time, never mind a next!

'But – but – but—' I'm doing a very good impression of a backfiring lawnmower.

'Let's just leave it,' he says. 'I don't want to make this into a big deal. I was just mentioning it.'

'For next time?' My voice drips with irony.

'Yeah,' he replies, apparently not noticing.

He buries his head in his laptop again.

I'm about to leave quietly when I catch sight of one of the antiques on a side table. The house is full of antiques, some conventional, others less so. This falls into the latter category: a toy bow and arrow. The bow is only two or three feet long and the end of the arrow is bound with faded red rope so there are no sharp bits.

I don't know what possesses me to pick it up now, given that I've passed it on countless occasions before and never given it a second thought. But, with Ryan's back to me, I pull the arrow against the bow, aiming it at his head as I suppress a giggle. Obviously I'm not going to let go. In any case, the last time I did archery in the Girl Guides the only thing I hit was my own toe because I kept dropping the arrow.

But the perfection of the moment – with the bow taut against my face and Ryan oblivious to my little joke – is nothing less than *delicious*.

'*Zo-eee! What are you doing?*'

I gasp and turn to see Ruby's horrified face. In the split second that I search for an excuse, my attention is diverted again.

'*Arrgh!*'

'What is it?' I revolve back to Ryan, heart pounding in my throat.

He is leaning forwards in his chair, groaning and holding both hands over his right eye.

'Oh dear – has something flown into your eye?' I ask optimistically.

'Yes – a three-foot fucking arrow!'

'Oh, God! It can't have! I'm a terrible shot!'

'Well, the fact that you're on form today isn't making me feel a whole lot better.'

'Are you sure it was me?' Okay, so I might be in a state of denial.

'I'm sure. Look!'

'*Arrrrrrggh!*' scream Ruby *and* Samuel, who has now joined us to see what the commotion is about.

Ryan's eye has swelled into something the shape of an ostrich egg and the colour of full-bodied beetroot soup.

Right. Don't panic, Zoe. Whatever you do, don't panic. This is a perfect opportunity to impress them with your swift and dynamic response to this emergency situation.

'I don't suppose you fancy another cup of coffee?'

Chapter 22

The bow-and-arrow incident didn't exactly do wonders for my working relationship with Ryan. In fact, the only positive thing I can say about it is that he didn't fire me. I was surprised, I must say, but more relieved than anything else. Being sacked for shooting the boss in the head doesn't sit well on anyone's CV.

However, the three-rounds-with-Mike-Tyson look meant Ryan had to cancel a week's worth of meetings, which gave him even more reason to stomp about like a bad-tempered bear with a hangover.

And since I'm on the subject, I've started recently to notice how much Ryan drinks. Admittedly, this might just be in comparison with Jason, who never drank at home. Like me, he preferred to save his recommended alcohol units and use them all up on a Saturday night before hitting a late-night curry house.

With Ryan, it isn't that he gets rolling drunk, just that when he comes home from work, at whatever time that might be, the first thing he does is to throw his laptop case into the corner of the hallway, loosen his tie, then dive into his whiskey with a glint of desperation in his eye. Our recycling bin permanently looks as if it belongs outside Yates's Wine Lodge after a brisk weekend's trading.

This, of course, is on the evenings Ryan spends at home. Often he is out with some mysterious woman. All I know about her is that she wears one hell of a lot of perfume. The fact that he comes home reeking of it may mean he's spending his nights at Macy's cardholder evenings trying out the new fragrances from Nina Ricci, but I doubt it.

'Zoe, can you make Scouse for dinner?' asks Ruby, as we arrive home from a day in the park with Trudie, Amber and the other children. Her accent makes the plain old meat and potato stew sound positively exotic.

'I will one day,' I tell her, hoping I can put off this request till next Easter at the earliest.

As the children follow me into the kitchen I notice that the answer-machine is flashing up a message. I press the button and go to get some pasta from the cupboard.

'Hey, Ryan . . . how's it going?'

The woman's voice is so husky it makes Mariella Frostrup's sound like Tweety Pie.

'It's Christina. From the other night . . .'

I drop the pasta packet and glare at the children.

'I just wanted to say, I think you and I had something real special going on . . .'

Oh, my God. They can't be exposed to someone whispering suggestive sweet nothings to their father.

'I'd really love to get together again because that thing you did to me . . . you know what I'm talking about . . .'

I dive across the kitchen and attempt to switch it off.

Unfortunately I'm not very strong on technology and, faced with an array of flashing buttons, I panic.

'That was ecstasy, Ryan . . .'

As I press the buttons frantically – and they refuse to obey me – I grapple with the phone.

'And it was definitely an experience I'd like to repeat . . .'

Oh, God, oh, God! Another tactic, Zoe.

'Is this the way to Amar-i-llo!' I shriek at the top of my voice. 'Fa la la la la la la pillow!'

Both kids stare at me as if I'm deranged.

'La la la la Amar-i-llooh!'

I continue bashing random buttons.

'Fa la la la la la la la!'

Finally, miraculously, it pays off and, mid-seductive murmur, the message stops.

'Ahem.' I cough, straightening my top. 'That was a friend of mine.'

Ruby frowns. 'I thought she said the message was for Daddy?'

'Er, yes. Well spotted,' I concede. 'She, um, is going to be doing some work for your dad. I recommended her.'

'What kind of work?' asks Ruby, suspiciously.

I scan the kitchen and spot Ryan's suit hanging in the corner. 'Some dry-cleaning. That's right. Yes. Dry-cleaning. She's the best in the business is my mate, um, Karen.'

'She said she was called Christina,' Ruby informs me.

'Oh, did she? Well, that's her professional name.'

'Dry-cleaners have professional names?' Ruby screws up her nose.

I usher her back to the table. 'Look, young lady, you ask too many questions. Now, what happened to that collage you were making for me earlier?'

'I couldn't find anything to do your hair with. We've run out of Brillo pads.'

Because I've already listened to at least some of the message from Christina there's no flashing light to alert Ryan later to its existence. Which, sadly, means I've got to do the job myself. I wait until both kids are in bed – at a miraculous eight forty-five, with less than one and a half hours' worth of pre-sleep tantrums – before I bring the subject up.

'Ahem,' I begin, as Ryan is downing his fourth bottle of beer. 'There was a message for you on the answer-machine.'

'Uh-huh,' he replies, as he surveys the contents of the fridge. 'Who from?'

'I'm not sure,' I mutter. Conversations between Ryan and me haven't been exactly world-beating and the thought of leaping straight to his bedroom antics doesn't seem a particularly good way to improve matters. 'You'd probably better listen to it yourself.'

He frowns as he pushes up the sleeves of his dark blue shirt – which I'm sure was once gorgeous but now looks as if it was last ironed at the turn of the century. 'Fine,' he says, approaching the machine. As he stands next to me, he gives his shoulder-blade a short, hard massage.

My eyes are glued to his fingers as they manipulate his golden flesh, which I can just see beyond the tired edges of his collar.

'Right!' I croak. 'I think I'll get an early night. Cheerio!'

Cheerio? Where did that come from?

'Zoe?' he says, as I reach the door.

'Er, yes?'

'There are no messages.'

'Oh,' I say, wondering whether I wiped it during my gymnastics with the machine earlier. 'Right. Er, maybe I imagined it.'

I head for the door.

'Wait . . . What did it say?'

I scrunch up my face, as comfortable with this as a bronze turkey feels three days before Christmas.

'Um . . . It was from a lady,' I tell him, hoping optimistically that that will be enough.

He opens the third button on his shirt. I find my eyes drawn to it – is his chest hairy or smooth? This is another issue I've thought about more than once recently. All bets so far are on hairy.

'And?'

'She was called Christina,' I offer.

He peers up at one of the lights above the oven. You can almost hear the cogs in his brain turning as he roots in the depths of his mind for information on exactly who Christina might be. As he leans on the work surface in contemplation, his collar moves and I can make out a shadow of chest hair. Ha! Knew it!

'O-kay,' he says. 'Thanks.'

I tear my eyes away from him and am about to walk through the door when he coughs. 'Zoe . . .'

I wince. 'Hmm?'

'If she phones again, and it goes onto voicemail, don't pick up, okay?'

'*Don't?*'

'I'd kind of like to avoid her,' he clarifies.

I'm sure he's embarrassed. 'Of course. No problem.'

He smiles at me. It's a strange, almost humble smile. A smile that seems to indicate appreciation of my understanding and discretion.

I find myself mesmerized by it, unable to move or say anything. I'm transfixed by his eyes as they gaze at me, for the first time, without a combative edge. Without the frown, he's so much more alluring, so much more captivating . . .

'Night then!' I say cheerfully.

'Sure,' he replies. 'G'night.'

When I get to my room, I snuggle into bed and con-template the whole Ryan business. My theory is this: the low-key attraction I have developed towards him is a defence mechanism. Having suffered the worst rejection possible – abandonment on my wedding day by a man I am truly, madly in love with – I'm latching on to the first good-looking bloke I come across, although he is arrogant, emotionally detached and permanently angry.

I suspect I go weak at the knees when Ryan looks at me because I'm trying subconsciously to prove to myself that I *am* capable of fancying a man other than Jason. That's it. It's *got* to be.

I'm now as convinced by this explanation as I am that my infatuation with Ryan's upper arms will pass as quickly as it developed. I pick up my Jackie Collins book, reassured that this is part of an emotional healing process. It might have been nice if my subconscious had picked on someone rather more appropriate than my boss.

I'm just about to get stuck into Chapter sixty-four, when my phone rings. It might be Trudie. She said she'd call this evening to talk about potential outings with the kids tomorrow. As I go to pick up, however, I catch a glimpse of the number flashing on the screen and gasp.

Because it isn't Trudie. It's a UK number – and one I know very well.

I haven't heard a peep out of Jason for months, despite my best efforts to contact him in the early days. Yet here he is, apparently phoning me now.

With my hand over my mouth and my heart racing so fast I'm surprised my bloodstream can keep up, I stare at the phone.

Christ – do I pick up?

No, no, I can't.

But I want to . . .

No, you bloody well don't, Zoe Moore. This is a man who not only jilted you but didn't have the decency to explain why. So don't be ridiculous. Really.

But I love him . . .

My finger hovers over the little green button, but before I can press it, the ringing stops. My mind is a whirl and I'm gripping the phone so hard my knuckles are white.

Okay, Zoe. Stay calm. Stay cool.

The best tactic here is to check if he's left a message. If

he hasn't, it's essential I don't give the incident a second thought.

I dial my voicemail fourteen times.

And each time it responds with the same five, unforgiving words: 'You have no new messages.'

I lie back on the bed and stare at the ceiling, trying to work out what to do. Every cell in my body is urging me to pick up the phone and ring him back. But something stops me. Is it pride? I don't think so. I lost all that after our wedding day, when I continued to phone him, refusing to listen to what everyone else was telling me: Zoe, he doesn't want you any more, so you've got to forget him and move on.

It wasn't easy. It took every bit of will I had to book that airline ticket to New York and tell myself I had to accept that I'd never see him again. That I had to build a new life without him.

That's the reason I mustn't phone him back: I've come this far without him and I've got to keep going. It's a question of self-preservation. I have no idea what he wants to say to me, but one thing I am certain of is that it will take me back to square one, back to the days of emotional turmoil when crying was the first thing I did in the morning and the last thing I did at night.

I switch off the phone decisively and, wrapping my sheet round my shoulders, shuffle to my open window. A warm breeze dances across my skin as I look up at the moon, so bright tonight that the trees are almost floodlit.

I try my absolute best to stop thinking about what happened. But my thoughts are dragged, kicking and screaming, back to Liverpool, back to everything it represents.

I glance down at the windowsill as a tear splashes on to it, followed quickly by another. With hot eyes and a lump in my throat, I know I'll never sleep.

Chapter 23

After I'd been told outside the church that my husband-to-be had stood me up, the rest of the day was a bit of a blur.

I remember the bridesmaids and ushers squabbling about who was to blame, and Win walloping her boyfriend with an already wilting bunch of calla lilies after he enquired whether the reception was still on.

I remember them nominating each other for the job of informing the hundred-odd guests that the show was over before it had begun.

I remember poor Dad wanting to stay with me, but finally being persuaded to go and break the news to Mum.

And I remember, while chaos broke out around us, Jessica shoving me back into the car and instructing the driver to hit the accelerator as if she'd just won a bit part in *The Sweeney*. 'What a bastard!' she kept exclaiming. 'A complete and utter bastard! I can't believe it. I mean . . . *Huh!* The *bastard!*'

Then she paused. 'Sorry,' she said, momentarily sheepish. 'I didn't mean to rant. You're the one who should be ranting, not me. Although . . . what a *bastard*! I just can't believe— Oh, sorry. You okay?'

I shrugged. 'I don't know,' I replied, so numb I felt anaesthetized. I remember thinking I wasn't crying so perhaps I must be okay.

'The thing is,' she continued, 'anyone who does this sort of thing really isn't someone you want to be married to, Zoe. What was he thinking? He mustn't have been thinking.'

I glanced down at my dress, my beautiful ivory silk dress that had come at such an eye-watering price that they should have thrown in a bottle of Optrex. There was a tiny snag on the skirt, right at the front. I picked at it with my middle fingernail and pulled gently. The fabric bunched.

'It's not as if he hasn't had years in which to dump you,' Jessica babbled. 'He could have done it six months ago and not put you through this. Or at least waited until after the honeymoon when he could have done the decent thing and got a divorce. It's not like it's hard, these days.'

I stared out of the window and suddenly wondered what poor Mum was doing. Probably shrieking loud enough for people sitting down to lunch in Newcastle to hear.

'I am going to *kill* Neil when I get hold of him,' Jessica huffed. 'As best man, it was his job to get the groom here – even if that meant binding and gagging him.'

Her phone vibrated. She had it slammed against her head so rapidly I didn't see her hand move.

'WHERE THE HELL ARE YOU?' I could picture Neil

cowering at the other end of the phone. To say that Jessica wears the trousers in their relationship hardly covers it. I don't think Neil even has any trousers.

'More to the point,' she continued, so forcefully it must have singed the hair round his ears, 'where's that bastard friend of yours?'

I couldn't hear Neil's response. But, as it turned out, I didn't need to.

'What do you *mean* you'll tell me about it later?' Jessica sounded one step away from ordering him to be beheaded. 'Tell me *now*. Neil? Neil! Don't you put that phone down – I mean it. I've never meant anything more in my life. If you put the phone down on me I'll—'

He'd put the phone down on her.

'Soddit,' she said. 'Soddit, soddit, soddit.'

We looked out of the window in silence.

'Was he with him?' I couldn't help asking, eventually. 'Jason, I mean.'

She sighed and nodded. 'He didn't tell me much. In fact, he didn't tell me anything. Oh, I'm sorry, love, I really am. This is horrendous. Absolutely bloody horrendous. I don't think I've ever known—' She wiped away a tear and sat, shaking her head and muttering like someone in the early stages of post-traumatic-stress disorder.

When we got to the house I realized, as I put my key in the front door, that I needed the loo. In fact, I was desperate. I'm talking every muscle in my pelvic floor working so hard it felt like a competitive sport. I remember wondering how I would have handled it had I been standing where I was supposed to be standing at that moment.

Going to the loo took longer than I'd anticipated, courtesy of my four-foot train and so much skirt it almost filled the room. As I was about to step out of the bathroom, I heard people coming in downstairs. My mother's voice was the loudest: 'What a pillock!' she bellowed. 'What a bloody, bloody pillock! And what a selfish bloody pillock at that! I suppose in Cheshire it's no big deal if a hundred and twenty-two asparagus tartlets go to waste. Or a hundred and twenty-two lemon mousses with curry.'

'Coulis,' corrected Desy.

'That's what I said!' snapped Mum. 'The point is they're all sat in a room along with a three-hundred-and-fifty-pounds-a-night disco man and twelve completely bloody useless cava lily centrepieces.'

'Calla,' corrected Desy.

'What?' said Mum.

'It's *calla* lilies,' Desy repeated.

'And that's before we even get on to the peach sugared almonds,' Mum continued, ignoring him. 'What exactly is our Zoe supposed to do with a hundred and twenty-two bags of peach sugared almonds?'

I attempted to open the bathroom door silently but the hinges had needed a squeeze of WD40 since 1991.

'Zoe? Zoe! Is that you?' yelled Mum, hurtling up the stairs, followed by Desy, my auntie Linda and various other members of the Slimming World/step-class posse.

'Oh, *looove!*' she yelled, flinging her arms round me

and squeezing me so hard she made my tiara fall off.

When she pulled away, her own hat – the Accessorize number that was a dead-ringer for a Philip Treacy – was wonky. It sent a stab through my heart.

My mum is usually nothing less than immaculate. She might be twenty years older than the average Wag, but her approach to self-maintenance would put Alex Curran to shame. I sometimes think she'd prefer to amputate her fingers than be seen in public with no nail polish.

At that moment she wasn't immaculate. At that moment, when she pulled away from me, grasping my arms as if I was about to abscond, she had so much mascara down her cheeks she might have been experimenting with the Gothic look.

'Mum, I—'

'Don't say *anything!*' she said, flinging her arms round me again with the grip of a Tae Kwon Do grand master. 'You don't need to say anything. That bloody pillock. I knew he didn't deserve you.'

'Mum, you loved him until an hour ago,' I pointed out.

She sniffed. 'I never liked his hair. Never trust a man who tints his own hair, that's what I always think. He did tint his hair, didn't he?'

I sighed and closed my eyes.

I could feel her about to protest again, but then she said, 'Oh, God, I blame myself.'

'Why?' I frowned.

'I should never have let this happen.'

Desy rolled his eyes and took a drag on his Embassy

cigarette. 'Zoe, how are you feeling?' he asked, blowing smoke.

'Me?' I said. 'Er . . . I don't know, really.'

Then they frowned. Had they each been asked to assess my mental state there and then I think I'd have spent the next twenty years locked up in a padded cell. Because, as far as they were concerned, I should have been wailing. I should have been calling Jason a bastard and a pillock and all the names under the sun. With hindsight – sorry, that word again – I was in shock. I must have been, because the tears did come later, buckets of them. All behind the door of my mum's sweltering spare room, which I moved into, feeling like a pathetic, overgrown teenager.

In the weeks following my wedding day, I did so much weeping my cheeks were as raw as two free-range chicken breasts. I listened to torturous love songs and wallowed in memories of our first kiss, our first weekend in the Lake District, the day we moved into our house.

But I never called him names, not even to myself. Because I still loved him. I knew I shouldn't. But I did.

Chapter 24

It's the natural instinct of all British nannies in the States to seek out others of their kind – even if they would make the most unlikely of chums back home. My new friend Felicity Bowdon-Clarke and I undoubtedly fall into that category. In fact, it would be fair to say we have about as much in common as Princess Michael of Kent and Kerry Katona.

I had worked in a lovely but average nursery in the suburb of a provincial city, while Felicity had been employed in super-rich Knightsbridge by the family of an industrialist so wealthy the patterns on their loo roll were probably Picasso originals. As far as I can remember, she's the first finishing-school graduate and High Court judge's daughter I've ever come across.

'Now, Nancy, watch carefully, please. Knife like so, fork like so,' she instructs, in a voice so cheerfully jolly-hockey-sticks that she can get away with saying almost anything.

As Felicity picks up Nancy's right hand and positions her fingers correctly, I should explain something: Nancy is *not* the five-year-old Felicity is employed to look after but the child's thirty-nine-year-old mother.

'Now, the American etiquette, as you know, is to cut a few bite-sized pieces of food, then lay one's knife across the top of the plate with the sharp edge of the blade facing in,' Felicity continues. 'The fork then changes from the left hand to the right, before eating commences.'

'Uh-huh,' replies Nancy, studiously.

'The European style begins in the same way as the American, in that one cuts by holding the knife in the right hand while securing the food with the fork in the left. The *difference* is that the fork remains in the left hand, prongs facing down, and the knife in the right. One proceeds to eat the cut morsels of food by picking them up with the fork still in the left hand. There. What do you think? Easy, yes?'

I'm just trying to work out how Felicity has managed to make something as straightforward as using a knife and fork sound like the worthy subject of an advanced lecture in applied science when she leaps in again. 'I do think this sort of detail is worth while, don't you, Zoe?' she asks, her smile broader than ever. 'I'm a firm believer in the importance of parents setting a good example. I've seen so many times what happens otherwise. If parents run a sloppy household, they end up with sloppy children.' Then she laughs. 'And, to put it bluntly, I don't look after anyone's slops!'

Felicity is supremely attractive: a slim, coltish redhead – think Nicole Kidman fifteen years ago. And, although her approach to childcare is about as progressive as that of a Victorian schoolmistress, it's hard not to warm to her.

'Okay, I think I got it now,' replies Nancy, in a broad east-coast drawl. 'Like this?' She holds up her knife and fork to Felicity for approval.

'*Parfait!*' exclaims Felicity. '*Félicitations!*'

'Hmm?' asks Nancy.

'Oh, don't worry, we'll get on to that another day.'

Nancy Magenta and her husband Ash made their money running a hairdressing empire that they sold last year to concentrate on developing a range of shampoo. They're not exactly typical of the Hope Falls residents who, I have worked out, fall mainly into two categories: deep-thinking intellectuals or high-flying City types. Judging by Nancy and Ash's success in life, you can only assume they're as sharp as they come. And, given that, you might think being retrained in the art of holding cutlery wouldn't be top of their priorities. Apparently you'd be wrong.

'Y'know, this is just the kind of added value a British nanny brings to a household,' Nancy tells Trudie, Amber and me as she flicks her hair behind a Versace-clad shoulder. 'I just knew the day we got Felicity we were right to hire one of you people. I mean, she has so much to give *culturally*.'

Nancy pauses momentarily in chewing her gum, which she's been doing so vigorously for the past half-hour that my jaw aches just to look at her. 'I don't tell you this enough, Felicity, but it is *so* great to have you here!' She leaps up to give Felicity a hug, apparently to celebrate her very existence.

'Yes, well, let's not get too carried away,' chuckles Felicity, unravelling herself from Nancy's grasp. 'Now, Tallulah, have you washed your hands and face in preparation for our day out?'

Tallulah, a cute, slightly tubby little girl with a Cleopatra bob and shy smile, nods obediently.

Less than an hour later we arrive at the park and Tallulah is loosening up a bit, thanks, largely, to her hitting it off spectacularly well with Ruby – as big a Bratz fan as she is. The pair skip to the swings as Felicity perches herself on a bench and smiles fondly. 'Tallulah's a lovely little girl,' she says.

'Do you like working for Nancy?' asks Trudie.

'Of course!' replies Felicity. 'I mean, no family is for ever, and I'm sure I'll go back to the UK at some point, but for the moment they're all wonderful!'

'They sound a lot better than the last bunch you worked for,' Amber says, nodding. 'From what you've said, I just can't *believe* anybody could be so materialistic.'

'I have nothing against materialism,' Felicity responds. 'In fact, I'd almost consider it a prerequisite. There's nothing worse than working for someone who's not prepared to part with any money.'

'You can't do this job for the cash,' Trudie points out.

'Of course not!' Felicity hoots. 'Although I am well paid.'

'Really?' I ask doubtfully.

She looks at me pityingly. 'There are people in Boston with JDs – that's a law degree – who make less than a good nanny,' she informs me. 'If you play your cards

right, as I have, you can get all sorts of benefits ...
health insurance, a country-club pass, personal trips
using your employer's frequent-flyer miles ...'

I haven't seen a sniff of anything like that from Ryan,
and from Trudie's expression, I can only guess that she
hasn't either.

'Of course it's all about being in demand,' Felicity
continues. 'Nancy knows that I'm often approached by
parents in the park offering to double what I'm making.
I had a note slipped under the windscreen wipers only
yesterday.'

I continue staring at her, stunned.

'Oh,' she adds hastily, 'I'd hate to give you the impression I'm in this job for the wrong reasons. I'm here
because I find working with children and their parents
very satisfying. When they're well behaved, that is.'

'It can get you down when they're not, can't it?' I leap
on to our first bit of common ground. 'I mean, Ruby
and Samuel are gorgeous – and perfectly behaved most
of the time – but bedtime is an absolute nightmare
sometimes.'

'I was referring to the parents,' Felicity replies. She
stands up and cups her hands round her mouth:
'*Tallulah! Tallulah! Over here now, please!*' The instruc-
tion is delivered at the pitch of a falsetto sergeant major
in charge of the deaf squadron. Tallulah drops her doll
and sprints over to us, eyes wide with anticipation.

'Now,' Felicity tuts gently, 'what did I tell you about
your clothes?'

'Um ...' Tallulah ponders, biting her lip. 'I'm not
sure.'

Felicity sighs as she takes a brush out of her bag and starts going at Tallulah's hair as if she's grooming an Afghan hound. 'I asked you to try to keep them clean,' she reminds her, smiling. 'You may be five years old but that isn't an excuse to start letting yourself go. Wait until you're your mother's age before you do that. Now, run along and be careful, darling.'

'Have I told you my family want me to go to the Seychelles with them next month?' Amber announces.

'You're kidding!' shrieks Trudie. 'You lucky thing! I mean, Barbara and Mike are great and everything but there's no way they'll be taking a holiday any time soon – let alone with me tagging along. They're just too busy for *vacations*, Barbara keeps telling me.'

I'm about to share with them that I was supposed to be going to Bermuda this summer, but decide against it. I'm enough of a professional not to dwell on such things. Even if I did come close to ceremonially burning my bikini a couple of weeks ago.

'Well, I'm not at all sure about it.' Amber frowns.

'What? Why not?' I ask.

'It's just . . . I mean, it's very difficult to reconcile the trip with my beliefs.' She's twiddling a dreadlock. 'They're planning to stay in a five-star hotel. I grew out of that sort of thing years ago. I prefer to travel meaning-fully, staying with the indigenous population preferably. In fact, I had a trip planned last year to stay with the Zulu people of South Africa. It was only because I broke my toe getting on the plane that it didn't happen.'

Trudie – who has been bouncing Andrew up and down on her knee in the most vigorous session of horsey-horsey you'd get outside a rodeo – pauses to look at her. 'Can I give you some advice, love?' she says. 'Drag yourself to the Seychelles, pull up a sun-lounger, order the biggest Piña Colada they've got and relax. Then, if you're still worried about your principles, give me a ring. I'll be over like a shot.'

Chapter 25

Despite his tender age, Samuel loves helping me with household tasks. Almost as much as his father doesn't. I've been in America for nearly two months now, and there aren't as many of these as there were when I first got here, thanks to our new cleaning lady, Daria (apparently they'd had several before I arrived – almost as many as there were nannies). But whether it's helping me to unload the dishwasher, sweep the floor after dinner or clear the coffee-table after we've been drawing, he plunges himself into each job with huge enthusiasm. He leaves a bit to be desired in the skill department but that hardly matters.

It all began a couple of weeks ago when I challenged Samuel to put away his toys faster than his sister could hers, then stood back to marvel at what a bit of competition does for a child's motivation. They both ran round the living room, tidying things away, as if they'd been possessed by the spirit of Mr Sheen.

Samuel's latest favourite is emptying the mailbox at the front of the house when the post arrives. He seems to remember this each day before Ruby does and begs

126

me to let him run outside and down the steps so that he can stand on tiptoe to reach up and get it.

This morning when he runs back to the house, his little hands are full of letters. Most of it is junkmail, catalogues and leaflets for things no one wants, but there are some bills too. At first sight, none looks as if it's for me, but I've come to expect that. Most of my correspondence is via email, which is far quicker and more practical. The only downside of checking my inbox is that I spend most of each day wondering whether Jason will have emailed me. When I first got here, I couldn't stop myself logging on at every opportunity with a pounding heart – which subsided the second I realized that, yet again, there was no word from him.

I was just getting this under control when I had his phone call. Since then, I've been logging on with shaking hands and sweat on my brow – pointless, because all I ever get are emails from Mum.

As I sort through the letters, I find an envelope near the bottom of the pile that is curious for no other reason than that there is neither a name nor an address on the front. It is made of particularly good-quality paper, but apart from that – and the lack of an addressee – it has no distinguishing features whatsoever.

Assuming it is another piece of junkmail I tear it open and remove its contents. But the second I catch a glimpse of the piece of paper, I realize it isn't junkmail, and that I'm not the intended recipient.

'What your letter, Zoe?' asks Samuel.

'Oh, um, it's from my daddy,' I lie, blushing pathetically.

'Can I have it?' he asks, reaching up.

'Oooh, er, no, I don't think that'd be a good idea.'

'I want a letter.'

'Sorry, Samuel, you can't have this one, sweetheart. Now, how about we do something else? Come on, what else would you like to do?'

His eyes light up with the cheeky glint of someone who has spotted an opportunity. 'Can I watch *SpongeBob?*' he asks, with a hopeful grin.

'Why not?' I reply, ushering him through the door.

He looks so surprised that I can tell he's already wondering whether it might be worth asking for a tub of ice cream and a bucket of popcorn too.

Now I know that the letter isn't for me, it would be unreasonable to continue reading it. Which is bloody annoying because, from the quick glance I caught, its contents couldn't have been juicier than if they were canned by Del Monte.

I head into the hall and really do intend to fold the letter up, return it to its envelope and leave it on the hall table to await its intended recipient.

Problem is, as I'm attempting to do this, I'm attacked by an insurgent group of rebel brain cells. Brain cells that camp out somewhere in my head and ambush me from time to time.

It is those brain cells that force me, against my will, to purchase and wolf Crunchie bars when I have vowed only hours earlier to follow a strict macrobiotic diet, as favoured by Gwyneth Paltrow.

It is the same brain cells that march me to the shops and compel me to use my Visa card on a new pair of strappy shoes, which are certain to bust my overdraft and match not a single item in my wardrobe.

It is those brain cells that are responsible for all manner of scurrilous decisions on my part. Of which sneaking Ryan's letter into a corner of the hallway so I can read it is undoubtedly one.

Darling Ryan,

It is weeks since I last wrote to you and it has taken all of my willpower not to write again before now. I am assuming there is a good reason why you haven't responded to my first letter. I don't know what it could be, but I'm prepared to give you the benefit of the doubt.

I saw you in the city on Tuesday, you know. You were having a business lunch with someone at that new place in Boylston Street. I was so tempted to come and say hello but I wasn't alone at the time so I couldn't.

You were wearing the black shirt I love you in so much. I couldn't help but notice. You really suit dark colours, Ryan, I always said so. It brings out the colour in those amazing eyes of yours.

You're probably wondering by now what this letter is all about and in some ways so am I. I suppose I just needed to make contact with you and reiterate what I said last time. To reach out to you and beg you not to ignore me. No, not beg. I don't beg, do I? It really isn't my style. But, then, I think you know that.

What is the case, though, Ryan, is that there is so much more to me that you don't yet know. What we started was just that – the start. The start of something beautiful, if you'll let it be. Please, Ryan, listen to your heart – and

*your head. We're great together and you know it deep
down. Just don't make the biggest mistake of your life by
not recognizing it, my love.*

   Yours for ever,
   Juliet
   XXX

'Can I read your letter, Zoe?' asks Ruby.

I jump and hide it behind my back, aware that I couldn't look more suspicious if I was wearing a false beard and glasses. 'Er, no, it's just a bill,' I say.

'You told Samuel it was from your daddy. I heard you.'

'It is.' I blush. 'My dad's called Bill. It's just that I think you'd find it boring, that's all.'

'You told me his name was Gordon,' she tells me.

'It's like living with Inspector Poirot round here.' I sigh. 'Look, it's a private letter, okay? Simple as that. And I would, just this once, like to keep it to myself. Is that okay with you?'

'Is it a love letter?' She grins. 'Come on, Zoe, is it a love letter?'

'No!' I tell her, shaking my head in mock exasperation. 'Absolutely not.' Well, I'm *half* telling the truth.

Chapter 26

My plan is simply to go out and buy some envelopes, put Ryan's letter into one, slip it in with the rest of the mail and pretend I've not seen it. I'm anxious to make sure he doesn't get the impression that I'm the sort of person who would wilfully disregard his privacy by reading what is obviously a very personal letter. Even if I *am* that sort of person.

The rest of the day, however, isn't just hectic, it's like a bad day in Bedlam times ten.

First, there is synchronized-swimming practice for Ruby, which I smugly deliver her to ten minutes early before realizing I've left her swimsuit in the hallway. By the time we get home and back, we're impossibly late and everyone else has miraculously graduated to some elaborate movement called the Oyster, while poor Ruby is still struggling to tread water.

She accepts this with incredibly good grace, but it doesn't take a psychology textbook and home tuition with Sigmund Freud to work out that she's upset. I feel terrible about this – but, sadly, it's only the start.

Next, we head for the tip down the road to throw

away some boxes of non-recyclable rubbish that have been cluttering up one of the cupboards in the hall since I arrived. Both children want to help and I see no reason not to let them. It's only when we're leaving that I marvel at how clean and clutter-free the boot looks – then realize that, actually, it isn't meant to.

In her enthusiasm, Ruby has also thrown into one of the skips a bag that contains half of Ryan's wardrobe, which I'd been supposed to take to the dry-cleaner's. Panic-stricken, I consider my options, recognize that there aren't many and settle on the only thing left open to me.

By the time I have jumped into the skip, located the offending item and am attempting to wade out again, I have a rusty bed-spring tangled in my hair, a generous portion of old pizza poking out of the top of my T-shirt and several burly blokes from the local authority standing at the side and threatening to have me arrested.

'I *love* having you as a nanny, Zoe!' Ruby giggles, as I slam my foot on the accelerator to make our getaway. 'Just wait till I tell Daddy!'

Shortly after this I come precariously close to reversing the car into a tree, Ruby falls over outside the house and nearly breaks her leg, and Samuel shoplifts a packet of condoms from the supermarket under the misapprehension that they are a new type of M&Ms.

The tantrums – which haven't been so bad over the last few days – start early at seven o'clock. To give Ruby and Samuel some credit, their excuses are becoming almost impressive in their inventiveness. Tonight Ruby announces there is a leak in her bedroom ceiling and she can't possibly go to bed in case she is dripped on.

'Ruby,' I say calmly, 'there is no leak in your bedroom ceiling. It couldn't be drier if it was in the middle of the Sahara desert.'

She sticks out her bottom lip.

'Mine drips too,' says Samuel, in what is either a display of solidarity with his sister or a blatant attempt to pinch her excuse. 'Drip, drip, drip!'

'No, it doesn't!' I shrill, in my merriest, most upbeat tone – although I'm as weary as someone who has trekked cross-country on a donkey for several days before realizing they've left the iron on at home. 'Now, what did you do with your pyjamas?'

'I don't like pyjamas,' Samuel informs me.

'Course you do, sweetie!'

'I don't.'

'But these are your favourites, Samuel! Look!'

'*Noooooooooo!*'

At that point I discover that my strict new rule of drinking alcohol no more than once a week – devised last night when I was ordering my third glass of wine on a girls' night out – is in serious jeopardy. The prospect of grabbing a bottle of beer and conversing on the phone with Trudie for a minimum of an hour and a half is too tempting.

At nine twenty-one, the moment finally arrives, when I creep upstairs and put my ear to each child's door and hear something sublime. Silence.

My shoulders relax, I take a deep breath and head downstairs, straight for the fridge. I refuse to be disheartened by the fact that, once again, Ryan has left an almost full plate of pasta on the work surface for the house-work fairy (i.e. me) to make disappear.

I have my hand on a bottle of Coors when I hear him coming into the kitchen. 'Oh, hi!' I say. 'Just trying to find a little snack for supper.'

But as I turn and glimpse his face, I see he's about as interested in whether or not I'm snaffling his beer as the weather forecast in the Galapagos Islands. 'Would you care to tell me what this is about?' he thunders. He's clutching the letter I found earlier today.

'What what's all about?' I ask angelically.

'*You've been opening my mail!*'

'No!' I splutter. 'Well, yes. I mean——'

'*Why* would anyone do that?'

The question is delivered with such force I could easily believe he's about three seconds away from turning into the Incredible Hulk.

'*Why* would someone come into my home and open my private mail?'

'I – I didn't mean to open it!' I know I sound pathetic.

'What? Your hand just slipped? You *accidentally* opened the envelope, *accidentally* took out the letter, then *accidentally* disposed of the envelope?'

'Well . . . *yes!*' I reply, hoping I'm maintaining a suit-ably dignified air, despite my cheeks feeling so hot you could fry an egg on them. 'The thing is there was no——'

'Oh, man!' he interrupts. 'You are a piece of work! You seriously expect me to believe that? I gotta tell you, I've seen some crappy behaviour from nannies before now but none as bad as this. I mean, what in God's name . . .'

As Ryan continues his tirade, I grow more and more indignant. Okay, I shouldn't have read the letter, but it really was an accident that I opened it. And, besides, do I really deserve this sort of berating after what I've had to put up with so far in this job?

With my own blood reaching simmering point, I know the only way to deal with this situation is swiftly and with singular aim: to demonstrate that Zoe Moore is not the kind of woman who puts up with such behaviour.

Empowered by this thought, I lift up my left hand and go to slam it down on the work surface, determined that the force of this – with my steely, authoritative glare – will shut him up immediately, then have him begging for forgiveness.

Sadly, I fail to factor into the equation Ryan's uneaten plate of pasta, which is in the way of my fist as I bring it down.

As my hand lands, the plate and its ribbons of tomato tagliatelle are propelled into the air and across the room in a firework effect, the likes of which I haven't seen since the opening ceremony of the last Olympics.

As the plate clatters on to the tiles and smashes into what must be eighty-odd pieces, my heart is thumping crazily and I'm almost panting with panic.

Right, Zoe, hold yourself together. Think of a sensible strategy with which to respond to this. Beg for forgiveness, maybe? Pretend it was always my intention to redecorate the walls this evening? *Run?*

Oh, shit . . .

Then I notice something. Okay, so it wasn't quite

what I had in mind. But Ryan – sporting a dollop of tomato sauce on his nose – is well and truly stunned into silence.

I straighten my back and frown at him. He's had an important meeting today – I can tell because he has shaved and is wearing an expensive white shirt that makes the skin on his neck look gloriously sun-kissed and smooth. My eyes are drawn to the erotic curve of his Adam's apple and a terrible mental image flashes through my mind – of my lips brushing it. I'm spellbound by the sensual contours of his cheekbones, his determined brow and his indecently full lips.

He's breathtaking, he really is. No matter how arrogant, angry or annoying he is, nothing can take that away from him.

But I can't let it distract me. 'I was *trying* to tell you,' I say, 'that your letter came in an envelope which had *no* name and *no* address on it. I did *not* know it was for you. And I certainly did *not* know the nature of its contents.'

He straightens his back, clearly reminding himself that *he*'s supposed to be annoyed with *me*. 'But now you do, huh?'

I shake my head at him silently, with the calculated expression of disappointment you'd see on a dog trainer whose King Charles Spaniel has just pooed on the carpet.

Before he has a chance to say or do anything other than feel uncomfortable, I turn and – ignoring the mess I've made – walk to the fridge. I open it and pointedly pick out not one, not two, but *three* bottles of beer. Then

I slam it and head for the door. 'I'm going to bed,' I announce.

I march upstairs, feeling a surge of elation. I have made Ryan shut up and listen to me. Unbelievable!

I'm just about to crack open a congratulatory beer, when I realize I've forgotten to bring anything to open it with.

Don't worry, Zoe. This is not a disaster. I can still get a bottle-opener without ruining the effect of my spectacular exit. The drawer where it's kept is at the side of the kitchen next to the door. So, even if Ryan is still in there, I can creep downstairs, open the door and scurry quietly back up with it before he notices me.

I'm in the kitchen with my hand in the drawer when I catch sight of Ryan on the other side of the room doing something that shocks me: he's wiping tomato sauce off the walls with a cloth and some kitchen spray. It isn't that he has never seen a bottle of cleaning fluid before: it's just that, the few times I've seen him examine one, it's with the sort of bewilderment you'd see on the face of a caveman who is attempting to assemble an IKEA flat-pack.

When he catches me looking at him, he stands up and reaches into his back pocket. 'Here,' he says, holding out the bottle-opener. 'I used it earlier.'

'Thank you,' I say curtly, taking it from him.

'Sure,' he replies.

I am about to march out of the room, when he's looking at me again and I feel a flush of heat at my neck.

He's smirking.

What has he got to smirk about? As I frown back, his

mouth twitches and I realize he's trying to suppress a giggle.

For some reason, the idea makes me smile – which triggers something in him. Laughter. Uncontrollable, slightly hysterical laughter that, it's clear, isn't going to stop, no matter how firmly he holds the back of his hand to his mouth.

Worse, it's infectious. I find myself joining in, chuckling at first, then full-on, unstoppable howling.

It becomes cyclical. Every time I think I've got myself under control, I catch sight of his face, which starts me off again. And him.

Eventually, with tears in his eyes, Ryan directs me to the door. 'Get outta here,' he manages, between snorts. 'Crazy woman.'

As I run giddily up the stairs, it strikes me that this is possibly the strangest thing that's happened since I got here. Oh, God, now I really need a beer.

Chapter 27

I must confess that it's been a number of years since I went to church for anything other than weddings, funerals or christenings. About twenty, to be exact. It's not that I don't believe in God, I do. I think. It's just that the level of conviction I had aged nine hasn't stayed with me. Besides, my grandma Bonnie is no longer around to tell me I'll go to hell if I don't turn up each week with freshly washed hair and shoes so shiny they dazzle half the congregation.

In America, church attendance seems to be at a far healthier level than it is in the UK. As the other nannies and I walk into St Stephen's, our neighbourhood Episcopalian church, and assemble our rabble of children near the back, the place is so packed you'd think they'd come to watch Frank Sinatra on the first date of a world tour.

'I really thought, when I started exploring the principles of Scientology, that I'd never set foot in a mainstream church again,' Amber tells me earnestly.

'When did you start exploring the principles of Scientology?' I ask.

'Last Tuesday.'

The church is a traditional one, and just being there plunges me into thoughts of my wedding day. Not that I got as far as being *inside* the church. But I still keep thinking about it all the same.

I often find myself drifting into a fantasy world, in which our usher Andrew – instead of dragging himself over to Dad and me to tell us that Jason had done a runner – smiles broadly and says, 'You look amazing, Zoe. Jason's a lucky man. He won't know what's hit him when he sees you walking down that aisle – although I know he'll be relieved. He's been here for the last thirty-five minutes.'

At that point the daydream usually disintegrates. Maybe picturing myself standing at the altar with Jason is a delusion too far. Deep down I know this sort of thing isn't good for me.

I'm dragged back to the here and now as an explosion of music fills the church to herald the arrival of the priest who, although he is surprisingly young, walks to the front with a serenely commanding air.

'Good morning to you all on this beautiful day,' he says, as the music dies down. 'I'd like to start by welcoming to St Stephen's anybody who is joining us for the first time.'

The priest, it is clear, doesn't fit the stereotypical image of a churchman. That of an off-duty Armani model, perhaps. Or George Clooney's dazzling younger cousin. And I'm clearly not the only one who's noticed.

Trudie leans over Samuel's head and beckons me. 'He's fit!' she hisses.

I nod sagely in an attempt to convince the woman in the next pew that she's relaying some theologically profound comment.

During the ceremony I find myself attempting to look as *au fait* with the proceedings as someone who attends four times a week and twice on Sundays. My rendition of 'What A Friend We Have In Jesus' is particularly convincing, I think, except for the bit where I accidentally turn over two pages of the hymn-book and end up singing 'How Great Thou Art' until Felicity prods my arm.

'Wonderful service, I thought!' she whoops afterwards, as we and the rest of the congregation pour out of the church. Her ponytail is so neat and perky today that you'd think she'd been groomed for a gymkhana. 'I'm so glad you've all come. I told you you'd enjoy it, didn't I? You have, haven't you?'

'I thought it was great,' says Trudie. 'And not just because the priest looked like Mr August on a *Hollyoaks* calendar either.'

'Now, my darling,' Felicity beams, bending down to Tallulah as we hover at the front of the church, 'straighten your back, like I told you. And let's fix this hat, shall we?'

She yanks at Tallulah's beret so that it's positioned at a jaunty angle. Today Tallulah is wearing white tights, patent-leather shoes and a stiff buttoned-up coat – the sort of ensemble you might expect Little Lord Fauntleroy to turn up in at a royal wedding. Something tells me it wasn't her mother who dressed her this morning.

'Oh, Zoe,' says Felicity, 'Tallulah and I were wondering if you're free for another play date this week. She's keen to perform the new piece I taught her on the piano for Ruby. What do you think?'

'Tuesday's good for us,' I tell her. 'I'll check my diary but I don't think I've got any high-powered meetings that day.'

'Marvellous, darling. We'll come to you?'

Ruby and Tallulah love their play dates – and I'm quite enjoying them too. Not least because since I've been spending so much time with Felicity I'm now able to reel off the correct manner of addressing a baroness at a cocktail reception, and I can tell you the French for 'Sorry, I'm allergic to caviar – do you have any truffles?'

'Felicity, Tallulah, how are you?' asks a soft American voice behind us.

'Vicar! What a wonderful service,' exclaims Felicity, gushing like a broken tap. 'Your sermon was a particular highlight. Tallulah and I were quite moved.'

'Well, that's great to hear,' smiles the priest, as he crosses his arms over his chest – which is so broad that I wonder if he spends every spare minute between prayers doing press-ups. 'And it's wonderful to see some newcomers, too. I'm Paul.'

Close up, Paul seems even younger than he did in church – he can't be any more than two or three years older than we are.

'Hi!' we say enthusiastically, and a slightly awkward silence ensues. It's filled by four-year-old Brett asking Amber if Taco Bells make her fart as much as they do his father.

'Do you go to church back home in England?' asks Paul.

'Oh, yes,' I fib, landing myself one step closer to eternal damnation. 'Well, when I can, you know.'

'Great! And how about you?' he says to Amber. 'I don't think I've seen you here before. Welcome to St Stephen's – it's great to have you.'

As Amber looks up, she flushes violently. When she meets his eye, it couldn't have been more obvious she has the hots for him if little love-hearts were floating round their heads.

'Um, I'm just here with Brett,' replies Amber, flicking back a dreadlock and attempting to pull herself together. 'I thought you had some interesting messages and everything but I'm into Scientology.'

'Oh, really?' replies the Reverend Paul, without batting an eyelid. 'I have a friend who's a Scientologist. L. Ron Hubbard's dynamic principle of man's existence is an interesting theory. We have some real in-depth discussions about it.'

Amber looks momentarily as if she's lost the use of her vocal cords. 'Um . . . good,' she replies.

'Clearly, I'm not a follower,' he smiles, 'but as someone who's had a lifelong interest in both philosophy and theology I find some of the questions Scientology raises fascinating – about whether the goal of life is simply infinite survival. Then, of course, you get on to Dianetics – the relationship between the spirit, mind and body. What's your view on that? Do you feel it provides some fundamental answers?'

'Um, definitely,' replies Amber. 'Yup. No doubt.'

'Well, I'd sure love to spend some time discussing it with you, Amber, but now I gotta go. So nice to have met you all. Come again, won't you?'

When he's out of earshot, Trudie turns to the rest of the group looking naughtier than a puppy that has pinched a chocolate éclair. 'He's *lovely!*' she exclaims.

'He's a man of God!' scolds Felicity.

'Yeah, but is he single?' Trudie winks.

'For goodness' sake, Trudie,' Felicity says reprovingly. 'You can't think in those terms about someone in the Reverend Paul's position. It's completely inappropriate.'

'Why?' protests Trudie. 'They're allowed to get married and everything, aren't they? Besides, I was just *commenting*, that's all. I'm already attached, as you know.'

'Good,' replies Felicity.

'Only I did think he had his eye on Amber,' adds Trudie, clearly unable to stop herself.

'Don't be ridiculous!' Felicity snaps.

'Why's it ridiculous? Come on, Amber, what do you think? Gorgeous, isn't he?'

'I . . . well . . . I mean . . .' Amber is flustered. 'He seems very nice but, fundamentally, he's a – a— Mainstream religion just isn't something I could ever—'

'Amber, Amber,' interrupts Trudie, putting a comforting hand on her arm, 'you don't need to say another word. Just give us the nod when you've come round to the idea and I'll set the two of you up together faster than you can digest a communion wafer.'

Chapter 28

After church, the kids and I head over to Trudie's for a cup of tea. We always enjoy this routine except that her tea tastes stewed and is sweetened so heavily that the enamel on your teeth erodes just from looking at it.

We pile into her mammoth people-carrier and I attempt to chat in the usual jocular manner, although the journey is death-defying. 'It can sometimes be tricky remembering to drive on the right, can't it?' I say diplomatically, as I cling for dear life to the edge of my seat.

'They say you're meant to get used to it, but I'm not sure I ever will, to be honest,' Trudie tells us, as she narrowly misses a 4×4. The driver winds down his window and throws us a hand signal that I'm confident doesn't mean 'have a nice day'.

'What a cheek!' she exclaims. ' 'Scuse me, kids, close your ears. JUST BOG OFF, WHY DON'T YA?'

'Some people have got no manners, have they?' I tut, as Trudie clicks on her indicator.

'Precisely my thoughts, love,' she tells me, as she checks for smudged lipstick in her rear-view mirror.

I'm coming to the conclusion that hedgehogs are

more alert to road safety than Trudie is. As we turn into the next street, she comes perilously close to careering into a pick-up truck. Her window is immediately rolled down in preparation for another tirade. Except what she does next is not what any of us was expecting.

'*Aaah! Bloody 'ell! It's you!*' She yanks on the hand-brake, leaps out of the car and dashes over the road to the driver.

She grabs his shirt collar and begins to kiss him as if she's attempting to lasso something stuck at the back of his throat. I pretend, for the benefit of passers-by, that I've never met her before in my life.

'It's Ritchie!' Eamonn exclaims. 'Ritchie, Ritchie!'

At that moment Trudie's lips part from those of her lover. She grabs him by the hand and drags him towards us. 'You've got to meet someone,' she says, leaning into my window.

Ritchie has skin the colour of a shiny chestnut, curly brown hair lightened by the sun and the biggest biceps I've seen outside a Desperate Dan cartoon strip. 'You must be Zoe.' He grins as he shakes my hand. 'I gotta tell you, this girl sure does speak highly of you.'

'Um, and you,' I say, which I'm aware is an understatement, given that his name makes an appearance in every other sentence.

'Really?' He squeezes her round the waist. 'Well, that sure is nice to hear.'

'As if you didn't know it already,' interjects Trudie, nudging him in the ribs so hard that anyone marginally less butch would end up in traction.

I spend the rest of the journey to the King household

confirming that, yes, Trudie probably is the luckiest person alive to have Ritchie as a boyfriend. We arrive as Barbara is preparing Sunday lunch.

For a high-powered City lawyer with the sort of salary that oil magnates dream of, Barbara King does domesticity pretty well. The tailored trouser suit I last saw her in has been replaced with a chic cotton skirt that falls elegantly below her knee, a fashionable fitted shirt and an apron so pristine I wonder why she'd bothered with it.

Her hair is as styled as it was for work and her makeup just as perfect, although there's no one to impress except us and a roast chicken the size of a well-built ostrich, which she's just taken out of the oven.

'My boys!' she cries, taking off her oven gloves and flinging her arms wide. 'Did you enjoy going to church?'

Andrew and Eamonn run into her arms, but remain noncommittal on the church issue. Barbara pulls back and scrutinizes their faces.

'Trudie.' She frowns. 'Have you dressed Eamonn in Andrew's pure wool sweater? Didn't I tell you he was allergic?'

'Oh,' says Trudie. 'Sorry.'

'If you only knew what this could do to him! I can see irritation marks already,' Barbara mutters. 'Eamonn, let Mommy remove that thing, will you?'

When Barbara has tugged the jumper over his head and satisfied herself that he's out of immediate danger, she returns to the lunch. 'Did you learn anything new at church today?' she asks, over her shoulder.

'Bog off!' giggles Andrew. 'Bog off! Bog off! Bog off!'

From the look on Barbara King's face, I'm guessing she's not impressed.

Chapter 29

It's ten twenty-four, my favourite time of night. The children are in bed so I can send emails, have my daily conference call with Trudie and attempt to take my mind off Jason by snuggling up in bed to find out who Lucky Santangelo is shagging in the next chapter of Jackie Collins's *Chances*.

But not tonight. Oh, no, sirree. Because while I have come to love looking after Ruby and Samuel, something still happens every so often at bedtime. Something that makes those otherwise adorable human beings turn into mini pit-bulls, determined not to be forced upstairs.

In tonight's case, this has included the usual pro-testations, excuses and elaborate lies, but for Ruby it has involved such a larger-than-average helping of hysteria I'm starting to wonder whether she really *has* got a bloodsucking monster in her wardrobe.

'*Nooooooo!* I won't go to bed, *nooooooo!*' she yells, pounding her fists on the banister.

'Ruby, listen to me, sweetheart,' I say, in desperation. 'This isn't doing you any good, it really isn't – you're exhausted.'

'N*ooooo, I'm noooot!*' she wails, sprinting into the living room.

I take another deep breath – my fourteenth of the evening. This is worse than usual. I have no idea why, but it is. I'm starting to despair about the apparent uselessness of my tried and tested techniques, involving calm voices, sticker charts and time out, and tears are pricking the backs of my eyes.

I find Ruby lying on the couch with her head buried in a cushion, sobbing relentlessly. I put my hand on her arm but she shakes it off.

'N*ooooooooo!*'

I take my fifteenth deep breath, put my head into my hands and force myself to think.

But I can't focus on practical solutions, just a succession of thoughts that prove I'm totally crap at this job.

What the hell if I've spent a few years looking after kids in a nice, well-organized nursery where I got to hand them back at the end of every day? That's hardly a challenge, is it?

And who gives a toss if I'm managing to maintain a calm tone and a composed manner when Ruby looks as if she wants to throw herself off a cliff and my own insides feel as if they're being torn apart?

There's no other explanation, Zoe Moore. You're a bloody failure.

Ruby sits up and scowls at me. 'Why are *you* upset?' she says accusingly, her bottom lip trembling.

'I'm not upset, sweetheart,' I tell her, hoping I sound convincing.

'Why are you crying then?'

I touch my cheek. It's damp.

'You've got no right to cry,' Ruby shouts. '*You*'ve got a mommy. I haven't.'

I'm so taken aback by this that I don't know how to respond. Then I say, 'Is that what this is about, Ruby? Is it because of your mommy?'

Ruby sniffs and wipes her cheeks. Then she nods.

'Oh, sweetheart.' I pull her towards me and wrap my arms round her.

At first, her tense little shoulders refuse to submit to my hug. But as I stroke her hair they relax, and she buries her face in my neck.

'M-Mommy used to put me to bed every night,' she tells me, her little voice wobbling. 'She – she used to read me a story and kiss my head and she'd be right next door if I needed her.' She stops and takes a breath. 'If I ever got scared, all I had to do was to go into her room and she'd be right there.' She looks up at me. 'But . . . she's not here any more. She's in heaven instead.'

Tears spill on to her nightdress. I feel a lump in my throat that makes it difficult to speak. 'I know, but when mommies are in heaven they are still there for their little girls,' I tell her, improvising as best I can.

She stares at me quizzically. 'They're looking down at you and making sure everything's all right,' I continue, through a blur of tears. 'And if you get scared, all you have to do is to close your eyes and picture your mommy and tell her what's wrong.'

'And she'll hear me?' asks Ruby.

'Of course.'

We sit for a minute, both silent, both thinking – I suspect – about the same thing. Ruby's mommy, up in heaven, no longer there to kiss her goodnight.

'It's hard sometimes, though,' says Ruby, her tears subsiding.

'I know, Ruby . . .'

'I mean picturing her. That's what's hard.'

'I suppose it's been a long time since you saw her, hasn't it?' I say. 'You know what? You should put a picture of her next to your bed. That way, whenever you want to talk to her, or even just think about her, you can.'

Her eyes widen. 'Really?' she says, brightening. 'I could do that?'

'Well, I don't see why not. If you'd like to, that is.'

She nods determinedly. 'I *would*. I *would* like to.'

So thrilled am I by the thought that maybe I'm Liverpool's answer to the baby whisperer after all that it's a moment before I register slight concern. It's prompted by something that's bothered me since I got here. *I haven't seen a single picture of Ruby's mother in the whole house.*

No wedding photo on the mantelpiece, no daft family pictures stuck on the fridge, no photo album in any of the drawers. In fact, if you didn't know better, you'd think she'd never existed.

'Okay,' I say to Ruby, 'perhaps I can speak to your daddy about it tomorrow night – if he's home – and we'll see if we can sort one out for you. How's that?'

'I know where there's a photo of my mommy,' she tells me, lowering her voice conspiratorially. 'Come on, I'll show you.'

As she stands up and grabs my hand, I feel suddenly uneasy.

'Ruby, I really think we should wait until I can talk to your dad.'

Her little face drops again. 'So I can't speak to my mommy, after all?'

I bite my lip. 'Oh, come on, then. Show me where it is.'

Chapter 30

The picture's in the utility room, tucked away at the back of a low shelf next to a camping stove collecting dust. It can't be that old because Ruby features in it, albeit as a baby, but it's tatty and dog-eared. Despite its condition, though, there's something immediately captivating about it.

Ruby's mom is a picture of youth and vitality, her long blonde hair cascading beyond her shoulders, her hazel eyes bright and alive. She's holding baby Ruby so close to her face that their noses are inches apart and their eyes locked. She has the unmistakable look of deep, thunderbolt love that mothers wear soon after their first child is born. The look of someone who has just discovered a part of their heart they never knew existed.

'Do you think she's pretty?' whispers Ruby.

'She's gorgeous,' I reply. And I mean it. She has a classically beautiful face, with full lips, lightly freckled skin and the bone structure of a supermodel.

I find a spare picture frame in a drawer in the hall – I

remember seeing it there ages ago. Ruby watches as I position the photograph in it and close the back. 'There,' I tell her. 'How's that?'

When she smiles, I know I'm back in business. 'Good,' she says decisively.

'I'm glad. Now, come on, let's get you tucked in.'

'Wait,' she says, and picks up the picture. She looks at it for a second, then plants her lips on the glass.

I feel my heart swell and am immediately reminded that this is about so much more than me trying to do my job well. This is about a little girl being able to give her mommy a kiss – which she hasn't done for nearly three years.

When Ruby snuggles down in bed and pulls the covers up to her shoulders, I lean down to kiss her. 'Night-night, Ruby.'

'G'night, Zoe.'

I'm about to leave when she pipes up again: 'Zoe?'

'Yes, sweetheart?'

'Thank you.'

By the time I get into my own bed it's almost eleven thirty. Sleep washes over me quickly and deeply . . . and the next thing I'm aware of is Ryan's voice. Which sounds like the equivalent of a helicopter taking off in my bedroom.

'Zoe? Come out here, I'd like to speak to you.'

I rub my eyes and look at the clock. It's seven twelve a.m., which means I've had almost eight hours' sleep. But it feels like only minutes since I dropped off.

'Zoe? Are you listening to me?'

I sit up in bed, feeling like a zombie who's been suffering from insomnia for the last week.

'*Zoe!*'

I leap up, straightening my pyjamas and scanning the room for a band to tie back my hair. I might be half asleep but I'm certainly not going to answer the door to Ryan looking like the Bride of Dracula on a bad day.

'Just a minute!' I reply, in a tone that's supposed to sound casual, but doesn't.

'zoe!'

I dive to the door and open it, regardless of the fact that I'm still minus a hairband.

'*Yes?*' I reply coolly.

He's about to speak when he glances at my pyjama top.

'Is something the matter, Ryan?' I ask calmly.

He averts his eyes pointedly and gestures to my pyjama top.

My eyes travel downwards.

Then I nearly faint.

Oh, fuck! Oh, fuck!

I was so tired last night that I managed to miss out two buttons when I put on my pyjamas. This wouldn't be such a big deal except that my left boob is poking through the hole.

I dive back into my room, grab my dressing-gown and wrap it round myself tightly.

'Sorry about that,' I mutter, my face burning. 'Um, what can I do for you?'

'Can I come in?' he asks. His expression tends to

indicate that he isn't after a cup of tea and a nice long chat comparing horoscopes.

My mind races – what have I got in my room that I might not want him to see? Top of the list is yesterday's knickers next to my bed, which he definitely must not set eyes on – even if I have just flashed him.

'I need to speak to you somewhere the kids can't hear,' he hisses.

I hesitate. 'Right. Sure. Just give me a second,' I say, diving back into my room and shutting the door. Outside, I hear him sigh again.

I scan the room as my heart pounds in an audacious attempt to break the world land-speed record. The offending knickers are kicked under the bed. The upper-lip dye kit on my dressing-table is chucked into the wardrobe. And, for some reason I can't put my finger on, I replace the Jackie Collins on my bedside table with Dostoyevsky's *Crime and Punishment*, a book I'd promised myself I'd read at some point in my life, but which I haven't got round to yet.

Within twenty seconds, the room is transformed into something I consider vaguely acceptable to Ryan's eyes. I open the door. 'Do come in,' I say, as if welcoming him for mulled wine and canapés.

Ryan enters and sits on the end of my bed. I plonk myself at the top. 'Right,' I declare brightly. 'What can I do for you?'

Chapter 31

Sitting at the top of my bed, I catch a glimpse of myself in my dressing-table mirror and my worst suspicions about my hair are confirmed. It looks as if it recently got tangled up in the blades of a combine-harvester. I gather it together and hold it, trying to concentrate on what Ryan's saying.

'Zoe,' he begins, with another heavy sigh. This morning he's wearing a pair of long vintage shorts that I've never seen before. As he leans forward and puts his elbows on his knees, they ride up and expose his tanned, muscular lower thighs. I glance at them momentarily but the image lingers in my mind.

'Yes, Ryan?' I say.

He looks at me directly and I see how weary he is. 'My kids like you,' he says softly.

'Oh!' I say, perking up. 'Well . . . thanks. I mean, good!'

He nods. 'My kids like you. And . . . and I . . .'

He's about to reveal his assessment of me.

'I think you're – you're . . .'

I lean forward anxiously, biting my lip.

'Well, it doesn't matter what I think,' he concludes.

'Right.' I feel deflated.

He looks down at his hands and scratches the side of a finger. The golden skin on one of his knuckles goes briefly pale.

'And it's because we . . . that is, *the kids* like you, that I'm going to be as diplomatic as I can be.'

I try not to raise an eyebrow, but the words 'diplomatic' and 'Ryan' aren't natural bedfellows.

'The photograph you put next to Ruby's bed last night.'

My heart nearly stops. I'd forgotten about it. But I know immediately that my reservations about it were justified. I also know that, whatever happened the other night, this is one conversation that *isn't* going to end in a fit of the giggles.

'Ah,' is all I can bring myself to say.

'Yes, *ah*,' he mimics. 'Well, I've removed it.'

'Oh.'

'And I'd like you to respect the fact that this is my house,' he continues. His voice, as deep and rich as ever, has a throaty quality this morning. 'If I'd wanted to decorate the place with pictures of my late wife, I would have. But I don't. And I believe that's my choice.'

'Oh, Ryan, listen . . .' I don't know exactly what I'm going to say. 'I mean, I didn't realize—'

'That's all I wanted to say about it.'

'Please let me explain—'

'No,' he interrupts.

I'm so taken aback that I nearly fall off the bed. I sit up straight and will myself to keep it together. Because I know that, whether Ryan likes it or not, I have to explain what happened last night. 'Please let me just tell you what Ruby said last night. *Please*.'

He hesitates for a second. 'Okay. What?'

I gulp. Right. Keep things calm, Zoe. Calm but succinct.

'She said the reason she never wants to go to bed is because her mommy's not here any more to kiss her goodnight.' The words tumble from my mouth. 'She said she can't picture her because she can't even remember what she looked like. She said she wanted to be able to talk to her because—'

'*Stop!*' shouts Ryan. 'That's enough. For Chrissake, that's enough.'

'But, Ryan—'

'I said that's enough. Now, *please*, just do things my way. For once.'

'Okay, okay.' I pull my dressing-gown tighter round me. 'I'm sorry.'

He nods slowly and takes a deep breath, then stands to leave.

Oh, well done, Zoe. Beautifully handled.

'I didn't mean to upset you,' I add awkwardly.

As he reaches the door, he turns. My eyes meet his and I'm shocked by what I see. They're filled with sorrow and, I'm certain, glistening with unspilled tears. Is he crying? Is Ryan really crying?

'You didn't.' He sniffs, and slams the door behind him.

Chapter 32

To: Zoemmoore@hotnet.co.uk
From: Helen@hmoore.mailserve.co.uk

Dear Zoe,

How are things? Sorry I haven't emailed for a while but, as I think your father told you on the phone the other day, I've been feeling really out of sorts lately. Absolutely everyone at work has had this stomach bug and I'm sure I'm coming down with it.

It's all I can think because I'm absolutely exhausted and have lost my appetite completely. I've never been a big eater, as you know, but when we went round to Dave and Angela's for a bite to eat the other night I could stomach hardly any of it. Still, I lost three pounds at Slimming World for the first time ever on a 'red' week, so it's not all bad news.

Anyway, Ian and Debbie next door have had their baby. It's a little boy, weighing ten pounds seven ounces, would you believe? Debbie's still feeling a bit tender after the birth. We saw her yesterday and she said it had been like trying to extract a watermelon from her private parts. Your father went a bit queasy. They've called him Harley. Harley Stan

Keanu Xabi Smith. Still, I'm sure we'll get used to it.

Thanks for sending the pictures, by the way. The children are gorgeous, especially Ruby with that lovely blonde hair. And the house looks wonderful – like something straight out of *Desperate Housewives*. Of course, I still think you'd have been better taking that job in the Wirral, no matter how good a boss you keep telling me Ryan is. That place in Neston was one of those multi-storey nurseries. That's what they call them, isn't it?

Oh, it's no good: I need to tell you about something.

Jason turned up at the house the other day. I was just coming in from work – after what had been a hellish day all round, not helped by Maurice Black from Payroll having scratched the side of the Astra as I was on the way out of the NCP – and he rolled up, just like that. Unbelievable. Wanted your address in America, apparently, and was quite insistent that we give it to him. Obviously we didn't. Your father sent him packing and I honestly hope I never set eyes on him again.

I hope I've done the right thing in telling you. You won't worry, will you? I think we managed to get rid of him, and after what your father said to him, I'd be amazed if he ever darkened our door again.

I've got nothing much else to tell you really, apart from the fact that I've picked out a new bathroom. It's almost identical to one in the Fired Earth catalogue *and* it's got a bidet. Your father's reaction was: what do we need a bidet for when we've got Andrex? Isn't that typical?

Lots of love,

Mum

XXX

Chapter 33

Considering my mum normally treats gossip as a competitive sport, I can't quite believe the lack of detail in her email about Jason having turned up at the house. What did he say, exactly? What was he wearing? Was he sheepish? Apologetic? And, more to the point, *why* did he come?

Why? Why? Why?

I can't ask any of these questions in my reply to her, of course. Dwelling on the issue would shatter the carefully crafted illusion that I'm successfully getting over him. That, now I'm in the US, he barely enters my thoughts.

It's laughable, really, because nothing could be further from the truth. I think about him all the time, between the welcome distractions of Ryan's biceps and decisions about the kids' dinner.

I'm constantly thinking about the small things: like how when he laughs, it's a full-on laugh, no half-measures, tossing his head back and submitting himself entirely to the moment.

I think about the precision with which he works when

he's cooking, his face a picture of intense concentration, even when he's making something as straightforward as spaghetti Bolognese. I think about him singing in the shower in a way no one else I've ever met can: his powerful, melodious voice belting out tunes to recording-contract perfection.

I think about these details and a million others. And I can't stop.

As well as the obvious problem that I'm still in love with him, it doesn't help that there are so many unanswered questions about our relationship. For example, I have no idea when it all went wrong. I've asked myself time and time again and come up with a different conclusion every time.

Then there's my unresolved suspicion that there must have been another woman. Jason insisted afterwards that there wasn't – not to me, because I've never seen him since that fateful day, but it wasn't long before his explanation filtered through to me via mutual friends: he just got cold feet. He couldn't go through with it. He'd realized I wasn't right for him.

Hearing all this made the weeks after the wedding so much more unbearable – because, although Liverpool has a population of around half a million, it can be a bit of a village sometimes. Ironically, it was one of the things I used to like about it. For example, I don't think I've ever walked into Keith's wine bar on Lark Lane without bumping into someone I know. I liked to think of it as comparable to life on the set of *Friends*, except that I bear about as close a resemblance to Jennifer Aniston as I do to a humpback whale.

The only problem with a village is that when there's something you don't want to talk about, it becomes difficult when you know it's the hottest topic around.

I know it's human nature to gossip. But I can't imagine anything attracting more speculation and discussion than my wedding day.

Bizarrely, though, the one person few people wanted to discuss it with was me. The look on their faces when they did end up talking to me – particularly if it was the first time they'd bumped into me since the day – was universally of pity, awkwardness, discomfort – a bit like the women in the Wind-eze adverts look when they're suffering from 'tummy troubles', except, of course, you can't buy something over the counter to stop you getting stuck in conversation with Zoe Moore.

I suppose it was only to be expected, but after a while the atmosphere around me, everywhere I went, became oppressive.

Even my relationships with my friends were affected. Jessica, whom I'd been so close to over the past few years, didn't know how to handle things post-14 April. The problem was that her fiancé Neil was Jason's best friend. When Jason and I were together, this cosy set-up had been great. When we'd split up, it was disastrous.

The once-easy conversations between Jessica and me became strained. As somebody who continued to be in regular contact with Jason, she was clearly burdened by a sense of disloyalty to me. That, and a permanent state of panic about what was and wasn't appropriate for her to reveal to me of what he'd said.

The result was a series of awkward get-togethers

between her and me in which she battled with her conscience about whether she should join in the ritual slagging-off of Jason, led by my mother, or whether, as someone who'd heard his side of the story, she should attempt a defence. Of course she never did, but I could see that that in itself made her feel guilty.

The point is, friendships can't survive that sort of thing – at least mine and Jessica's couldn't. And while I'd never go so far as to say I no longer count her as a friend, our relationship fizzled out somewhere along the way. We'll send each other Christmas cards, I'm sure, but I don't expect much more than that.

As for Mum and Dad, they were another story. I don't know what I would have done without my dad. Typically, he put a brave face on it and offered the sort of quiet support I needed. I'm not talking about anything fancy. I'm talking about cups of wallpaper-paste-strength Horlicks at bedtime. I'm talking about handling estate agents as sympathetic as plankton. And, above all, I'm talking about keeping my mother under control. Which cannot have been easy because she didn't handle things well.

I don't blame her for being upset, of course: 14 April was her big day as well as mine. And she was right about the sugared almonds being hard to shift.

While I didn't – and don't – blame anyone for any of it, after a while I wanted a break from it. A new start. So when I read an article in a magazine one day about women who'd used the skills they'd acquired in the UK to move abroad, it got me thinking.

In many ways, I was about as likely a candidate for

moving overseas as Gordon Ramsay is for the title of Miss World. I'd never done anything like it before. But as I checked my text messages for the fifty-third time that day to see if Jason had tried to contact me – and saw he hadn't – I knew that enough was enough. I had to get away.

But there's one flaw in the clean break I've tried to make with my old life. You can travel across an ocean to escape. But you can't escape your thoughts.

Chapter 34

Barbie and Action Man are having extensive plastic surgery, courtesy of a bumper tub of Play-Doh. Action Man is blessed with an extra leg, while Barbie has had breast enhancements so wonky that if she were real she'd have a strong case for medical negligence. It might not constitute a traditional Saturday-afternoon craft session, but it's certainly keeping the children occupied while I get on with making their late lunch.

As I look up from my tuna melts, however, I know immediately that the peace is about to be broken: Ryan enters the kitchen clearly more stressed than ever.

'Zoe,' he says, 'I have a favour to ask you.'

I try to stop myself looking puzzled. Ryan doesn't normally think of his requests as 'favours'. He normally thinks of them as things I should do automatically. Or he doesn't think of them at all.

'Er, okay. What is it?' I hope I don't seem too suspicious.

'You don't have to look so suspicious.'

'I don't,' I say. 'I mean, I'm not.'

'It might be something nice,' he continues defensively. 'In fact, it *is* something nice.'

Now I'm definitely suspicious. 'Er, right. What?'

'I need you to come out with me tonight,' he announces.

I drop my knife. As it clatters to the floor, I come within an inch of amputating my little toe. Ruby gasps and jumps up, squashing Barbie's boobs into the table. 'Daddy, are you and Zoe going *on a date?*' she squeals.

'No!' we reply in unison. My cheeks are suddenly very hot.

'I have a black-tie dinner to go to,' Ryan explains. 'An extremely important black-tie dinner. One I can't afford to miss. And the *person* who was supposed to be coming with me has let me down.'

'Right,' I reply half-heartedly. There probably isn't a woman I know who wouldn't jump at the opportunity for a date with someone who looks like Ryan. But I'm acutely aware of how inappropriate the semi-lustful feelings he arouses in me are and have started to think that I *must* do more to keep them in check.

I know they're nothing more than the result of my broken heart, but that doesn't make them acceptable, given that he's my boss. To go on a date with him, as Ruby says, is asking for trouble.

'Um, couldn't you try someone else?' I add.

'I have. It's too late in the day.'

'So I'm the last resort, am I?'

He ignores me.

'Who's going to look after the kids?' I ask.

'Uh, I'll phone Barbara King and see if they can stay over,' he says.

'Barbara King?' I ask. He *must* have lost his marbles. I know Trudie wouldn't mind, but Barbara's another matter. She'd have more fondness for a serial killer than she has for Ryan.

'Yeah, why not?' he asks.

'I didn't think you two got on.'

'We don't. But I'm not asking her to spend the night with *me*, I'm asking her to spend it with my kids. She thinks she's the perfect neighbour. Now she can prove it.'

'But I can't go!' I leap in, as he picks up the phone.

'Why not?'

'I – I have absolutely nothing to wear!'

The second I say this I kick myself. To a bloke's ears, this line is like trying to get out of jury duty because you've developed a zit. But not only is it crucially important to me, it also happens to be true.

When I packed for the US, I never imagined I'd go out anywhere particularly swanky, at least nowhere more glamorous than the local bar. And just because I plan to be here for a year, it doesn't mean there was any more room in my suitcase than there would have been for a two-week trip to Majorca. So, the posh dresses stayed behind, while the jeans came with me.

'You'll need to do better than that,' Ryan tells me.

'So what am I supposed to go in?' I'm exasperated now.

'Don't worry,' he says. 'I'll fix it for you.'

I must look worried.

'Relax,' he insists. 'We'll find something great for you to wear.'

Suddenly my spirits rise as it dawns on me what he's suggesting. I'm thinking Richard Gere. I'm thinking Julia Roberts. I'm thinking that seminal moment in *Pretty Woman* where he takes her to Rodeo Drive and spends a fortune on getting her kitted out. I'm thinking, *Yippee!*

'Okay, okay,' I say, rolling my eyes. 'I suppose I'll do it.'

'Good.'

'You owe me one,' I add, trying not to sound as cheerful as I now feel.

As Ryan picks up the phone to negotiate with Barbara King about the children staying the night, I consider whether to go for purple or red. Purple is definitely my colour, but red is so much more versatile – or so *Grazia* magazine always says. What am I thinking? Red, purple, who cares? As long as it's new and it's on Ryan's credit card, it doesn't matter.

'I can't thank you enough,' Ryan is saying to Barbara, through gritted teeth. He's about to put down the phone when he hesitates. 'Oh, and one more thing,' he continues. 'I'm sending Zoe over right now. I need you to loan her a dress.'

Chapter 35

I love coming into the heart of Boston, with its awe-inspiring combination of gorgeous old public buildings, lush parks and huge, glistening skyscrapers. Top of my list of favourite places is Newbury Street, filled with elegant art galleries I keep meaning to visit, smart restaurants I wish someone would take me to, and top-notch boutiques in which I'm forever window-shopping. (I do so hoping that the assistants might have me down for the wealthy daughter of a British diplomat, not just someone who can't afford one of their carrier-bags.)

It's here that I find myself for Ryan's dinner, which is taking place in the swishest hotel in the city, a magnificent 1920s landmark at the end of the street, overlooking the Chanel boutique on one side and Boston Common on the other. I know I should be revelling in the occasion, its glitz and glamour, and as I step into the lobby I try to emulate the confident, sassy stride of the other women.

Only it isn't happening.

Barbara King's strappy stilettos don't help. She's the equivalent of a British size six. I'm a five. A small difference, I'd thought, but as I discovered – when I stumbled down the porch stairs and almost head first into a shrub – an absolutely crucial one.

We are greeted at the door by a pouting blonde, with a waist the size of my upper arm, and directed to the grand ballroom.

'This way,' says Ryan, opening a door for me. 'Oh, and – you look ... um ... nice, by the way.'

He catches my eye as he says this and my stomach flutters wildly. I almost kick myself: how ridiculously naïve and primeval. Aside from my determination to end my infatuation, Ryan's words are evidently the manifestation of some management technique he picked up on an expensive course his company sent him on – words designed to keep up my spirits in the face of adversity. Because the fact is I *don't* look nice: I look as if I've been given a makeover by a lunatic with severe colour blindness.

As well as the ill-fitting shoes, I have to contend with wearing the skimpiest dress I've ever been near in my life, an item that would be too small to cover a bulimic guinea-pig, never mind me and my unshakeable sixteen and a half pounds.

It became clear while I was getting ready that this dress was too revealing for me to wear in its original state so I customized it with the help of several safety-pins, which are now holding bits of fabric in place so that I can retain at least a degree of modesty.

It's just about working. I've got a pin under each armpit, two at either side of the waist and one at the back. But if any of them decides to pop open during the evening, I'll find myself in an impromptu acupuncture session.

'I hate this dress,' I mutter, through a fixed smile, as I stumble over another step.

'You look great,' Ryan replies. 'Hey – I'm serious.'

I feel an alarmingly pleasurable sensation in my groin. Oh, get a grip, Zoe!

I wanted to try on at least six other outfits in Barbara King's wardrobe, but she slapped my wrist as if I was a naughty six-year-old reaching for sweeties. The floor-length black Valentino was out of the question. The purple Roberto Cavalli too. I was flashed a don't-even-go-there look over the red YSL *and* the cream D&G. Not that I'd have fitted into any of them. But they would have been better than this hideous yellow number, in which I feel like the star turn at a lap-dance bar.

Furthermore, you know how all the magazines say that gorgeous underwear does wonders for your confidence? Well, the only knickers I had that weren't in the wash was a pair of novelty Wonder Woman briefs I got in a Secret Santa at the nursery four Christmases ago.

Need I say more?

What makes this immeasurably worse is that Ryan has scrubbed up so well this evening that every woman in the room will be drooling over him, including – and, God, I hate admitting this – me.

He's sexier than any 007 in his tux. His shoulders seem even broader, his stomach even tighter. His clear eyes and burnished skin stand out all the more against the crispness of his shirt. The slight roughness of his hands is in beautiful contrast with the formality of his attire. He smells sensational and I can't work out why. It's the same aftershave he usually wears, but with undercurrents of something else that I spent an insane proportion of our journey here attempting to identify.

In short, he has never been more desirable, more dripping with sex appeal. He is the embodiment of masculine perfection.

For which I feel like kicking him in the shin.

As we walk into the grand ballroom, I grab a glass of champagne from the first passing tray and take a deliberate sip.

'Come on,' instructs Ryan. 'Let's go and talk to some people. Don't worry – I'll introduce you.'

I throw back the rest of my champagne and, heart pounding like a demon percussion instrument, scuttle behind Ryan, telling myself not to panic. To stay calm. To remember that I can be as refined, elegant and cosmopolitan as anyone else in this place. Even if my dress does resemble a duster.

'Ryan, how are you?' booms a voice. We turn round, and a tall, handsome bloke with silver hair and a Paul Newman smile shakes Ryan's hand.

'Michael, good to see you,' Ryan responds. 'Zoe, this is Michael Ronson.'

I'm aware that we've somehow ended up among a group of people the size of a wedding reception – and that I'm blushing for no fathomable reason.

'And these are Catherine Manford, Jack Bishop, Victor Hislop, James Sorbie, John Kaplovski and Terri Costa,' Ryan continues.

As they nod and smile politely, I'm hit by a powerful,

rogue thought, which convinces me immediately that I can read every one of their minds – and there's only one thing going through them: what the *hell* is that girl wearing?

Stop it, Zoe! Just remember, you can be as sophisticated as the next person.

'Hiya!' I shrill, as I grin inanely and – to top off the effect – begin waving. '*Lovely* to meet you all! It really, really is! What a great place! Ha . . . wow!'

'Um, Zoe's from England,' offers Ryan.

They nod and say, 'Oh,' and 'How nice,' and 'Great.' There is an awkward pause.

As a waiter offers me another glass of champagne, I take it and attempt to break the silence. 'We'll all be pissed at this rate!' I hoot. Everyone stares at me silently. I get the impression they're not bowled over by my outstanding social grace.

'Um, so, how're things, Ryan?' asks Michael Ronson, as the others go back to their own conversations.

'Hey, not bad, under the circumstances. Like everyone else, we've had some difficult announcements to make recently, the economy being as it is. It's a tough old world out there right now.'

'You got it,' agrees Michael. 'The market sure is up and down.'

'The *Boston Herald* seems to be permanently on our case too, but that's a different story,' Ryan continues. 'How 'bout you guys?'

'Much the same.' Michael nods. 'Hey, did you hear about Jerry Caplin over at Everright's?'

'Did I ever.' Ryan rolls his eyes. 'That guy's crazy.'

176

I stand in silence, grinning, my eyes following one and then the other. Occasionally, I nod knowingly, as if I'm best buddies with Geoff over in the New York office and, like them, am up to my eyes in the challenges involved in the world of corporate communications.

'Tsk, tell me about it,' I find myself muttering at one point. But, you see, I've got to try. I'm feeling about as useful to this conversation as a suckling pig at a vegetarian dinner party.

'Zoe, this must be so dull for you,' says Michael finally.

'Oh, no!' I gush, as if I'd happily have his babies because he's bothered to talk to me. 'I don't mind at all!'

'What do you do for a living?' he asks.

'I'm Ryan's nanny. Or rather, Ryan's kids' nanny.'

Michael nods.

'This is the first time he's let me out in public,' I add.

Michael's eyes glaze over so rapidly that he looks as if he's being cryogenically frozen. 'Sure,' he mutters. 'Good. Well, Ryan, great talking to you. Catch up soon, buddy.'

'Sure thing,' Ryan replies.

'Don't worry,' he tells me, when Michael has gone – I wonder whether he's reassuring me or himself. 'This part of the evening is all about business. People will loosen up soon.'

'Oh, I'm sure.' I smile unconvincingly. 'Really, it's not a problem.'

But after three-quarters of an hour of networking all I can think of is networking my way out of the door and back to the house.

Chapter 36

The organizers have put us right at the front of the room on an elaborately decorated table boasting a massive centrepiece of black feathers, purple roses and crystals. It's all so dazzling and I know I should be enjoying myself, but the whole experience is proving as pleasant as colonic irrigation during an A-level maths exam.

As we arrive at our table, Ryan introduces me to the woman on his left. 'Zoe, this is Matilda Levin, our vice-president of marketing,' he says. 'Matilda, meet Zoe.'

Matilda is a willowy brunette, so immaculately turned-out she must class moisturizing as one of her hobbies. 'Zoe,' she smiles, holding out a hand, 'very pleased to meet you. You must be the lawyer Ryan's been dating.'

'Ooh, er, no,' I mumble.

'Oh,' she says, raising an eyebrow. 'The accountant?'

'No.'

'The interior designer?'

'No. No – no!' I splutter. 'Sorry. I'm the nanny.'

'Oh. Sorry. I didn't know you were dating a nanny.' She smiles at Ryan.

'I'm not,' he replies.

'I'm just *the* nanny,' I clarify. 'I mean, Ryan's kids' nanny.'

'Oh,' she says, still smiling. 'Fascinating. Where are you from?'

'England, for my sins.' I smile back.

'I love England! We've just got to have a chat!'

I feel overwhelmed with relief that I've found someone to talk to, until Matilda grabs Ryan's arm. 'But first, Ryan, I need to bounce something off you about the media packs we've put together. I've been trying to catch you all week . . .'

The pair are quickly engrossed in another bewildering conversation as I stand there, twiddling my bag. My fingernails now resemble the ends of a doggie chew.

'Hello, how are you?' says a voice behind me. 'I'm Gerald Raven.'

I turn and find a big, gentle-looking man behind me, with short white hair and a Santa Claus belly. 'I'm Zoe Moore,' I reply. 'I'm Ryan's children's nanny.' I've decided that this will be my new tactic: to announce who I am immediately and give them the opportunity to bugger off to someone more important.

Gerald Raven doesn't move. 'Really?' he says. 'They're two beautiful kids.'

'Oh, you know them?'

'Sure. It feels like only yesterday that Ruby was born. Such a great kid – especially after what she's been through.'

'She is,' I agree, amazed – and relieved – to have found

someone prepared to talk about a subject I actually know something about.

'Now, young lady,' he says, raising an eyebrow, 'you don't sound like you come from these parts.'

'No,' I smile, 'you're right. You can tell I'm from California, can you?'

He laughs. 'Let me guess. England? The north?'

'Yep.'

'No, wait,' he continues. 'I can do better than that. Is it Manchester? No, no, it's Liverpool, isn't it?'

My eyes widen. 'That's impressive. You're the first American I've met who could even tell my accent was northern. At least three people tonight thought I was Irish and one Australian. But to get the city as well, wow! Ten out of ten.'

'Well, I should probably let you into a secret – I'd feel like a cheat otherwise.'

'Oh?'

'My mom was a Scouser.'

'You're kidding!'

Within five minutes, I've discovered that Gerald Raven's mum was a seamstress from Speke (three miles from where I grew up) and met his dad – a GI – during the Second World War at nearby Burtonwood. They moved to America after 1945. And the rest, as they say, is history. Within minutes I feel overwhelmingly close to this man. I've never met him before, but the fact that his mother was born in my city makes me feel as if I've found a soul-mate.

'Hey, big guy,' says Ryan, appearing out of nowhere

and hugging Gerald. 'I obviously don't have to do any introductions.'

'Oh, you needn't worry about us,' I tell him. 'So, you two work together, then?'

'Yes, Zoe,' Ryan says. 'Gerald is the president of BVH Systems. Which means he's probably the most important guy in this room.'

Chapter 37

Well, sitting next to Gerald was probably the best bit of luck I've had all week. If I'd hired my own personal PR man for the evening, he couldn't have bigged me up more than Gerald has. He's spent the evening regaling everyone with such affectionate stories of Ye Olde Liverpool – 'Zoe's hometown and that of my dear old mom, too' – that everyone is now looking at me as if I'm some sort of fascinating artefact. Which beats being a freak in a canary yellow dress.

I have to admit that a couple of glasses of wine have helped me relax a little too. But I'm taking it steady – the last thing I want tonight is to get so drunk I risk making a show of myself.

'So, how do you find working for Ryan?' whispers Gerald, as we get to dessert and Ryan is engaged in conversation with Matilda to his left.

'Oh, well, that's an interesting question.' I try to think of an appropriate response. *He's a nightmare but I can't keep my eyes off his bum* doesn't seem quite right. 'Well, the kids are great. I love looking after them. And, as you said earlier, they've been through so much and it's nice to be able to give them a bit of normality.'

'I bet you're great with them,' he says. 'But that wasn't what I asked.'

'Oh?'

'I asked what it was like working for Ryan.'

'Ah.'

'Ah,' he echoes, with the hint of a smile.

'Well, he's fine.' I smile back. 'Really.'

'Good,' he says. 'Because some people find him a little difficult.'

'Um . . .'

'You don't have to say anything,' he continues, 'but let me tell you this. Ryan is a good guy. The best. Deep down, he's the most decent, hard-working, loyal person you could ever hope to meet. And he *loves* his kids. But, recently . . . well, since Amy's death, he hasn't been himself.'

I feel a stab of guilt. 'It must have been terrible for him.'

'They were great together. To be honest with you, I don't think he's ever gotten over her death. He's always been a strong guy, but it seemed to make him go into meltdown. Privately, I mean. Outwardly, he's become a real tough nut to crack.'

'Tell me about it,' I find myself saying.

'But don't let his manner fool you,' Gerald continues. 'He just needs time. And a little support. That's why someone like you is so important.'

'Me?'

'Sure you,' he says. 'How long have you worked for him now?'

'Oh, only a couple of months.'

'Well,' says Gerald, 'that's a record. From what I hear, Ryan's nannies don't usually last longer than a week. So, ten out of ten to you too.'

I smile, but I can't help feeling about as comfortable with this as being told I have a key role to play in the negotiation of the next major international treaty on human rights. I'm here for the kids, not for Ryan. And I'm here for myself. If he needs somebody to get him back on track, I'm the last person qualified to do it.

I'm just wondering whether or not to break this to Gerald when the band launches into song, indicating it's time for people to start letting their hair down.

'I don't suppose you'd care to dance, would you?' he asks.

I break into a sweat. I might be well on the way to being slightly, and happily, pissed, but there's no way I'm getting on the dance floor looking like this. 'Er, I'd love to but I'm going to nip to the loo first. You don't mind, do you?'

'No problem.' He pats my hand. 'I'll catch you later.'

I'm on my way to the ladies' when someone leaps out in front of me. 'Well, hi, little English girl!'

It's one of the men from the group Ryan introduced me to at the start of the evening, a slightly rotund bloke in his early thirties with dark, unruly curls that remind me of my aunty Carol's old Westmorland terrier. Now, let me think, was it Jim Bishop or Victor Kaplovski?

'Er, hi. It's Jim, isn't it?' I say, confident I've plumped for the right name.

'Jack. But I'll forgive you.'

184

To my horror, he slides his arm round my waist with such a degree of familiarity you'd think we were on our fifth date. 'If you'll come and dance with me, that is,' he adds.

'Oh, I don't dance,' I tell him, wriggling out of his grip. 'I've got two left feet. There are penguins who can salsa more impressively than I can.'

'Well, that's okay,' says Jack, attempting to put his arm back round my waist. 'Because I'm quite happy to stay here and get to know you better. So, you single?'

'Er . . . um . . . ah . . .' I'm buying time to think of an intelligent way to avoid the question. 'Are you?'

'Oh, yeah, baby. I ain't ready for commitment. My middle name is Fun. I'll have to assume from your answer that the same goes for you, too?'

'Well, that's a *big* assumption.' I frown.

'I'm a *big* guy,' he replies.

'Hmmm,' I mumble, crossing my arms but trying to keep smiling while I plot my escape.

'No matter anyway,' he continues, 'because I think you and I are made for each other.'

'Well, I'm not sure *I* do,' I splutter.

'Jeez, you English girls can flirt! The dress is *greeeat!*' He's staring down my top with the sort of expression Scooby Doo wears when he's about to devour a six-foot-high sandwich. I cross my arms tighter. 'I just love voluptuous girls. There ain't nothing worse than a girl who don't like her food.'

'Thank you. You really know how to sweep someone off their feet,' I reply, 'but I must get going now. Sorry. I'm off to the loo.'

'The *loo*?' he exclaims, as if I've just come out with the funniest line since John Cleese and the Germans. 'The *loo*! What a blast! I'll wait right here for you.'

I dart towards the toilet. When I get there I decide to delay returning to the table for as long as possible in case I get groped again *en route* by Jack Whatsisname. I'm touching up my makeup at the mirror when Matilda Levin joins me.

'So, what's it like working with the Blue-eyed Boy?' She smiles.

'You're the second person tonight who's asked me that,' I tell her.

She smirks. 'People will be wondering which camp you fall into – the he's-a-complete-bastard-and-has-no-redeeming-features camp or the he's-a-complete-bastard-and-still-manages-to-be-totally-gorgeous camp.'

I try not to look shocked.

'Oh, don't worry, honey.' Matilda laughs. 'Personally, I think you must be a saint to *live* with him.'

'Well, he's not that bad,' I say, unwilling to give the impression that I can't stand up to him. 'I mean, he has his moments but . . . his kids are great. It's only them I really deal with.'

'Uh-huh,' she says. 'Well, just so's you know, I think Ryan likes you. I can tell from the way he was talking about you earlier.'

'He was talking about me?' I ask, alarmed.

'Sure. But he doesn't give much away. Anyway, just take a piece of advice from me.'

'Oh?'

'If you do get it together, keep your head screwed on.

Ryan is a real ladies' man, these days, but as far as he's concerned, women are objects of pleasure to be used and discarded. It's great while it lasts – but Ryan Miller is trouble with a capital T. Believe me.'

'Oh, really, there's nothing going on between us – and nothing ever *will* be going on between Ryan and me and – well, honestly, the very idea is just ridicu—'

'Stop!' Matilda grins. 'The lady protests too much! All I'm saying is, watch yourself. And I'm only saying it because I've been there. Ryan and I were an item once.'

'Right,' I mutter. But I can't stop myself asking the next question: 'So, which camp do you fall into?'

'Honey,' she shrugs, 'I change my mind every day.'

Chapter 38

Jack the Westmorland terrier lookalike is still hovering when I leave the ladies'. The second he sees me he pounces, as if I'm a walking tin of Pedigree Chum. 'So, how about that dance? Come on, I can tell you can't resist me.' He's trying to be clever in a cute, tongue-in-cheek kind of way.

It isn't working. 'Whatever gave you that idea?'

'Call it animal magnetism.' He winks, prompting another visual image of Auntie Carol's dog. 'Come on, that's what you were thinking too, wasn't it?'

'Sort of,' I mutter. 'Anyway, must run.'

'Not so fast.' He grabs my elbow. I wriggle my arm in an attempt to shake him off, and at that moment Ryan appears.

'What's going on?' he asks. He doesn't seem impressed. 'You okay, Zoe?'

'I'm fine. Really,' I insist, sounding as tough and post-feminist as I possibly can.

'She's fine,' echoes Jack.

'Good,' says Ryan. 'Although I'll bet she'd be even

more fine if you stayed away from her for the rest of the evening.'

'What?' exclaims Jack. 'We were just talking, for Chrissake, Miller. What the fuck is wrong with that?'

There is barely a flicker on Ryan's face as he steps forward. 'When a lady makes her wishes clear,' he whispers menacingly, 'my advice to you is that you respect them.'

'What the—'

'Just stay away. That's all.'

As Ryan ushers me back to our table, I glare at him. 'Thank you for that. But, just for the record, I'm *not* some sort of wimp.'

'I didn't think you were.'

'You could have fooled me.'

'Oh, so you were happy having Jack Bishop salivating into your breasts, were you?'

My cheeks redden so rapidly I must look as if someone's lit a bonfire inside my head. I pretend it isn't happening. 'Well, no, but that isn't the point. In fact—'

'So what's wrong with me rescuing you?' he interrupts.

'I didn't *need* rescuing,' I point out.

'*You* could have fooled *me*.'

I sit down sulkily and try to look as if I'm not responding with a clever remark because I'm taking the moral high ground rather than because I can't think of one.

'Look, I'm sorry, okay?' He sighs. 'I didn't mean to imply you couldn't handle yourself. But he's an asshole. Now . . . drink?'

He fills my glass with wine and I try to stop myself smiling.

'What's so funny?' he asks.

'You're not an easy person to live with, Ryan,' I tell him. 'And you've done plenty of insensitive, annoying, irritating things since I got here. Believe me. That wasn't the worst of them.'

'So what are you saying?' he asks, defensively.

'I'm just saying,' I continue, 'that was the first time I've ever heard you say sorry.'

'And?'

'I like it.' I smirk.

He puts down the wine bottle and is about to protest again when I flash him a glance.

'Okay. I'll shut up, shall I?' he says.

Chapter 39

'So, is this evening proving to be as bad as you thought?' asks Ryan. He's smiling but I get the impression that for once he cares how I respond.

'I never said it was going to be bad,' I reply.

'You didn't need to,' he says. 'Your reaction this afternoon was enough to give a guy a complex.'

'I don't think I'm in any danger of that,' I can't resist saying.

My libido has gone into overdrive as I sit with Ryan, alone at our table, watching people on the dance-floor. The lights have dimmed and the table is a scene of post-dinner dishevelment, the once pristine white tablecloth now covered with red-wine stains and bits of Brie that have fallen off the cheeseboard.

We're sitting inches apart and Ryan has discarded his dinner jacket. His bow-tie is still on but he has loosened it, and he's playing with the label on an empty Chablis bottle. As the lights from the dance-floor skip across his face they reveal features I've never noticed before. The shadow of a scar next to his left eye. A faint mole just above his jaw.

With one too many glasses of wine sloshing around in my bloodstream, my hormones seem to burst into action every time his arm so much as brushes against mine.

'I'd be lying if I said I didn't feel like a fish out of water, though,' I continue. 'I mean, look at me. I'm not exactly experienced when it comes to events like this.'

'For the record, I don't think anyone would have guessed,' he reassures me. 'And, besides, what does it matter?'

'It doesn't, I suppose. I still feel an idiot sometimes, though.'

He shakes his head dismissively. 'Listen. I remember one of the first dinners I attended when I started out in this business. I was wearing the most ridiculous tux you can imagine – I'd borrowed it from a friend's dad. It was at least two sizes too small and the trouser legs were halfway up my ankles. I'm convinced Woody Allen would have struggled to fit into it, never mind me.'

I can't help but laugh.

'It could have been worse, though. I *almost* followed my buddy's advice and wore a carnation in my button-hole.'

'A carnation?' I giggle.

He nods. 'People would have thought I'd got lost from a wedding reception.'

'So your buddy wasn't an expert, then.'

'He was a mechanic,' he says, 'so why I thought I should listen to him I don't know. Still, we've all got to learn somehow. I didn't grow up in a world of fancy parties and five-star hotels – it was new to me at the time.'

'Oh,' I say, surprised. 'What sort of world did you grow up in?'

I don't know why but I'd had Ryan down as someone who'd had a firmly middle-class upbringing. I'd assumed he was a rich kid who'd grown up in exactly the sort of neighbourhood he lives in now. Apparently not.

'Well, I was born and raised in the country,' he tells me. 'My dad – when he was still around – was a farm worker and my mom worked in a grocery store.'

'When he was still around?' I ask.

'They divorced when I was ten. But that was fine because I never got on with my dad – nobody did. He was a bully. And Mom was better off without him.'

'You get on well with her, then?'

'Got,' he corrects me. 'She's no longer with us. But, yeah, in answer to your question, she was kind, loving, desperately hard-working. A great mom in every way.'

'How long ago did she pass away?' I ask tentatively.

He studies the Chablis label. 'She died when I was twenty-one, of lung cancer.'

'I'm sorry,' I say, rather pathetically.

He shrugs. 'I just wished she could have seen me graduate from college.'

It's no wonder Ryan's eyes always seem so sad. He's had more heartbreak in his life than anyone should have to deal with.

He turns and catches me looking at him. I blush and reach for a bottle of mineral water. As I unscrew the top to pour it into my glass, I realize it's empty. 'So . . . how does the son of a farm worker end up going to college?'

I say. 'From what I hear it's ridiculously expensive over here.'

'It is, compared with the UK,' he concedes. 'Am I right in saying you don't have to pay over there?'

'You do, these days,' I tell him, 'but it's nothing like as expensive as it is here.'

'Right. Well, I was one of the lucky ones and won a scholarship. I worked hard, got good grades and, hey, the formula's simple. Here I am.'

'I bet your mum would have been really proud of you,' I tell him.

'I hope so.'

'Any brothers or sisters?'

'No, I'm an only child.'

'Me too,' I say.

'Really?' he says, surprised. 'I don't know why but I imagined you having brothers and sisters all over the place.'

'All over the place?' I grin.

'Oh, tons of 'em!' he replies, smiling. Which starts my stomach fluttering, just as it always does when he smiles. I don't know why this is – perhaps because his whole face comes to life; perhaps because it happens so rarely.

'Maybe it's because of what you do for a living,' he continues. 'I pictured you as the kind who'd always looked after other kids when you were growing up.'

'Nope. I hate to shatter your illusions,' I tell him. 'Besides, it might have put me off.'

'True,' he concedes. 'So, if you're an only child, that means – like me – you're pampered, socially dominant and spoiled.'

'Intelligent and conscientious is what I read.'

'Really?' He laughs. 'I must remember that one.'

As he pours me another glass of wine, it strikes me how much I'm enjoying talking to him. He's so much more than a tight bod and a pair of sparkly eyes when he wants to be. He's likeable. He's funny. Good looks aside, he's one of the most charismatic men I've ever met. I wonder why he can't be like this all the time, and stop myself. It's probably a good thing he isn't. God knows how I'd handle myself if he was.

Then something else occurs to me. I haven't thought about Jason all night.

Chapter 40

About an hour after my chat with Ryan, it occurs to me that, somewhere along the way, the evening has taken a significant turn for the better. My outfit, for a start, has begun to grow on me. In fact, what on earth was I worried about? I look positively – almost certainly – *gorgeous*.

So what if I'm showing a bit more flesh than everyone else? They're all gorgeous in their own way. I'm gorgeous in mine. Gorgeous, gorgeous, gorgeous! I can't put my finger on why I'm feeling so positive, but I'm not complaining about it.

'Now, where's that bottle of wine gone?' I wonder.

'Would you like another top-up, young lady?' asks Gerald.

'Oops!' I exclaim. 'Did I say that out loud?'

'You did.' He smiles. 'You're sure you wouldn't prefer some water?'

'Ooooh, *nooooo*!' I reply, throwing my head back to emphasize the point. The room goes so wobbly that I almost fall off my chair. 'How boring would that be?'

Gerald smiles again. 'Okay,' he replies, topping up

my glass, but only halfway. 'You never did give me that dance you promised. Why don't we go and do that now?'

It suddenly occurs to me that Gerald might think I'm a bit drunk. I mean, I can't deny I've been enjoying the wine, but I've only had three glasses – oh, no, hang on, four . . . or was it five? No, five was what I'd had just after I'd come back from the loo. God, that means I must have had . . .

The point is, I've always prided myself on being able to hold my drink – even if everyone I try to focus on is swaying as if they're on an Irish Sea ferry.

'All right, Gerald,' I reply, leaping up and holding out my hand. 'You're on.'

'You sure you're ready for me?' Gerald grins.

'Let's knock 'em dead!' I reply, feeling so confident that if Gerald had asked me to dance in front of a capacity crowd at Shea Stadium I'd reply: 'Pass me my leotard.'

I sashay into the centre of the room, my shoulders shimmying like Jennifer Grey's in *Dirty Dancing*, even if I have to use some serious imagination to make Gerald morph into Patrick Swayze. Nevertheless, with the band in full swing, before I have a chance to think about it, he's whisking me round in a waltz so jaunty it causes two of my hair slides to fall out.

I don't know whether it's our brilliant dancing, or simply that he's the boss of one of the biggest companies in Boston, but before long the eyes of everyone in the place are on us as we spin round the room.

I spot Ryan standing at the side with some of his

colleagues and wave as I swirl past, hoping he's as impressed as I feel sure everyone else is. Admittedly, Gerald is doing the leading, but nevertheless, I'm good. Bloody good. We must be because as I glance up I realize we couldn't be receiving more attention if Gerald was perfecting an advanced break-dancing routine.

'You're a great dancer.' Gerald grins.

'Oh! Do you think so?' I reply modestly, bouncing around like a spring lamb who has just discovered what her feet are for. Feeling on top of the world, I prepare to do a snappy little manoeuvre Ginger Rogers would have been proud of, which involves pinging away from my partner, then straight back into his arms.

However, something comes to my attention. Something that is immediately alarming. No, strike that. Potentially catastrophic.

One of the safety-pins keeping the side of my dress together has latched on to the lining of Gerald's dinner jacket. I can't work out how it's happened. All I know is that I'm stuck.

Ohmigod, ohmigod, ohmigod.

The first vision to flash into my head is that of a gaping hole in Barbara King's outfit if I attempt to part from Gerald. But I'm being optimistic: the dress is so flimsy that, with one false move, the whole thing will be whipped off faster than Barbara Windsor's bra in *Carry On Camping*.

Panicking, I stumble across the dance-floor, glued to Gerald's torso, as the music gets faster and faster. I look down at the safety-pin, my pulse approaching the point of cardiac failure, beads of sweat pricking my forehead.

'Oooh, ah, Gerald . . .' I pant, pressing my torso to his.

'How's about something a bit more fancy, eh?' He winks, oblivious to my plight as he swings me round to the rapturous applause of our growing audience.

'Whoooa!' I cry, as I realize our bodies have parted slightly, his jacket and my dress pulling away from their respective owners in a, frankly, terrifying fashion.

I grab Gerald's back and pull myself into him, attempting simultaneously to concentrate on my feet, which have been treading on his toes so much in the last two minutes I'll be surprised if he doesn't end up in plaster.

'Gerald, whoooooa – I—' I begin, but now he has us doing the quickstep, with the whole room gathered round the dance-floor, clapping and cheering so loudly he can barely hear me.

He swings me round as I gasp, the room spinning, the safety-pin digging into my skin, echoes of the applause whirling through my head.

'Now, honey,' Gerald whispers gleefully, 'we're coming to the end here. I'll bring you in tight, then spin you away from me.'

Suddenly I find it difficult to breathe. Because I know exactly what he's talking about. I also know exactly what pirouetting away from Gerald at the speed he has in mind may result in. And I'm afraid my new-found confidence doesn't stretch to doing the full monty in front of five hundred of Ryan's most important business contacts.

'Gerald, I – *nooo!*' I pant, blood pumping, face on fire.

'Don't worry, honey, the crowd'll go wild for it,' he assures me.

'No, I mean—'

As he pulls me in, I reach, fumbling, into his jacket like an extremely poor pickpocket on her first practice run.

'*Here we go, honey!*' he cries.

As Gerald propels me away from him I realize that the safety-pin is still stuck. I tug as he propels. He propels as I tug. And finally, to the whoops of the onlooking crowd, I feel my dress rip, just a little, enough to release me from Gerald's jacket.

Which should be good. Except I'm tugging so hard that when it happens, instead of twirling gracefully away from him, I'm catapulted backwards with the force of an Apollo space-shuttle launch.

As I slide on my backside across the dance-floor, I seem to go on for ever – past the feet of several guests . . . past the waiters . . . past Ryan . . . past his colleagues.

When I finally come to a stop, in a crumpled heap with my legs akimbo, at the feet of Jack the Westmorland terrier, I wonder for a split second whether I've got away with it. Maybe, just maybe, I looked like Jayne Torvill, when Christopher Dean pushed her elegantly across the ice during their Olympic medal-winning routine to Ravel's 'Bolero'. I look up into Jack the Westmorland terrier's eyes.

'Nice pants.' He sniggers, as Wonder Woman grins up

at me. Fumbling, I pull my dress down to cover myself and scan the room. The band has stopped playing. The crowd is stunned into silence.

And Ryan looks ready to throttle me.

Chapter 41

When I wake up the next morning and look at my clock, it's gone ten. I sit up and rub my eyes.

The swift change in my head's centre of gravity makes it feel as if it has been smashed repeatedly against a breeze block. But that's not the worst of it. As last night's events wash over me, I feel physically sick. Again.

I'm sure I read somewhere that one of the definitions of an alcoholic is someone who regrets behaviour that has occurred while they've been drinking. The thought is so depressing that I want to curl back into my bed and never get up. I'm already an emotionally befuddled runaway, a biceps-obsessed neurotic and a failed dieter. I can't cope with being an alcoholic as well.

I dress as quickly as I can, but it still seems to take me twenty minutes just to pull my jeans on. As I traipse down the stairs, I'm hit by continual flashbacks of the night before. Of my godawful dress. Of Jack the Westmorland terrier. Of Ryan's smile during what was probably the most successful conversation we've ever had. Then of Wonder Woman's to anyone who cared to look.

I'm dreading seeing Ryan so much that part of me is tempted to run back upstairs, pack my bags and leave immediately. But that would be the wimp's option. And I've disgraced myself so much already, I know I wouldn't be able to live with myself if I did that.

I have little recollection of the car journey home last night, except that Ryan and I were largely silent and it took every bit of willpower I could summon not to throw up every time we went round a corner.

As I push open the kitchen door, Ryan is sitting in front of his laptop while the kids are glued to the television. He doesn't look up.

'Morning,' I attempt, but it comes out as little more than a croak.

'Zoe! Zoe!' Ruby cries, as she leaps up and hugs me. 'How was your date?'

I glance at Ryan, who stiffens visibly.

'It wasn't a date, sweetie,' I manage, through raw vocal cords. 'But it was . . . interesting. Thanks.'

'Can we do some drawing? I'll do a picture of you in your pretty dress.'

'Okay,' I mutter, sliding into one of the kitchen chairs and shielding my eyes from the sunlight streaming through the windows. 'Why don't you go and get your crayons?'

As Ruby scuttles away, I turn to Ryan – head down, silent. 'Thank you for picking up the children from Barbara's,' I say.

'Uh-huh,' he replies.

I look down at my hands and pick off a loose sliver of nail polish.

'I'm sorry, Ryan,' I say quietly, my heart heavy with dread.

He takes a second to respond. 'Don't worry about it,' he says flatly, his eyes not moving from the screen.

'I feel terrible if I've, you know . . . embarrassed you. Or let you down . . . or anything,' I continue. 'I mean, I know I have. And I feel dreadful about it. I really do.'

He doesn't reply at all this time. The silence is excruciating.

I take another deep breath. 'If you want to sack me, I'll understand. It won't take me long to book a flight and—'

'Zoe,' he interrupts, finally looking up from his computer, 'if I'd wanted to sack you I'd have done it long before now. I don't.'

I feel a wave of happiness, closely followed by a wave of nausea. 'Thank you,' I mumble.

'I just won't be taking you to one of those dinners again,' he continues.

I drop my eyes in shame.

'At least, not without sending you out first to buy you some better underwear.'

Chapter 42

My darling Ryan,

You always have been a little on the naughty side – you know that's partly what I like about you. But now you're being just a bit too naughty. My last few letters were intended as an olive branch, an opportunity for you to realize the error of your ways. They were not meant to be ignored. I am therefore deeply disappointed that you appear to have done just that.

Let me remind you of something, Ryan, something that is very relevant to me, if not to you. You and I slept together. Several times. I am not the sort of person to go around sleeping with people – several times – then moving on to someone else. What we had meant something. Something big. And just giving up on it is not an option – not for me anyway.

But aside from the way I feel, let's look at you, Ryan. I brought some light into your life – I know I did – in a way that you hadn't experienced since before Amy's death. I am your salvation, Ryan. You only have to wake up and realize it. Give me a chance. You and I could

*have a real future together. Deep down, you know it
makes sense.*

*Finally, most importantly, Ryan, don't ignore me. Not
again.*

    Yours for ever,
    Juliet
    XXX

This time, I didn't open the letter. It was among Ryan's
washing, stuffed into the pocket of his Levi's. Which is
not particularly clever on his part because anyone could
have found it. Well, anyone rifling through his trousers,
that is. But, hey, it's not like I *want* to rifle through his
trousers.

It's now a week since the most humiliating incident
of my adult life and things still aren't back to normal –
whatever that is. If Denise Robertson of *This Morning*
was advising on the situation I just know she'd say that
Ryan and I need to work hard at putting this unfortunate incident behind us. Which *I* am trying to do. But
it isn't easy, given that Ryan has gone into one of his
smouldering moods.

Then there's the laundry. Even though Ryan finds
plenty of time to run, work and womanize, he still can't
fit washing his socks into his schedule. After the dinner
last week, though, I don't feel as though I'm in a position
to complain.

'How's life in the Miller household?' asks Trudie.
We're on our fortnightly trip to what has become our
favourite bar in Hope Falls, waiting for the others to
join us.

'It would be more fun working for Vlad the Impaler,' I tell her.

Tonight, Trudie is wearing a pair of *Dukes of Hazzard* shorts and a stylish turquoise top, both of which are small enough to be part of Mothercare's spring collection for four-year-olds.

'He's not up to his old tricks, is he?' she asks, fiddling with her Wonderbra to plump up her boobs. 'Go on, spill the beans.'

'Oh, it's nothing in particular.' I sigh. 'I just managed to make his permanently bad mood even worse.'

'I'm sure he doesn't mean it, love,' she says, in what I assume is an attempt to reassure me.

'I know,' I concede. 'But, selfish as this may sound, part of me doesn't particularly care whether he *means* it or not. The point is that he's a nightmare to live with.'

'Maybe he's just trying to hide the fact that he likes you.'

I laugh incredulously. 'Please explain the twisted logic behind that statement.'

'I never claimed to be logical, love,' she grins, 'but that woman at the dinner said he liked you, didn't she? Well, I agree with her – I get that feeling, too, every time I see him with you.'

'You're obviously both barking mad,' I insist.

Nevertheless, part of me feels glad to hear this. At its most basic level, this is because I don't want Ryan to replace me with a more effective, sophisticated nanny and send me back to the UK.

But I know it's more than that. There remains a stupidly primitive part of me that can't help fancying him, no matter how badly behaved he is. And while I know this is my warped way of trying to get over Jason, I don't want to fancy someone who can't stand me.

Okay, so the little fantasies I occasionally have about Ryan will never become reality. But I'd like to think that if they did he wouldn't immediately regret it. And, yes, I'd like Ryan to think of *me* as attractive. There are times when he looks at me, in a way that sets my heart racing. I have no idea what the true meaning of those looks is, but it would be nice to think that a fraction of the sexual frisson I feel every time he's in the room is reciprocated.

'Ryan will have said some positive things about me to Matilda Levin so he could save face,' I tell Trudie.

'How do you mean?'

'I wasn't his first choice of date for that night,' I explain. 'I was probably the zillionth. But there's no way he'll have wanted his colleagues to think he'd been lumbered with some sad act wearing a dress not fit to clean the windows with. So he obviously talked me up a bit.'

'You're paranoid. That dress was great. I didn't think it was too revealing at all.'

'Trudie, I could have gone to that do in a see-through basque and hung on to more of my modesty.'

'Fair enough. But I was talking about *before* you flashed your knickers. I hope you'd had your bikini line done.' She reaches over her shoulder and scratches her back so violently you'd think she had fleas.

'What's up with your skin?' I ask.

'Oh, it's these things.' She pulls off her anti-smoking

patch and flicks it into an ashtray. 'They're so annoying. And not just because I'm still dying for a fag every time I come out for a drink. It's been months now since I gave up and beer still doesn't taste right without a Benson & Hedges.'

'You'll get used to it,' I tell her.

'Anyway, stop changing the subject,' she says. 'I can't believe Ryan's that bad.'

'He has his moments, believe me,' I insist.

'Well, if he's that bad, why are you still here?'

Suddenly I'm lost for words. The answer is so straightforward, yet so complicated. I'm here because I was jilted. I'm here because I'm trying to get over a broken heart. I'm here because being back in the UK represents nothing but grief.

I haven't told Trudie about my wedding day, even though we've grown so close. From the outset I was determined not to let anyone out here know about it, not because I wanted to be mysterious, but because I needed a break from talking about it. And I know I could never reveal to anyone that I'd recently been jilted and expect them not to ask questions.

Yet as I sit next to Trudie tonight, I feel differently about it. I don't know why but I do. 'Can I tell you something, Trudie?'

'Course, love. What?'

'I've not talked about this since I left home . . .'

She frowns. 'You can talk to me, you know you can.'

I smile. For the first time in months, I know I *have* got someone to talk to – someone to *really* talk to. Someone who'll understand. And there aren't many people like that. I take a deep breath. 'Well, something happened that—'

I've barely started when a voice from the other side of the bar stops me in my tracks: *'Where's my girl?'*

It's Ritchie. And as Trudie leaps to her feet, her face is so lit up with happiness she could have had her own float at the Blackpool illuminations.

'Hiya, gorgeous!' she cries, throwing herself into his arms so he can swing her round, not caring how precariously close her wedges come to knocking over everyone's stools. Then they kiss – so passionately I barely know where to look – before Ritchie pulls away from her.

'Hey, kid,' he says to me. 'How's it going?'

'Good.' I smile. 'Fine.'

'Sorry, love,' says Trudie, straightening her hair, which now looks like she's spent several hours rolling round a haystack. 'What were you saying?'

'Oh, nothing. Really. Ritchie, let me get you a beer.'

Chapter 43

Ritchie can't get his head round Felicity. It might be because while most men focus on her looks – as opposed to her endearing but undeniable eccentricity – he is so loved-up with Trudie that they don't have any effect on him. The result is that every so often you catch him staring at her as if she's got more screws loose than a reject wardrobe.

'You see, Ritchie,' Felicity declares, with her usual joviality, 'I'm not saying that the American accent necessarily equals incorrect pronunciation. Lots of Americans speak perfectly good English. Such as . . . hmm . . . Well, the point is, it's not about one's *accent*. It's so much more than that.'

'Uh-huh,' smiles Ritchie, tolerantly. 'You guys wanna get another beer?'

'Why not?' says Amber, who is wearing a big Paisley skirt and so much ethnic jewellery she looks like Mr T at Woodstock. 'I'll have a Budweiser.'

'Are Scientologists allowed to drink?' asks Trudie.

'Um, I think so,' mutters Amber, glaring at the bottle she's just seen off. 'Although, now you mention it, I'm not sure. Oh, never mind, it wasn't going very well anyway.'

'Why not?' I ask. 'Don't tell me, Tom Cruise hasn't made an appearance at church yet.'

'That'd piss me off too,' adds Trudie.

'I wasn't just jumping on some celebrity bandwagon, you two,' says Amber, innocently. 'I was searching for spiritual fulfilment.'

'We're only teasing you, love,' says Trudie, putting her arm round her affectionately. 'Anyway, it's funny you should mention spiritual fulfilment because I know someone who specializes in that very thing – and he's just walked through the door.'

Before Amber has a chance to object, Felicity is waving as if she's trying to flag down a taxi on New Year's Eve. 'Oh, Vicar! Vicar, *do* come and join us!'

'Hey, guys.' The Reverend Paul smiles as he approaches us. 'How are you all?'

'We're great,' says Trudie, 'although we didn't expect to see you here. Aren't you meant to spend Saturday nights at home praying?'

He laughs. 'I'm here meeting an old friend from out of town so I think God might forgive me. Just this once.'

'Let me get you a drink, Reverend,' says Ritchie, taking his arm away from Trudie's waist to dig out some cash.

'Oh, thanks,' replies Paul. 'I'll have an orange juice.'

'Nothing stronger?' asks Ritchie.

'Oh, why not? You've twisted my arm.'

Trudie nudges Amber. 'This is looking even more

promising,' she whispers, as Amber's cheeks turn a ferocious red. 'You might be able to get him drunk and seduce him.'

Chapter 44

Ryan was once so secretive about his love life that I'd almost become convinced he was dating a member of the secret service. And, to be honest, that suits me fine. I'm not sure I want to hear the gory details of his relationships.

So, as I stand in the hallway, having been collared while I'm still in my dressing-gown, I can't help feeling uneasy about the conversation we're having.

'The thing is,' he tells me, 'I've been seeing this woman.'

'O-kay,' I say, twirling my dressing-gown belt round my finger.

'She's called Kristie, and she was the one who was meant to be coming to the black-tie dinner instead of you the other week.'

I try not to resent her.

'I won't go into details,' he continues, 'but the reason she stood me up was that she was a little pissed at me because . . . well, because she wanted to meet my kids.'

He pauses.

'Oh, right,' I mutter, still twirling.

'And I didn't want her to.'

'Um, right.'

My dressing-gown belt is now wound so tightly round my finger that it has turned the shade of a raw Cumberland sausage.

'But I've decided maybe I should give it a go,' he continues. 'I mean, it's not that Kristie and I are particularly serious. It's just that it's been three years since . . . Well, maybe I need to introduce the kids to *the idea*.' He pauses.

'Right.' I can't help hoping this is the end of the matter. But Ryan is expecting some sort of feedback. He obviously doesn't realize I'm about as qualified to give romantic advice as a celibate cactus.

'Well, I think you're probably right,' I declare. 'Why are you telling me this?'

'Because I'm going to introduce them today,' he replies.

'Oh . . . oh, well, good,' I say.

I feel my mood lift: if Ryan's taking the kids out for the day I can see if Trudie's available for that shopping trip to Filene's Basement – a spectacular Boston discount store selling designer goodies you can pass off as something you picked up in Selfridges.

'Yes, that really is good news,' I continue. 'It'll be nice for you to spend some quality time together as a family and—'

'You're coming with us,' he interrupts.

'*Me?*' I exclaim. 'I mean, sorry, but why do you need *me?*'

'I'm sure everything will be okay,' he carries on,

ignoring me, 'but I just think there's a remote chance they might find it a little unsettling. I hope they won't, but they might. And if they do I need you there.'

'To do the settling.'

'You got it,' he replies cheerfully, heading up the stairs.

Chapter 45

Kristie is a Cindy Crawford lookalike, with cheekbones like window-ledges and a body so toned she must spend seven hours a day doing *Buns of Steel*. She's stunning. And it's not hard to see why Ryan might find her appealing. The kids, on the other hand, despise her the second they set eyes on her.

'What are your favourite subjects at school?' she asks, sounding so awkward you can almost hear her voice creaking with the strain.

'Samuel's too little to go to school,' Ruby informs her sulkily. 'He's only three.'

'Oh.' Kristie purses her lips.

We're sitting on a blanket at Boston Common, having been for a trip on a swan boat and had an enormous picnic.

Kristie only ate two rocket leaves and a piece of cracker that looked like something you'd feed a rabbit on appetite suppressants. I can't help reflecting on this guiltily as half a cold pizza and several helpings of Doritos sit heavily in my own stomach, whose bulges

I've been trying unsuccessfully to mask by keeping my arms crossed for most of the afternoon.

It strikes me that if Jason and I were to meet now for the first time he'd never be attracted to me. He isn't one of those men who appreciate women's curves. Although he never said anything when I put on a few pounds, it was obvious he preferred me on the skinny side. God knows what he'd think if he could see how bad my cellulite is, these days.

'Well, how about you?' Kristie continues, trying to engage Ruby in something approaching a conversation.

She shrugs and doesn't answer.

'Go on, Ruby,' I coax. 'Tell Kristie how much you love art.'

'Art, huh?' says Kristie, trying again. 'I used to like art at school too. That was a long time ago, though.'

Ruby doesn't say anything.

'I bet you can't guess how long?' asks Kristie.

'Two hundred years?' Ruby shrugs impishly. I flash her a disapproving look, Ryan suppresses a smile and Kristie clearly wants to strangle her.

'No,' she replies, smiling with gritted teeth. 'Not that long ago, as I'm sure you know, really.'

'Kristie brought a Frisbee with her,' announces Ryan, as he stands up and brushes the grass off his jeans. 'How about a game? Come on, Ruby.'

'Frisbee's dumb,' she replies. Fortunately, Samuel isn't quite so contemptuous. He jumps up to join in. 'I play, Daddy, I play!'

'You're not being mean to Kristie, are you?' I ask Ruby, when they're all out of earshot.

'No!' she protests.

'Okay, that's fine,' I say. 'But you should give her a chance.'

'Why?' She pouts.

'Because your daddy has to have *friends*,' I reply, as she climbs over and sits on my knee. 'And you should be nice to them.'

'She's not his *friend*,' she tells me, turning up her nose. 'She's his *girlfriend*. There's a difference.'

'You're right.' I nod. 'Sorry if I underestimated your powers of observation. But, Ruby, it would help your dad to be happy if he had some company like Kristie. And him having a girlfriend isn't that bad, is it?'

'It is if it's *her*.'

'Well,' I say, 'I think she's perfectly nice, really I do. And if your daddy likes her, then—'

'I wouldn't mind him having a girlfriend if it was you.'

My heart skips a beat. 'Ruby, sweetheart, that isn't going to happen. Your daddy and I are just friends.'

'But you're much prettier than she is,' she says.

'Oh, well, I don't know about that . . .' I smile modestly, choosing not to see this comment as a blatant fib designed to bring me round to the idea.

'And Daddy's never grumpy when you're around.'

Yeah, right.

'At least, he's not quite so grumpy now you're around. Really,' Ruby insists, eyes wide.

The others come bounding over and Samuel dives on top of me, determined to find a place on my knee. 'I played Frisbee, Zoe!' He couldn't look more pleased with himself if he'd just passed his driving test.

'I know – I saw you! You're such a big grown-up boy, aren't you?'

'Not a little boy,' he reiterates seriously.

'No, definitely a big boy,' I confirm.

'Very big boy,' he repeats.

'Very, very, very big boy,' I say, kissing him as he collapses into giggles.

When I look up, Kristie's staring at me as if I'm chief policy adviser to the Antichrist.

'Um, wasn't that clever of Kristie to buy you two a Frisbee?' I say, in a flimsy attempt at distracting every-one and getting Kristie on-side. But Ruby doesn't rise to the bait. And, unfortunately, another hour's worth of my encouragement seems to do nothing for Kristie's popularity.

The only let-up is when Samuel is eventually per-suaded by Ryan to go with Kristie to feed the ducks while Ruby stays behind to ride her bike. Ryan and I start to tidy up the leftover picnic, which is such a mess you'd think it'd been consumed by a herd of wildebeest at a teenage house-party.

'What do you think?' Ryan asks. 'Of Kristie, I mean.'

'Oh . . . well, she's fine,' I say, putting some part-regurgitated fairy cake from Samuel's plate into a bag. I can't help feeling a twinge of something approaching jealousy at this line of questioning. 'Nice, I mean.'

Ryan sniffs. 'Anything else?'

'She's very attractive,' I tell him truthfully.

'Yeah,' he says. 'She's okay.'

He abandons the picnic, sits down, picks up a small branch and starts to scrape the bark off it with his Swiss

Army knife. The muscles in his forearms ripple. I try to look unmoved.

'What I meant was, how do you think it's gone – with the kids?' he asks.

I try to think of a way to put this diplomatically. 'I'm sure they'll warm to her. Sooner or later.'

Ryan snorts. 'You Brits really are masters of the put-down, aren't you?'

'What do you mean?'

'"I'm sure they'll warm to her,"' he mimics. 'That's your way of saying she's shit with the kids and they hate her.'

'I didn't say that.' Heat rises to my neck.

'You didn't need to.'

This isn't the worst thing Ryan has said all week or, indeed, since I got here. Maybe it's just one comment too far. Whatever, there's something about it that makes me want to dump the plateful of now soggy brownies on his head and garnish them with a cherry.

'Ryan,' I say, ignoring my heart, which is doing championship-standard flick-flacks. 'What's *with* you?'

'Hmm?'

'I said, what's *with* you?'

I'm hoping I sound tough, but my hands are shaking so much I feel about as tough as Jemima Puddle-duck.

'I've come here today, although I've not had a day off in Christ knows how long,' I splutter, 'and I've played the perfect chaperone, the perfect diplomat. I've tried my best to get Ruby to like your girlfriend. And despite all this, you're *still* having a go at me.'

If Ryan is shocked by this outburst, he doesn't show it.

'Can I remind you that *I* employ *you*, Zoe?' he points out.

'If only you treated me like an employee,' I grumble, 'and not like a slave.'

'I pay you, I give you a roof over your head, and in return you're expected to work for it,' he replies. 'What's wrong with any of that?'

'Nothing,' I mutter, reminding myself that I need this job. 'Really, nothing. I just . . . just . . .'

'Just what?' he says.

My lip starts to wobble uncontrollably. I take a deep breath and pull myself together. 'Ryan, I work my arse off in this job. And I don't mind that. It's just . . . well, I can't help finding it infuriating that you don't – ever – say, "Gee, thanks, Zoe."'

'So you want me to start sending you flowers now or something?'

'No!' I cry in frustration.

'So what *do* you want?' he yells.

'I just want you to stop being such a bloody tosser!' I scream.

As soon as I've said it I'm torn between thinking I've lost my mind and that I'm doing the right thing.

Because while I feel sorry for Ryan – I feel desperately sorry for him – nobody seems prepared to tell him that he can't go around treating people as he does.

He stands up and I know immediately that I've riled him. 'I have no idea what a tosser is,' he replies, 'but if I am one, I don't give a shit.'

'Well, you should.'

'Why?'

'Because you've got two gorgeous kids who love you and they don't deserve a tosser as a father,' I tell him. 'They deserve someone who's a good role model and a—'

'A good role model?' he interrupts.

'Yes, a good role model who—'

'You're saying I'm not a good role model?'

'Stop putting words into my mouth!'

Suddenly, I realize Ryan isn't listening.

Instead, he's looking towards the lake, his face filled with confusion and anxiety. Then Kristie's running towards us. And she's screaming.

'What the fuck . . .' Ryan begins.

'It's the kid!' shrieks Kristie, hysterical. 'He's drowning!'

Chapter 46

As Ryan drags Samuel's limp little body out of the lake, there's so much adrenalin running through my veins I feel sick. 'I don't know CPR,' he mutters frantically.

I swallow. I've never done this before. Not on a real child. The training I got during my studies involved mouth-to-mouth resuscitation on a doll that could trace its parentage to a large jelly mould. Not a real child. Not Samuel.

'I do.' I move Ryan out of the way.

Everything seems to be happening in slow motion as, robotically, I put Samuel into the right position, hoping desperately I'm remembering this correctly. Kristie is still screaming hysterically about how she only turned her back to take a phone call. Ruby is standing behind me, sobbing, her bike abandoned by the picnic blanket. Ryan is the only one not making any noise. He's kneeling beside me, his face so drained of colour he looks supernatural.

'Do you know what you're doing?' His voice is so terror-stricken I barely recognize it.

'I – I think so,' I reply.

But I don't *know*.

All I know is that I'm probably Samuel's best hope.

Please, God, make that good enough.

I put a shaking hand on Samuel's forehead and the other under his chin to lift it. Then I bend down and listen to his breathing. But even with the wailing in the background, I can tell there isn't anything to hear. His chest is still.

Panicking, I look inside his mouth, then close my lips over his, telling myself to keep a grip on the situation, not to lose it, to stay calm.

Except I can't focus and my whole body is shaking and sweating like that of a recovering heroin addict.

I count to five as I begin the mouth-to-mouth, forcing any thoughts, other than those concerned with my task, out of my head. I pull away and check his pulse, praying I'll feel something. But there's still nothing.

Please, God, help me. Please, God, help Samuel.

I'm trying to stay on auto-pilot, trying my best to keep cool. But it's no good: panic is taking over and my shaking has become so bad I can barely steady myself enough to do the mouth-to-mouth.

'Don't let him die, Zoe,' whispers Ryan. 'Please don't let him die.'

My head swirls with Ryan's words, Ruby's crying, Kristie's wailing. And Samuel's grim, agonizing silence.

God Almighty, give me the strength to do this. Please, God. Please.

I take a deep breath and close my eyes.

I can do this, can't I?

I can do this.

ZOE, YOU CAN DO THIS!

I don't know why or how but suddenly the noise around me fades into nowhere.

ZOE, YOU CAN DO THIS!

I lean down and start the mouth-to-mouth again. After five breaths, I pull back and check Samuel's pulse. My fingers are on his windpipe but I still can't feel anything. I try lower down – maybe I haven't got them in the right place.

ZOE, YOU ARE NOT GOING TO LET HIM DIE!

I take another deep breath, then lean down to put my mouth to Samuel's again.

One breath.

Two breaths.

Three breaths—

Suddenly, Samuel's chest rises. I lean back, shocked, stunned, amazed, as his little face splutters back to life.

Water is gushing from his mouth. He's coughing wildly.

Then he's crying. He's crying and crying and crying.

It's the best sound I've ever heard in my life.

Chapter 47

I've never liked hospitals. Since the death of Grandma Bonnie six years ago, they've held few positive connotations for me, no matter how devoted or friendly the staff. I even hated driving Jason to A and E when he broke his arm playing badminton at the end of last year. Admittedly, this was partly because its unfeasibly contorted angle made me wince, but the lengthy wait in a room that resembled a prison cell – with two dodgy blokes exuding suspicious smells – didn't help.

Although Jason was the injured party, he seemed far more cheerful than I was. I teased him afterwards that he saw his breakages – there were three in the left arm – as a badge of honour.

'Well, I wouldn't be much of a sportsman if I never ended up in hospital.' He grinned.

'I don't know whether you're immensely brave or completely daft.' I smirked as I kissed him on the way out. Just thinking about it makes me feel an overwhelming pang of longing for him.

If I was hoping that American hospitals would be any more appealing than British ones, that idea was quashed

227

the moment I walked through the door and was assaulted by a distinctive medicinal whiff. Then there is the fact that we're here because of what happened to Samuel. Frankly, there's nothing positive you can say about that. Except, of course, that he's alive.

Thank God, he's alive.

'He's settled well, but he'll need to stay in at least overnight,' the doctor tells Ryan. 'But the important thing is that he'll be fine. You saved his life.'

Ryan's complexion is marginally less ghostly now, but his expression is numb. 'It wasn't me,' he whispers. 'It was Zoe who saved his life. It was Zoe.'

'Well, Zoe,' replies the doctor, putting his hand on the back of my chair, 'you should be real proud of yourself. The little guy wouldn't be with us if it wasn't for you. You did everything right.'

I force a smile, but I'm feeling so wiped out I'm sure I must look like a zombie.

As the doctor closes the door of Samuel's room behind us, I look down at his little round face as he lies fast asleep on the bed. He's still pale too, but compared with how he looked when Ryan pulled him out of the water, he's a vision of health and vitality.

Ruby is also fast asleep on a couch in the corner of the room, a blanket wrapped tightly round her. I offered to take her home hours ago, but she was determined to stay and I think Ryan's glad of our company.

'Well,' I drag myself up from my chair, 'do you fancy a coffee? I'm sure I saw a machine out there somewhere.'

Ryan shakes his head. I'm about to walk through the door, when his voice interrupts me. 'Zoe.'

I stop.

'Can you sit down again for a minute?' he asks.

I walk back to my chair quietly so I don't wake Ruby or Samuel. 'What is it?' I ask.

His cobalt-blue eyes are glazed with unspilled tears. 'I'm sorry,' he says slowly, as he wipes them. 'I'm so sorry.'

'Forget it,' I whisper. 'It was just a row. And I said things that were—'

'No,' he replies. 'I don't just mean about the row. I mean about everything. I mean about . . . *how I am.*'

'Oh,' is all I can manage.

'I know what I'm like to live with. And yet you put up with it. *With the way I am.* And I guess what I'm saying is . . . you shouldn't have to put up with it.'

Now I bow my head, fiddling with a cord at the side of Samuel's bed. This conversation *should* feel awkward but somehow it doesn't. 'I'm not going to tell you I've found my whole time here easy,' I whisper.

'I know,' Ryan admits, 'and I . . . I don't feel good about it. Believe me.'

I look up into his eyes. He's as handsome as ever, but so pale. My heart starts to beat faster and I curse myself at the inappropriateness.

'Zoe,' he continues, 'you should know that you're probably the first person I've met since Amy died that I actually, really . . . *liked.*'

Suddenly my chest feels tight and I realize I've been holding my breath for so long my cheeks must be about to turn blue.

'You're kind, Zoe,' he continues, as I listen in silent

229

astonishment. 'You're funny. You're *great* with the kids. That's before we even get on to the fact that you've just saved my son's life.'

As I sit there, shell-shocked, so many things are whirling in my head yet I have nothing to say.

'I've been an asshole. And I know I don't deserve your friendship. But please just know how sorry I am.'

I feel a dry lump in my throat as Ryan reaches across the bed and gently clutches my hand. His is big and strong but his fingertips are soft. As I gaze at the contours of his knuckles, my heart beating wildly, he squeezes. There is something about the way he does it that makes the tears I didn't know were welling spill out of my eyes. They rush down my cheeks and on to the blanket next to Samuel's foot. Just watching them soak into the fabric makes me say something without even thinking about it. 'I want to go home.'

As soon as I've said it, I don't know why I did. Perhaps the intensity of the moment reminds me of how much I miss it. Of how much I miss Jason. Of how *desperately* I miss him.

'I want my mum and dad,' I whimper. 'I want to hear a Scouse accent again. I want to drive on the left. I want to watch what Leanne Battersby's doing on *Coronation Street*. I want a massive breakfast with HP sauce. I want . . . I want . . . Well, that's all.'

I glance up at Ryan, who looks as though I've stabbed him in the heart.

He stands up and walks silently round the bed to my side. Then he leans down and – to my even greater astonishment – wraps his arms round me. They feel so powerful and strong that they take my breath away. I am overwhelmed with shock and desire as warmth spreads through my body and I struggle to keep my pulse under control.

I close my eyes and, my emotions all over the place, eventually persuade my shoulders to relax. As he pulls me closer, I register how glorious the warmth of his skin feels against mine. I allow my wet cheek to drop to the muscular curve of his shoulder and luxuriate in the sensation. My head is a cyclone of confusion but my body's reaction is one of unequivocal yearning.

Ryan strokes my hair away from my face and I can feel his mouth next to my ear. His breath is soft and sweet. 'Don't go,' he whispers. 'Please don't go.'

Chapter 48

Later in the week I wake up in the middle of the night dreaming about the wedding again. There is cold sweat on my forehead and I feel so clammy that if my mother was there she'd accuse me of coming down with something.

I hardly sleep after that, tossing and turning as if the bed has been invaded by a swarm of morris-dancing ants. By the time I drift off, it feels as if I've had only a minute's sleep before I'm woken by Ruby and Samuel knocking at my door. 'Come in,' I croak, sounding as if I've inadvertently left my tonsils somewhere else.

When the door opens, Ryan is standing there with a tray of scrambled eggs, tomatoes, mushrooms, bacon, toast, a cup of tea and a paper. 'Oh, Jeez – I forgot something,' he mutters. He produces something from his back pocket and plonks it on the tray.

It's a bottle of HP sauce.

Chapter 49

If they'd made museums like the Boston Children's Museum when I was little, I'd have wanted to spend my life there. Trudie, Amber, Felicity and I have been there all morning with our entire crew, who have been so excited you'd think someone had been surreptitiously slipping e-numbers into their organic pear juice.

We've been taking apart toasters in a section called Johnny's Workbench, investigating the laws of science with a golf ball, and are now in Kid Power, which is about different ways of exercising. They should be exhausted, but if anyone suggested stopping for a rest I'm sure the kids would think they needed psychiatric treatment.

'You not joining in, Felicity, love?' Trudie asks, as she slips off her cork wedges and prances on to an interactive dance-floor with Andrew and Eamonn skipping behind her.

'Oh, I'll sit this one out,' says Felicity, cheerfully, straightening the collar of Tallulah's cardigan. 'This isn't the kind of dancing I specialize in.'

'Don't tell me you've got qualifications in that as well?' I ask.

'Only a few.' She beams. 'Grade eight in ballet, seven in jazz – just enough to get by, really. My real passion is ballroom, though. Did you know that the Viennese Waltz is so fast and complicated that some schools insist on teaching it privately rather than in classes?'

'Er . . . of course.'

'Well,' she continues with conspiratorial glee, 'between you and me, while I could never comment on this personally, I'm told *my* Viennese Waltz is enough to make gentlemen weep.'

'Why? Do you tread on their toes?' Trudie shouts.

'Very droll, Trudie,' Felicity concedes.

It's always slightly odd to hear Felicity refer to the men in her life. In contrast to Trudie – whose love life is such a hot topic it's positively inflammable – Felicity gives the impression that her attitude towards the opposite sex is rather like her attitude towards *foie gras*: she can take it or leave it.

Trudie once attempted to interrogate her about her romantic history, but while we got some mildly juicy titbits (lost her virginity at twenty-one to the son of one of her father's shooting companions), she insists she's focusing on her career. Trudie couldn't have been more appalled if her tea had been spiked with Domestos.

'Now, Tallulah, my darling,' Felicity says, as she leaps up and claps her hands, 'I spotted a wonderful basket-weaving area earlier that I know you'll love. Shall we?'

By now the children are as giddy as a pack of hyenas

having their feet tickled. Even Amber has joined them on the dance-floor and is lolloping around performing what she insists is a traditional *bhangra* dance she picked up when she was travelling in India. To me it looks like some of the moves you see at three a.m. in the Ministry of Sound.

Tallulah glances at Ruby, who is now near-hysterical with laughter. 'Um, okay,' she replies reluctantly.

'We won't be long, Zoe!' Felicity shrills, as they disappear round a corner.

Trudie bounds back to me, out of breath, as she pulls her tiny vest top over her belly. 'Christ, are there any paramedics in here?' she wheezes.

'Never mind that,' I say. 'Now I've got you by yourself, I demand that you tell me about your night out with Ritchie. Did the "date of the decade" live up to expectations?'

Last night hadn't been just any old night on the tiles. Ritchie had organized an overdraft-busting restaurant, booked a taxi and given Trudie strict instructions to wear the most glamorous item in her wardrobe.

The result was more feverish anticipation on her part than if he'd been flying her to Paris in his private Learjet.

Yet Trudie's frowning. 'I wish you hadn't asked that.'

'Why? What's the matter?' I ask, hardly able to believe she isn't bursting to fill me in with every last micro-detail.

'Don't repeat this?'

'Of course not.' I'm a bit worried now. 'What is it?'

She sighs and inspects her hands. Her bright pink

nail polish has started to chip round the edges. 'Ritchie asked me to marry him.'

'Ohmigod!' I cry. 'Ohmigod, ohmigod! Wow, Trudie! This is great!'

Halfway through my frenzied monologue I pick up on her mood and pull back the reins on my congratulations. 'Or . . . not great?' I ask, trying to work out why she has the expression of someone on their way to identify a body.

'Hmm, great or not great? Bloody good question.'

'Oh, God, you're right. It's far too soon. I wasn't thinking, I just—'

'It's not too soon,' she interrupts.

'Oh. Then why?'

She doesn't say anything.

'I know we're good friends, Trudie, but my powers of telepathy aren't quite as tuned as they might be.'

'Sorry, love,' she says. 'Look, it's good in one sense, obviously.'

'In the sense that you adore him?'

'Yeah.'

I roll my eyes. 'Well, for God's sake, what other sense is there?'

'Ssssh!' she hisses, glancing round to check that no one can hear. 'I *can't* marry him.'

'You're not already married, are you?'

She tuts. 'No.'

'Um – you've secretly signed up to become a nun?'

Trudie looks down at her vest top and hot pants, both of which appear to have been on a boil wash for the past six days. 'What do you think?'

'Okay . . . *Why?*'

'First, let me tell you something about Ritchie. He loves kids. He's great with Andrew and Eamonn – I mean, *really* great, better than their own dad. Even before he proposed last night, he'd been going on about us starting a family and stuff. I mean, Ritchie just cannot *wait* to have kids.'

'And?'

'Well, he thinks I'd make a great "mom", as he says.'

'You would.'

'Well, don't be so sure,' she replies.

'Don't you want kids?'

'Yeah, but—'

'I've seen you with Andrew and Eamonn. You're amazing with them. How can you think otherwise?'

She bites a nail. 'When I was little, I got sick.' Her eyes blur. 'I had leukaemia.'

It takes a couple of seconds for the words to filter into my brain. 'You . . . you're kidding?'

She shakes her head and continues so matter-of-factly we might have been talking about a bout of Chickenpox.

'I was only four,' she says. 'Spent ages in and out of hospital. Nearly drove my poor old mum and dad out of their minds. Mum was convinced I wasn't going to make it – I mean, you would be, wouldn't you? Having your four-year-old daughter get cancer isn't something anyone plans for.'

'God, Trudie.'

'Well, the really unbelievable thing is that I pulled through. "I'm A Survivor!"' she sings, not quite as tunefully as Destiny's Child.

'You're amazing, Trudie,' I tell her. 'I knew it the minute I met you.'

'Yeah, well,' she shrugs, 'I don't know about that. I beat the disease, got the all-clear and grew up to lead a completely normal life.'

'So, what's this got to do with Ritchie?'

'I was just getting to that, love. Cancer's a bloody cruel disease, Zoe, don't ever doubt it. And although I beat the bugger at four years old, it left me with a memento. A little thing to make sure I never forget it was there.'

Somehow I know what's coming next.

'I can't have kids, Zoe. I've had all the tests. No matter how much I want them – no matter how much *Ritchie* wants them – I can't ever have kids.'

Chapter 50

Ryan's no saint, so if I'd thought that what had happened the other week would turn him into the world's greatest housemate overnight, I'd have deserved a reality check as big as the Isle of Wight.

But – and there's a big but – since I put my first-aid training to use and his son came back from the brink of death, I get the feeling that a couple of matters have been put into perspective for him. And the manifestation of this is that he's shown such an improvement that if I was writing his half-term report he'd get a gold star.

The downing-whiskey-like-it's-going-out-of-fashion has stopped. The stomping-round-the-house has *almost* stopped. The arriving-home-at-three-a.m.-reeking-of-perfume *hasn't* stopped – but what the hell? Nobody's perfect.

In fact, last night he didn't get in until about five thirty and I have ascertained – from the whiff I caught of his shirt when I was doing the laundry this morning (yes, I still do that) – he's dating the woman who wears Estée Lauder Pleasures again. She hasn't made an appearance for at least six weeks.

Anyway, crucially, in addition to most of his bad behaviour stopping, a load of other things have started. Like spending lots of time with his kids. Like having fun. Like, wait for it, laughing.

Yes, Ryan laughs so much now that he's started to look like a man who has remembered how to enjoy life. He even manages to make me laugh regularly, something I'd once have considered as likely a prospect as Nicole Richie winning an international prize for her contribution to molecular science.

Ruby and Samuel have noticed a dramatic change. This week alone, he has been home from work every night before six, which has enabled him to play baseball in the garden, sit down to paint at the kitchen table, or even just watch a movie on TV. In fact, he's done so much with the children recently, I've sometimes felt we're living with a Butlin's Redcoat.

The effect of all this on the children has been incredible. Ruby has a permanent sparkle in her eyes, and every night this week – with the exception of one wobble on Tuesday – she and Samuel have been tucked up in bed, blissfully exhausted and fast asleep by eight twenty.

And my job has become *so* much easier.

Tonight I'm considering what to give the children for dinner when I hear the door slam. My shoulders no longer tense involuntarily.

'*Daddy!*' shout Ruby and Samuel, as they dive into his arms like two overactive puppies.

'Wow,' I say. It's just gone five. 'You're early.'

'They let me out for good behaviour.' He smiles.

'Well, I was about to start cooking – you can join us for dinner, if you like?'

Ryan grimaces. 'I tasted that HP sauce the other day,' he teases. 'I have a few doubts about your culinary tastes.'

'What a cheek!' I gasp, and the children collapse into giggles.

'No, no,' he protests. 'I was going to offer to take you all out to dinner.'

'Really?' squeals Ruby, jumping about with such excitement you'd think he'd said we were relocating to Disney's Animal Kingdom.

'Really? Really?' adds Samuel.

'Yes, *really*, *really*,' replies Ryan, picking him up and throwing him into the air as if he were no heavier than a blow-up beach ball.

I dash upstairs and open my wardrobe to survey the options. What the hell does one wear to go out for dinner with one's boss and young charges? Are we talking cocktail dress and heels? No, no, no. Cocktail dress and heels are definitely out – not least because I don't want flashbacks to the last time I wore such an ensemble.

After an intensive search through my wardrobe, I settle on an outfit I bought recently that's made for an occasion like this – that is, when I haven't a bloody clue what to wear: linen trousers and a floaty, angel-sleeved print top, as worn by Kate Hudson in a recent edition of *Allure* magazine (although I bet hers wasn't thirty-five dollars from H&M).

I set about applying my makeup, a demanding and subtle process by anyone's standards. Overdo the

Clinique soft-finish foundation and I risk being exposed as the sort of sad-act who gets so worked up at the prospect of a bit of dinner that she's emptied her entire wardrobe looking for something to wear. Underdo it and it'll look as if I've stopped off on the way back from Wal-Mart.

When I meet Ryan in the hallway, he looks at me as he opens the door for the children. As usual, my knees go wobbly.

'You've lost weight, Zoe,' he says.

I stop in my tracks. 'What?'

'You've lost weight,' he repeats.

I'm stunned by this statement and almost buckle under the weight of my gratitude. Ryan might as well have informed me I have eyes like starlight, lips like dewdrops and the body of a Greek goddess.

'Oh, do you really think so?' I ask, as nonchalantly as I can, my cheeks glowing like the end of *ET*'s finger. 'I haven't been on a diet or anything . . . and, well, I used to be much thinner than this, honestly.'

'You look great.' He smiles, and my heart dances with happiness. 'Now, come on, Ruby – hop in.'

Here's the ridiculous thing. I *hadn't* been on a diet. Which can only lead me to one conclusion: the more effort you put into slimming, the less weight you lose.

And Ryan's right – I have lost weight. Granted, I'm still not back to my normal size, but I'd estimate I've shifted at least half a stone, possibly more.

I walk into the restaurant feeling like Miss World after a spa day.

Dinner is at Legal Seafoods, a Boston institution to

which Ruby and Samuel have never ventured until now. Ruby rises to the challenge of being at a 'posh restaurant' by putting on a funny *faux*-British accent and holding her knife and fork so daintily she keeps almost dropping them.

She orders rainbow trout and seems disappointed when it comes. Rather than the exotic, colourful creature she'd imagined, it's just a big fish. Now that I'm a successful, health-conscious slimmer, I decide to opt for a Lite Clam Chowder.

It's Ryan's west-coast oysters that create the biggest stir.

'Euurgh! Daddy!' cries Ruby, as Ryan picks one up.

'Euurgh! Daddy!' echoes Samuel.

Funny, but watching Ryan slip an oyster on to his tongue has quite the opposite effect on me.

'Look, they're delicious.' Ryan grins. 'Zoe thinks so too. Don't you, Zoe?'

I blush. Not wanting to reveal that I've never eaten one, I slide an oyster into my mouth. 'Delicious!' I exclaim, swallowing what feels like a lump of salty slime. 'You don't know what you're missing.'

Samuel's in fits of giggles, but Ruby couldn't have looked more appalled if we'd eaten our own unwashed socks accompanied by a compôte of bathwater. 'You guys are gross,' she says, picking at a bread roll.

As the evening wears on, I come to the conclusion that eating out is such an unqualified success that Ryan should consider doing it every other day – and don't hesitate to tell him so.

But it's not just the kids. I've enjoyed it too. And at

nine, when we're still at our table, waiting to be picked up by our taxi, I realize what a nice warm glow I'm feeling tonight. I put it down to the bottle of wine Ryan and I have shared.

'God, stupid me,' he says, out of the blue.

'You haven't forgotten your keys?'

'No, no. Something else. A toast. Raise your glasses, kids.'

They hold their glasses so high that Samuel nearly spills his orange juice on his head.

'To Zoe,' says Ryan. 'Our life-saver.'

Chapter 51

At eleven o'clock the kids are fast asleep and I've retired to my bedroom. I'm just settling beneath the covers when I hear footsteps thudding down the stairs. When I hear it again I sit up in bed and frown. Only this time, Ryan – I presume it is Ryan – is running *up* the stairs.

He's doing it so loudly I'm convinced he's going to wake Ruby and Samuel. I jump out of bed to find out what's going on. Except when I open the door the sight that confronts me is *not* what I was expecting.

Ryan is at the top of the stairs, his back to me, heading for his bedroom. Other than a towel so small it wouldn't cover the modesty of Elmer Fudd, let alone that of a six-foot-two-inch man, he's buck naked.

That he's also dripping leads me to surmise that he must have been running downstairs for a clean towel. As he tramps across the landing, I find myself rooted to the spot.

Then he drops the towel.

I gasp.

It's a silent, panicky, squeaky gasp, partly driven by the terrifying prospect that he might turn round and

245

find me gawping at his backside, and partly because I *am* gawping at his backside.

'Shit,' he mutters, picking up the towel. He throws it over his shoulder and continues towards his room.

I clap my hand over my mouth as my eyes guiltily devour the contours of his naked wet body. I am horrified by myself but I can't stop. I take in the beads of water clinging to his broad, tanned shoulders and – *oh, God, I can hardly breathe* – his bum.

Ryan's bum is world class.

I mean, some bums are good, but this isn't just good. Michelangelo at the height of his creative powers couldn't have created a better one.

Suddenly, accidentally, I breathe out. It sounds like a short burst of gas from a helium balloon. Ryan stops. I bite my hand, squirming, praying he hasn't heard me.

He looks to the side.

Sweat pricks my forehead. My fists are clenched so tightly that if I had half-decent nails I'd need hospitalizing.

But he doesn't turn.

I have no idea whether or not he heard me – all I know is that he continues on his way, shutting his bedroom door behind him.

I close my eyes and breathe a heavy sigh of relief. Finally I pull myself together enough to scuttle back into my room, shut the door, jump into bed and pull the covers up to my chin.

I try to read my book. But something odd keeps happening. Every time I get to the bottom of a page, I realize I haven't taken in a word of it.

Chapter 52

It's a week before I've stopped thinking about Ryan's backside.

'It's not even like I fancy him, for God's sake,' I tell Trudie on the phone one night.

'Yeah, yeah, yeah,' she says. 'So you keep telling me.'

'It's true!' I squeal.

I don't know why I'm trying to convince myself of this. Perhaps it's because what started as amorous flickering whenever I caught sight of Ryan's upper arms has developed into a disarming obsession involving images of his posterior. And how the hell can I be lusting after Ryan when I'm still plagued by pangs of pure, wholesome love for Jason? Defence mechanism or not, it's bothering me.

'Are you sure you don't fancy him?' she asks.

'Of course I am,' I tell her. 'How can I possibly fancy him when it's only relatively recently that I wanted to kill him?'

'You must've seen the light.' She sniggers. Teasing me about this is now clearly a sport for her.

'Don't be ridiculous.'

'Okay – you've seen his arse.' She giggles. 'That was obviously enough.'

I can't help smiling – but that doesn't stop me leaping at the opportunity to change the subject. Besides, there are far more important things to talk about than Ryan's body.

'How are things with Ritchie?' I ask, tentatively.

'Oh, you know,' she says, noncommittal. 'Okay, I suppose.'

Oh dear. Until the other week, if I'd asked for Trudie's assessment of her relationship with Ritchie, she'd have said they made Romeo and Juliet look like Jack and Vera Duckworth.

'It's not the same since he asked me to marry him,' she confesses. 'He's changed. I mean, on the surface we're both pretending nothing's different – but we know it is.'

'Well, in what way has it changed?'

'Oh ... nothing you could put your finger on. But it's like, before, he was clear in his head that we loved each other equally. Now I think he feels the balance has changed. Like because I didn't leap at marrying him, he's got to pull back. To stop being so affectionate and loving and ... Well, now I'm overcompensating so much I'm like a Labrador on heat. It's pathetic.'

'It's probably just a pride thing,' I offer.

'I *hope* it's a pride thing.'

'But you didn't say no, did you? When he asked you to marry him, I mean.'

'No ... no, I didn't,' she admits. 'But look at it from his point of view. When you're down on one knee in the middle of a restaurant, a lukewarm "Oh, er . . . okay, we'll talk about it," isn't quite the response you'd want.'

'There must be a way round this,' I tell her. 'He must understand where you're coming from. Talk me through his reaction when you told him you couldn't have kids.'

There's a pause and I wonder if something's wrong with my phone. 'Trudie?'

'You've got to be joking, love.' She says it as though I've lost my marbles so comprehensively they're probably stuck on the easternmost ridge of Everest. 'I haven't told him *that*.'

'Why not?'

'I've told you why not,' she continues. 'Because he adores kids. Because he's desperate for a family. He'd drop me like a stone the second he found out.'

'But what if it's not as big a deal to him as you think?'

'It *is*,' she says.

'But what if it's not?'

'It *is*,' she repeats.

'Look, he loves you, doesn't he, and—'

'Yes, but— Barbara's on her way in. I'll have to dash. Take care – and thanks for sharing all the juicy details about Ryan's bum. I'll have some bloody good dreams tonight.'

Chapter 53

Ryan has done lots of things recently that have surprised the kids. Not to mention things that have surprised me. But none more so than this.

It's an average Friday in October, which means I was expecting not to see him until at least tomorrow morning after he'd been up at dawn to go for his daily run. He'd have had only three hours' sleep after a *different* sort of marathon session with an Elle MacPherson lookalike doused in Dior Addict.

But in the middle of the afternoon my mobile rings and his number appears on the screen.

'Hi, Ryan. Everything okay?'

'Sure. Where are you?'

'At the grocery store, before we pick up Ruby from school. Samuel couldn't get through the afternoon without Oreos. He's been really good today so I decided to treat him.'

'Well, can you get back here after you've got Ruby?'

'Here?' I ask, wondering where he could be referring to.

'The house.'

'You're at the house?'

'I *do* live here,' he points out, not unreasonably.

'Well, I know,' I concede. 'But you haven't been home at two-thirty on a Friday since I met you. I'd have suspected you were phoning from the Outer Hebrides before I'd thought of your own living room.'

'Okay, okay. Point taken. But that's exactly why I'm here now. I've got a surprise. For the kids.'

When we get home, Ryan is in the hallway with two large holdalls at his feet. 'Okay, you guys.' He's trying, and failing, to stop himself smiling. 'Come here a second.' He lifts Ruby up in one arm and Samuel in the other. 'How would you like to go on a little vacation?'

Ruby's eyes almost pop out. 'Really?'

'Vacation! Vacation! I love a vacation!' sings Samuel.

Ryan looks at me and smiles. 'It's not Bermuda,' he says hesitantly, 'but I'd love you to come too, Zoe.'

It emerges that Gerald Raven, Ryan's boss and my one-time dance partner (the less said about that the better) has let us borrow his vacation home in New Hampshire. Apparently, this is something he's been offering Ryan for the last three years but, until now, he's never taken him up on it.

When we arrive there later that evening, I can't help thinking this is a mistake on Ryan's part. Big-time. I had pictured my aunt Linda's static caravan in Cleveleys, complete with nursing-home-chic net curtains, mattresses so lumpy they could host a mountain-bike rally and an 'unparalleled view' backing on to the site rubbish bins.

Gerald's holiday home has to be seen to be believed.

It's surrounded by scenery so stunning – aspens, sugar maples and cedars of the most incredible, fiery colours – that if you saw it in a brochure, you'd think the photograph had been touched up. Then there's the house itself: a huge, luxurious wooden affair, with a veranda at the back wide enough to accommodate a gala dinner.

'This place is gorgeous,' I say, as Ruby and Samuel skip round the main room excitedly. 'I can't believe you've never bothered coming here before. You must be mad.'

'Questioning my sanity again.' Ryan tuts. 'Maybe you've got a point this time, though.'

'Daddy, Daddy,' squeals Ruby, 'when are we going on the horses?'

'Whoever mentioned anything about horses?' he teases her.

In fact, horses were the sole topic of conversation during the entire drive here. We've probably talked more about horses in the last few hours than the chief executive of William Hill does in a month.

'I didn't hear anything about horses. Did you, Zoe?' asks Ryan.

I shake my head. 'Nope. Not me. I can't stand them.'

'Oooh,' squeals Ruby. 'You said we could go on them. Dadd-eee! Zo-eee! Please!'

'Okay, okay,' says Ryan, kissing her head. 'Horses tomorrow morning – first thing. Promise.'

Appeased, Ruby plays happily with Samuel on the veranda while Ryan cooks steaks for us all, then serves them with a salad so big and elaborate it makes any effort of mine look like something at which a hamster would turn up its nose.

After dinner, with a watery sun on the horizon and chilled beers in our hands, Ryan and I play cards with the children. At stake is a bumper pack of M&Ms evenly distributed at the start of the game – but after less than forty-five minutes Ruby and Samuel are wiping the floor with us. How much that's down to their card-playing skills and how much to the fact that they keep sneakily swiping the chocolate from across the table, whether they win or not, I couldn't comment. But by the end of the night they have so much on their faces they might have spent the day in the quality-control department of Willy Wonka's factory.

'Isn't gambling illegal at your age?' I say, putting my arm round a gleeful Samuel.

'It's certainly immoral,' Ryan interjects. 'So you two should go to bed before someone arrests Zoe and me for not looking after you.'

By the time I've got both children into their pyjamas, milky drinks drunk and teeth brushed, I start to wonder how easy it'll be to get them to bed. Ruby is so excited at the prospect of waking up to go horse-riding you'd think she was gearing up for the Grand National.

'How long do you reckon before Ruby's up again?' I whisper, as Ryan closes their bedroom door.

'Hmm . . . thirty seconds?'

But thirty seconds pass. Then five minutes. And ten minutes later when we peep through the door, we hear something neither of us was expecting. Silence. Ruby and Samuel – without coaxing, persuasion or bribery – are sound asleep.

Chapter 54

I'm not what you'd call a horsy type. I grew up in the middle of a city, for God's sake. The only horses I came into contact with were outside football grounds with police officers sitting on them.

Okay, so that's not the entire story. I did have five months' worth of lessons every Saturday when I was ten. Our neighbour Susan Hamilton's daughter Sally had just reached grade two on the piano, so I was packed off to the stables in Harthill Road every weekend to be moulded into a Jilly Cooper character. I wasn't awful, exactly, but I breathed a sigh of relief when the Hamiltons moved to West Kirby and I was allowed to stay at home and watch Trevor and Simon on *Going Live!* instead. While the lessons lasted, I got by. But there's one crucial difference between then and now: fear. As in, I had no fear then. Now I'm so terrified I can feel my teeth chattering like one of those plastic sets you wind up.

As we saddle up with the help of our instructors, the creature I've been lumbered with – ironically named Tiny – is so big I can't quite believe that getting on top of him is humanly possible. I've seen daintier dinosaurs.

'Tiny's great with beginners,' says my instructor, a redhead called Cindy with thighs that could crack walnuts. 'Even those who aren't naturally . . . athletic.'

She's spent the last half-hour throwing snide comments like this in my direction and flirting with Ryan. It's starting to get to me.

'I'm not a beginner,' I inform her again. 'I *have* had lessons.'

'Oh, sorry.' She sniggers. 'It was just that when you put your hat on back to front I assumed . . .'

I sniff defensively. 'That's the way we wear them in England.'

'Whatever.'

'But, hey,' I continue, ignoring her, 'when in Rome, as they say . . .'

I pull my hat on the right way this time and, out of the corner of my eye, catch Ryan smiling at me.

I watch as he proceeds *confidently* to check the saddle on his horse, then *confidently* leap on top of it, before *confidently* parading him round the stableyard. It's evident that Ryan couldn't be more expert at equestrian matters if his mother was Princess Anne.

I'm torn about what to think. On the one hand his rural credentials are showing me up big-time. On the other he's as sexy as hell on that horse.

I've never been one for cowboy films, but the sight of Ryan today has made me realize where their appeal might lie. With his powerful thighs resting against the horse's sides and his shirt-sleeves rolled up so that his arms are on show, he's a vision of rough-and-ready athleticism. Which isn't helping my concentration one bit.

'You all set?' He smiles enthusiastically.

'Um . . . nearly!' I smile shakily. 'Did you do a lot of riding when you were younger?'

'Sure.' He shrugs. 'But, hey, Zoe, don't worry. Your instructor's going to be right with you. I'm told they look after beginners real well.'

'I am *not* a beginner,' I insist, putting my foot into one of the stirrups and attempting to swing my leg over Tiny's back. 'I'm just a bit rusty, that's all.' After five goes, I realize I look like an arthritic Jack Russell trying to wee against a fencepost. Worse, Ryan leaps off his horse and tries to help by putting his hands on my backside and shoving my entire weight on top of Tiny. It's the most ungainly movement that Cindy has ever seen, judging by her expression.

'I wonder if I wouldn't be better on something more like that one,' I suggest, pointing at Ruby's mount.

'Let me get this straight,' asks Cindy. 'You want the pony the six-year-old is on?'

'It doesn't have to be that one in particular.' I bristle.

'You'll be fine,' she purrs, as she pats Tiny, prompting him to shudder and me to grip the front of the saddle so tightly my knuckles are white. 'Tiny's a gentle giant.'

We set off on our trek across the countryside, Ryan leading the way. Samuel and Ruby are next, their instructors – a lovely bloke called Robbie and a shy seventeen-year-old called Lauren – walking next to them and holding the reins. Then there's me and Cindy – who very publicly tells me off for not stopping Tiny eating the foliage.

'Oh, it won't do him any harm,' I tell her, as if I'm

allowing him to do it because I'm a benign animal-lover and not because Tiny refuses point-blank to go in any direction I want him to.

'It's poisonous,' she tells me.

Fortunately, Tiny decides to move on anyway as I force myself to try to chill out. Even after we've ridden for about half an hour or so, however, I'm still experiencing the adrenalin rush of a would-be suicide standing on Beachy Head with their toes hanging off the edge.

'The countryside's beautiful, isn't it?' Ryan remarks, as his horse drops back next to mine.

'Oh, yes,' I say, wiggling round on my saddle in an attempt to emulate the easy-going poise of a Texan ranch-owner who started riding shortly after emergence from his mother's womb. 'And no better way to see it, eh?'

'I'm glad you've relaxed a little,' says Ryan. 'The kids are having a fantastic time. I'd have hated it if you'd been uncomfortable.'

'Me?' I exclaim. 'Me? Ha! Uncomfortable? That's a laugh, eh, Tiny?'

In a gesture designed to show how entirely comfortable and confident I am, I attempt to pat Tiny's neck. But as I lean over and my hand makes contact, I lose my balance.

In fact, that doesn't quite cover the spectacular movement involved as I plunge sideways from the saddle, lose a stirrup and am left, part unsaddled and gripping Tiny's mane for dear life.

'Waah!' I yell.

Tiny decides he doesn't like the idea of a nine-and-a-half-stone lunatic flailing about on top of him like a giant squid. And instead of standing still so that someone can rescue me, he takes matters into his own hoofs – and speeds up.

'Waah!' I wail, clinging to his neck.

'Just stay calm,' my instructor shouts unhelpfully, as Tiny pounds into the distance and my arse slips even further down the side of the horse.

I can't concentrate on anything at this point except the thunder of Tiny's hoofs as I'm thrown up and down like an oversized rag-doll in a tumble-dryer and my muscles burn as they attempt to grip hard enough for me to stay on.

Which isn't, it turns out, hard enough.

As I feel myself sliding further down Tiny, getting closer and closer to the ground, I fear for my life. My fingers slip through his mane and I know that's it: I'm about to be snuffed out. Snotty Cindy and her galvanized-steel upper legs will be the last thing I ever see.

But suddenly I become aware of something happening at my side. Someone is riding alongside me. Someone is grabbing Tiny's reins.

'Whoooa!'

Miraculously, Tiny slows down. Even more miraculously, he eventually stops.

I release my grip and land in a puddle, like a sack of King Edwards thrown off the side of a cargo ship. I close my eyes, overwhelmed with shock and relief.

When I open them again, Ryan is kneeling next to me.

'Who was it you took lessons from?' he asks. 'Clint Eastwood?'

Chapter 55

I have never in my life had so many bruises. I'm lying in a hot bath, semi-comatose, staring hazily at a pair of legs that might belong to a character from *Reservoir Dogs*. All this from a quiet trek through the countryside on Tiny, the 'gentle giant'.

I reach for the soap and groan as pain shoots through my side. To be honest, it's not just that it hurts so much that bothers me. It's that, despite being completely naked, I look like I'm wearing Joseph's Technicolour Dreamcoat.

I close my eyes and my mind drifts. I imagine Jason tending my wounds. He was always good at that sort of thing.

A few months after we'd met, I fell down the stairs at a nightclub and, as well as giving me a piggyback to the taxi rank, he took me to his place. While I lay on the couch watching the room spin, he emerged with the most comprehensive first-aid kit I'd ever seen and doused the graze on my leg with Savlon. I don't know how much help it was medically but it made me feel better.

I'd kill to have him here now. Although I suspect he'd need more than one bottle of Savlon this time.

'Zoe, do you need any help in there?' shouts Ryan, through the door.

'No!' I yell in horror, scrambling out of the bath and reaching for my dressing-gown. 'No, no! I'm absolutely fine, honestly. Be out in a sec!'

When I hear Ryan pad away, I peer dolefully into the mirror. I may be clean – no longer covered from head to toe with mud – but my face is so scratched I look as if I've been wrestling with a hawthorn bush.

I sneak into my bedroom and pull on clean combat pants, an old T-shirt and my big cosy hoodie – which I love, even though my mum insists it's the sort of thing you'd see someone wearing while they were robbing an off-licence.

I walk through the living room and on to the veranda, where Ryan is attempting to win back the Hershey bars he lost to Ruby earlier. Samuel is finishing a drawing he and his sister have obviously been working on while I was in the bath.

'Hey, that's a nice picture,' I tell him. 'What is it?'

'It Zoe,' he says proudly. 'Zoe and a horsy.'

Samuel's artistic skills, even with Ruby's help, are abstract. But I can work out enough to see that they have drawn a horse – with what appears to be a large heap of yesterday's catering slops next to it. Apparently that's me.

'You weren't impressed with my riding skills, then?' I ask, ruffling his hair.

'You not meant to fall off, Zoe,' he tells me.

'How're you feeling?' asks Ryan. 'You look a lot better after your bath.'

'Oh, I'm fine,' I reply. 'I feel like a total prat but, hey, I'm used to that.'

'It's almost endearing.' He grins. 'Not quite. But almost.'

'Oh, well, that's not bad, I suppose. I mean, I'd prefer devastatingly sophisticated – but almost endearing is probably more than I could have hoped for under the circumstances.'

There must be something about the air in this part of the state, because at bedtime the miracle that happened last night is repeated and the children go happily to bed with little fuss.

'Are you bribing them or something?' I ask Ryan.

'A full day of fresh air was all they needed,' he says. 'Plus the fact there's no more chocolate left.'

'What do you fancy for dinner?' I ask. 'It's my turn – you cooked last night.'

'Hey, don't worry. You go chill out.'

'Really?'

'Really. Sit down. I'll bring you some wine. I bought a nice bottle earlier.'

Ryan goes into the kitchen as I flip through Gerald Raven's CD collection. There aren't a hell of a lot of classics, but I do find a dusty *Best of Billy Joel* CD. I put it into the player and skip the first few tracks until it reaches my favourite. 'She's Always A Woman To Me' still makes the hairs on the back of my neck stand on end – even though it hasn't appeared on Radio 1's play-list for at least thirty years.

I head outside to the veranda and breathe in the countryside. Soon, Ryan appears with a glass of red wine the size of a soup bowl. 'I love this song,' he says.

'Me too,' I reply. 'It's the most perfect definition of how completely *bonkers* love can be, isn't it?'

He laughs. 'I may not have used the word "bonkers" but you're absolutely right. He loves her not just *in spite* of her flaws but *because* of them. That takes a real dreamer. I can relate to that.'

I raise an eyebrow. 'You don't strike me as much of a dreamer, Ryan.'

'No? Aw, maybe you just don't know me very well.'

Then something occurs to me. How can it be that, despite the bruises, despite the complete loss of dignity, despite everything else . . . I feel weirdly happy?

'What are you smiling at?'

'Oh, nothing. Well . . . I was just thinking that, you know . . .'

'What?'

'I'm enjoying being here.'

He smiles again. This time, it's a broad, unequivocal smile the likes of which used to be such a rare sight on Ryan's face. 'I'm enjoying you being here.'

Chapter 56

It's one a.m. I'm drunk on life. Oh, okay, and a fair amount of red wine.

Tonight, by the now fading glow of an exhausted oil lamp, Ryan and I have talked about everything from whether Dostoyevsky's *Crime and Punishment* is worth reading (he assures me it is), to whether soccer is the world's superior sport (he assures me it's not). We've been through whether most people still believe in marriage and whether or not Botox is a good thing. We've discussed whether Brits and Americans have more in common than Brits and other Europeans, and speculated on whether Ruby will grow up to be president (her last but one ambition) or Hannah Montana (her latest).

We've talked about Ryan's childhood in Michigan and mine in Liverpool, the two summers he spent travelling (once to the Far East and then to Australasia), and a weekend I once spent in Barcelona.

'So, come on, secretive Zoe,' he asks, topping up our glasses. 'What's your big love story? What exactly is the deal with you and boyfriends, lovers, significant others?'

'I'm not secretive.'

'Come on,' he says, raising an eyebrow. 'What else could have brought a beautiful, bright young woman halfway round the world?'

I'm stunned.

'What's up?' he says worriedly. 'Did I say the wrong thing?'

'You think I'm beautiful?' I ask, immediately cursing myself.

The light flickers on Ryan's face making him unfeasibly perfect. His eyes are like clear, deep pools and his strong features contrast with the softness of his mouth. Just looking at him makes my question seem ridiculous. Yet he frowns. 'Of course you're beautiful, Zoe.'

It's only as my eyes meet his that I notice how hard my heart is now pounding. As heat spreads through my blood, the wine I've consumed buzzes through my body, and I find myself unable to concentrate on anything but the contours of Ryan's face.

With my body tingling outrageously, the next thing I know is that Ryan is closer to me than he was a second ago. He reaches out and puts his hand behind my neck. As he pulls me towards him I find myself going willingly – and soon his cheek is next to mine, our skin is touching and his breath is whispering against my ear. 'Of course you're beautiful,' he murmurs.

My eyes ping open as my head swirls with thoughts. Sane, sensible, pre-half-a-gallon-of-Zinfandel thoughts.

This is my boss, *for God's sake. My boss.*

This is wrong on so many levels.

265

Wrong, wrong, wrong.

But before I know it something happens that I couldn't have stopped even if I'd wanted to. Which, at this precise moment, I don't.

Ryan's lips brush mine, sending shockwaves through me. As we melt into each other, I submit to his taste, his touch, and feel as giddy with lust as I am with wine. His fingers run across my back, setting off tiny fireworks on my skin, and his lips caress my neck, leaving behind a faint but delicious trail of wetness. His arms surround me. They feel amazing. *I* feel amazing. And yet . . .

'Ryan, I—' I pull away, breathless. 'I'm not sure we should be doing this.' I don't mean it to sound as corny as it comes out.

His eyes are so filled with desire that another bolt of lightning shoots through me.

'I know,' he replies, and I pull him towards me.

Chapter 57

I wake up with a start in the middle of the night. No, a near cardiac arrest.

Ryan is on his back with his arms round me. Our legs are entwined like the tendrils of a hundred-year-old oak tree. I lift my head from his chest. We're in his bedroom. It's pitch-black. I'm still drunk. The facts of this situation hit me as if I've been walloped in the face with a frying-pan.

I am in bed with my boss.

I am in bed with Ryan Miller.

And all I've got to cover my modesty are a teensy pair of knickers, a Liverpool women's ten-kilometre-run T-shirt and about four hundred bruises.

I take a deep breath in an effort to slow my heartrate. It makes Ryan stir. He pulls me tighter to him so my face is snuggled into his neck. I know what I should do. Scrap that – what I've *got* to do. I've got to leap out of bed, leap into my *own* bed, and reconsider my employment options at the first opportunity.

As if sensing my thoughts Ryan, still half asleep, kisses my head and rubs his foot against my ankle. I close my eyes and submit to the shiver of electricity it sends through me.

At least I didn't have sex with him.

He stirs again, his hand lazily moving up my T-shirt and I feel a wave of heat between my legs.

Thank God I didn't have sex with him.

His fingers brush my breast, his lips finding my cheek as my skin tingles with excitement.

Having sex with him would be totally, utterly, completely disastrous.

I feel a growing bulge pressing against my hip and hear myself let out a tiny groan of pleasure.

I sit bolt upright with my hands on my head. 'Ryan – I *absolutely, definitely can never, ever have sex with you!*' I squeal.

He sits up in shock, as if a chorus of can-can girls has high-kicked its way into the bedroom. It takes him a moment to catch his breath. 'Okay. No problem,' he says softly, brushing a hand over my hair. 'No problem.'

He kisses my head and we lie down again as he pulls me towards him, cuddling up to me.

At least that's cleared up.

Chapter 58

I spend the next day trying to behave normally – as if last night never happened. It's the only professional thing to do.

This is quite difficult, given that I also devote a large amount of time to replaying Ryan sliding his warm palm across my thigh. And slowly moving his hips against mine. And doing all manner of entirely inappropriate but knicker-wettingly sexy things that make me blush every time I think of them.

Disconcertingly, he acts with nothing but composure all day. And while it would be going too far to describe him as cool, I don't get a sense that he's overjoyed about what happened either. He behaves as he did yesterday. To look at him, you'd never guess it had happened. Which I know is the precise effect I'm aiming for but, dear God, how does he do it so well? Why can't he give a little more away? And what the hell does he *think* about the whole thing?

As we load up the car in the middle of the afternoon and get ready to go home, Ryan picks up Samuel and gives him a hug.

'I love you, Daddy,' Samuel says, kissing his lips.

'Aww, I love you too, buddy,' replies Ryan, clearly touched. 'And I've had a fantastic time with you guys this weekend.'

'Can we do it again, Daddy?' asks Ruby, strapping herself into her booster seat.

'I'd love to,' says Ryan.

'Which part? The horses?' asks Ruby.

'For sure,' he replies. 'The horses, the card-playing . . . and one or two other things.' He's smiling at me now. 'I'd love to do it all again,' he says.

My heart leaps and I scramble into the passenger seat, wishing I could control my heartrate. Yet by the time we reach home a couple of hours later, I'm consumed by paranoia.

Did I misinterpret an innocent comment by Ryan as him flirting with me? Am I imagining he fancies me when last night only happened because I was the only female within a twenty-five-mile radius?

Later in the evening, as I unpack my bag behind the closed door of my bedroom, I tell myself to get a grip. Haven't I already promised myself that the fantasies I've been having about my boss must remain just that? I remind myself that my feelings towards Ryan are superficial. Lustful thoughts, raunchy dreams, escapism. What I think and feel about him is nothing like the deep, pure love I have for Jason. How could I have considered acting on it?

I hear a knock on my door as I'm tucking my bag beneath my bed. 'Come in,' I reply.

The door opens and it's Ryan. My heart is pounding again.

'The kids are asleep,' he tells me, shutting the door behind him.

'Oh, really? God, that country air must really have got to them.' I laugh nervously. 'Listen, I'm glad you stopped by.'

'Oh?'

'Yes. The thing is . . . um . . . about last night.'

'I had a nice time.'

'Well,' I continue, determinedly, 'that's as may be, but with you being my boss and everything, I'm not sure it was a good idea. Besides, there are certain things I've been through in my life recently that may have affected my judgement. My emotional life, that is. And on top of that it would be terrible if Ruby and Samuel found out. That's aside from the fact that—'

'I agree,' he interrupts.

'What?' I reply, shocked. 'Oh, well, good.' I suddenly want to slit my wrists. 'I mean, yes – it was ridiculous, wasn't it?' I babble. 'Stupid of us, really. I couldn't regret it more, and I'm sure you feel the same. So irresponsible—'

He is right in front of me now. 'No, I mean, I agree with what you said about Ruby and Samuel,' he whispers, gazing into my eyes as he strokes a strand of hair off my face. 'I don't mean I regret it. I *don't* regret it.'

I return his gaze and my legs go weak. 'D-don't you?'

'Of course not,' he says.

Then he bends down and kisses me. It takes my breath

away and I panic about the effect that will have on my technique. But as his fingers glide through my hair and, with the other hand, he pulls me into his hard body I soon stop worrying about that.

Chapter 59

Three weeks and two days after our weekend in New Hampshire, I have sex with Ryan. That's three weeks and two days after I promised myself I wouldn't. And . . . *Oh, God!* It's the most sensual experience I've had in my life. More tender than I thought it could be. More electrifying than should be possible. It's gorgeous. Mindblowing. Loving. Amazing.

I'm torn between feeling as guilty as hell and having a lottery-win-level spring in my step.

The one thing we are both agreed on is that this thing – this affair (*argh! Is it an affair?*) – has to be kept secret from Ruby and Samuel. The reason they can't know about it is obvious and doesn't need to be spelled out by either of us: this is one of Ryan's flings, which, logic tells us, can only end in the same way as the others. And that's fine when it only involves two grown-ups. But the prospect of Ruby and Samuel finding out makes the stakes far too high.

Both Ryan and I know I could never be just another girlfriend, particularly where Ruby's concerned. So

Jane Costello

when it ends – because *it will end* – Ruby knowing about it would not help matters.

Anyway, that's the theory. The practice of keeping it secret from them isn't always easy.

Especially when Ryan pulls me towards him behind a door and sneaks a languorous kiss when no one is looking. Or pushes my hair to one side and brushes his lips across my ear as I'm attempting to peel the spuds over the kitchen sink. Or grabs my hand the second the kids are in bed and wraps his arms round me with such tenderness that I feel bereft when eventually he moves.

All that said, I still don't feel confident I'm doing the right thing by engaging in this liaison.

I worry constantly about having such a meaningless dalliance solely to get over the love of my life. I worry about how one-dimensional such behaviour is. How lacking in anything like the depth and breadth of my seven years with Jason. And, as old-fashioned as this may sound, I worry about the sort of girl it makes me.

On the other hand, I cannot deny that fooling around with Ryan is making me feel utterly *fantastic*. I walk about in a permanent state of semi-elation, my heart beating in anticipation of the snatched moments I have with him.

In many ways, this is understandable, given my recent history. It's as though I've spent months detoxing on alfalfa seeds and melon before being presented with a giant Galaxy Easter egg. I know it isn't good for me but, God, it's delicious.

Ironically, one of the side effects of all this is that I'm *really* losing weight. The extra pounds I was shedding

274

gradually are now falling off at such an accelerated pace I'm almost back to my original size.

'You're in love,' Trudie declares, as we drink iced coffee in Barbara King's conservatory. 'The only other way you could lose four pounds in a week would be a bout of dysentery.'

The children are playing happily in Andrew and Eamonn's enormous sandpit. So far they've created a 'castle' that looks like a semi-detached in Wigan and some soldiers that appear so severely dehydrated they're having trouble staying upright.

'I'm not in love, Trudie,' I tell her. 'Really. I'd tell you if I was, but I'm not.'

'Well, Christ, you're doing a good job of looking like it.'

I sigh and gulp some coffee. The fact is, I cannot be in love with Ryan Miller. I fancy him. I'm having plenty of fun with him. But, much as it pains me to say this, I'm still in love with Jason. No matter how hard I'm trying not to be, I am.

Chapter 60

To: Zoemmoore@hotnet.co.uk
From: Helen@Hmoore.mailserve.co.uk

Dear Zoe,

The new bathroom is a disaster. Your dad insisted on going with a local firm and look where that's left us: with a whirlpool bath that doesn't whirl and a power-shower with about as much oomph as a leaky hosepipe. Still, the tiles are nice. I got them to copy the ones in the Center Parcs brochure and they've very nearly done it. Apart from the dolphins, that is – there's one corner of the shower in which several of them have been decapitated. But they were half price.

I've got an appointment at the doctor's next week – this feeling faint and tired business isn't letting up at all. I went on some website yesterday and I've narrowed it down to one of two things: wheat intolerance or pancreatic cancer. So we'll wait and see.

I only hope it gets sorted out soon because it's driving me mad. Linda, the woman who sits opposite me at work, was in the middle of telling me about going to see *Dancing on Ice* at the arena and I nearly dropped off. Still, she's bloody boring when she wants to be. How many times can you listen to an anecdote about a triple pike, even if it does involve a pair of split trousers?

We haven't really talked about this until now, but have you decided when you're coming home for Christmas yet? There's only seven weeks to go, you know! I could do with you being at home at least a few days beforehand – not least to keep your father's decorating in check! You know he never listens to me about how to do a tree tastefully. Last time he was let loose on one he used so much spray snow the fumes set Desy's asthma off and he nearly ended up in A and E.

I assume you'll come at least a week before but, whatever, can you remember to pick up a new bottle of Tia Maria from Duty Free? Great Aunt Iris cleaned us out last year.

Love,
Mum
XXXX

Chapter 61

Ryan is in the kitchen preparing dinner, and the world has come to a temporary standstill.

'What is it with men and cooking?' I shake my head in amusement. 'I'm sure this pot roast will be fantastic, but it does feel like we're in the presence of Marco Pierre White when the Michelin judges are about.'

Ryan has given us a running commentary on every ingredient he's put into the dish – all five of them – and is playing up to his audience of me, Ruby and Samuel so much that he's clearly expecting a round of applause.

'I don't know what you mean.' He smirks. 'I'm doing pretty well. In fact, I should do this more often – I'm obviously a culinary genius.'

At least he's being tongue-in-cheek – I think.

I pick up Samuel and let him peep into the pot.

'I want pizza,' he says. From his expression you'd think he was confronting the rotting carcass of a recently deceased rodent.

A chuckle escapes me.

'This is a nutritious, home-cooked meal!' says Ryan,

pretending to be offended. 'It will be nothing less than delicious – isn't that right, Zoe?'

'It'll be gorgeous, kids,' I tell them. 'And, if not, we can sneak out to McDonald's afterwards.'

Ruby giggles.

'Traitor,' Ryan mutters.

Suddenly we hear a voice at the front of the house.

'Hello? Er, um . . . hiya?'

It sounds like Trudie, but quieter. She usually announces her presence at a volume only matched by the horn of a four-hundred-ton freight container. 'Have I got five minutes before dinner?' I ask Ryan.

'Sure.'

Trudie's in the hall, wearing a short flowery dress, the sort of thing that, on a different person and in a different size, would look like one of those stylishly mumsy Boden numbers. Trudie manages to look like an off-duty *Playboy* centrefold.

'How are you doing?' I ask. 'I've been meaning to give you a shout about whether you fancy coming to the cinema with the kids this week but— Hey, what's up?'

Trudie is never pale. That's partly because she's such a fan of Fake Bake tanning products she makes the average Wag's complexion seem positively Elizabethan. But tonight pale is exactly what she is. Pale and worried. 'You got a minute?' she asks, her lip trembling.

'Of course.' I lead her into the living room. 'Can I get you some juice or something?'

As soon as I say it I realize she needs something significantly stronger than that. Like a beta-blocker or five.

She shakes her head.

'What is it?'

She lets out a shaky breath. 'Where do I start?'

'The beginning?' I offer.

'Okay,' she says. 'The beginning . . . Well, let me *begin* with Ritchie.'

'What happened?'

'He came over today,' she tells me, 'and said he wants to spend the rest of his life with me – but if I don't want the same there's no point in wasting any more time together.'

I fold my arms. 'So, what did you say to him?'

'I tried to explain – well, sort of explain – why I didn't leap at the chance of marrying him.'

'So you told him about not being able to have kids? That that's all you're worried about?'

'That's all?' she cries incredulously. 'Zoe, this is a massive thing for anyone, not least someone who talks constantly about how he can't wait to start a family.'

'I know, I know. I didn't mean that,' I tell her, regretting my lack of tact. 'Sorry, I . . . You did tell him, didn't you?'

She bites her lip and looks out of the window. 'I told him I love him – *really* love him – and that that hasn't got anything to do with why I won't say yes to his proposal right this second and that . . . I just needed to think a couple of things through and . . . well . . .'

'But you did tell him?'

'Well . . .'

'Trudie?'

'Not exactly. No.'

'Oh, Trudie.'

'Zoe, think about it. If I start telling him about my problems – that I can't have kids – there's only two ways it can go. One, he leaves me. Two, he stays with me, and I ruin his life by not giving him the one thing he really wants.'

'But—'

'Don't go there,' she interrupts. 'That's not even the half of my trouble at the moment.' Her face crumples and tears flood down her cheeks.

'Oh, God. What else?' I ask, putting my arm round her.

'It's Barbara.'

'What about her? What's she done? There can't be a problem with your work. You're brilliant with Andrew and Eamonn. And they love you. And—'

I stop. Her lips are still quivering.

'It's my own fault,' she sobs. 'All my own fault.'

'What is, Trudie? *What*'s your own fault?'

'After Ritchie left,' she says, between sniffs, 'I was so upset I put the twins in their play-pen in front of *Jo-Jo's Circus* and went upstairs to my room.'

She pauses.

'Go on.'

She looks down at her hands. 'I'd given up smoking before I came out here – honest, Zoe, I really had. Or, I thought I had.'

Oh, God.

'I *thought* I'd kicked the habit. Honestly I did.'

Oh, God.

'But I remembered I had one fag left in a pack of Marlboro Lights buried in the bottom of my suitcase.'

Oh, God.

'I was so stressed out about Ritchie I just found myself rooting around for it. I was like a woman possessed. I swear I was so desperate that if that fag had been the last one in a machine I'd have paid a hundred and forty quid for it.'

Oh, God.

'So I'm leaning out of my bedroom window, smoking,' she continues, 'and it was great. It was really bloody great. The ciggie was as stale as hell, tasted like a camel's armpit . . . but great.'

'Go on.'

'And I'm taking my last drag and just about to put it out . . .'

'When Barbara caught you,' I finish for her.

She nods.

'Oh, God,' I say.

Smoking is absolutely against the rules for any nanny, these days, in virtually every country in the world. However, that goes doubly in the US. And it goes triply for Barbara King, a woman so obsessed with protecting her children from toxins of any sort it's a wonder she hasn't issued them with purification masks.

'I'm guessing she didn't take it very well.' I know that just the thought of one stray molecule from that cigarette smoke making its way into one of her children's lungs will have been enough to make her apoplectic.

'No, she didn't,' Trudie continues, wiping even more tears from her cheeks. 'Zoe, she sacked me. Which means I'm not only being booted out of my job, I'm being booted out of the country.'

Chapter 62

I don't think Ryan's pacing is doing much to help Trudie's nerves, not given the state she's been in for the last two hours.

He used to do a lot of pacing when I first arrived. He hasn't done it for a while – not for ages, in fact. But he's doing it now. Not as manically as he used to, I'll admit: this is more of a pensive stroll across the living room while he thinks up a plan. All he'd need is a cigar and he'd be a dead ringer for Hannibal from *The A Team*.

'I'm going to see Barbara,' he announces, pausing mid-stride.

Trudie sniffs and takes such a large gulp of the beer I've just handed her that I'm surprised there's anything left in the bottle afterwards. 'It won't do any good.' She sighs. 'Honest to God it won't. You don't know Barbara and smoking. She might as well have caught me injecting crack cocaine.'

'That's ridiculous,' says Ryan.

'No, it's not. I think she's right.' Trudie starts to peel the label off her beer bottle. 'I told her I was a non-smoker and I betrayed her trust.'

'But you *were* a non-smoker when you applied for the job,' I persist. 'You'd given up by then, hadn't you?'

'Well, yeah. But only twenty minutes earlier,' confesses Trudie.

'But you haven't had one since you got here, have you?' asks Ryan. 'Before now, I mean.'

'No.' Trudie shakes her head decisively. 'In fact, I was doing bloody well till my patches ran out and I forgot to get some new ones. That's PMT for you. I'd forget my own name at certain times of the month.'

Ryan pulls on a sweater. 'Well, I meant what I said. This is ridiculous. And somebody needs to do something about it.'

Trudie and I flash each other a look as Ryan heads for the front door, then slams it behind him so hard they must have felt it in Kentucky. The children rush to the window to watch. I'm about to instruct them not to be nosy, but decide against it and huddle up beside them with Trudie.

Ryan is crossing the road towards the Kings' house with utter determination. I can't help feeling impressed. Then he stops, turns, heads back towards us and in through the front door.

'You changed your mind?' I ask, trying to hide my disappointment.

'Course not,' he replies, striding to the coffee-table and picking up the bunch of lilies I'd put there earlier today. The stems dripping, he goes into the kitchen, opens the fridge, picks out a swanky bottle of Californian white and departs.

This time, he makes it to Barbara King's front door.

When she opens it and sees him, she couldn't have looked less enthusiastic if he had been the neighbourhood's new rag-and-bone man trying to flog her some second-hand pan-scourers. Ryan responds by producing the flowers from behind his back. She seems entirely unmoved.

'This is never going to work.' Trudie sighs.

'My daddy will save you, Trudie,' Ruby assures her.

Trudie tries to smile, but is about as convincing as a fifteen-year-old mongrel at Crufts.

But she's about to be surprised.

Within five minutes, Barbara King's expression has softened to such an extent I'm convinced her last Botox session has only just decided to kick in. She invites Ryan in.

'Well I never . . .' I grin.

'Go, Daddy!' says Ruby, triumphantly.

'Daddy! Daddy! Daddy!' squeals Samuel.

Excitedly, we settle down to wait for him. And we wait. And wait. In fact, we do so much waiting that this whole thing becomes less of a drama and more like watching a two-hour Open University programme about advanced vacuum-cleaner mechanics. Things become so dull that the children end up plodding to bed virtually by themselves.

'He's been in there a bloody long time,' I tell Trudie, once they're safely tucked up.

Then a thought flashes into my mind. 'You don't think he's . . .'

'What?' asks Trudie.

'You don't think he's . . .'

'*What?*'

'Seducing her.'

Trudie's eyes widen. 'God, I know he wanted to do me a favour but I didn't mean him to prostitute himself.'

Just then a car pulls up, and I recognize it instantly as Mr King's. I start to panic on Ryan's behalf – perverse, to say the least.

'Shit!' Trudie exclaims. 'I hope he doesn't catch him with his pants down in the living room!'

I frown at her.

'What I mean is, I hope he hasn't *got* his pants down in the living room. If he *has*, it would make things so much worse than—'

'Trudie,' I interrupt.

'Yep. Don't worry. I'll shut up.'

We turn back to the window. Except now there's nothing to see. In fact, there's nothing to see for ages. And ages. And ages.

The next thing I know, I'm waking with a start as our front door opens. Trudie and I have fallen asleep on the sofa and I'm dribbling like a hungry St Bernard. The clock says it's ten to midnight.

Trudie rubs her eyes as we stand up and the living-room door flies open. It's Barbara King, with Ryan behind her. She looks as if she's spent all day at a wine-tasting session and forgotten to spit.

'Tshhrudie,' she slurs, leaning on Ryan's shoulder. Her eyes are so crossed you'd think they'd fallen out with each other. 'Tshhrudie, you and I need to have a talk.'

'I know, Barbara, I know. I'm so sorry. I really am sorry. It was all my fault and you were right to throw me out. But I love my job. And I love Andrew and Eamonn. And I love being here next to my mate Zoe. And I love this country. And, and—'

'Sssssh!' instructs Barbara, attempting to press her finger to her lips but prodding it up her nose. 'We'll go through all this tomorrow. The point is I've had a shange of heart. You can come back.' She throws her arms open and leans in to hug Trudie, who catches her before her face becomes acquainted with the living-room carpet. 'Shall we go home, Tshhrudie?'

Trudie beams and squeezes her arm round her. 'Let's do that, Mrs K.'

Ryan and I watch as Trudie and Barbara weave their way back to the house, where Mr King is waiting at the door to greet them. He waves to Ryan and Ryan waves back. I turn to him, my mouth ajar. 'What *happened* over there?'

'I made friends with my neighbours, that's all. And I just pointed out what a great nanny Trudie is and how much their kids love her. And, well, that was it.'

'Come on,' I say sceptically. 'There must have been more to it than that. How did you get so friendly?'

He says nothing.

'You must have flirted with her?' I ask, trying to look unbothered by this scenario.

'Maybe.' He smirks. 'But it wasn't that either.'

'Oh?'

'I've promised to mow my lawn.'

'No!'

He nods. 'Every goddamn week.'

Chapter 63

Ruby and Samuel used to watch so many cartoons on TV that they were in danger of growing up believing the world was populated with little yellow people like the Simpsons. Not any more. Life is no longer dictated by the whims of the programme schedulers. *SpongeBob SquarePants* is no longer a powerful, omnipresent force in our lives. And they no longer sit and stare at the screen for hours, as if they've been put under a spell. As far as they're concerned, they've got more interesting things to do.

By the way, I don't say this to be smug. I'm not saying I'm Jo Frost. And I should confess that *something more interesting* recently involved giving Barbie's hair a funky new look with a pair of craft scissors (Samuel) and painting Spiderman's head with my Tropical Sunset nail polish (Ruby). But, still, we've come a long way.

However, that's not to say both children don't still enjoy the odd *bit* of television. And, with the weather having turned so wet and cold it has felt like Skegness in November recently, we're in the mood for getting cosy and doing nothing more energetic than a rigorous session of channel-hopping.

Ruby has taken control of the remote and landed on something that caught her attention immediately: James Bond. 'Does everyone in Britain dress like him, Zoe?' she asks, staring in wonder at Roger Moore's tuxedo. It's *The Spy Who Loved Me* – made in the late seventies, which means everyone's lapels are so wide you could park a Volvo on them.

'Not all the time, sweetheart.'

She turns back to the television, where Barbara Bach is on screen in a dress like something you'd find hanging over the windows of a bungalow. 'She's pretty, isn't she?' muses Ruby.

'Yes, she is,' I agree, glancing to Ryan at the other end of the couch.

His face breaks into one of his heart-stopping smiles and my neck flushes. Which still strikes me as weird, and not just because of my lingering heartbreak over Jason. It's weird because Ryan and I have done things together that are significantly more intimate than a coy smile. Yet such a simple expression – which isn't suggestive, or racy – has a physical effect on me that is nothing less than profound.

My train of thought is broken as the famous 007 theme tune crashes out of the TV speakers and both kids lean forward in anticipation.

'Now, that's a real man,' I declare, as Roger Moore scoops Barbara Bach into his arms having rescued her from super-baddie Jaws. 'Despite the dodgy hairdo and mahogany complexion.'

Ryan chuckles and – with the children clearly not about to be distracted by anything short of a seismic wave – leans over to me. 'I'd do that for you,' he teases, kissing my ear.

I pull back. 'No way.'

'Way,' he insists. 'No problem at all.'

'Well,' I say, 'given we're unlikely to find ourselves in the sea off Sardinia any time soon, fortunately for you you're not going to be forced to prove yourself.'

He's about to protest again when my phone rings.

'Give your mom my love,' says Ryan, sitting upright again.

With Christmas rapidly approaching, she has been phoning me so often her next quarterly bill is set to rival that of a FTSE 100 company. I'm about to answer my mobile when I glance at the screen. The blood drains from my face. The number is as instantly recognizable now as it was when he last tried to contact me.

'What is it?' asks Ryan.

'Oh, um, nothing,' I mumble. 'Just my mum, like you said. I'm going to take this outside so I don't disturb you.'

When I'm out of the living room, I stumble up the stairs with all the grace of an inebriated donkey. I reach my room, my finger hovering over the answer button. It keeps hovering. And hovering. Chewing my lip, I pray for strength – but end up taking a chunk out of my tongue. Finally, I answer. 'Hello?' I croak. 'Jason? Hello?'

Chapter 64

I'm too late. He's rung off. I slump on to the bed, my mind reeling so wildly I can barely focus on my light shade.

I know I should be relieved, and part of me is. I think.

Coming out to the States was supposed to represent a clean break with my past and talking to Jason won't help in that respect.

The sensible part of me also knows that he should have phoned me back on one of the countless occasions I tried to contact him immediately after the non-wedding. He had his chance. *Chances*.

I've promised myself I'll be a strong, focused, independent woman, who doesn't dwell on her past. And I know, having come this far, that the worst thing I could do would be to indulge Jason – or myself – in a long conversation that reopens old wounds.

Yet part of me is desperate to do just that.

I have so many questions to ask him I could out-interrogate Jeremy Paxman. Like, what happened to him that day? And was there really no one else involved? When did he decide he wasn't going through with it?

And, more to the point, *why* did he decide he wasn't going through with it?

But the thought that I could just pick up my phone and hear his lovely, familiar voice saying my name is too much to bear.

My eyes bore into my mobile as I pull up the last number dialled. I'm going to do it. I know I shouldn't but I am.

I'm milliseconds from pressing call when there's a knock on my door.

Panicking, I shove my mobile under my pillow and lean back against my headboard as if I'm on a sun-lounger waiting for someone to come and rub in some factor fifteen.

I must look ridiculously shifty.

'Everything okay?' Ryan is mildly concerned.

'Yes, of course!' I declare. 'I just came up here to have a chat.'

He doesn't say anything.

'With . . . my auntie,' I add.

He still doesn't say anything. My eyes dart round the room for inspiration and land on the mountain of toiletries on my dressing-table.

'My auntie . . . Lil-let.' Oh, Christ. I've named my imaginary aunt after a tampon.

Ryan frowns. Then smiles.

He walks over to the bed, puts his hand behind my neck and kisses me, making my pulse thump with desire.

'You're so beautiful today,' he whispers, running his fingertips across my cheek.

'Am I?' I ask, bewildered. I have no makeup on and a spot is developing on the side of my nose.

'Absolutely.' He smiles. Then turns to leave, and hesitates.

'I didn't know you had an aunt – what? Lil-let?' he says.

'Hmm,' I reply.

'She . . . French?'

'No . . . er, yes. No.'

Ryan raises an eyebrow.

'I mean . . . she's Belgian,' I bluster.

'You got family in Belgium?'

'Oh, yes.' I wish my mouth would close and not open again until I've managed to cultivate a brain. 'Tons of them. Big beer-drinkers. And chocoholics.'

Shut *up*, Zoe.

'Anyway . . . I thought I'd come up here to take the call because Auntie Lil-let doesn't half go on sometimes,' I add, rolling my eyes.

'Oh?'

'Mmm,' I continue. 'She's going through the menopause and is having terrible hot flushes. That was what she phoned about – so, obviously, I didn't want to have *that* talk with Ruby and Samuel in the room.'

There's another pause.

'Apparently it's the chocolate,' I add, cursing myself.

'What's the chocolate?'

'The hot flushes. The chocolate sets them off something rotten.'

'Really?'

'Mmm, oh, yes, she—'

I stop. Ryan is staring at me, clearly not believing a word of this rubbish.

'Well,' he says finally, 'pass on my regards next time you speak to her. I'm going down now. I just wanted to check you're okay.'

'Me? Ha! Fine. Absolutely fine and dandy. Couldn't be better.'

He smiles. I try to smile.

And when he shuts the door behind him, I stare at the phone. What was I thinking? What the *hell* was I thinking? I wipe off the last received-call number – *Jason*'s phone number – and turn it off.

'Ryan,' I shout, opening the door. 'Hang on a sec. I'm coming too.'

Chapter 65

Nights out on the town with a priest are not something I've had many of before now – and I suspect the same goes for Trudie, Amber and Felicity. But Paul is unlike previous churchmen I've encountered. At least, he's nothing like the Reverend Derek Crapper, who was at St Michael's, Woolton, in the days when I last attended regularly. He was a lovely man who had sideburns you could have scrubbed a step with and a gentle, caring manner. Lord knows, that was a miracle, given the stick he must have received growing up with that name.

Looking back, he also had a body odour so potent that one whiff almost took the lining off your nasal passages, but he was so nice it didn't matter.

For the Reverend Paul Richardson, however, this isn't an issue. He's lovely too, but he smells of Hugo Boss and tonight he's wearing his dog collar over a stylish black shirt and a pair of jeans that flatter his backside in a manner some might think shouldn't be allowed for a man of God.

'So, um, what do you think of Paul?' Amber asks, as she helps me carry the drinks back to our table. She's trying so hard to make the question appear idle that she sounds as though she's been brushing her teeth with turps.

'I think he's fantastic. Kind, intelligent, great fun to be around. Why do you ask?' I add, as if I didn't know.

'Oh, no reason,' she says.

I smile.

'Don't look like that,' she adds, blushing. 'I know you all think I'm attracted to him, but I'm not, I promise you.'

'Course,' I say.

'Apart from anything else, our moons are mismatched.'

'Your what?'

'Moons. I'm a great believer in Vedic astrology, after all the time I spent in India. Under the Kuta system, you can measure the flow of consciousness between two people and how this energy harmonizes in the relationship.'

'And your energy isn't in harmony with Paul's?'

'Our lunar mansions are all over the place.' She sighs. 'Of course, it's not meant to be an indicator of *complete* karmic compatibility . . .'

'Oh, well, then.'

'Hmm,' she says doubtfully.

'Of course, if you *did* like him, none of that stuff would matter, would it?' I point out.

'Of course it would, Zoe,' she tells me pityingly. 'Two people getting together whose moons aren't aligned would be like trying to mix . . . I don't know . . . something really oily with something really watery.'

'Oil and water?' I suggest.

'Well, exactly. It wouldn't work.'

I'm grinning inwardly about this conversation until I sit down. Trudie and Felicity both look utterly miserable.

'You okay?' I whisper to Trudie.

'Yeah, yeah.' She nods – but it couldn't be clearer that she's not. 'Why didn't you bring Ryan out with us tonight?'

'Oh, because someone's got to babysit. Anyway, it's nice just being out with friends.'

Between you and me, I'm fibbing so outrageously I'm surprised my nose isn't a foot long. Ryan did toy with the idea of getting someone in, but as soon as he found out that this was largely a girls' night out he seemed to go off the idea.

I'm not concerned about this, especially since nobody – Trudie aside – knows about our fling. So it makes sense to avoid doing anything as suspicious as inviting Ryan out with us.

'How's Tallulah, these days?' I ask Felicity. 'Ruby's missing her – we haven't seen you for a week.' I'm attempting to spark her into conversation, but she's been so uncharacteristically low-key tonight that I suspect nothing short of jump leads would work.

'Oh? Ah, fine,' she replies, with a flicker of her usual smile.

'Is it right you're teaching her French?' asks Trudie.

'Yes,' says Felicity, clearly trying to brighten up. 'She's very good, actually. And her mother's picking up the odd word. I fear we won't get very far, though, given that

Nancy has only just stopped pronouncing the *z* in *chez*. But she *is* trying.'

'Fantastic!' I exclaim, glad she's warming up a bit. 'I hope you're bringing them to Ryan's Christmas party.'

This is a venture Ryan only announced last week. It was Ruby's idea initially, but Ryan has embraced it wholeheartedly, which I can only take as proof that he's enjoying being able to talk to his neighbours without teetering on the edge of Armageddon.

For my part, I can't wait, not least because Ryan's got somebody in to do the catering. I already have my outfit planned. Flattering wide-leg trousers and black cashmere top with plunging neckline. It's chic in an effortless way, although it took a day-long intensive search of every retail outlet in Boston to find it.

'Christmas party?' asks Felicity, her fragile smile disappearing. 'Ryan's having a Christmas party?'

'Well, yes. Um, you've got your invitation, haven't you?'

'No, Zoe. We haven't.' Felicity makes an attempt to look cheerful while she delivers her reply, but it doesn't work.

'Oh. Well, maybe they haven't gone out yet.'

'We got ours,' Trudie points out unhelpfully.

'And us,' Amber pipes up.

I look over to the Reverend Paul for help. He nods. My eyes widen.

'Oh, God, sorry, Felicity,' I say, suddenly flustered. 'It must have been an oversight, it really must. I know we put you on the list. Ryan must have forgotten to send you an email. But, please, consider yourself invited. Really.'

'No, no!' she declares, holding up her hand like a traffic warden and grinning widely as if that was the last thought on her mind. 'Really, don't you worry about me, Zoe!'

'But, Felicity, I—'

'No! We won't come! Don't worry!'

'Honestly, Felicity,' I attempt to butt in, 'you *were* invited. You *are* invited!'

She pauses for a second. 'I wouldn't want to come if I wasn't welcome.' She's smiling in a wobbly, wounded way.

'You *are* welcome,' I insist.

She pauses. 'Am I?'

'Absolutely,' I say.

'Well, that's wonderful.' She beams. 'I'll have to check my diary, of course, but you can pencil me in.'

The subject comes up twenty minutes later when Trudie co-ordinates a trip to the ladies' with me so she can touch up her makeup – which she likes to do with as much regularity as a toddler undergoing training visits the potty.

'Christ, it's a good job you discovered Felicity'd been left off the invite list to Ryan's party,' she tells me. 'She would have never forgiven him.'

'I know. I just hope it really was an accident and Ryan didn't leave them off on purpose. Maybe he doesn't get on with Nancy and Ash.'

'They get on with everyone,' says Trudie, dismissively. 'Besides, Ryan's making an effort to be the world's perfect neighbour at the moment, from what Barbara

tells me, so he would never have not invited them deliberately. Anyway, I'm just glad it's sorted. Felicity's been
in a funny mood all night.'

It's typical of Trudie to be thinking of others when
her own life isn't exactly a bed of roses. 'And how are
things with you?' I ask.

She shrugs. 'Oh, you know – so-so. I mean, things
with Barbara are great, don't get me wrong. Ryan worked
a miracle there.'

'You and Ritchie?'

'There *is* no me and Ritchie. We haven't spoken since
the other day.' I wonder what to say next – but Trudie
gets there before me. 'He won't return my calls.' Her face
crumples.

'Oh, Trudie.' I put my arm round her. I'm fully aware
that my response is as woefully inadequate as attempting
to put out a house fire with a water pistol, but it's
difficult to know what more to do.

We spend the next ten minutes in the loo, sobbing
and hugging, sobbing and hugging. When she decides
she's ready to go back into the bar her skin is so blotchy
she looks like she's had an allergic reaction to her face
powder.

'I didn't mean to upset you, Trudie,' I tell her, as we
head out.

'Don't be daft, love. I feel better for having a good old
blub. I don't know what I'd do without you, really I
don't.'

However, the second we're outside the ladies', I spot
someone at the other side of the bar who, I know, will
change the course of the evening dramatically.

I nudge Trudie, but she's rifling through her pink-sequined bag, trying to locate a nicotine patch to join the other four she's got plastered under her top.

I nudge her again.

'Hang on, love, I think I've got one,' she says, pulling out a small, plaster-like item. 'Oh, bollocks. That's one of my nipple covers.'

'Trudie,' I hiss, nudging her so hard in the ribs that she yelps.

As she looks up, Ritchie walks towards us, unfaltering. They stand facing each other, silent, and for a second you could have cut the atmosphere with a knife.

'Hiya, love,' Trudie whispers eventually. 'How ya doing?'

Ritchie reaches out to grab her hand, which, despite her attempts to seem calm, is trembling uncontrollably. 'Trudie,' he murmurs, 'I'm here to try again.'

Chapter 66

The bar is bustling. People are paying about as much attention to Trudie and Ritchie as they would a busker at a U2 concert. That is, until Ritchie produces a ring. I'm not sure whether he intends his proposal to be quite so public, but the woman to his left is not overly concerned about that. Because when she works out what he's about to do, her reaction is so over the top you'd think he was asking *her* to marry him. 'Oh, my Gaaad!' she hollers. 'Oh, my Gaad! He's going to propose! Ssssh, everyone, he's going to propose!'

The whole bar comes to a standstill and gawps at Ritchie.

'Uh, Trudie,' he begins, as he sinks on to one knee – Trudie looks as if she's about to walk the plank. 'You're the only woman for me, honey. I know I'm making a fool of myself, but you're worth it. I love you, Trudie, and I'll ask you to marry me again and again and again, if need be. I want you. I want you to have my babies. So please, Trudie, what do you think?'

I wince at Ritchie's penultimate sentence.

'Er, yeah . . . about that.' Trudie glances round the

302

room, her eyes scanning a sea of expectant faces. Then she looks at Ritchie.

'Trudie?'

'Er, well ... Yeah, why not?'

I drop the bottle of Budweiser I appear to have inadvertently stolen. It shatters on the floor in front of me, leaving my new jeans covered with beer and foam seeping between my toes.

'Are you saying *yes?*' asks Ritchie, standing up with an expression of such incredulity he looks close to passing out.

'Er ...' she scans the room again '... YES!'

I give her ten out of ten for conviction.

Ritchie scoops her into his arms as the whole bar erupts at the sort of volume you'd expect to hear standing next to a 747 on take-off. 'Drinks are on me!' he yells, spinning Trudie round and causing her handbag almost to throttle an innocent passer-by. When he finally puts her down, he leans over the bar to grab a bottle of champagne and I give Trudie a look.

'Don't look at me like that,' she hisses.

'Like what?' I whisper. 'I wasn't looking like anything. I just—'

'What?'

'Well, the thing that stopped you saying yes the first time – are you going to tell him?'

She takes a deep breath. 'Course I am. I just need to find a suitable time to—'

But before she can get the words out, she's engulfed in another kiss so passionate Ritchie's lips must be on fire.

'Well, I gotta say, that's a pretty good way to end a

night out,' says the Reverend Paul, as he pats Ritchie on the back. 'Way to go, you guys. Well done.'

'Where's Felicity?' I ask no one in particular.

'Oh,' Amber frowns, 'I'm not sure where she went. She was here a minute ago when Ritchie proposed. Then she stood up and said she had to go.'

'Is she all right?' I ask.

'Dunno.'

I contemplate going after her, but Trudie's at my side again. 'It's no good,' she whispers. 'You're right. I've got to tell him. I can't do this.'

'Trudie, wait—'

'No, Zoe,' she replies. 'I need to speak to him.'

I watch as Trudie takes Ritchie's hand and leads him out of the bar, wondering how the hell he'll react to her news.

Chapter 67

I close the front door quietly and wonder if Ryan is still up, but hear nothing. I feel a stab of disappointment. Creeping upstairs, I spot that his light is off and know I ought to head for my own room. I mean, I'm not desperate, am I? Surely I can manage to go one night without snuggling up to Ryan and running my fingers across the curve of his back. Besides, it will be the perfect opportunity to do my new beauty regime. I've vowed to stick to it since I filled in a magazine quiz yesterday and discovered my slackness in this area is set to leave me with the face of Dot Cotton by the time I hit thirty-five.

I go to the bathroom, intending to cleanse my face of all makeup, then apply gentle, clinically formulated toner (which looks suspiciously like coloured water), moisturize, brush my teeth with whitening toothpaste and settle down for a full night's sleep.

Oh, sod it.

I enter Ryan's room, take off my clothes and slip into bed next to him, warming my skin against his. I wrap an arm round his torso and press my cheek to his neck.

His smell – so clean and sexy it's a shame it can't be bottled – sends blood pulsing through my body and I find myself pushing my hips against him. He stirs and turns towards me in his half-sleep, pulling me in tightly as his leg wraps round mine. 'You're back,' he whispers, his mouth so close I can taste the toothpaste on his breath.

'I didn't mean to wake you,' I reply, stroking the side of his face with my thumb.

'Yeah, yeah,' he murmurs, kissing me slowly.

'Okay, so I did.' I smile as our bodies move against each other in a slow rhythm.

'Hey, I'm not complaining.' He kisses the side of my face, sending butterflies across my skin.

'No?'

His fingers glide across my back, radiating warmth. He brushes his lips against my ear. 'Definitely not.'

We make love until morning, late enough to be precariously close to the time when the children are due to wake.

We dress slowly – between kisses – and while Ryan pulls on his T-shirt, I find myself raising a question I've thought about a lot lately. 'You never talk about your wife,' I say softly.

Ryan, T-shirt half on, stops what he's doing and I wonder whether bringing this up was a mistake. I search his eyes anxiously.

'I know.' He finishes pulling on the T-shirt and sits on the bed next to me. 'I never used to think of myself as one of those guys who couldn't express their feelings.

But I guess I've proven comprehensively since Amy died that that's exactly what I am.'

He pauses.

'It might help to talk about her sometimes,' I offer, but as the words tumble from my mouth, I realize what a hypocrite I am. I haven't talked about Jason – or my cancelled wedding – to *anyone*. Not properly, anyway. And yet somehow this feels different, in another league. What Ryan has been through puts my problems in the shade.

Ryan nods, as if he believes what I'm saying – he just doesn't know how to do it. Then he stands up and goes to the window, his back to me.

'We met when we were both just out of college,' he says, keeping his voice steady. 'I'd played the field a lot. Never found anyone I wanted to get serious with. Then I met Amy and all that changed.'

'What was she like?' I ask.

He turns slowly, leans on the window-sill and smiles, transported back to another time, another place. 'Smart. Funny. Forthright. She would never have taken any shit from me.' He laughs.

'No?' I smile.

'Uh-uh.' He shakes his head fondly. 'The way I was when you first met me, the *mess* I was, she'd have hated that. She'd have said, "For Chrissake, Ryan, pull yourself together. Get a shave and stop being such an asshole."'

'Don't be so hard on yourself,' I tell him. 'You went through a lot. Not many people have to cope with being widowed and left with two young children.'

'I didn't handle it well,' he insists. 'Right from the beginning, I didn't handle it well at all.'

I don't say anything.

'When I got the call to say she was in hospital, she'd been in a car crash, I – I . . .' He pauses to gather his thoughts. 'It's difficult to describe what I was feeling. I just couldn't take it in. I *wouldn't* take it in – wouldn't believe it. She'd only been on her way to collect her friend, Keeley, less than five miles away. They were going shopping and I was watching the kids. Samuel was still real young and – well, you know how demanding tiny babies can be on their moms. This was supposed to be an afternoon off for her.'

'So what happened?' I ask.

He closes his eyes and lets out a long sigh. 'It was a head-on collision with some guy who'd just held up a 7–11. He was driving like a maniac, turned a corner without looking and basically ended up in the windshield of Amy's car.'

'Did *he* live?' I ask.

'No. And it's a good thing, 'cause I'd have killed him otherwise.'

I bite my lip.

'Sorry,' he says, lowering his eyes.

'Nobody can blame you for feeling like that.'

'Anyway,' he continues, 'by the time I got to the hospital I can't remember much, except I was screaming and shouting like a lunatic, demanding to know why the doctors weren't doing more to save her. The fact was she died instantly. There was nothing they could have done.'

'And where were Samuel and Ruby while all this was happening?'

'Keeley – Amy's friend – came over to look after them. She was amazing, with hindsight. It was she who had to tell Ruby what had happened. I was just . . . too freaked out. And the worst thing is, I never even see her, these days. She waved at me once when she saw me across the street in the city but I got away from her as quickly as I could. I guess that sums up my attitude to the whole thing since it happened. To pretend it never did.'

'That's why there are no pictures of Amy.'

He screws up his nose. 'This is stupid . . . simplistic – but the fact is that it's always hurt too much looking at her, talking about her, thinking about her. So I guess, without even knowing it, I decided early on I wasn't going to do any of that. Which I know isn't good for the kids and probably isn't all that good for me either.'

'You're talking about her now,' I point out.

'Yeah, I am.' He pauses. 'And, actually, it feels okay. Good, even.'

I smile.

'You know,' he continues, turning back to the window, 'I think Amy would have approved of you, Zoe.'

'Really?' I'm taken aback.

'Yeah,' he replies. 'She would.'

I feel sudden panic about this statement, about whether I've misinterpreted what Ryan might be expecting from this relationship. I mean, yes, I like him a lot. And, okay, spending time with him certainly beats moping in my mother's spare bedroom.

But he's not Jason.

I look up at him again and tell myself I'm imagining

309

things. He has poured out his heart to me because the timing is right for him to do so. He's moving on – he'd do the same with anyone. No, this is still very much a fling, for him and me.

Suddenly the creak of the door breaks my train of thought and Samuel's unruly blond curls appear round it like the top of a vanilla ice cream. 'Zo-eee?' he mumbles sleepily. 'I want Cheerios. Please.'

Ryan walks over to him, picks him up and gives him a huge hug. 'Zoe and I are coming downstairs now, Buster, so we'll get you some, okay? She was in here having a talk with me about something.'

Just as I get downstairs, I'm contemplating when to go over and see Trudie when my phone beeps to announce the arrival of a new text message.

'Don't pick yr hat yet, lv,' it reads. 'Weddings off.'

Chapter 68

Less than half an hour later Trudie comes over. Her eyes are so bloodshot from crying she might have spent the last twenty years drinking vodka for breakfast.

'He can't have called it off just like that?' I ask.

'No, no, he didn't,' she clarifies. 'He says he still loves me. But he wants time to work out what he needs to do.'

I sigh as we wander outside to collect the mail. 'You did the right thing,' I say, feeling about as qualified to give advice on the matter as Tinky Winky.

'I was right to accept his proposal in a packed bar, then drop a bombshell on him twenty minutes later?' she says. 'I take it you're kidding?'

'Okay, your timing wasn't great,' I admit, 'but lots of people would have done the same thing in that bar. I mean, talk about pressure. That woman in the blue top looked ready to garrotte you if you'd said no.'

'Maybe. But the thing is . . . Are you all right? Zoe, what's up?'

'What? Oh . . .' I stare at the letter in my hand. 'I've told you about these funny letters Ryan's been getting.'

'Yes, I remember you saying.'

'Well, it looks like he's got another.'

'Christ!' Trudie exclaims. 'Have you asked him about them? I mean, you two are an item now, so it'd be perfectly reasonable.'

'We're not *an item*.'

She raises an eyebrow. 'Whatever you say, love.'

It's much later in the day, when the children are tucked up in bed, that I finally get to speak to Ryan. 'You had another of these today,' I tell him, strangely sheepish as I hand over the envelope.

He's about to take it when he realizes what it is. 'Shit. I thought they'd dried up.'

He takes the envelope and stuffs it into his back pocket, then carries on looking for a beer in the fridge. I feel about as satisfied with his response as someone who's queued up at a customer-services department for three hours only to find it closed.

When I first saw one of those letters I was mildly intrigued. Back then, I was nothing more than an observer in Ryan's life. They were a jigsaw piece in an incomplete picture I had of him: bad boy, womanizer, alluring scoundrel.

But now that I'm *more* than an observer, I can't help feeling something else about them, something I don't like.

What Ryan and I have may be little more than an extended holiday romance, an amorous diversion from the realities of life, but the reappearance of these letters represents a dark reminder of his past – and potentially his present. They are a reminder that, no matter how convincing he is when he snuggles up to me, no matter how loving and tender he appears, Ryan is no boy-next-door.

The writer of these letters, whoever she is, once found solace in his arms as I do. And, no matter how silly this is – *for God's sake, I'm still in love with someone else!* – that makes me feel strangely insecure. Jealous, even. And it isn't nice.

'Um . . . who are they from?' I ask, trying to be non-chalant.

He spins round and scrutinizes my face. I'm clearly about as good at nonchalance as I am at lion-taming.

'It's someone I had a *thing* with one time,' he tells me. 'A very brief thing. It was absolutely nothing. No big deal. Really.'

'She doesn't seem to think so,' I can't help pointing out.

'Well, I know, but I have a very simple tactic. Ignore her letters. They're really not a big deal.'

'What if she finds out about me? I'm not going to have some bunny-boiler trying to get me, am I?'

'Nah,' he says dismissively. 'She's a psycho, but I'd back you in a fight any day.'

I feel about as reassured as someone who'd just found out Sweeney Todd had been assigned to do their cut-and-blow.

'Don't *worry*,' he stresses. 'Anyway, she doesn't know about you.'

Don't worry. Words guaranteed to make me worried.

'Okay, then.' I can think of only one way to put my

mind at rest. 'If you're convinced she doesn't know about me, maybe I could see the letter.'

'What? You don't want to—'

'Ryan, I won't sleep otherwise,' I interrupt. 'Come on, humour me.'

'I can think of far better ways of humouring you.' He smiles.

I reach into his pocket. He snatches the letter out of my hand so rapidly he nearly takes my fingers with it.

'I'm really worried now.'

'Okay,' he concedes. 'You win. But at least let *me* open it.'

I watch as he rips open the envelope and stares at the page. His expression is difficult to read.

'Well?'

'You don't want to see this.' He puts the letter behind his back.

'I do!' I squeal, attempting to wrestle it off him.

'No, really you don't,' he says, twisting away from me again.

'Yes, really I do,' I reply, knowing I'm as likely to defeat Ryan physically as Cherie Blair is to win the Eurovision Song Contest.

'No, you—'

'Ryan!' I snap. 'If you don't let me see that letter I'm only going to think it's about ten times worse than it probably is. So, show me it, will you?'

He hesitates. Then, slowly, he brings the letter round to where I can see it and, reluctantly, hands it to me.

The Nearly-Weds

Ryan
You bastard. You absolute bastard.
    And do you know what makes this so much worse? She
is at least two dress sizes bigger than me.
    Juliet

I look up at him, my mouth ajar.
'Okay,' he says. 'So maybe she does know about you.'

Chapter 69

To: Zoemmoore@hotnet.co.uk
From: Helen@Hmoore.mailserve.co.uk

Dear Zoe,

I cannot believe you're not coming home for Christmas.
I *cannot believe* it!

After all we've been through this year, I'd thought at the very least we could sit down as a family and have a nice Christmas together. Is that really too much to ask? I mean, it's not as if I haven't sat back and let you go off to America without so much as batting an eyelid. Publicly, anyway. I've just sat at home worrying myself sick but not saying a word because your father wouldn't let me.

If you're concerned about seeing Jason out and about, then don't be. I haven't so much as bumped into him in the street – and neither has anyone else. It is as if he's disappeared off the face of the planet. Which is fine by me. Mars would be the best place for him.

I know this probably won't make the slightest difference to your decision, but I was intending to tell you something when you came home. Something extremely important that I found out at my appointment with Dr Ahmed yesterday. It isn't pancreatic cancer or wheat intolerance but I promise you it's just as serious. So much so that I really don't feel I can break the news to you in an email. Or over the phone. But if you can't even be bothered coming home, then I won't bother telling you.

So I hope you're satisfied, young lady, that's all I can say.
Mum

Can my mum really be seriously ill?

The thought flickers fleetingly across my brain. Then I remind myself that her hypochondria is nothing less than world class. She once had an ingrowing toenail and thought it would result in amputation.

No, I'm absolutely confident that when Mum says she has something as serious as pancreatic cancer she could be referring to anything from a lingering migraine to nits.

That doesn't make me feel any better about the email, though. The absence of kisses at the bottom stabs my heart.

The truth is I *agonized* about whether or not to go home for Christmas. On the one hand, I think I would have liked to see Mum and Dad. (Oh, God, just saying 'I think' probably makes me an even poorer excuse for a daughter than I already am.) But there's no doubt about what the overriding theme of my return home would have been – the wedding. And, to be honest, I want to spend Christmas talking about the wedding about as much as I want to retrain as a mortician.

The other reason for my anxiety about going back is

an even simpler one: Jason. I'd be as desperate to bump into him as I would be terrified to do so. And, frankly, at this time of year I'd prefer to be bursting with festive cheer than with raging paranoia, thank you very much.

So, in the end, my decision just sort of happened. To describe it as a decision makes it sound more deliberate than it was. I couldn't decide what to do so I didn't do anything. Which means I'm still here, with less than a week to go to Christmas and no practical way of getting home even if I wanted to. Every flight to Manchester will undoubtedly be booked by now, with the exception of seats so pricy an oil baron would need a second mortgage to get one.

But that doesn't stop me feeling rotten. And I've got to put my mind at rest by finding out what this mystery illness of my mother's is.

The time difference forces me to wait until the next morning to phone home and I do so while I'm making the kids' breakfast. Mum answers after three rings.

'Hello, Zoe.' She sounds suitably wounded.

'Mum, what's all this about you being seriously ill?' I ask. 'What's the matter with you?'

'I never said I was— Look, I just said *it was serious*. I never said I was being immediately hospitalized or anything like that, so you don't need to worry.'

'So what is it?' I insist.

She sighs. 'It's not something I want to discuss on the phone.'

'Right,' I say, through gritted teeth, trying to hide the fact that I want to throttle her.

'It's just not the sort of thing you talk about in a long-distance phone call,' she continues haughtily. 'So, if you're that intrigued, you'll have to come home for Christmas like any normal daughter would.'

'Mum, are you blackmailing me?' I ask, unable to conceal my annoyance.

'No!' she cries, outraged.

I pause for a second, thinking. 'Put Dad on,' I say decisively.

'He's not here,' she informs me. 'And, anyway, he's under strict instructions not to discuss my medical issues with you so there's no point in trying to go down that route.'

'You're a very frustrating woman sometimes, Mum,' I tell her.

'Ha!' she squeals. 'I'm frustrating? You're the one who's left me with precisely four and a half pounds too much of organic bronze turkey, thanks to your no-show.'

I take a deep breath. 'Look, Mum, just tell me something. This thing you've got that Dr Ahmed has diagnosed, is it going to kill you?'

'No.'

'Is it going to leave you in any way significantly debilitated?'

'No.'

'Right, then,' I say. 'I'm going now.'

'Zoe,' she says, before I disconnect the call, 'it isn't anything to worry about, this thing. It's just . . . I wanted to talk to you about it in person, that's all. Oh, it doesn't matter, it's not urgent. You'll be coming back soon after

319

Christmas, won't you, even if it's not for Christmas itself?'

'Y-yes,' I say unsurely.

'Right, then,' she says. 'We'll have a chat then. And don't worry, will you?'

Chapter 70

The party was gearing up to be the social highlight of my month until I saw a printout of an invitation shortly after Ryan emailed them. Apparently, with the backing of both children, he took the crucial decision to introduce a theme to the event that I feel distinctly uneasy about.

'Does it *have* to be fancy dress?' I ask him.

'I thought you Brits loved costume parties. We usually only have them at Halloween. But the kids convinced me it'd be a good idea to have one now in your honour,' he grins.

'Great,' I reply.

'Do you still have nothing to wear?' he asks.

'No,' I say despondently.

'Well, that's okay,' he says brightly. 'There's a great little store in the city that I know you'll be able to get something from.'

'Oh, er . . . I'm sure I've left it too late now,' I cough. 'I mean, I'm happy to sit out the "fancy dress" bit.'

'What?' asks Ruby, incredulous.

'*Nooooo, Zo-eee!*' squeals Samuel.

'You can't be the only one not to join in,' Ruby pouts.

Oh, God. I *hate* fancy dress. I've hated fancy dress since I went to Louise Bennett's sixth birthday party dressed as a cocker spaniel, my mum having thought I was supposed to go as 'something furry'. When I got there every other girl was dressed as a *fairy*.

'It's all right for you lot,' I tell Ruby. 'Your outfits are fantastic.'

Ruby is going as Island Princess Barbie and Samuel is going as Dash from *The Incredibles*, after Ryan took them to choose their costumes last week.

'And so will yours be, Zoe,' she beams.

I wish I felt quite so enthusiastic.

I start with the store Ryan recommended but find it closed. So, I proceed to traipse round every costume emporium the entire state of Massachussetts has to offer, but by four thirty. I'm still out of luck. Until I reach one final store – which is open. The problem is, it's not exactly overflowing with choice.

'So, these are *really* the last two you've got in my size?' I ask the storekeeper impatiently. 'Really?'

'Yeah, hon. Really,' he drawls.

'I mean, you haven't got something a bit less . . . full-on?'

He shakes his head.

I'm picturing my perfect fancy-dress outfit as I speak. I'm thinking Princess Leia, cool, a little bit retro, and with the added bonus of *everyone* having fancied her in their youth.

'Nothing from *Star Wars*?' I ask, hoping to jog his memory.

'We've got a Jabba the Hutt left, but it's not in your size,' he tells me.

'Oh. So, it's these two then, is it?'

'Uh-huh.'

I look at the first choice and decide on the spot that it's out of the question. It's a saucy nurse's outfit, the sort of thing Benny Hill's sidekicks wore in the early 1980s.

Which leaves me with the other. Not exactly what I had in mind, but at least I won't be showing as much flesh as I would with the alternative.

The store assistant looks at his watch.

'I suppose I'll have this one, then,' I say, heaving the costume on to his counter.

'Sure,' he replies, clearly relieved to be getting rid of me.

By the time I've humped the outfit back to Hope Falls, I'm exhausted and never want to look at it again. I'm also having second thoughts about whether or not I should have given Jabba the Hutt a go.

'What did you get, Zoe?' cries Ruby, rushing to the door.

'I'm really not sure about this,' I mutter, unwrapping my parcel.

'Wow!' exclaims Samuel, as I unfold it. 'Wow! Wow! Wow!' But he seems to be the only one who's impressed.

'It's, um, nice.' Ruby smiles diplomatically.

'Oh, God, it's awful, isn't it?' I grimace.

'It's great,' Ryan whispers, kissing me when the kids are looking the other way. 'You'll be in it and that's all that matters.'

Chapter 71

Ruby and Samuel have put up so many garlands around the place that the living room looks like a grotto.

Ryan is dressed – heart-stoppingly – as a cowboy. When I first see him I wonder if he somehow sensed my private fantasies while we were horse-riding in New Hampshire. I don't give the issue too much thought, though. I'm too busy admiring his bum again.

When the first people arrive, Ryan goes to greet them at the door. On the way he turns to me. 'You're not dressed yet,' he points out.

'Are you really making me go through with this?'

'Come on, Zoe!' squeals Samuel. 'Costume! Costume!'

Ryan frowns. 'If you feel bad in it then don't. I want you to enjoy yourself.'

Suddenly I feel like the world's biggest bore. Everyone else is getting into the spirit of things and I'm obsessing about whether or not I look daft. At a fancy-dress party, for God's sake.

'No, you're right,' I decide, determined not to be a party-pooper. 'It's only a bit of a laugh, isn't it? I'll go upstairs and slip on my costume now.'

In the event, it's about as easy to 'slip' into this particular costume as it is to cha-cha across a tightrope in a pair of Christian Louboutin studded booties. It takes me no less than forty-five minutes to get ready. I consider popping my head round the door to see if anyone could come up and help – Trudie, ideally – but all I can hear is people mingling happily.

When my costume is finally in place, I squeeze out of my bedroom, make my way across the landing and peer down the stairs.

I see Barbara and Mike King dressed tastefully in Roman togas and curse myself for not having come up with the same idea. All I'd have needed was a couple of sheets and that pair of ethnic flip-flops I got from New Look in Manchester airport.

Still, too late now.

Nancy, Tallulah's mum, has come as Cruella de Vil, and is stunning in a long black wig and Dalmatian coat. Her husband, Ash, is dressed unoriginally as a Hell's Angel, and little Tallulah is a teddy bear.

I scan the room for the other nannies and spot Felicity in the corner. She's wearing a sixteenth-century-style dress, all bodice and ribbons, a beautiful creation that wouldn't have looked out of place in *Shakespeare in Love*. Her long red hair is tousled into ringlets down her back, her green eyes accentuated by soft, smoky makeup. In short, she looks totally and utterly gorgeous.

'Oh, God,' I mutter, doubts about my outfit kicking in once again.

I put one of my feet on the first stair to get a better

view of everyone else. There's a nun, an angel, a jester, a 1920s flapper and a woman from Ryan's work dressed as a character from *The Matrix* who looks particularly fantastic. In fact, they *all* look fantastic.

What the *hell* was I thinking? I just *cannot* go down dressed like this. I *will not* go down dressed like this.

I'm suddenly hit by a flash of inspiration and Plan B. A brilliant Plan B, actually. I can turn round, put on my jeans and dig out my old bandanna (the one I use to keep my hair off my face when I'm doing my makeup) to tie round my neck and pass myself off as Calamity Jane.

Perfect! I can't *believe* I didn't think of it earlier!

Relief sweeps through me as I turn round – when something goes wrong. Horribly wrong.

Perhaps it's because I've never attempted to turn round at the top of a flight of stairs wearing a pair of webbed rubber feet. Whatever it is, something happens to the foam padding at my knees that tangles it with a leg – or a foot, or maybe even my tail. God, have I got a tail?

The next thing I know, I've got this horrendous time-standing-still sensation. I'm conscious of losing my step – and falling – and bumping – and falling – and bumping. The only positive thing I can say about the experience is that, with all my padding, it doesn't hurt much.

But, believe me, that's little consolation.

As I land in a heap at the bottom of the stairs, the head of my costume having half come off and one of the feet lost altogether, I wonder why I can't hear anything and why everything is pitch-black.

I sit up and attempt to straighten my head so I can at least see through the eyes.

Tallulah is standing in front of me, sobbing. 'Mommy!' she gasps. 'Mommy! Look what happened to Big Bird. Is he dead?'

Chapter 72

'I never even liked *Sesame Street*,' I grumble, after my Big Bird costume has been abandoned and I've tracked down Trudie.

'You're sure you're not injured?' she asks, genuinely concerned.

'No, that's about the only positive thing I can say about that costume,' I reply. 'All the rubber made such good padding I could have fallen down the southern face of Krakatoa and remained bruise-free.'

The party's in full swing and everyone's getting into the festive spirit. Mike King has had at least six glasses of mulled wine and keeps having to be reminded to keep his toga closed.

Trudie and I have spent the last hour with scores of children, rehearsing an impromptu nativity play in which absolutely nobody would agree to be the donkey. We've had to make do with Eamonn as a zebra.

'I was lucky to find this costume,' Trudie says.

She's in the nurse's outfit I turned down at the fancy-dress shop. It was small in the first place but on Trudie, well, I'm surprised she wasn't arrested on the way here.

'It was the last one in the place. I can't believe no one wanted it, can you?'

'No,' I lie, straightening my bandanna and picking a crusty bit of exfoliator off it.

I remind myself that things could be worse.

Poor Trudie hasn't heard from Ritchie since his aborted proposal in the bar and – despite her Oprah-worthy attempts to tell everyone she's 'moving on' – she hasn't been very convincing.

'Hey,' Trudie nudges me, 'have you seen those two?'

Amber is engaged in deep conversation with the Reverend Paul.

'I don't care what Amber says,' I say, 'there's *definitely* chemistry between them.'

'You're not looking hard enough,' Trudie points out. 'I don't think she's trying to deny it any more.'

Puzzled, I look again – and realize exactly what Trudie's talking about: they're holding hands.

'They're not!' I exclaim. 'They didn't! They couldn't! They're an item?'

Trudie sniggers. 'Amber apparently decided – despite the non-alignment of their moons – that their stars were on the same trajectory so that made it okay. Or summat like that.'

I'm shaking my head when I feel someone jab my shoulder sharply.

'I haven't seen Ryan this whole party,' Felicity declares, looking as happy as someone who's just had their wheels clamped. 'Can you tell me where he is, please?'

'Er, I'm not sure,' I say. 'I last saw him getting some

more beers from the garage but . . . Is there anything I can help you with, Felicity?'

'I doubt it,' she snaps, and turns on her heel.

'Have I done something to offend her?' I ask, bewildered.

'No idea, love.' Trudie shrugs. 'She's not said anything to me. I was with her one afternoon last week so I'm sure she would have mentioned it if there was something wrong. Oh, speaking of which, I meant to tell you . . .'

'What?'

'I'm really sorry, but I let slip about you and Ryan.'

'Oh, Trudie,' I groan. 'What if she tells Tallulah and *she* tells Ruby and Samuel? We didn't want them to know. I mean, it's only a fling.'

'I know, I know,' Trudie insists. 'But she'll definitely keep it quiet. Honestly, I made her swear on her Laura Ashley shoe collection she wouldn't breathe a word of it to anyone. Sorry, love.'

I'm annoyed with Trudie. But somehow I can't bring myself to be *too* annoyed – she's one of those people I find it impossible to be cross with.

However, I do want to satisfy myself that Felicity will keep her mouth shut. I follow in the direction she went, through the throngs of people in the hall and down the corridor to the kitchen. I spot her from behind, her hand on her hip and one arm leaning on the door frame.

'So, how do you like my outfit?' she's saying to someone, before I have a chance to approach her. 'Appropriate, don't you think?'

'How's that?'

I recognize the voice from the kitchen immediately. It's Ryan's.

I find myself shuffling backwards behind the pillar in the hallway so that I can hear what they're saying without being seen. It's the sort of thing people do in Agatha Christie films – and I almost kick myself for not dressing up as someone from *Death on the Nile*.

'You mean you can't tell?' Felicity laughs. 'Oh, darling Ryan, my darling, darling Ryan. You Americans really should read more. I'm Juliet, of course. As in *Romeo and Juliet*. As in the pet name you gave me.'

My blood runs cold. Juliet. Never mind Juliet as in *Romeo and Juliet*. How about Juliet as in Ryan's letter-writer? It can't be true. Surely to God Felicity isn't behind those?

'My recollection,' replies Ryan sternly, 'is that *you* gave yourself that nickname. I told you I'd read more Steinbeck than Shakespeare.'

Felicity throws up her hands in despair. 'You're such a spoilsport. Well, I don't care what you say, you're still my Romeo. There's no wriggling out of it. But, then, that's not all you are, is it?'

'Felicity,' Ryan snaps, with a sharpness that could have sliced a lemon, 'I don't have time for this. I have guests to attend to.'

'You're a liar as well,' she states.

'That's enough. I'm not having this conversation.'

'Charming, I must say.' She tuts. 'And to think you didn't even invite me to the party. After all we've been through.'

'You're right,' he replies. 'I didn't invite you. So how come you're here?'

'I was invited by your new girlfriend.'

Ryan doesn't say anything.

'Does poor little Zoe know what a liar you are yet?'

Ryan still doesn't speak.

'No,' she responds for him. 'I bet she doesn't. I bet she's caught up in the whirlwind romance you caught me up in too, isn't she? So, when are you going to throw her away like yesterday's trash? Because that's what happens to all of the women in your life, isn't it, Ryan? You hook them in with the I've-got-such-an-injured-soul-because-of-my-poor-dead-wife routine. Then you seduce them. Then you get bored with them. Then you dump them. That's right, isn't it?'

'Well, maybe, Felicity. Maybe you've managed to analyse my personality. Maybe you know me better than anyone else after only two fucks and—'

'Three!' she squeals.

'Whatever. The point I'm making is, you *don't* know me. You don't know what's going on in my life. And I don't want you to, either.'

Then his voice softens. 'Listen, I'm sorry I hurt you. I'm genuinely sorry. Because I didn't mean to. Really I didn't.'

'Well that's hardly any conso—'

'But, as I've told you before, it wasn't anything more than . . . Look, Felicity.' He sighs. 'It's over. And I'd just like to get on with my life without any more of those letters. Please.'

He sounds genuinely regretful, as if he's reaching out

to her to see reason and hopes, perhaps naïvely, that there can be some sort of resolution to this. But if Felicity was a cartoon character I suspect steam would be coming out of her ears.

'Can I point something out to you?' she snaps. 'About Zoe and about me?'

'If you must,' he says wearily.

'I attended the Institut Villa Pierrefeu finishing-school. I speak four languages. I have prospective employers fighting over me. *And* I am a perfect size four. *She*, on the other hand, is a comprehensive-school flunkey who – when she's not dressing as a seven-foot yellow canary – is dressing from Dorothy Perkins!'

'Dorothy Perkins?' Ryan repeats, mystified.

Felicity nods, as if she's just revealed something tantamount to my having contracted a deadly contagious disease.

I'm waiting for Ryan to jump to my defence. To say he doesn't give a toss that I dressed as Big Bird – in fact, he thought it was the best costume since someone won an Oscar for *Moulin Rouge*. To say that he thinks Chanel is overrated and, actually, he'd choose a woman who dressed at Dorothy Perkins any day of the week.

To say something – anything – that tells Felicity once and for all what he really feels about me. I'm waiting with such bated breath my lungs feel like they're about to implode.

'Whatever,' he replies.

'Whatever?' repeats Felicity. For the first time in this conversation, I feel almost as exasperated as she clearly does.

'Felicity, you've nothing to be jealous of when it comes to Zoe,' he continues.

'I never said I was jealou—'

'It's just a fling,' he interrupts. 'Nothing more than a fling.'

Chapter 73

I creep backwards and lose myself in the packed hallway until I stumble across Trudie. She's with Ruby, Samuel, Eamonn and Andrew and they're singing such a tuneless version of 'Silent Night' that I'm amazed everyone's eardrums remain intact.

'You okay to watch Ruby and Samuel for a bit longer?' I ask, surprised to hear my voice wobbling. 'I need to go for a walk.'

'Course.' She nods. 'Something up?'

'Oh, nothing. I'm feeling a bit light-headed after my fall. A bit of fresh air might do me good.'

I make my way through the house, feeling claustrophobic and numb. I'm suffocated by the colour and noise of the party – glasses clinking, children laughing, music pounding.

I feel a flicker of relief when I spot the conservatory door, which opens on to the garden, and I head towards it single-mindedly.

'Hey, Zoe,' I hear someone say. I feel a hand tighten on my elbow and turn hazily. It's Amber.

'You've heard about Paul and me, then?' she whispers, with a beaming smile.

'Oh, er, yes,' I reply vaguely. 'I – I'm really happy for you, Amber. I thought you'd make a good couple.'

'We do, don't we?' she says dreamily. 'You were absolutely right. I mean, cosmically speaking, we're not a perfect match but . . . well, he's lovely. And I suppose that's all that matters.'

I try to smile and feel guilty that it proves so difficult. I'm happy for Amber, really I am, but her budding relationship is the last thing on my mind. 'When did you get together?' I manage. It's the only question I can think of.

'We've been going out for a couple of weeks now. I bumped into him while I was shopping and we went for a coffee. He's one of the most fascinating people I've ever met,' she continues. 'He's . . . *deep* in a way I've never encountered before.'

'Deep,' I repeat.

'Mmm.' She nods. 'Deep *and* nice. It's a wonderful combination. So, what about you, Zoe?' she asks. 'Hasn't there been anybody over here who's taken your fancy? I'm sure you haven't been short of admirers.'

I glance up and see Ryan entering the room as he uncorks a bottle of wine. He catches my eye and smiles. Suddenly I feel dizzy. 'Uh, sorry, Amber, I need to step outside for a minute,' I tell her.

'Are you okay? You're a bit pale.'

'I'm fine,' I mutter. 'Honestly. Thanks for asking.'

As I step outside, I breathe deeply and the cold air fills my lungs. I head towards the bottom of the garden where no one can see me, Ryan's words echoing in my head.

I know I've said it myself time and time again, but hearing *him* say it had stung so badly.

It's only a fling . . . nothing more than a fling.

I fight back tears and gaze up into the dense, cloudy sky. Why am I so bothered about it? Isn't it exactly how *I'd* seen our relationship? Suddenly I hear footsteps behind me and spin round, hoping and dreading in equal measure that it might be Ryan.

But it isn't. It's Felicity.

'I saw you creeping off, you know.'

Her staccato voice grates on me.

'Right,' I reply coldly. In the light of what I overheard her saying, this isn't much of a comeback. But I'm afraid that if I try to say anything else I'll cry.

'You heard what I said, didn't you?' she asks.

I nod.

'I'm sorry, Zoe,' she offers, lowering her head.

'Are you?' I ask, hoping I sound at least a *bit* formidable now. Not like someone who'd lose at conkers with a five-year-old.

'Yes,' she replies. 'I am. But let me explain something to you. What Ryan did to me was so *awful*, he's turned me into a – a *monster*. I'm convinced of it. And I'm not a monster, Zoe, really I'm not. You know that, don't you?'

'What about all those weird letters?' I say, exasperated. 'Forgive me for saying this, Felicity, but that isn't my definition of well-balanced behaviour.'

She bursts into tears. I don't just mean a little sniffle,

either. I mean spontaneous, uncontrollable, struggling-for-breath crying. It's one of the most disturbing things I've ever seen. I hadn't thought Felicity was built with tear ducts until now.

'I – I know,' she manages, between sobs. 'You're – you're absolutely r-right. B-believe me, if you'd told me a year ago that I'd be sending letters to my unrequited love I wouldn't have believed you. It's not very . . . dignified, is it?'

'No, Felicity.' I sigh. 'It's not.'

'I loved him, Zoe. I really, really loved him. I don't know if you can understand that. Have you ever loved someone who didn't return it? Have you, Zoe?'

Have I ever loved someone who didn't return it? Oh, God, if only she knew. Despite an acute sense of irony, I feel compelled to put my arm round her. As I reach over to her and pull her towards me, I'm shocked by how fragile she feels. Her shoulder is so bony I'm surprised an anatomy student hasn't mistaken her for a study aid.

'Let me tell you something about unrequited love, Zoe,' she says. 'It hurts like mad.'

I close my eyes. 'I probably understand more than you think,' I mutter.

Felicity has acted like a fool, but I understand the torture she's been through. I understand what it's like to be consumed by desire for someone you were once so close to – but you know will never be yours again.

'Do you, Zoe?' She sniffs. 'Do you understand?'

'Yes, I do.'

'Can I tell you something?' she continues, with reddened eyes.

'Of course.'

'And, believe me,' she says, 'I say this with no hidden agenda now. I'm saying this as your friend.'

I nod reluctantly.

'All those things I said to Ryan back there – I said them because I was angry and hurt.'

'I know.'

'A lot of it was nonsense – the things I said about you were awful.'

'Look, don't worry about it,' I say dismissively. 'It's water under the bridge.'

'*But*,' she interrupts, 'there was one part of it I meant. One part of it, Zoe, is absolutely true.'

I pull back and study her face. She's completely sincere. There's no doubt about that.

'Ryan is using you, Zoe. That's what he does. I don't think he can help it. When I was with him, I followed a long line of women he'd been out with after Amy's death. Women he used then threw away without a second thought. The fact is, he's not in love with you or me or anyone. Unfortunately I think he's still in love with his wife.'

'You've got Ryan and me wrong, Felicity,' I tell her finally. 'Ryan and I . . . it's just a—'

'A fling?'

I don't answer.

'That's exactly what I thought when he and I were together, Zoe. But isn't he getting under your skin? Aren't you starting to miss him when he's not there? To enjoy the feel of his arms round you a little too much?'

'I – I don't know.'

'The point I'm making, Zoe – as your friend and nothing else – is that if you don't get out *now* you'll end up as hurt and as damaged by it as I am.'

Chapter 74

I head back into the house to look for the children, so disoriented by everything I've heard in the past hour that I feel as if I've stepped off a merry-go-round.

As hurt and as damaged . . . as I am.

One thing is for sure. After 14 April – my wedding day – I've had quite enough of that sort of thing to keep me going until Christmas 2080, thank you very much. So have I really been getting drawn into another relationship that so obviously represents trouble it almost has flashing lights?

It can't be true, surely. Ryan is supposed to be a distraction from my woes, a bit of light relief – not another problem.

Oh, God. I could be one of those weird, dysfunctional women who only ever get together with *bad men*, who thrive on the drama of being used and abused.

I hadn't thought I liked being used and abused. I'd always thought my dream man would be someone who'd want to shower me with love and kisses and always put the toilet seat down. But maybe not.

Maybe a pattern's emerging. First Jason leaves me

standing at the altar, and now Ryan's only in it for a bit of fun and is bang on course to leave me heartbroken. But how can I be heartbroken when it's only a fling? It *is* a fling, isn't it? Oh, God, I'm sick of that word.

I stomp into the hallway and spot Ryan with Barbara King, who has been hitting the mulled wine with almost as much purpose as her husband has.

I watch as she drains her glass, slams it on the table beside her and throws her arms round Ryan like a sex-starved groupie who hasn't had a sniff of a Y chromosome since 1904.

As she takes off his cowboy hat and whispers in his ear, I can't help thinking it's a gesture some might call overly friendly. In fact, it couldn't be more friendly if she had her hand down his chaps.

My eyes widen as Barbara, presumably neither noticing nor caring if anyone is looking, lowers her hand to Ryan's backside, her manicured fingers squeezing one of his buttocks like it's her personal executive-stress ball. Then she stands on tiptoe and kisses his ear.

My chest tightens and I don't want to watch this any longer.

I rush into the living room in search of Trudie, desperate for someone to confide in. But when I get there, I can see she's got other things on her mind.

'Zoe! Zoe!' squeals Ruby, jumping up and down. 'Trudie's going to get married and I'm going to be a flower-girl!'

Trudie lets go of Ritchie's hand and holds out her fingers to me. She's wearing a delicate diamond ring you can tell is beautiful even though her hand is shaking so much you'd think it was experiencing turbulence.

'Is it – is it true?' I gasp.

Trudie's eyes are awash with tears and, although she tries to speak, her lip is trembling too much to let her.

'Yeah, it's true,' Ritchie answers for her. 'I've found the greatest woman in the world. There's no way I'm letting her go.'

'You really don't mind about the—' she begins.

'Sssh,' he whispers, clutching her hand. 'We can always adopt.'

With her mascara blurring, Trudie grins so widely she looks as if she might faint.

'Well done, you,' I say, hugging her as my own eyes fill again. 'Bloody well done.'

'Thanks, love,' she mutters, pulling back. 'But are you okay, Zoe? You still look a bit funny after your fall.'

I'm sure I'm an appalling friend for saying this, but despite Trudie's amazing news, the rest of the evening drags. Badly.

When we finally get rid of the last guest and put an overexcited, overtired Ruby and Samuel to bed, Ryan tries to put his arms round me. But I wriggle away.

'Is everything okay?' he asks, concerned.

'Oh, yeah,' I say dismissively. 'I'm just knackered, that's all. Do you mind if I help clear up in the morning and head for bed now?'

'Of course not,' he says, a hint of dejection in his eyes.

When I get into my room, I open the window and a whoosh of cold air hits my cheeks as if I'm caught in the path of a snow machine. I pull my duvet round me as I collapse into bed. I try to close my eyes but I feel far too agitated to sleep.

I'd somehow convinced myself that being with Ryan would help me get over what happened this year. But how empty it feels now, how pointless.

Who even wants a fling when it's with someone who's going to allow Barbara King to become intimately acquainted with their bottom, and when you're just one in a long line of women?

As I sit up again, my eyes are drawn to something poking out from behind my chest of drawers. I climb out of bed and retrieve it. It's the OK! magazine I bought in England on the day I left, all those months ago. The cover has coffee stains all over it, but as I leaf through the crumpled pages, I'm transported home so rapidly it's as if someone's opened a floodgate.

Suddenly I long to be in Woolton, ironing my uniform for nursery tomorrow and making sure I pack an apron to keep it clean during Christmas decoration-making season. I long to be kissing Jason goodnight as I head upstairs to bed, leaving him to watch the end of *Match of the Day*. I long to be drawing the curtains my mum made for us and jumping into bed to read a Jackie Collins until I drift off, stirring only momentarily when I feel Jason slip in next to me.

Suddenly I feel so homesick I ache.

I'm jolted out of my thoughts as a sound invades the silence. My mobile is ringing.

I suspect it's Trudie, wanting to talk about her engagement. But I can't bring myself to listen to her now, I really can't. I lean over to grab the phone and try to work out whether I can cut it off without her knowing. But it isn't her number on the screen.

It's Jason's. And for once I don't have a doubt in my mind what I'm going to do.

Chapter 75

'Jason. How are you?' My voice sounds remarkably calm, considering that my heart is pounding so hard it feels ready to leap out of my chest and tap-dance across the dressing-table.

Suddenly there's a loud crash, followed by so much clattering I have to hold the phone away from my ear. Then it stops.

'Zoe?' His voice is instantly recognizable, instantly familiar, instantly heart-stopping. 'Zoe, are you there? Sorry about that. I dropped the phone.'

Jason is uncharacteristically nervous, which throws me.

'Zoe? You are there, aren't you?'

'Yes,' I reply, then can't think of anything else to say.

'Zoe, I've thought about making this phone call every day for the last eight months. In fact, I've phoned you a few times but – well, I've always been cut off.'

I'm still stumped for something to say.

'But now that I've managed to get hold of you,' he continues, 'I don't know where to begin.'

Hearing Jason again is like the first sip of champagne

346

after months of abstinence. It's as delectable and irresistible as it's risky. I find myself craving him, longing to be with him in person. Despite this, I have to start with the obvious question. There's no alternative.

'How about telling me why you stood me up on our wedding day?' I ask.

'Of course,' he says awkwardly. 'Well, that's a good question. A question I've asked myself every second of every day since. All I can say is, it was a moment of madness.'

There's another silence.

'Are you saying you regret it?' I ask.

'*Yes*,' he says, with more than a hint of desperation. 'Yes, I regret it. It was insane.'

'Insane?'

'Utterly crazy,' he continues. 'I don't know what came over me or how to explain it.'

'Well, try.'

'Okay, okay. The truth is, I was scared. I can't put my finger on why – but I was. I suppose it was just the idea of being with one person for the rest of my life. It kept nagging at me.'

'It's called marriage, Jason,' I tell him flatly.

'I know, I know! And marriage is something I wanted. That I *do* want. But the day before the wedding, well, I was terrified. Really bloody terrified. Which is stupid because you and I had been together for so long that, logic tells me, we would have been fine for much, much longer. For ever, in fact. But that didn't stop me feeling . . . claustrophobic. Panicky. Fraught—'

'Oh, stop!'

347

'Sorry.'

I immediately wish I hadn't jumped in. I want to get to the bottom of all this, don't I? 'No,' I say. 'Carry on.'

He takes a breath. 'Right,' he continues. 'Well, the thing is, Zoe, I'd been fine about the whole getting-married thing. I mean, I loved you and was just happy to be with you without all the bells and whistles of a bloody big ceremony. But I knew you wanted to do it and that was fine. In fact, it was more than fine. But my feelings towards the whole thing seemed to change the closer we got to the day. And by the morning, when Neil and I were getting ready, it was like I was in shock. I couldn't bring myself to put my suit on. I just stood there, unable to move, unable to do anything except panic and listen to Neil getting more and more hysterical as time went on.'

I still don't say anything.

'Are you still there?' he asks.

'Yes.'

'Well, it got to ten past two and I still didn't have my suit on and all I could do was lie on my bed and try not to think about it. Try not to think about you going through what you must have been going through. I just wanted to close my eyes and block everything out.'

He pauses again.

'This isn't making me feel any better,' I lie.

'Isn't it?' he asks anxiously. 'No. I don't suppose it is. I mean, why would it? I ruined your big day. How could I possibly make that better?'

He sounds like a little boy. Hurt and bewildered because he's done something catastrophic that he can't reverse. Despite everything, I find myself wanting to reach out and hug him. To feel his arms round me. But there are 3,500 miles of ocean between us.

'Zoe,' he mumbles, 'I'd do anything to get you back.'

I hesitate. Then, 'How can you say that after what happened? After what you did?'

'Because I know now – more than ever – that I love you,' he says. 'You're the only woman I'll ever love. I know I'll never be able to turn back the clock, but I wish I could. My life's over without you, Zoe.'

'Don't be daft.'

'I mean it,' he insists. 'What I want more than anything in this world is the chance to start again with you. For you and me to get back what we had. I know I don't deserve you, but I thought you ought to know how I feel. I couldn't have lived with myself if I hadn't told you.'

I slump back on the bed, close my eyes and think. In fact, I think so much my head starts to hurt.

But no matter how hard I try, I can't help but come to one conclusion. A conclusion I know my friends, my family, my former colleagues and all the guests who turned up on my wedding day would consider so certifiably insane that nothing short of a full-frontal lobotomy would help me now.

But everyone deserves a second chance, don't they?

Chapter 76

I only have to touch Ryan's shoulder and he stirs.

'Hey,' he murmurs, with a sleepy smile. 'I was hoping you'd change your mind. I can't seem to make it through the night without you any more.'

I'm sitting on the edge of his bed, fully dressed. It takes him a second to notice this, but when he does he sits up and rubs his eyes. 'What is it? Is something the matter?'

'No,' I whisper. 'It's just—'

'Why are you dressed?' he asks, bewildered.

'Ryan, there are some issues I need to sort out back home,' I tell him. 'A couple of things have happened and I need to . . . well, I need to deal with them.'

'Okay,' he says slowly, putting his hand on my arm. 'Is there anything I can help with?'

'No,' I reply. 'I just need to go home. Quickly.'

Realization sweeps across his face. 'You're not leaving now?'

I gulp. 'There's a flight that leaves in a few hours,' I tell him. 'I couldn't believe they had a spare seat so close to Christmas but they did – so I ought to take it. There won't be another chance to get home until after Boxing Day, I'm sure.'

He stares at me, incredulous, and I feel the need to give him some sort of explanation.

'My mum's not very well,' I blurt out, feeling guilty for using my mother's hypochondria as an excuse.

'Is it serious?'

'I – I don't think so,' I mutter, 'but I probably ought to get home to make sure and . . .' I take an envelope from my back pocket. 'This should explain some things, Ryan,' I tell him. I hand it over and he takes it, his eyes not leaving mine. 'Something happened before I came here that I didn't want to discuss with anyone. So I haven't. Not with anyone. It was all too – too painful. But I hope you'll understand when you read it.'

He looks down at the letter. 'You are coming back, aren't you, Zoe?' he asks.

I bite my lip. 'I – I've left a message with the nanny agency asking them to send a replacement as soon as possible. So, whatever happens, you won't be without childcare.'

'Zoe,' he frowns, 'it's not about the childcare, for God's sake.'

Tears well in my eyes.

'I – I feel awful not being able to say goodbye to Ruby and Samuel,' I continue, pretending not to have heard him. 'Will you please give them a kiss for me and tell them I'll phone them as soon as I can? I've written them a letter too and their Christmas presents are in the cupboard next to my bed. I haven't had time to wrap them, I'm afraid, but—'

My rambling runs out of steam and I want to get out of here before the tears in my eyes spill out uncontrollably.

I'm about to leave, when Ryan kneels up on his bed and grabs my arm. Then he cups my head in his hands and kisses me as tenderly, as passionately, as beautifully as ever.

I know it's the last time we'll kiss like this and the thought overwhelms me. Despite what Felicity said. Despite what I saw Barbara doing to him. Despite how much I love Jason.

The next thing I know, tears are pouring down my cheeks and I can't stop kissing him, no matter how swollen my mouth and wet my skin.

Eventually I manage to pull away.

'I'm sorry.' I back towards the door and tear my eyes away from his bewilderment. 'I'm really sorry.'

The cab is waiting outside when I get downstairs, its engine purring. As I shut the door behind me, I lift my bag and am taken aback by how heavy it is. I feel as if I'm dragging the dead body of a large yak.

When I reach the front garden, I gaze up at Ruby's window and my stomach lurches. I just hope to God the note I've left for her and Samuel makes them realize how desperately I'll miss them: those two gorgeous children who – no matter where I end up in life – I will never, ever forget.

I think about hugging them in the mornings, their soft baby skin as warm and sweet as freshly baked biscuits, their eyes full of energy and excitement. I'm praying they're not too upset when they wake up and find I'm not there. I really couldn't bear to upset them. Yet, somehow, I know that's exactly what they'll be. Those two small children, who've already lost a mother and are now losing . . .

I feel a hard lump rise to my throat and I fight back more tears. I grip my suitcase and tell myself not to be so stupid. I'm their nanny, for God's sake, not their mum.

I hesitate. Oh, Zoe, are you doing the right thing?

I haven't a bloody clue.

The taxi driver gets out and attempts to help me put my bag in the boot. Even with both of us working on it, he complains it nearly gives him a hernia. 'The airport, right?' he checks, as I slump in the back.

'Please.'

'You going home for Christmas?' he asks, as we turn out of the road.

'I'm going home for good.'

'Awww,' he groans. 'You mean old Boston didn't get under your skin enough to keep you here?'

'You know what it's like,' I reply. 'Home sweet home, as they say.'

'Yeah, yeah. So where you from?'

'Liverpool,' I tell him. 'In England.'

'*Liver-pooohl*,' he replies, in what I can't help thinking is a closer approximation of a remote African dialect than my own accent. I suppress a smile.

'Wasn't that where the Beatles were from?'

'The very same.'

'My wife used to have a crush on Ringo Starr.'

'Really?' I reply.

As he drones on, I can't bring myself to listen. All I can think about is the taste of Ryan's mouth and the feel of his hands on my skin.

The flight is uneventful. The most exciting it gets is a couple of hours after take-off, when I've finished my in-flight breakfast and am entertaining myself by stacking the plastic cup, cartons, cutlery and sachets. By the time I've finished, every item is satisfyingly secure, neat and tidy.

As I hand it to the stewardess, an empty yoghurt carton, a plastic fork and an unopened orange juice clatter on to my tray. 'Oh, Jeez! I am so, so sorry!' blusters my neighbour, as she leans over me to scoop up the stray items. 'I really, really am. Oh, Jeez!'

She's in her mid-twenties, with olive skin and a short, funky haircut.

'Oh, man!' she mutters, as she attempts to lean into the gap between our fold-down trays to reach her spoon and nearly dislocates her shoulder.

'Hey, I'll get it,' I tell her, folding up my tray. As I bend to pick up the spoon I catch a whiff of a heady combination of at least seven duty-free perfumes.

With the spoon safely ensconced in the stewardess's trolley, my neighbour leans back in her seat and blows a stray hair out of her face. 'Thank you.' She smiles, rolling her eyes.

'Not a problem.' I chuckle.

'This is my first time out of the US,' she confides.

'Really?' I say, trying my best to look surprised.

'I'm taking a year out to travel. Manchester's my first stop – my dad has family there. Got a job lined up. You know the score.' She shrugs.

'Well, good for you,' I say, meaning it. 'I hope you love it, I really do.'

'Thanks. Hey, I don't suppose you know whether or not I need one of these, do you?' she asks, brandishing an immigration form. 'I took one earlier but haven't got a clue if I'm supposed to fill it out.'

Chapter 77

When I walk through Arrivals at Manchester airport, I find myself scanning my surroundings for Jason. It's been months since I last saw him, but I know he won't have changed. My heart is galloping as I look around, desperate to locate his tall familiar frame, his dark hair and the smile that could win anyone over.

Only it's difficult to see much through the sea of people – and as my eyes dart from person to person, I start to panic. Why the hell isn't he here? He knew which terminal I was flying into, didn't he? He hasn't left me in the lurch again, surely! Oh, God, I'm not sure I could take it . . .

I rifle through my hand luggage for my phone but suddenly spot a hand waving through the crowd. A voice is calling my name. Someone is hurtling towards me.

Only it's not Jason.

'Zo-eeee! We're here!' Mum elbows her way through the crowds using the sort of guerrilla tactics she usually reserves for the January sales. 'Zo-eeee! Over here!' She flings her arms open and propels herself into me with the force of a prop forward. 'My little girl! Oh, my little girl! Oh, I've *missed* you!'

Dad is hovering behind, his arms filled with her belongings, including what looks like a new bag, a dripping umbrella, her Whistles coat and his car keys. She's put on a little weight since I last saw her, but all in all looks as polished as ever. 'Hello, love,' he says cheerily. He attempts to peck my cheek, but Mum gets there first again.

'Ohhh!' she hollers, squeezing me so hard that I'm concerned for my vital organs. 'Oh, I've missed you!'

'Sorry, but can you move along, please?' interrupts a member of the airport staff, who doesn't look sorry at all. 'You're blocking the access route here.'

Mum disengages herself from me – momentarily at least – then links my arm and shuffles me towards the car-park pay point. 'We've got so much to organize, but you don't need to worry about *anything*. I've made up your bed already so—' She stops for a second. 'Gordon! What *are* you doing? Carry Zoe's bag, for goodness' sake!'

'Oh, no, it's fine, honestly,' I insist. The suitcase alone is enough to give Dad the backache of an overworked pack-horse.

'Don't be ridiculous, Zoe,' she says, thrusting it on to Dad, whose knees almost give way. 'After that long flight you're bound to be jet-logged.'

'Lagged,' corrects Dad, poking his head over Mum's coat.

'What?'

'I was just saying you meant jet-lagged.'

'Now,' Mum grins, ignoring him, 'things we need to organize. Well, we'll discuss it in more detail when we get home. You'll have a rest first. But you mustn't worry because I've started to make a list.'

I'm in the back of Dad's Vauxhall Vectra and halfway down the M62 before I can get a word in between Mum's wittering. It's so incessant you'd think she was being sponsored. 'How did you know to come and pick me up?' I ask.

'Jason, of course,' Mum says brightly. 'He wanted to come himself but he had a meeting to go to. It was a very important one otherwise he would have been here. And, anyway, we didn't have much on.'

As we trundle along the slow lane of the motorway, I wipe my sleeve across the condensation on the window and peer out. It's hard to see anything because of the drizzle, but everything looks so cold and grey it's like watching a fifty-year-old portable telly.

'How are you feeling, Mum?' I ask.

'Hmm . . . Not bad, not bad at all now.' She beams.

'Good. So what was wrong with you that you couldn't tell me over the phone?'

She pauses for a second. 'Don't you worry about that for now. We'll have a chat later. Let's just concentrate on one thing at a time, shall we?'

'Fine.'

'Now,' says Mum, 'I don't know if I did the right thing, but I've left a message for Anita at the nursery today to ask if your old job's still going. Of course, you might want to go for something a bit better now. All that experience you got in America must be worth something.'

Dad switches Radio 2 on as Terry Wogan introduces a Coldplay song. Mum switches it off again.

'Jason's coming round as soon as he can get away from work,' she continues, turning round to grin at me. 'D'you know? I'm *so* pleased you two have had a reconciliation. I knew you were made for each other.'

Something isn't right about this. Something definitely isn't right.

'Is something the matter, love?' asks Mum.

'I don't know,' I mutter. 'I suppose I'm just surprised at your reaction – about Jason, I mean.'

'Whatever makes you say that?' she gasps.

'You thought he was the devil incarnate last week,' I point out. 'I was dreading telling you I'd arranged to meet him because . . . well, I thought you'd think I was doing the wrong thing. You know, after what happened with the wedding and everything.'

I catch a glimpse of Dad's expression in the rear-view mirror. He isn't saying anything. I can tell immediately that this is *exactly* what he thinks.

'Oh, Zoe, we'd have to be pretty churlish to take that standpoint, wouldn't we?' Mum laughs, giving Dad a nudge. 'I mean, perhaps if he hadn't taken such drastic steps to prove he means it this time, I might be sceptical. But you can't doubt his motives now.'

'No,' I mutter again, still distinctly uneasy.

'*Not now he's booked the register office and everything.*'

For a moment I wonder if I've heard her right.

Whether she's really just said what I think she has. But as I play it back in my mind – and become convinced that she has – I realize that a full fifteen seconds have passed without me taking a single breath.

'And I have no doubt he'll go through with it this time,' she continues. 'A nice small service. Just a handful of us. No big hoo-ha like last time. Yes, it'll be fine. Lovely.'

I try to swallow but my throat seems to have closed. 'What did he tell you exactly?' I manage.

'Oh, Zoe, for goodness' sake.' She tuts. 'He had a proper heart-to-heart with us and told us *everything*. That you and he are back together. That you'll get married at a register office – because it was that big old church and all those people that scared him off last time. Oh, and that it's happening two weeks on Thursday.'

Suddenly I feel the last mouthful of in-flight hash brown rise up my oesophagus. 'Right.'

'Oh, sorry, sweetheart,' Mum says. 'He probably didn't tell you he was going to let us into your secret, did he? Well, don't worry, we're not going to breathe a word. There's only me and your dad who know. And he only told us because he knew we'd never believe he was sincere about you getting back together other-wise.'

'Mmm.'

'Everything all right, love?' Dad asks.

'Oh, Zoe,' Mum interrupts, before I have a chance to answer. 'Don't look so taken aback. As I've said, it's our little secret. Jason told us how important it was not to

360

tell anyone – and we won't. I haven't even told Desy, for goodness' sake.'

'And that really is a first,' adds Dad.

Chapter 78

Jason's new apartment is on the fourteenth floor of one of the gleaming new developments that have sprung up on the banks of the river Mersey in recent years. An old-fashioned part of me has always loved the stretches of the waterfront that won it World Heritage status – the vast docklands and imposing neo-classical buildings that are a permanent reminder of its grander past.

But the glistening skyscrapers – like the one Jason lives in – have added a surprising new dimension to the city's beauty and charisma. A boldness about the future that suits it more than anyone who grew up here could have imagined.

As the lift makes its way up to Jason's apartment, my stomach is doing back-flips. I peer at my reflection in the mirror and feel a wave of relief. Okay, so after a long-haul flight and very little sleep my skin might not be glowing, but I'm slightly tanned and, more importantly, I've lost the weight I'd put on. My eyes have their shine back and my hair is satisfactorily glossy. For the first time in ages I feel good about the way I look, comfortable in my skin. I just hope Jason agrees.

362

As I knock on his door, my heart is beating so fast that if I were undergoing medical tests right now I'd have the same heartrate as a hamster.

A couple of seconds later, it opens.

And there he is.

The man I wanted so desperately to be my husband. The man I thought had rejected me but now wants me back. My lover. My friend. Jason.

'How are you, sweetheart?' He grins.

'I – I'm fine,' I breathe, my voice wobbling.

We stand in front of each other, neither of us knowing what to say. Finally Jason takes the initiative. 'Come here,' he says softly, leaning forward to hug me. But as I move to reciprocate, my sleeve catches in the door frame. Awkwardly, I tug it out and try again.

He wraps his arms round me and I attempt to submit to their reassuring familiarity. I wait to be overwhelmed by happiness and security, as I used to be. I close my eyes and squeeze him.

The first thing that runs through my head is how small his physique feels compared with Ryan's. My frame isn't used to slotting into it any more. We're two pieces of a jigsaw that don't quite fit. After a few seconds, I pull away and look into his eyes. 'I've missed you,' I tell him.

He kisses me. 'Me too. Now, come on in and let me make you a coffee.'

At first the conversation is strangely stilted, even though there's so much catching up to do. It's as if the depth and intimacy of what we discussed over the phone while I was back in the States never happened.

'So . . . there were no delays on your flight or anything?' Jason asks, as we sit next to each other on the sofa, his arm draped awkwardly round my shoulders.

I feel like a fifteen-year-old in the back row at the cinema. 'No, none at all,' I reply.

'Good.' He nods. 'That's good.'

'Mmm,' I agree.

Oh, this is no good. After twenty minutes of small-talk, I'm getting agitated. And, surely, with good reason. Jason hasn't yet mentioned that he has rearranged our wedding. For two weeks on Thursday.

'Jason.' I turn to him and look into his eyes. 'My mum told me something when she picked me up. Something I thought you might have raised with me by now.'

'Ah,' he replies. I can tell he knows what I'm talking about. 'Did she?'

'She said you've rearranged the wedding. Is that right?'

Suddenly his face bursts into life. 'Well, I was hoping to tell you myself.' He beams. 'I was waiting for the right moment. Your mum was supposed to be sworn to secrecy. But, well, never mind that. So, what do you think?'

What do I think? That's a bloody good question. Clearly I should be delighted. I've got every right to be a bit nervous too, of course, but delighted first and foremost. Only as I weigh delight versus nervousness, the latter wins hands down.

'Clearly, I'm . . . um, *delighted*,' I offer.

'Fab! I knew you would be! Oh, sweetheart, this is going to be better than any wedding you could have imagined.'

'I'm a little nervous, though, given what happened last time,' I continue.

'What?' he says, as if I've broken his train of thought. 'Nervous? Well, yeah, I can understand that. But, believe me, you've nothing to be nervous about this time. Absolutely nothing. Okay? Okay, sweetheart?'

I gulp. 'Of course.'

I know it'll be a while before things feel normal again. I mean, I'm bound to feel twitchy. It's been a very stressful time. That's why I feel weird about the impending wedding. And about Jason. A hell of a lot has happened since April.

But that doesn't mean I'm still not *certain* he's the man for me. I just need to give myself time to adjust. That's it.

'Can I have another cup of coffee?' I ask, feeling the need to stand up.

'Sure, I'll make you one,' he says, leaping up attentively.

'No, I'll do it. Do you want one?'

'Nah,' he says. 'Just sort yourself out.'

I head towards the open-plan kitchen. It only takes a few paces and I'm there. It's not exactly generously proportioned, this flat. In fact, it's about as bijou as a broom cupboard.

'When did you move in here?' I ask, rooting around for the coffee.

'Oh, a couple of months ago,' he says proudly.

'Gorgeous, isn't it? I can just picture us settling here, can't you?'

'Oh,' I say, a bit surprised. 'You wouldn't want to move into a house, then, like before?'

'Nah. Why would you, when you can get a place like this for the same amount we'd be paying for a mortgage?'

'So you wouldn't want to *buy* anywhere again?'

'Who needs that sort of commitment at our age?'

'Isn't getting married a *commitment*?' I can't help pointing out.

'Yeah, course.' He laughs. 'That's different.'

His mobile rings and he picks it up, then heads into the bathroom – which is so sparkling that I felt guilty just sitting on the loo earlier.

I abandon my coffee-making and go to the window to gaze out across the waterfront. The view is spectacular. The Mersey and the Charles river are nothing like each other, really, but I get another flashback to Boston.

I'm desperate to phone Ruby and Samuel to say sorry for leaving so abruptly. To say I miss them. To say hello. I'm also desperate to stop thinking about my last kiss with Ryan. The feel of his body against mine, his lips, his—

When Jason walks back into the room again, he has a leather coat in his hand.

'New coat?' I ask.

'Yeah. Nice, eh? That was Neil on the phone asking us if we'd like a quick drink with him and Jessica. Do you fancy it?'

I shake my head. 'I'm shattered. That time difference, it's a killer. Do you mind if I get some sleep?'

'Oh, okay.' He looks disappointed.

'You go on, though,' I add.

'You're sure?'

'Of course.'

He walks across the room and puts his arms round me. I'm relieved that they feel less foreign than they did before. 'God, I'm glad you're back, gorgeous. I really am.'

'Me too.' I sigh.

Then he prises me away from him and walks to the door, stopping to brush a non-existent fleck of dust from the hall table.

'Oh, Jason . . . I'm just going to make a call to America,' I say. 'I have a couple of loose ends to tie up.'

'No problem. As long as it's not to a boyfriend.' He winks.

I flush so violently I must look temporarily menopausal, but fortunately he closes the door without glancing back.

I pick up the phone and dial the number, my throat so dry that cacti could thrive in it. It rings four times before someone picks up.

'Hello?' It's a little voice I recognize immediately.

'Hello, Ruby, it's Zoe.' I feel ashamed of myself even before the words are out of my mouth.

Chapter 79

'They're sending another nanny tomorrow,' Ruby says, her voice wobbly but defiant. 'But I've told Daddy I don't want another nanny. I only want you. And so does Samuel.'

I try to contain my emotions, but speaking to Ruby is almost too much for me. 'I'm sure your new nanny will be wonderful,' I say. 'Really I am.'

'That's what Daddy said too.' She sniffs. 'But he doesn't understand. He keeps saying that you were no different from all the other nannies and that the next nanny will probably be even better. But it's not true. I know it's not.'

Logic tells me that Ryan has said this to make Ruby and Samuel feel better, but a surge of dismay nearly knocks me over.

'Well, we'll just have to see, won't we?' I say. 'But I bet that in less than a week's time, you won't feel so bad.'

'I wanted you to be our mommy, Zoe.'

I try to find my voice without allowing any tears to escape, but it's like trying to hold back a tidal wave with a cocktail umbrella. 'That wasn't going to happen, sweetheart,' I croak. 'Your daddy and I were just friends. We were very good friends, who got on with each other very well, but just friends all the same.'

'No, you weren't,' she says accusingly.

I pause. 'What do you mean?'

'You kissed,' she said. 'I saw you.'

'Oh, er . . . did you? Where?'

'In the kitchen while Samuel and I were playing outside.'

'Oh, well, that was just a friendly kiss,' I insist. 'Nothing more, honestly.'

'It didn't look like it. It was how James Bond kisses ladies.'

We've been well and truly rumbled. 'Oh, er, right . . . well, perhaps.'

'I told Daddy about it too,' she continues. 'He says it was no big deal. But I don't believe him. It wasn't no big deal, was it, Zoe?'

I hold my hand over the phone for a second. 'I don't know, Ruby,' I whisper, more to myself than to her. 'I mean—'

Suddenly I hear a commotion at the other end of the phone and Ryan's voice in the background.

My stomach is churning as I hear him take the phone from her.

'Hey, Zoe.'

'Hello, Ryan.' About as original as a leather handbag in a Thai street market, but I can't think of anything else to say.

There's a short but excruciating silence.

'Well, you gave me a hell of a shock,' he begins. 'I couldn't believe what I read in your letter.'

I swallow.

'I mean – wow,' he continues. 'You sure were keeping some secrets.'

'Yes,' I reply numbly. 'I suppose I was.'

'It made me feel terrible,' he said.

'It made *you* feel terrible? Why?'

'I was an asshole when you first got here. A total asshole. And you had to put up with all that while you were going through hell yourself.'

'You weren't that bad.'

'I'm sure I was.'

There's another silence, but I don't feel such an overwhelming urge to fill it this time.

'So, this guy Jason.' His voice sounds weird as he says his name. 'You're giving it another go with him?'

'Yes,' I reply.

My response is decisive and unapologetic. That might seem strange, given that Ryan is the man I've been sleeping with, but I feel no need to tiptoe round the issue to avoid hurting his feelings. Not because I *want* to hurt his feelings – that's the last thing I want – but because I'm certain I won't.

He will forget our fling as quickly as he forgot about all the others. And I don't hold that against him, not for a second. I'd always intended it should be nothing more than a bit of fun – and that's exactly what it was.

'Okay,' he says awkwardly.

I consider going on to tell him that I'm getting married in just over two weeks' time. Yet, for some reason, I think I've said enough. Aside from not wanting him to think I'm a complete nutcase, it doesn't feel right. I don't know why, but it doesn't.

'Well,' he continues, 'if you believe it's the right thing to do, you gotta do it. And you got nothing but my best wishes.'

His breeziness confirms everything.

Ryan will have another woman on the go before the week is out, I'm certain of it. Maybe even Barbara King if she has her way.

As we politely say goodbye and I put the phone down, I remind myself that this is not something I should be dwelling on, not now I'm about to be knee-deep in wedding planning again.

Yet I have a lump in my throat. And it won't go away.

Chapter 80

Mum's pesto chicken and pine nuts looks suspiciously good. There's no doubt, although it's bubbling convincingly in her Le Creuset casserole dish in the oven, that it originated from Marks & Spencer. I wonder how she managed to dispose of the foil tray and cardboard packaging without any of us noticing.

'Can I help?' I ask.

'No!' she insists, dropping a packet of French beans over her marabou mules as she tries to juggle two pans of boiling water. 'All under control!'

I lean against the Welsh dresser. 'I'll set the table, then, shall I?' I ask.

'Good idea,' she pants, blowing hair out of her eyes.

She spends the next twenty minutes running around the kitchen with the frantic air of a decapitated chicken.

'Are you sure I can't help?' I ask helplessly, as pans are spilled and sauces are whisked across the tiles.

'All under control!' she sings, her face getting redder.

I perch on the edge of a chair.

'Can I help at all?' asks Dad, wandering in.

'All . . . under . . . *control!*'

Dad flashes me a look. 'I tried,' he whispers.

By the time dinner's on the table, Mum is so hot and bothered she's having to mop her brow with the hem of her pinny – a shocking-pink number with 'Yummy Mummy' written in big letters across it.

'There.' She sits down with a satisfied smile. 'All done. I said we were under control, didn't I? Now, French beans, Zoe?'

God, it's weird being at home.

This is where I've lived for most of my life yet I feel like a foreigner. From the labels on the milk cartons to the oversized, brightly coloured money. It all seems strange – so familiar and yet not.

'So, love, are you excited about the wedding?' Dad asks.

I smile, grateful for the question. It's the first time Dad has mentioned this since I flew home and I can tell it sticks in his throat. He's only bringing it up for my benefit.

Because, while he was more than happy to give his unequivocal blessing when I was getting married to Jason the first time, the second time is a different matter.

This has bothered me. Dad has never been the sort of father to disapprove of just about anything. Every milestone of my development – the first lipstick I bought, getting my ears pierced, my first night out at the pub – led to a low level of hysteria from Mum, but Dad was the opposite. 'She's more sensible than we ever were,' he'd argue, to her exasperation.

Yet he disapproves of the impending wedding. There's

no doubt of it. He's said nothing about it until now – but he doesn't need to.

'Yes, Dad,' I say. 'I am. Very excited.'

'Well, I for one can't wait!' adds Mum, with a grin. 'Jason's always felt like a member of the family and this is just going to confirm it.'

Dad coughs and flashes her a look. I try to work out what he's trying to say to her.

'What's up?' I ask.

Dad turns to Mum. 'Don't you think it's time you let Zoe into your news?' He seems strangely nervous as he reaches over and holds Mum's hand tenderly.

Mum looks all hot again. 'I suppose I better had,' she says, after she's finished her mouthful. Even then she's hesitant, almost as if she's stuck for words. It's not an affliction I'd usually associate with my mother.

'Zoe,' she begins, 'you know I told you I found something out from Dr Ahmed recently?'

'Yes,' I say.

'Well, that conversation we had over the phone when I said it was something serious? I wasn't joking.'

My throat goes dry. Oh, God. Oh, God, no. It can't really be serious, can it? I'd convinced myself Mum was being a hypochondriac.

'What is it, Mum?' I put down my knife and fork.

'At least, it's serious in that it's going to affect our lives quite a lot. My life. Your father's. And yours, for that matter.'

I get a wave of nausea. Grandma Bonnie died of breast cancer when she was in her fifties. Mum is only forty-four. That's it, isn't it? I know it.

'What *is* it, Mum?' I ask, desperate for her to put me out of my misery.

She turns to Dad and squeezes his hand. Then she smiles. 'I'm pregnant, love,' she tells me. 'You're going to have a little sister or brother.'

Chapter 81

'Bloody hell,' sighs Trudie on the phone the next day. '*EastEnders* is boring, compared with your family.'

I snort. She's not wrong, though. A little sister or brother. I can still barely believe it.

'So how do you feel about it? It must be weird, given your mum's old enough to be a grandmother.'

'Oh, God,' I splutter. 'Don't tell her that if you ever meet her, whatever you do.'

Trudie giggles.

'In answer to your question, though, I'm chuffed to bits, I really am. I can't say it wasn't a surprise, but I'm ridiculously pleased. I always wanted a sister or brother, and now I'm going to get one. Admittedly I'll be changing their nappies instead of borrowing CDs from them, but still.'

'So is there anything else you need to tell me?' she asks teasingly. 'You know, apart from you having just got back together with the man who jilted you – oh, and your mother being up the duff.'

'What did you have in mind?' I giggle.

'Oh, I don't know,' she continues. 'I don't think

anything could shock me now. You had any affairs with high-profile politicians?'

'No,' I say decisively.

'Any secret love-children?'

'No.'

'A sex change?'

'No.' I laugh.

'I still can't believe you never told me about your wedding – I mean the wedding you never had,' she continues.

This is the fourth long-distance phone call we've had in less than a week, and the fifth time she's mentioned that in the last ten minutes.

'I know, I know, and I'm sorry,' I say, meaning it.

'Bloody 'ell, love, I'm not asking you to be sorry. I just mean I feel awful you couldn't confide in me. I must have been so wrapped up in my own problems.'

'It wasn't that. And I did try once when we were out one night, but Ritchie turned up. Not that that matters. Honestly, Trudie, the reason I came to the States was to escape even having to think about being jilted, never mind talk about it.'

'So you sure you're doing the right thing now?'

'Yeah,' I reply. 'I mean, yes.'

Trudie pauses for a second. 'Look, tell me to butt out here but you don't sound a hundred per cent convinced.'

'I am. Honestly, Trudie – I *am* convinced.'

I can't help squirming, though. The truth is, I *do* want to get married next Thursday. Jason and I have spent a lot of time together since I returned and things are definitely slotting back into place.

If I'm entirely honest, I'd have to admit that I remain *slightly* jumpy about things. Part of me wonders whether it's too soon, whether I need more time to get used to the idea. Again. But logic tells me that this is one man I spent seven years wanting to be married to. That hasn't changed – I know it. And I'm certain that any reticence I feel is only because of what happened last time.

In the light of this, taking the bull by the horns and going ahead with this marriage – whether it feels rushed or not – is the right thing to do. No doubt about it.

'I'm sure, Trudie,' I say. 'If I sound a bit funny, it's just that – well, after what happened last time, I can't help being nervous about it. That's all. It's only to be expected.'

'And you love him?' she asks.

'Of course.' I laugh. 'I wouldn't have leaped on a plane and flown back here at the first opportunity if I didn't, would I?'

'Okay. Fine. Okay.'

'I do wish you could be here for the wedding, though.'

'I know, but – well, hang on a minute,' she says. 'Maybe there is a way . . . I've been promising my folks I'll come home for a week at some point – I've just never got round to booking it. And they're going ballistic because I'm not there for Christmas. Maybe I could combine the two . . .'

'Really?'

'I don't see why not. I'm due for a break soon and Barbara was saying to me only the other week she'd prefer me to take it before the end of the holiday season.'

I feel a surge of happiness so powerful I'd cartwheel across the living room if I wasn't terrified about leaving skidmarks on Jason's carpet. Then another idea strikes me.

'Listen,' I say. 'Since you're going to all this effort to come to my wedding and everything, I wonder if I could make a little request?'

'Anything.'

'How do you fancy being my bridesmaid?'

She lets out a scream that nearly deafens me.

'Is that a yes, then?'

'Bloody right it is. Oooh, Zoe, I've never been a bridesmaid before. Oh, my God, I'm going to wet myself! This is fantastic! Oh, and don't worry, I'll get a gorgeous dress. It'll be well classy, believe me.'

'Trudie,' I tell her, 'I'd have expected nothing less.'

Chapter 82

'What is this again?' Desy whispers to me, during Christmas dinner.

'Roasted carrots with a honey-mustard glaze,' I tell him, sticking my fork into a mound of orange gloop that looks less like a root-vegetable dish than radioactive waste. 'It's Mum's personal interpretation of something from her new Jamie Oliver book.'

'Oh,' he says sceptically. 'What happened to Nigella? I thought she was Nigella's biggest fan after last year's triumph.'

'I know, but the Christmas pudding came out wrong the other week so she's disowned her,' I tell him. 'Nigella is now, officially, unreliable. The fact that the pudding had been boiled for twenty-two hours solid and she'd forgotten to put any suet in it apparently had nothing to do with it.'

Desy and I stifle a giggle. Loyally Dad refuses to join in.

Mum approaches the table wearing her new Missoni-inspired blouse (from Zara) and with a jug of gravy she's been whisking for the last twenty minutes to remove some of the lumps.

Unfortunately, as it slides over Dad's turkey like molten lava, I fear nothing short of a cement-mixer would save it now.

'Now, Zoe,' says Mum, sitting down and carefully positioning her paper hat, 'don't eat too many of those roast potatoes. You were like a whale when you went to America, and now you've lost all that weight, I just *won't* let you put it back on – not with less than a week to go until your big day.'

'I haven't eaten anything yet,' I protest.

'Your mum's right,' pipes up Jason. 'I mean, you're lovely as you are. Obviously I think that – I'm marrying you.'

Everyone giggles a little too much.

'I'm just saying,' he continues, 'no one wants to look fat on their wedding day, do they?'

'No – it'll be up to me to do that!' howls Mum, patting her tummy.

Jason grins. 'Aw, you're barely showing yet, Mrs M. How far gone are you?'

'Five months.' She smiles. 'But I didn't start showing with Zoe until I was almost seven. It's in the genes. Grandma Bonnie was exactly the same.'

'You must be over the moon,' he says.

'Well, I can't say it didn't come as a bit of a surprise,' she laughs, 'but, yes, we're delighted. Now, Zoe, sprouts?'

I glance at the large spoonful of snot-coloured mush in her hand. 'Um, I'll just have a roasted parsnip,' I say. I happen to know the parsnips are a shop-bought emergency side dish, something Mum kept in the freezer in the unlikely eventuality that her Delia version went wrong. Which it did.

'A roasted parsnip?' Mum explodes. 'Are you *kidding*? Do you know what the fat content is in those things? Stick to the sprouts, for goodness' sake. There's only eight calories in each of those.'

'Eight calories? Oooh, steady on, Zoe,' says Desy, sarcastically.

'It is Christmas,' I point out to Mum. 'All I'm after is a parsnip, not a Chinese banquet for ten.'

Jason smiles encouragingly.

'You'll thank us when you look at your photos in years to come. Now, here you go,' Mum adds, ladling an alarmingly large portion of sprout mush on to my plate. 'Oh, and make sure you go easy on the gravy, won't you? Although I see you've not had any. Good girl!'

My mum's relationship with Jason has gone a bit weird since I came back. Weird, as in conspiratorial. I know why: without Mum on side, Jason knows he'd struggle to pull off a second attempt at a wedding. I can't pretend I'm not starting to find it nauseating, though.

'Now, Jason, about next week,' Mum continues, 'do you know whether your mum's going to be wearing the same outfit as last time?'

'She said she was going to buy something new. She thinks it's bad luck otherwise.'

'Precisely my thoughts,' Mum agrees. 'So I've bought a new silk dress in ultraviolet. I've only got a little bump so far, so I can get away with one I saw in Cricket. So, could you just tell her if she's going to buy a new outfit not to get one in ultraviolet? It'd be awful if we turned up in the same colour.'

'Sure.' Jason nods.

'I mean, I'm not saying she can't wear anything with a purply tone. Lilac would be fine. She might even try jacaranda. Anything but an ultraviolet, is all I'm saying.'

'There's only going to be a couple of people there to see it, remember,' I tell her gently. I'm concerned she's forgetting the wedding isn't going to be like the first one we planned.

'I *know* that, Zoe. But it's still your big day. And we're still going to be having our photos taken.'

I lean over to grab a Yorkshire pudding and Mum slaps my hand so hard and fast it's like watching Mr Miyagi in *The Karate Kid*. For a second our eyes lock.

'Have this,' I mutter, reluctantly putting the Yorkshire pudding on Jason's plate.

Suddenly my phone rings. I glance at it briefly and see a US number. 'Won't be a sec,' I say, leaping up from the table and scuttling into the living room to take the call. My heart is pounding as I answer the phone.

'Hello?'

'Happy Christmas!'

It's Trudie. I'd recognize those dulcet tones anywhere.

'Hi,' I say.

'Oooh, bloody 'ell, you're not exactly full of the Christmas spirit,' she observes. 'Were you expecting someone else?'

'No, no. Not really. Honestly. Thanks for phoning, Trude. Happy Christmas to you too. Sorry, I thought it might have been . . . Ruby.'

'Oh, I've just seen her,' she tells me. 'She's got your present by the way – those little pink shoes. She's wearing them. Over the moon with them, she is. As is Samuel with his train.'

'Did you see Ryan?' I find myself asking, trying to sound casual.

'Yeah, hon, I did,' she says. 'I get the feeling he's missing you.'

'Really?'

'Yeah, their new nanny isn't much good. The kids don't get on with her and have virtually refused to leave the house with her. Bedtime's a nightmare too.'

'Oh.' I curse myself for feeling disappointed that she's only referring to my nannying skills.

'Anyway, hon, listen,' she says, breaking my train of thought, 'as well as saying Happy Christmas, obviously, I thought I'd let you know my flight's booked. I'll be coming into Manchester on Tuesday.'

When I put the phone down, I hesitate before going back into the dining room. Why can't I stop thinking about America?

Oh, stop it, Zoe. Just stop. You've come all the way home to get what you wanted. If ever there was a time to get on with things, stop worrying and appreciate what you've got, it's now.

I sit down at the table and put my hat back on as Mum is dotting brandy butter over the Christmas pudding. It no longer looks mass-produced – earlier, I spotted her bashing its giveaway smooth surfaces with the back of a wooden spoon.

'Oh, I nearly forgot,' she says, scuttling away. She returns with a pot of something she plonks on my mat. 'I got you a Müller Light, love,' she says. 'I thought it best under the circumstances.'

Chapter 83

Having sex with Jason again is nice.

Not as passionate as it was with Ryan. Not as adventurous. Not as hot and breathless and ... but, look, it really is nice. I know you never get magazines like *Cosmo* comparing good sex with a cosy pair of slippers, but I honestly believe there's a lot to be said for it.

Excitement and passion are easy to muster up when you've only just met someone. Having a lasting sexual relationship requires so much more. The way Jason touches me, the position he chooses, the way he shudders when he comes ... They might be oh-so-familiar but familiarity is what I crave. And as I lie in his arms gazing at the rain belting his bedroom window, I'm certain our sex life will get better with time.

Particularly when I manage to stop those bloody images of Ryan invading my thoughts ...

'That was nice.' Jason strokes my hair.

I can't help feeling disappointed at the description, hypocritical though that is. 'Yes,' I agree. Then I roll on to my side and prop myself up on an elbow. 'It wasn't ... disappointing, was it?'

386

'Course not,' he says, a little too forcefully. 'It was lovely. Just like it used to be.'

To be fair, sex between Jason and me was never the sticky, sweaty, heart-thumping affair popular with Hollywood film-makers. And, if I'm entirely honest, before I met Ryan I often used to think that, as a pastime, it was overrated. A touch of the Emperor's New Clothes. That's not to say I didn't enjoy it. I just never understood why some people found it so all-consuming.

'Just think,' Jason continues, 'in three days' time, you and I will be lying in this bed as man and wife.'

He'd said exactly the same thing a few days before our last wedding day. The thought makes me feel ill.

'You are going to go through with it this time, aren't you?' I ask hesitantly.

He rolls over and mirrors my position.

'Zoe, listen to me,' he says intently. 'There's no way I'm going to let you down this time. You do know that, don't you?'

I bite my lip. 'I never thought you would last time.'

'I know, I know,' he says, running a hand through his hair defensively. 'And believe me when I say I'll never forgive myself for it. Never. But I'm going to spend a lifetime making it up to you. You're going to be the happiest married woman in England, I promise.'

He leans over and kisses my forehead. I smile and turn on to my back, gazing up at the ceiling. There was a time when my heart swelled with affection for Jason when he said that sort of thing. I used to gaze into his eyes and marvel at how lucky I was.

The things he's saying to me now are no less caring or

poignant. Yet in my darker moments I have to admit that they're not having the same effect. I keep trying to make them, but they don't.

I've told myself not to worry about it too much. I know it will only be a matter of time before things are like they used to be. I've just got to stop comparing Jason with Ryan and remind myself of all the wonderful things that made me fall in love with him in the first place.

'I'm going to jump into the shower,' I announce, throwing back the covers and leaping out of bed.

Jason is lying on his back now and puts both hands behind his head. 'God, I've missed that bum.' He grins.

I smile and kiss his lips, then pick up my clothes and head for the bathroom. I pause. 'Did I really fold these up?' I ask.

'No, I did,' he says. 'An untidy house is an untidy mind.'

'I know,' I frown, 'but is your mind supposed to be *tidy* when you're in the throes of passion?'

'I wouldn't have been able to concentrate if I hadn't done it. Anyway, you never used to complain.'

He's right. I didn't. So why the hell am I now?

I know the answer to that one: I'm comparing him with Ryan again.

Which is ridiculous because on this issue Jason wins hands down. Ryan is a man who drops towels on the floor, leaves the dishwasher unemptied and discarded pizza boxes on the sofa. It drove me insane, especially when I first lived with him.

I feel like shaking myself. For God's sake, Zoe. Women can't stand living with men like Ryan – men who don't notice mess and don't care if they do. In this respect Jason is the perfect man. In fact, he's beyond perfect. He doesn't just clear up his own mess, he clears up mine too. I should be overjoyed.

When I get into the shower, I turn it to a colder setting than usual, hoping it will knock some sense into me.

I don't know how long I spend in there, but there's something pleasingly distracting about the cold jets pummelling my goose-pimpled skin as I attempt to get things straight in my mind.

Come on, Zoe. Are you or are you not in love with Jason? This is make-your-bloody-mind-up time.

I pick up the shampoo and pour a dollop on to my hand, then massage it vigorously into my scalp. After a few seconds, I can hardly believe I asked myself the question.

Of *course* I'm in love with Jason.

I've spent more than seven years being in love with him. The upheaval of the last eight months is bound to have affected me – but that doesn't mean, deep down, that I love him any less.

What's really annoying is that I only ever got involved with Ryan as a defence mechanism, as a bit of fun to distract me from the trauma I'd been through. How the hell did it become so much of a distraction that I can't stop thinking about our affair even now it's served its purpose?

As I rinse off the shampoo and start on the

conditioner, I make a promise to myself: no more thinking about Ryan. Full stop.

If I really concentrate on this, he'll soon be nothing more than a distant memory, and Jason and I will be happily married with our whole lives in front of us. Which is exactly what I've always wanted. Isn't it?

Chapter 84

My preparations for this wedding couldn't be more different: last time, there wasn't a bridal magazine known to woman that I hadn't subscribed to for at least a year and a half in advance. I visited every wedding emporium in the north-west of England – and one or two beyond – just to find the perfect pair of shoes. I attended bridal fayres in their dozens, searched endlessly on the Internet for innovative table decorations and tried on more tiaras than the Queen.

The timescale now means things have to be low-key. But it's not just that. Something has changed in me. I can't bring myself even to look in a wedding shop. Maybe I've become cynical. Maybe part of me is determined not to go over the top in case Jason decides not to show up again.

By the way, I don't think he'll do that.

In fact, I'm certain he won't. But that it's even a possibility is undoubtedly affecting me. Which is probably why my promise – that I won't let thoughts of Ryan enter my head – has been broken. Arrgh! There I go again!

I head over to Coast, one of my favourite shops in the Metquarter, and browse through its rails. There is a day and a half to go before I get married and I still don't know what I'm going to wear. I'm not worried, though. In the scheme of things, it isn't important. And as someone who spent a month and a half's wages on a full-length silk number I got to wear for approximately an hour and twenty minutes last time, I think I'm qualified to judge.

What I'm certain of is that, this time, I'm not going for a traditional wedding dress. I want something that reflects the tone of the nuptials. Understated. Unfussy. Something you'd struggle to recognize as anything to do with a wedding.

When I was chatting this through with Trudie last night, we agreed that an elegant, sophisticated suit, perhaps in cream, would do nicely. However, I'd forgotten that once you've pictured an item of clothing in your mind it's *impossible* to find it.

I've been in the city centre for what feels like hours and am no closer to finding something suitable. I pick up a strapless red dress and examine it. Gorgeous, but not what I'm after.

With twenty-five minutes to go before the shops shut, I decide to cut my losses and head back to a place I was in earlier. Instead of buying 'the one', I will buy the one that was closest to 'the one', as it were. It's not perfect, but it's *okay*. And it's in the sale, which makes me feel a bit better.

Chapter 85

The night before the wedding, Trudie and I go out for a drink in one of the bars on Allerton Road – but for some reason I'm not in the mood for it.

'You all right, love?' she asks, looking concerned as I take a sip of the same glass of red wine I've been struggling with for the last hour and a half.

'I think I'm coming down with something,' I tell her, as I pull out a tissue.

'It's this bloody weather. Everyone you see seems to have a cold at the moment. It's like a permanent reminder of why we left the UK.'

After a couple of hours I'm utterly drained and ready to go home. I feel guilty about being such appalling company, especially when she's flown all the way over just for me. But I can't help it.

Back at Mum's house, I climb under the covers feeling so tired I imagine I'll be flat out for the next eight hours. But it doesn't happen like that. My sleep is fitful, broken by dreams that leave me even more restless and disturbed. Particularly one.

In this dream, it's my wedding day – tomorrow. I

arrive at the register office and everything seems to go according to plan. My parents are beaming with pride. My outfit is fabulous. And Jason – this time – turns up.

But there is a spanner in the works. His name is Ryan.

The registrar asks me if I, Zoe Maureen Moore, will take Jason Peter Redmond to be my lawful wedded husband and the words 'I will' are on the tip of my tongue. But I'm stuttering and stammering so much it's as though I'm trying to deliver a speech through a mouthful of peanut butter. I can't get the words out.

But it doesn't matter.

Because the door bursts open and flies off its hinges.

The whole room gasps. I swoon. And there he is, standing at the door in a James Bond tuxedo with a .45 revolver in his hand. Ryan.

I run towards him and, as the rest of the room melts away, he gathers me in his arms and kisses me so passionately and hard and sexily that, quite frankly, in a movie it would be X-rated.

Finally, he pulls away and says, 'Come on, the Aston Martin's outside.' We speed away through the streets of Liverpool, then drive off the Pier Head and into the Mersey, which – *really* bizarrely – is as blue and clear as the sea off Koh Samui. At this point, the car morphs into an underwater pod, Ryan pops open a bottle of champagne and proceeds to take me to heaven and back so comprehensively I doubt I'd be able to walk for a week afterwards.

Then I wake up, sweating, shivering, cursing myself. And realizing that my nose is running.

Chapter 86

I'd always thought it was one of the unwritten laws of nature and the universe that brides did not catch colds. Certainly, I've never seen a wedding photo in all my twenty-eight years on earth in which either of the happy couple has a snotty nose so raw and crusty from blowing that they look like they need skin grafts.

But apparently it can happen. It does happen. In fact, it has.

'No better, then?' asks Trudie, handing me the second-to-last Super Duper Ultra Soothing Balm tissue in the box. The gentlest blow fills it, and I need another to clean up the debris from my face.

'Doh,' I say, chucking the tissue into my overflowing bin. 'I mean, *no*. Not so far, at least.'

I open the next box and dab one on my eyes to stop them streaming. 'I'll have to redo my makeup,' I say. I peer at my blotchy skin and can't help thinking it would be easier to give Shrek a makeover.

'Maybe you should leave it until the last minute,' advises Trudie. 'I mean, this is our fourth go – we'll run out of foundation at this rate.'

I head for my full-length mirror, hoping to reassure myself. But I look awful. In fact, I couldn't look more awful if I'd just taken part in a competition to dive through hedges backwards and won.

My suit, the one I'd pictured as elegant and sophisticated, is neither. I have spent the last twenty-four hours trying to convince myself, with a little help from Trudie, that it might not be perfect but it is *okay*.

As I stand in front of the mirror now, all I can focus on is how *not* okay it is. There are so many creases at the top of my thighs you'd think I'd just stepped off a twenty-hour flight. Its horrible shiny finish stretches across my bum and displays more cellulite than you'd find in a liposuction clinic's waste container. 'Oh, God,' I complain, and grab another tissue.

Trudie sighs. 'Have another glass of champagne,' she tells me. 'It might help bung you up a bit.'

'I don't think I'm meant to be drinking with the tablets I'm taking for my cold.'

'Oh, rubbish. They always say that to cover their arses. It might give you a bit of an extra buzz, but nothing more.'

'I'll take your word for it.' I knock back a mouthful. I couldn't feel worse than I do already.

Suddenly the door bursts open. 'Only me!' Mum has never believed in knocking. 'So, what do you think of the ultraviolet?' she says, twirling round. It's immediately obvious to Trudie and me that this is a rhetorical question: her expression indicates that she thinks she looks like Linda Evangelista. Which, I have to say, isn't unwarranted – she's stunning.

'Mum, you're beautiful,' I tell her, and lean forward to kiss her.

'Ooh, not too close, love.' She pulls back to make sure my nose doesn't drip on her.

'Sorry,' I mutter. 'You do look amazing, though, Mum. That colour's definitely you.'

'It is, isn't it?' She smiles. 'And all the better now I've just had it confirmed that Jason's mum isn't wearing anything similar. She's gone for cappuccino, apparently. I'm not sure her complexion can take it at her age, but there you go. It's up to her.'

I feel another urge to blow my nose and reach over to grab a tissue. Mum frowns. 'Don't worry, Zoe,' she says earnestly.

'Don't worry about what?' I ask.

'Your nose,' she says. 'That photographer fellow said he knew how to do hairbrushing.'

'You mean airbrushing?' I ask.

'That's what I said, love. Hairbrushing – just like the celebrities. You might look like Rudolph now, but by the time we've finished with you, you'll be giving Scarlett Johannesburg a run for her money, I promise.'

Chapter 87

Mum's gone on ahead to the register office, which leaves Dad, Trudie and me. As we get into the taxi I notice how different I feel this time. Not nervous. Not even particularly excited. Just numb.

Before you start wondering, this isn't cold feet. The combination of my medicine and three glasses of champagne is so powerful it would have tranquillized a woolly mammoth.

'You okay, love?' Dad squeezes my hand.

'Course,' I say, forcing a smile. 'Just a bit . . . dizzy, actually. I think it might be my tablets.'

Suddenly Dad looks incredibly worried. 'You're certain about this, aren't you?'

'What do you mean, Dad?' I ask, shocked.

'I mean, you're certain you're doing the right thing? That you love Jason? That you're meant to be together?'

I hesitate as I let his words sink in. 'God, Dad, I . . . of course I am. Of course.'

'Only—'

'*Dad*,' I interrupt. 'I'm sure.'

He looks into my eyes. 'Okay, love. Okay.'

There is virtual silence for the rest of the journey. No giggly excitement. No banter with the driver. So little jollity, in fact, that when we stop at some traffic lights next to a funeral car I can't help noticing that the passengers in it look as if they're having considerably more fun than we are.

'Are you going on honeymoon?' Trudie pipes up. 'I've just remembered I never asked you.'

'No. Jason doesn't want to. He'd booked a stag weekend in April for his friend Jimmy's wedding and we can't afford both.'

'Oh.' Trudie turns to gaze out of the window again.

When we arrive at the register office in Old Hall Street, the car pulls in at the side of the road. I open the door and begin to get out. But with just one foot on the pavement, I'm ambushed.

'*Have I got a surprise for you-hoo!*' whoops Mum, dragging me along as if I'm a large sack of Maris Pipers.

'Wh-what?' I stammer, wiping my nose and removing the sixth application of foundation from my top lip.

'The *Echo* are here, Zoe, the *Echo*! You're going to be a front-page splash!'

'What?' I ask, hoping I've misheard her. 'Who invited them?'

'Oh, don't worry about that!' Mum cries. 'Come on, Zoe! Every girl your age would love to be popped!'

'You mean papped, Mum.'

'That's what I said. What they do for *OK!* magazine. You're easily as pretty as some of the Wags. I mean, look at that one in the paper the other morning – I've seen better legs on an uncooked chicken.'

A nervous young reporter is hovering outside the glass doors chewing the end of her pencil like a hungry mongrel chomping its way through a piece of beef. I grab Mum's arm and attempt to stop her. 'Mum,' I snap, 'I don't *want* to be in the *Echo*. Really, I don't.'

'Of *course* you do!' she cries, rolling her eyes in despair. 'You love the *Echo*, Zoe.'

It was bad enough when Mum took out a classified advert in the paper to 'celebrate' my twenty-first birthday – by sharing with the world a picture of me as a chubby toddler lifting my skirt up and showing off a fetching pair of brown-and-orange-striped knickers.

'This wedding is supposed to be low-key,' I tell her. 'I don't want the whole of Merseyside reading about it in the paper.'

'Don't be silly,' she scolds, clearly convinced that this is the chance of a lifetime. 'They thought it would make a lovely article, a young woman left at the altar finally getting her man.'

My heart sinks.

'I can see the headline now,' Mum continues gleefully, '"SECOND TIME LUCKY AS BRIDE ZOE BOUNCES BACK". Oh – that's quite good! I should do this for a living!'

'So it *was* you who invited them.'

'Er, now, let me introduce you to Michelle,' says Mum, ignoring me. 'She's a journalist.'

'Um, hi. I'm Mandy.' The reporter offers me her hand. 'I'm, um, not quite a journalist yet. I'm on work experience. But your mum's right. The newsdesk are really keen on your story.'

'Look, I— Sorry, but I don't want to do this,' I tell her

apologetically. 'I wanted to keep things low-key. No one knows about this wedding yet. I really am sorry.'

'Oh,' she says dejectedly. 'Well, never mind. It's your day. I do understand.'

'Thanks—'

'It's just . . . I was hoping this would be my big break. They were planning to use the story on page three. I was going to use the cutting to get into journalism college.'

I sigh.

'Don't worry.' She sniffs. 'Working in Netto isn't that bad.'

I groan. 'Oh, God, all right. Be quick about it, though.'

After a two-minute interview and three hastily composed photographs – all of which Mum managed somehow to pop up in – I usher her inside, blow my nose again, and attempt to pull myself together.

'Make sure you turn your phone off,' Dad tells me.

'Oh, yeah. Of course,' I say, feeling queasier than ever.

I'm about to take my phone out of my little satin bag when I feel an overwhelming urge to ask Trudie something. 'Trudie,' I whisper, 'I don't suppose . . . I mean . . .'

'What?' she asks.

'Did you tell Ryan you were coming over for my wedding?'

Trudie hesitates for a second. Then she nods. 'Yeah, hon. I did. You don't mind, do you?'

'No,' I assure her, feeling my spirits lift momentarily. 'I just . . . So he knows I'm getting married? He knows I'm getting married *today*? *Now*? *Here*?'

She nods again.

'Okay. I just wondered, that's all.' I bite my lip as I look at my phone. There are no missed calls.

We enter the main entrance hall and are greeted by a fluffy-haired woman who, despite the tight-fitting navy skirt suit, still reminds me of Mrs Beeton.

'Zoe?'

I nod.

'I'm one of the assistants. You're in there.' She indicates a room to her right. 'Jason's waiting for you. He's very excited.'

So, this time he turned up.

I know I should feel elated, but I don't. I just feel weird. Tense. Those bloody sinus tablets have a hell of a lot to answer for.

'You ready, love?' asks Dad.

'Ready as I'll ever be.'

The huge doors open simultaneously.

Jason turns and beams.

His parents exchange a contented glance.

And Mum dabs her eyes with a tissue, like she does at the end of *The Sound of Music*.

I glide to the front of the room, feeling as if I'm having an out-of-body experience. When I reach Jason, Trudie and my dad fall back. Then the registrar begins talking. He talks and talks. But I can't take in what he says because I've got champagne and medicine swirling round my system and all I can hear are four little words: *Ryan, where are you?*

I turn and glare at the door, repeating the words slowly and silently as tears prick the backs of my eyes.

Ryan. Where are you?

Then, as if I'm waking from a dream, I hear the registrar saying my name, imploring me to respond. But before I get the chance, another thought charges into my head, like a white knight who isn't in the mood to be argued with. It's something I've known all along, deep down.

I want Ryan.

I need Ryan.

Christ almighty, I'm in love with Ryan!

'Zoe?' Jason grips my arm. 'What's going on?'

I turn to the door again, willing it to burst open.

But it doesn't. And I have to come to terms with a truth so unbelievably disappointing that it shocks me to the core: Ryan isn't going to rescue me.

'Shit,' I hear myself saying. 'Shit, shit, and double shit.'

'Zoe, you're scaring me,' says Jason. 'Is everything all right?'

I realize – just as I feel the urge to blow my nose again – that I've got to tell him what has only just become clear to me.

'Doh, Jason,' I say. My nose got the better of me.

'What?' he asks.

'No,' I repeat. 'Everything's not all right.'

His eyes widen and there's a collective gasp.

I turn back to the door, still hoping. It remains resolutely shut.

If no one is going to rescue me – if *Ryan* isn't going to rescue me – I'll just have to rescue myself.

'Trudie, can I have another tissue?' I ask, holding out

my hand. There's a sigh of relief as she hands me one.

'God,' mutters Jason, 'I thought for a second you were about to say you weren't going through with it, not that you just needed to blow your nose.'

Everyone collapses into giggles. The registrar, Trudie, my mum, Jason's parents . . .

'Jason,' I say, 'that *is* what I meant. I don't want to go through with it. I'm sorry, but I really don't.'

Chapter 88

Mum is banging on the door of the register-office lavatory so hard I'm convinced her fist is about to burst through it. 'Zoe!' she howls. 'Zoe! Come out here *this instant*! This is your mother talking and – and you're to do as you're told!'

I unravel another piece of loo roll and blow my nose. It's cheap, crinkly paper, so far from my Super Duper Ultra Soothing Balm tissues that when I wipe my nose it feels as if it's laced with fibreglass.

'Zoe!' cries Mum, her voice rising to the pitch of a battling alley cat. 'This is *ridiculous*, young lady. We know you're in there.'

Next I hear Trudie's voice.

'Listen, Mrs Moore,' she says softly, 'why don't you have a cup of tea and let me have a go?'

'With respect, Trudie,' says Mum, sighing, 'Zoe is *my* daughter. What she needs at this moment is her mother. So, if you'll please—'

'Just give us a minute, will you, Mum?' I interrupt, through the door.

'Zoe!' she squawks. 'Never mind *give you a minute*! Get

out here this instant and get down that aisle. We've only booked a twenty-five-minute slot, which means you've got precisely two and a half minutes to get your act together. The next wedding's waiting outside. Now, get your skates on, girlie!'

I take a deep breath, then stand up and open the door. 'Mum—'

She grabs my arm and attempts to pull me towards the exit, but I clutch the loo door like a stroppy toddler who won't go to bed.

'What are you *doing*?' she shrieks, dropping my arm, but not the subject. 'Come *on*! You've got to be quick!'

I stand my ground. 'Please let me say something, Mum.'

'But—'

'Ssh!' I hold my finger authoritatively to my lips. 'Ssh. Don't say a word until I've finished.'

'Zoe, I—'

'Ssh!' I repeat, my finger to my lips again.

I don't think I've ever told my mum to ssh! before. Despite the circumstances, a tiny, wicked part of me enjoys it.

Mum purses her lips. Then, reluctantly, she nods.

'The first thing I want to say to you, Mum, is that I'm very sorry for what you've been through. No mother of the bride should have to go through two weddings without her daughter ending up married at either of them.'

'Well, you can easily change that—'

'Mum!' I hold up my finger again. Her mouth closes – but with so much effort it's like watching someone trying to shut the boot of an overpacked Mini.

406

'But I've got to do what I think is right,' I continue. 'And the fact is that – that Jason isn't the man for me.'

'Is this your idea of getting revenge on him?' she asks sternly. 'For standing you up the first time?'

'No, Mum. It's not. I was angry about what Jason did. In fact, I was devastated. But I *forgave* him – I forgave him to the extent that I was willing to try again. At least, I thought I was.'

'So why the big turnaround?' She's exasperated.

I sigh. 'Jason's . . . lovely. In fact, I'm sure he'll make someone a great husband. But, Mum, it's this simple. I don't love him any more.'

'But you *do*,' she pleads. 'Zoe, you've loved him for seven years!'

'That's just it, Mum. I don't. Not any more. I thought for such a long time we'd be together for ever. But sometimes it doesn't work out like that. I loved him once, but I've changed. Perhaps we've both changed. And while I love you dearly, Mum, on this occasion you're going to have to let me do what I think is right. And trust me.'

Mum's lip wobbles and she pulls out her tissue. 'I do trust you,' she mutters, blowing her nose.

'Yes, but you sometimes treat me as if I'm still a little girl, Mum.' I put my arm round her. 'And I'm not. I'm twenty-eight years old. I'm a grown-up.'

'It's only because I love you.' She sniffs.

'I know, Mum,' I say, squeezing her.

Mum nods with such conviction that her hairpiece threatens to fall off. 'You're right, Zoe. Of course you're right. And I've got to admit . . . your dad's been right all along.'

'What do you mean?' I ask.

'I suppose he's always known you could stand on your own two feet. I felt like strangling him when he said he thought going to America would be good for you. I couldn't understand it. I accused him of not caring about you as much as I do. But I know, really, it's not that. And it probably has been good for you.' She sighs.

'Oh, Mum.' I hug her again.

She squeezes me, then pulls back. 'I'm so proud of you, Zoe,' she continues. 'I probably don't tell you as often as I should, but I really am. When I had you at sixteen, so many people looked down their noses at us. They said me and your dad would never last – and that you'd turn out like some hooligan or something because you'd come about as a result of a teenage pregnancy. But you're clever, you're beautiful, you're everything I ever wanted in a daughter. I'm so lucky to have you.'

I'm choked. I've always known how much my mum loves me, yet I've never heard her say anything like this before. I smile, just as she glimpses herself in the mirror and gasps. 'This bloody hairpiece,' she huffs, tearing it off and throwing it into the bin.

Then she turns back to me. 'Well, I suppose I'd better go and tell everyone you won't change your mind.'

She walks to the door, and is about to open it when she hesitates. 'Just one other thing, Zoe.'

'Yes, Mum?'

'Is someone else involved? Is that the reason you did this?'

I glance at Trudie. But I don't know why she'd know the answer.

Is someone else involved? Let's see . . .
Am I in love with someone else?
Yes.
But is he in love with me?

I picture myself standing at the front of the register office, turning expectantly to look at the door. Which had stayed shut.

'No, Mum,' I admit, my throat tightening. 'There isn't anyone else involved.'

As Mum heads back through the doors, Trudie grabs my hand. 'Come on, you and I need to get out of here,' she says.

I take a deep breath. 'Bloody right.'

Trudie goes first, and we make our way towards the exit. We're about three feet from it when I see Jason. He looks furious.

'I'm sorry,' I say, my heart pounding. 'I'm really, really sorry.'

'I suppose you think I deserve this, do you?' he asks, fists clenched.

'No,' I tell him truthfully. 'I don't think that. Neither of us deserved it.'

He snorts.

'I don't know what to tell you, Jason, except I didn't mean to hurt you. Just like I know you didn't mean to hurt me. So I'm sorry,' I repeat. 'I'm so, so sorry.'

It's all I can think of to say. But it's clearly not what Jason wants to hear. I turn away, desperately sad, and go to the door.

'Zoe,' he shouts.

I spin round and meet Jason's eyes.

He takes a deep breath and frowns. 'Good luck,' he says.

Chapter 89

Trudie and I stumble down Old Hall Street, both shivering but not feeling the cold. We spot a taxi and she waves her arms as if she's trying to flag down a jumbo jet.

As we clamber into the back, she says, 'So, hon, where do you want to go?'

'Haven't a bloody clue.'

'Take us to a pub,' she instructs the driver. It's an executive decision.

'There are about nine hundred in this city, love.' He grins. 'You might want to narrow it down.'

'Anywhere you like. Somewhere nice. You choose.'

Five minutes later, we arrive at the Baltic Fleet, a proper, cosy pub with cask ales and roaring fires that practically singe your eyebrows. When we walk in I claim a spot in the corner while Trudie heads for the bar.

I gaze into the flames until she returns with two enormous whiskies. 'Get that down you,' she says to me.

Whisky isn't something I've ever particularly drunk. As I take a sip I can't help thinking it tastes like a glass of windscreen de-icer. But its warmth spreads through me and I can't deny it helps.

'Well, what a day you've had,' she says.

'All my own doing.'

'I get the feeling you were a bit railroaded into this wedding. Am I right?'

'Maybe,' I concede. 'But do you know the most pathetic thing about it?'

'What's that?'

'I think I'm in love with Ryan. No, scrap that. I know I am.'

'You don't say,' she replies ironically. 'But why's that pathetic? He might love you too.'

'I don't think so.'

She frowns. 'Well, for Christ's sake, if this experience has taught you anything it must be to follow your gut feelings and not keep quiet.'

'Hmm.'

'So phone him and tell him.'

I look down at my drink and back at her. Just the thought makes me feel queasy again. But I have another sip. A big one this time. 'You're right,' I say, as my blood races with adrenalin. 'You're absolutely right.'

Suddenly I get an overwhelming feeling that this phone call will be the most important one I ever make. That I'm going to tell Ryan I love him and to hell with the consequences. I dip my hand decisively into my bag – and realize immediately that my phone isn't there. 'Oh, bugger. I've left my mobile in the loo at the register office. It's probably sitting on top of the Tampax machine.'

'Here, use mine,' offers Trudie, rooting in her bag. When she produces the phone, it's vibrating.

'Christ, I've got about ten missed calls,' she exclaims, pressing answer. '*Hiya?*'

I can just about hear a muted voice and Trudie gestures to me that she's going to take the call outside so she can hear properly. I watch, mildly intrigued, as she stands by the door for a good ten minutes, gesticulating like an over-excited football manager.

When she plonks herself down on the stool next to me, she looks strangely twitchy.

'Everything okay?' I ask.

'Hmm?'

'I was just asking if everything's okay?' I repeat. 'You seem a bit funny after your phone call.'

'Me? No, I'm fine,' she says, almost too dismissively. 'Er, I was just giving someone directions.'

'To where?'

She clears her throat and shifts in her seat again. 'Er, Primark. The one in Barnsley. Er, I'm just going to get some Scampi Fries – do you want some?'

'No. Can I borrow your phone?' I ask desperately. I know that if Trudie doesn't give it to me soon, I risk bottling out of the whole thing faster than you can say 'world's biggest wimp'.

'Just give us a sec!' She darts to the bar and I gaze into the fire again, its heat stinging my eyes. As I shuffle my stool sideways, I sense Trudie next to me again.

'Oh, all right, then. I'll have some dry roasted peanu—'

It isn't Trudie.

413

It's the last person I ever expected to walk into the Baltic Fleet pub, Liverpool, just as I'd settled on the bar snack I wanted.

He's not wearing a tuxedo.

There isn't a .45 revolver in sight.

But, I can say categorically that I'd prefer this person to be standing here more than anyone else on the planet. And I'm not talking about James Bond.

Chapter 90

As Ryan sits on the stool next to mine, my pulse is racing wildly.

'I was late,' he says.

'I can't believe you're here.' I search his eyes, desperate to read his expression.

'My plane was delayed. I should have arrived in plenty of time.'

'In plenty of time for what?' I am barely able to believe this conversation is happening.

'Your wedding,' he whispers, reaching for my hand.

'But you weren't invited,' I find myself saying.

He smiles. 'I know that. I was going to do something very . . . well, discourteous.'

'Oh?'

'I was going to try to stop you getting married.'

I hear myself gasp – a short, sharp, this-can't-honestly-truly-be-happening gasp – so audibly that the bloke at the next table looks momentarily concerned that I'm about to be taken hostage.

'The plan was I'd arrive this morning at your mom's

house, finally tell you how I feel about you and beg you to be mine.'

'And when did you make this plan exactly?'

He looks at his watch. 'About twenty-three and a half hours ago,' he tells me. 'But I've been wondering how to get you back since the day you left.'

'Only you didn't make it on time.'

'No,' he admits. 'Not much of a hero, am I?'

I smile and finally look up into his eyes. With the light from the fire flickering on them, they're more mesmerizing than ever. Just gazing into them makes me feel weak with happiness. 'Actually, you haven't done too badly. I mean, you still came. Okay, your timing's a bit out, but nobody's perfect. Besides, fortunately for you, luck was on your side.'

'How's that?'

'I didn't go through with it.'

'I heard.' He smiles. 'So, when exactly did you make this plan?'

I look at my watch. 'Oh, about an hour ago. But I've been wondering how to get you back since I left.'

With my eyes moistening, I suppress another urge to blow my nose, determined that my overactive nasal passages will not ruin this moment.

'Why did you leave?' he asks.

I close my eyes and take a deep breath. 'I thought I felt something for Jason that – that now I know I didn't.'

He nods.

'But it wasn't just that,' I admit. 'I overheard you at the party talking to Felicity, telling her that what you and I had was nothing but a fling. Then I saw you with

Barbara King and it looked like she was going to be your next conquest.'

He raises an eyebrow.

'I also thought . . . I'd never replace Amy. I suppose I thought lots of things, Ryan.'

I press a tissue to my nose in as ladylike a fashion as I can.

'Can I tell you something, Zoe?' he says, squeezing my hand. 'I was a wreck before I met you. I was self-centred and boorish. I didn't appreciate my kids and I was on my own personal collision course. I didn't think life had anything left to offer me. Then you came along. And you changed everything.'

'Me?' I ask.

'Of course you. You rescued me. You rescued my kids. You taught me how to laugh again. You made me enjoy waking up in the morning. You gave me my life back, Zoe.'

I swallow.

'And I'll tell you something else.'

'What?' I ask.

'I love you for it. And the weird thing is, that's not the only thing I love you for. I love you for sliding across the dance-floor at my black-tie dinner. I love you for throwing my pasta all over the kitchen. I love you for dressing as Big Bird when everyone else was trying to be sexy.'

He reaches out and tenderly tucks my hair behind my ear, then studies my face. 'Nobody was sexier than you.'

'In a Big Bird costume?' I ask doubtfully.

'Feathers obviously do it for me.'

'But what about what you said to Felicity?' I ask. 'And

Barbara King? You – you seemed to be getting very . . . I don't know . . . *cosy* with her at the party.'

He frowns. 'Zoe, telling Felicity I was madly in love with you would have been the worst thing possible,' he explains. 'She's *insanely* jealous. I didn't want to rub it in for her sake, but more than anything I wanted to protect you. I honestly thought downplaying our relationship was the best way to handle it. I'm sorry if it turned out that it wasn't.'

Suddenly I feel silly. 'No,' I say, shaking my head. 'You're absolutely right. I . . . I understand now.'

'As for Barbara,' he continues, 'she was so drunk she would have made a pass at a tree-trunk. Part of me didn't want to upset her by making a big deal of it – especially since we'd only recently made friends. The second she tried to kiss me, I marched her back to her husband and – as diplomatically as possible – suggested he took her home. You must have left the room too soon to see that.'

I nod.

'The fact is, I've never wanted Barbara,' he tells me. 'I've never wanted *anyone* since I met you.'

'Really?' I ask.

He sighs. 'There's something else too.'

'What?'

'I loved my wife, Zoe, really loved her. But she's not here any more. And it's taken me years to grasp that it's okay to move on. That loving somebody else now isn't against the rules.'

I bite my lip.

'And there's another simple fact,' he adds. 'I can't

help loving someone else. I can't help loving you.'

'Ryan, I'm so sorry I left,' I blurt out. 'I didn't know what I was doing, I—'

'Sssh,' he says, as he pulls me to him.

Tears spill down my cheeks, but before I get a chance to wonder where they've come from, Ryan and I have our arms round each other so tightly it feels as if we'll never let go.

Then he loosens his grip. As his mouth finds mine a surge of emotion rushes through me. His kiss is so tender, so beautiful, so glorious, I want it never to end. Particularly since, for the first time today, my nose has dried up.

'They didn't have any dry-roasted,' announces Trudie. 'So I got you some Quavers instead. Only, I'm guessing you don't want them any more.'

Ryan and I unravel ourselves and laugh.

'Do you mind if we don't?' he says.

'Course not.' She grins. 'Don't worry about me.'

Ryan grabs my hand. 'Come on, I've got a cab waiting outside.'

'Not an Aston Martin?' I ask.

'Not exactly.' He frowns. 'It's something called a Mondeo. The seats smell of vomit and the driver belched the whole way here. That's not a disappointment, is it?'

'I smile. Nope. It's absolutely perfect.'